# Falkner
### A Novel

*by*
Mary W. Shelley

# Falkner
## A Novel
### by Mary W. Shelley

Copyright © 2024

All Rights reserved.

No part of this publication may be reproduced, stored in a retrieval system, or transmitted in any form or by any means, electronic, mechanical, photocopying or Otherwise, without the written permission of the publisher.
The author/editor asserts the moral right to be identified as the author/editor of this work.

ISBN: 978-93-61151-33-0

Published by

# DOUBLE 9 BOOKS

2/13-B, Ansari Road
Daryaganj, New Delhi – 110002
info@double9books.com
www.double9books.com
Tel. 011-40042856

This book is under public domain

# ABOUT THE AUTHOR

English novelist Mary Wollstonecraft Shelley is most renowned for her revolutionary book "Frankenstein; or, The Modern Prometheus." Shelley was born in London on August 30, 1797. Her parents were feminist author Mary Wollstonecraft and political philosopher William Godwin. Her upbringing was severely impacted by her mother's early death after she was born. When Mary Shelley, her future husband Percy Bysshe Shelley, Lord Byron, and others participated in a storytelling competition in the summer of 1816, famously known as the "Year Without a Summer", she had the idea for her most well-known work, "Frankenstein." "Frankenstein," which was published anonymously in 1818, is regarded as one of the first works of Gothic and science fiction. Tragedies in Mary Shelley's personal life included the passing of her husband and multiple children. Up until her passing on February 1, 1851, she carried on writing, editing, and participating in literary societies. Mary Shelley faced hardships during her lifetime, yet her impact lives on, and she is acknowledged as a trailblazer in the Gothic and science fiction genres.

# CONTENTS

CHAPTER I ............................................................................. 7
CHAPTER II ........................................................................... 12
CHAPTER III .......................................................................... 19
CHAPTER IV .......................................................................... 29
CHAPTER V ........................................................................... 37
CHAPTER VI .......................................................................... 42
CHAPTER VII ......................................................................... 48
CHAPTER VIII ........................................................................ 56
CHAPTER IX .......................................................................... 63
CHAPTER X ........................................................................... 67
CHAPTER XI .......................................................................... 72
CHAPTER XII ......................................................................... 76
CHAPTER XIII ........................................................................ 87
CHAPTER XIV ........................................................................ 93
CHAPTER XV ......................................................................... 97
CHAPTER XVI ...................................................................... 105
CHAPTER XVII ..................................................................... 111
CHAPTER XVIII .................................................................... 119
CHAPTER XIX ...................................................................... 127
CHAPTER XX ....................................................................... 136
CHAPTER XXI ...................................................................... 140
CHAPTER XXII ..................................................................... 146
CHAPTER XXIII .................................................................... 153
CHAPTER XXIV .................................................................... 161

CHAPTER XXV ............... 166
CHAPTER XXVI ............... 174
CHAPTER XXVII ............... 182
CHAPTER XXVIII ............... 196
CHAPTER XXIX ............... 205
CHAPTER XXX ............... 211
CHAPTER XXXI ............... 219
CHAPTER XXXII ............... 224
CHAPTER XXXIII ............... 227
CHAPTER XXXIV ............... 234
CHAPTER XXXV ............... 238
CHAPTER XXXVI ............... 243
CHAPTER XXXVII ............... 248
CHAPTER XXXVIII ............... 253
CHAPTER XXXIX ............... 257
CHAPTER XL ............... 262
CHAPTER XLI ............... 269
CHAPTER XLII ............... 273
CHAPTER XLIII ............... 280
CHAPTER XLIV ............... 286
CHAPTER XLV ............... 294
CHAPTER XLVI ............... 301
CHAPTER XLVII ............... 307
CHAPTER XLVIII ............... 312
CHAPTER XLIX ............... 319
CHAPTER L ............... 323
CHAPTER LI ............... 328
CHAPTER LII ............... 335

# CHAPTER I

The opening scene of this tale took place in a little village on the southern coast of Cornwall. Treby (by that name we choose to designate a spot whose true one, for several reasons, will not be given) was, indeed, rather a hamlet than a village; although, being at the seaside, there were two or three houses which, by dint of green paint and chints curtains, pretended to give the accommodation of "Apartments Furnished" to the few bathers who, having heard of its cheapness, seclusion, and beauty, now and then resorted thither from the neighbouring towns.

This part of Cornwall shares much of the peculiar and exquisite beauty which every Englishman knows adorns "the sweet shire of Devon." The hedges near Treby, like those round Dawlish and Torquay, are redolent with a thousand flowers; the neighbouring fields are pranked with all the colours of Flora—its soft air—the picturesque bay in which it stood, as it were, enshrined—its red cliff's, and verdure reaching to the very verge of the tide—all breathe the same festive and genial atmosphere. The cottages give the same promise of comfort, and are adorned by nature with more luxurious loveliness than the villas of the rich in a less happy climate.

Treby was almost unknown; yet whoever visited it might well prefer its sequestered beauties to many more renowned competitors. Situated in the depths of a little bay, it was sheltered on all sides by the cliffs. Just behind the hamlet the cliff made a break, forming a little ravine, in the depth of which ran a clear stream, on whose banks were spread the orchards of the villagers, whence they derived their chief wealth. Tangled bushes and luxuriant herbage diversified the cliffs, some of which were crowned by woods; and in "every nook and coign of 'vantage" were to be seen and scented the glory of that coast—its exhaustless store of flowers. The village was, as has been said, in the depth of a bay; towards the east the coast rounded off with a broad sweep, forming a varied line of bay and headland; to the west a little promontory shot out abruptly, and at once closed in the view. This point of land was the peculiarity of Treby. The cliff that gave it its picturesque appearance was not high, but was remarkable for being crowned by the village church, with its slender spire.

Long may it be before the village churchyard ceases to be in England a favoured spot—the home of rural and holy seclusion. At Treby it derived a new beauty from its distance from the village and the eminence on which it was placed, overlooking the wide ocean, the sands, the village itself, with its gardens, orchards, and gayly-painted fields. From the church a straggling, steep, yet not impracticable path led down to the sands by way of the beach; indeed, the distance from the village to the church was scarcely more than half a mile; but no vehicle could approach except by the higher road, which, following the line of coast, measured nearly two miles. The edifice itself, picturesque in its rustic simplicity, seemed at the distance to be imbosomed in a neighbouring grove. There was no house, nor even cottage, near. The contiguous churchyard contained about two acres; a light white paling surrounded it on three sides; on the fourth was a high wall, clothed thickly with ivy: the trees of the near wood overhung both wall and paling, except on the side of the cliff'. The waving of their branches, the murmur of the tide, and the occasional scream of seafowl, were all the sounds that disturbed, or rather harmonized with, the repose and solitude of the spot.

On Sunday, the inhabitants of several hamlets congregated here to attend divine service. Those of Treby usually approached by the beach and the path of the cliff, the old and infirm only taking the longer but more easy road. On every other day of the week all was quiet, except when the hallowed precincts were visited by happy parents with a newborn babe, by bride and bridegroom hastening all gladly to enter on the joys and cares of life—or by the train of mourners who attended relation or friend tothe last repose of the dead.

The poor are not sentimental—and, except on Sunday, after evening service, when a mother might linger for a few moments near the fresh grave of a lately lost child—or, loitering among the rustic tombs, some of the elder peasants told tales of the feats of the dead companions of their youth, a race unequalled, so they said, by the generation around them. Save on that day, none ever visited or wandered among the graves, with the one exception of a child, who had early learned to mourn, yet whose infantine mind could scarcely understand the extent of the cause she had for tears. A little girl, unnoticed and alone, was wont each evening to trip over the sands—to scale with light steps the cliff, which was of no gigantic height, and then, unlatching the low white gate of the churchyard, to repair to one corner, where the boughs of the near trees shadowed over two graves— two graves, of which one only was distinguished by a simple headstone, to commemorate the name of him who mouldered beneath. This tomb was inscribed to the memory of Edwin Raby, but the neighbouring and less honoured grave claimed more of the child's attention—for her mother lay beneath the unrecorded turf.

Beside this grassy hillock she would sit, and talk to herself, and play, till, warned home by the twilight, she knelt and said her little prayer, and, with a "Good-night, mamma," took leave of a spot with which was associated the being whose caresses and love she called to mind, hoping that one day she might again enjoy them. Her appearance had much in it to invite remark, had there been any who cared to notice a poor little orphan. Her dress, in some of its parts, betokened that she belonged to the better classes of society; but she had no stockings, and her little feet peeped from the holes of her well-worn shoes. Her straw bonnet was died dark with sun and sea spray, and its blue riband faded. The child herself would, in any other spot, have attracted more attention than the incongruities of her attire. There is an expression of face which we name angelic, from its purity, its tenderness, and, so to speak, plaintive serenity, which we oftener see in young children than in persons of a more advanced age. And such was hers: her hair, of a light golden brown, was parted over a brow fair and open as day: her eyes, deep-set and earnest, were full of thought and tenderness: her complexion was pure and stainless, except by the roses that glowed in her cheek; while each vein could be traced on her temples, and you could almost mark the flow of the violet-coloured blood beneath: her mouth was the very nest of love: her serious look was at once fond and imploring; but when she smiled, it was as if sunshine broke out at once, warm and unclouded: her figure had the plumpness of infancy; but her tiny hands and feet, and tapering waist, denoted the faultless perfection of her form. She was about six years old—a friendless orphan, cast, thus young, penniless, on a thorny, stony-hearted world.

Nearly two years previous, a gentleman, with his wife and little daughter, arrived at Treby, and took up his abode at one of the moderate-priced lodging-houses before mentioned. The occasion of their visit was but too evident. The husband, Mr. Raby, was dying of a consumption. The family had migrated early in September, so to receive the full benefit of a mild winter in this favoured spot. It did not appear to those about him that he could live to see that winter. He was wasted to a shadow—the hectic in his cheek, the brightness of his eyes, and the debility apparent in every movement, showed that disease was triumphing over the principles of life. Yet, contrary to every prognostic, he lived on from week to week, from month to month. Now he was said to be better—now worse—and thus a winter of extraordinary mildness was passed. But with the east winds of spring a great deterioration was visible. His invalid walks in the sun grew shorter, and then were exchanged for a few minutes passed sitting in his garden. Soon he was confined to his room—then to his bed. During the first week of a bleak ungenial May, he died.

The extreme affection that subsisted between the pair rendered his widow an object of interest even to the villagers. They were both young, and she was beautiful; and more beautiful was their offspring—the little girl we have mentioned:—who, watched over and attended on by her mother, attracted admiration as well as interest, by the peculiar style of her childish, yet perfect loveliness. Every one wondered what the bereaved lady would do; and she, poor soul, wondered herself, and would sit watching the gambols of her child in an attitude of unutterable despondency, till the little girl, remarking the sadness of her mother, gave over playing to caress, and kiss her, and to bid her smile. At such a word the tears fell fast from the widow's eyes, and the frightened child joined her sobs and cries to hers.

Whatever might be the sorrows and difficulties of the unhappy lady, it was soon evident to all but herself that her own life was a fragile tenure. She had attended on her husband with unwearied assiduity, and, added to bodily fatigue, was mental suffering; partly arising from anxiety and grief, and partly from the very virtues of the sufferer. He knew that he was dying, and tried to reconcile his wife to her anticipated loss. But his words, breathing the most passionate love and purest piety, seemed almost to call her also from the desolation to which he was leaving her, and to dissolve the ties that held her to earth. When he was gone, life possessed no one attraction except their child. Often while her father, with pathetic eloquence, tried to pour the balm of resignation, and hopes of eternal reunion, into his wife's heart, she had sat on her mother's knee, or on a little stool at her feet, and looked up, with her cherub face, a little perplexed, a little fearful, till, at some words of too plain and too dread an import, she sprung into her father's arms, and clinging to his neck, amid tears and sobs, cried out, "You must not leave us, papa! you must stay—you shall not go away!"

Consumption, in all countries except our own, is considered a contagious disorder, and it too often proves such here. During her close attendance, Mrs. Raby had imbibed the seeds of the fatal malady; and grief, and a delicate texture of nerves, caused them to develop with alarming rapidity. Every one perceived this except herself. She thought that her indisposition sprung from over-fatigue and grief, but that repose would soon restore her; and each day, as her flesh wasted and her blood flowed more rapidly, she said, "I shall be better to-morrow." There was no one at Treby to advise or assist her. She was not one of those who make friends and intimates of all who fall in their way. She was gentle, considerate, courteous—but her refined mind shrunk from displaying its deep wounds to the vulgar and unfeeling.

After her husband's death she had written several letters, which she carefully put into the postoffice herself—going on purpose to the nearest post-town, three miles distant. She had received one in answer, and it had the effect of increasing every fatal symptom, through the anguish and excessive agitation it excited. Sometimes she talked of leaving Treby, but she delayed till she should be better; which time, the villagers plainly saw, would never come, but they were not aware how awfully near the crisis really was.

One morning—her husband had now been dead about four months—she called up the woman of the house in which she lodged; there was a smile on her face, and a pink spot burnt brightly in either cheek, while her brow was ashy pale; there was something ghastly in the very gladness her countenance expressed; yet she felt nothing of all this, but said, "The newspaper you lent me had good news in it, Mrs. Baker. It tells me that a dear friend of mine is arrived in England, whom I thought still on the Continent. I am going to write to her. Will you let your daughter take my little girl a walk while I write?"

Mrs. Baker consented. The child was equipped and sent out, while her mother sat down to write. In about an hour she came out of her parlour; Mrs. Baker saw her going towards the garden; she tottered as she walked, so the woman hastened to her. "Thank you," she said; "I feel strangely faint—I had much to say, and that letter has unhinged me—I must finish it to-morrow—now the air will restore me—I can scarcely breathe."

Mrs. Baker offered her arm. The sufferer walked faintly and feebly to a little bench, and sitting down, supported herself by her companion. Her breath grew shorter; she murmured some words; Mrs. Baker bent down, but could catch only the name of her child, which was the last sound that hovered on the mother's lips. With one sigh her heart ceased to beat, and life left her exhausted frame. The poor woman screamed loudly for help as she felt her press heavily against her: and then, sliding from her seat, sink lifeless on the ground.

# CHAPTER II

It was to Mrs. Baker's credit that she did not attempt to investigate the affairs of her hapless lodger till after the funeral. A purse, containing twelve guineas, which she found on her table, served, indeed, to satisfy her that she would be no immediate loser. However, as soon as the sod covered the gentle form of the unfortunate lady, she proceeded to examine her papers. The first that presented itself was the unfinished letter which Mrs. Raby was engaged in writing at the time of her death. This promised information, and Mrs. Baker read it with eagerness. It was as follows:—

"My dearest Friend,

"A newspaper has just informed me that you are returned to England, while I still believed you to be, I know not where, on the Continent. Dearest girl, it is long since I have written, for I have been too sad, too uncertain about your movements, and too unwilling to cloud your happiness, by forcing you to remember one so miserable. My beloved friend, my schoolfellow, my benefactress; you will grieve to hear of my misfortunes, and it is selfish in me, even now, to intrude upon you with the tale; but, under heaven, I have no hope, except in my generous, my warm-hearted Alithea. Perhaps you have already heard of my disaster, and are aware that death has robbed me of the happiness which, under your kind fosterage, I had acquired and enjoyed. He is dead who was my all in this world, and but for one tie I should bless the day when I might be permitted to rest for ever beside him.

"I often wonder, dear Alithea, at the heedlessness and want of foresight with which I entered life. Doomed, through poverty and my orphan state, to earn my bread as a governess, my entrance on that irksome task was only delayed by my visit to you; then under your dear roof I saw and was beloved by Edwin; and his entreaties, and your encouragement, permitted my trembling heart to dream of — to possess happiness. Timidity of character made me shrink from my career: diffidence never allowed me to suppose that any one would interest themselves enough in me to raise the poor trembler from the ground, to shelter and protect her; and this kind of despondency rendered Edwin's love a new, glorious, and divine joy. Yet, when I thought of his parents, I trembled—I could not bear to enter a family where I was to be regarded as an unwelcome intruder; yet Edwin was already an outcast—already father and brothers, every relation, had disowned him—and he, like I, was alone. And you, Alithea, how fondly, how sweetly did you encourage me—making that appear my duty which was the fulfilment of my wildest dreams of joy. Surely no being ever felt friendship as you have done—sympathizing even in the untold secrets of a timid heart—enjoying the happiness that you conferred with an ardour few can feel, even for themselves. Your transports of delight when you saw me, through your means, blessed, touched me with a gratitude that can never die. And do I show this by asking now for your pity, and saddening you by my grief? Pardon me, sweet friend, and do not wonder that this thought has long delayed my letter.

"We were happy—poor, but content. Poverty was no evil to me, and Edwin supported every privation as if he had never been accustomed to luxury. The spirit that had caused him to shake off the shackles his bigoted family threw over him, animated him to exertions beyond his strength. He had chosen for himself—he wished to prove that his choice was good. I do not allude to our marriage, but to his desertion of the family religion, and determination to follow a career not permitted by the policy of his relations to any younger son. He was called to the bar—he toiled incessantly—he was ambitious, and his talents gave every promise of success. He is gone—gone for ever! I have lost the noblest, wisest friend that ever breathed, the most devoted lover, and truest husband that ever blessed woman!

"I write incoherently. You know what our life in London was—obscure, but happy—the scanty pittance allowed him seemed to me amply to suffice for all our wants; I only then knew of the wants of youth and health, which were love and sympathy. I had all this, crowning to the brim my cup of life—the birth of our sweet child filled it to overflowing. Our dingy lodgings, near the courts of law, were a palace to me;

I should have despised myself heartily could I have desired anything beyond what I possessed. I never did—nor did I fear its loss. I was grateful to Heaven, and thus I fancied that I paid the debt of my unmeasured prosperity.

"Can I say what I felt when I marked Edwin's restless nights, flushed cheek, and the cough that would not go away? these things I dare not dwell upon—my tears overflow—my heart beats to bursting—the fatal truth was at last declared; the fatal word, consumption, spoken: change of air was all the hope held out—we came here; the churchyard near holds now all earthly that remains of him—would that my dust were mingling with his!

"Yet I have a child, my Alithea; and you, who are incomparable as a mother, will feel that I ought not to grieve so bitterly while this dear angel remains to me. I know, indeed, that without her life would at once suspend all its functions; why, then, is it, that while she is with me I am not stronger, more heroic? for, to keep her with me, I must leave the indolence of my present life—I must earn the bread of both. I should not repine at this—I shall not when I am better; but I am very ill and weak; and though each day I rise, resolving to exert myself, before the morning has passed away I lie down exhausted, trembling, and faint.

"When I lost Edwin, I wrote to Mr. Raby, acquainting him with the sad intelligence, and asking for a maintenance for myself and my child. The family solicitor answered my letter; Edwin's conduct had, I was told, estranged his family from him; and they could only regard me as one encouraging his disobedience and apostacy. I had no claim on them. If my child were sent to them, and I would promise to abstain from all intercourse with her, she should be brought up with her cousins, and treated in all respects like one of the family. I answered this letter hastily and proudly. I declined their barbarous offer, and haughtily, and in few words, relinquished every claim on their bounty, declaring my intention to support and bring up my child myself. This was foolishly done, I fear; but I cannot regret it, even now.

"I cannot regret the impulse that made me disdain these unnatural and cruel relatives, or that led me to take my poor orphan to my heart with pride, as being all my own.

What had they done to merit such a treasure? How did they show themselves capable of replacing a fond and anxious mother? How many blooming girls have they sacrificed to their peculiar views! With what careless eyes they regard the sweetest emotions of nature! never shall my adored girl be made the victim of that loveless race. Do you remember our sweet child? She was lovely from her birth; and surely, if ever angel assumed an earthly vesture, it took a form like my darling: her loveliness expresses only the beauty of her disposition: so young, yet so full of sensibility; her temper is without a flaw, and her intelligence transcends her age. You will not laugh at me for my maternal enthusiasm, nor will you wonder at it; her endearing caresses, her cherub smiles, the silver accents of her infantine voice, fill me with trembling rapture. Is she not too good for this bad world? I fear it, I fear to lose her; I fear to die and to leave her; yet, if I should, will you not cherish, will you not be a mother to her? I may be presumptuous; but if I were to die even now, I should die in the belief that I left my child another mother in you—"

The letter broke off here, and these were the last words of the unfortunate writer. It contained a sad, but too common story of the hard-heartedness of the wealthy, and the misery endured by the children of the high-born. Blood is not water, it is said, but gold with them is dearer far than the ties of nature; to keep and augment their possessions being the aim and end of their lives, the existence, and, more especially, the happiness of their children, appears to them a consideration at once trivial and impertinent, when it would compete with family views and family greatness. To this common and iniquitous feeling these luckless beings were sacrificed; they had endured the worst, and could be injured no more; but their orphan child was a living victim, less thought of than the progeny of the meanest animal which might serve to augment their possessions.

Mrs. Baker felt some complacency on reading this letter: with the common English respect for wealth and rank, she was glad to find that her humble roof had sheltered a man who was the son—she did not exactly know of whom, but of somebody, who had younger sons and elder sons, and possessed, through wealth, the power of behaving frightfully ill to a vast number of persons. There was a grandeur and dignity in the very idea; but the good woman felt less satisfaction as she proceeded in her operations—no other letter or paper appeared to inform or to direct. Every letter had been destroyed, and the young pair had brought no papers or documents with them. She could not guess to whom the unfinished letter she held was addressed; all was darkness and ignorance. She was aghast—there was none to whom to apply—none to whom to send the orphan. In a more busy part of the world, an advertisement in the newspapers would have presented itself as a resource; but Treby was too much cut off from the rest of the world for its inhabitants to conceive so daring an idea; and Mrs. Baker, repining much at the burden fallen upon her, and fearful of the future, could imagine no means by which to discover the relations of the little orphan; and her only notion was to wait, in hopes that some among them would at last make inquiries concerning her.

Nearly a year had passed away, and no one had appeared. The unfortunate lady's purse was soon emptied—and her watch, with one or two trinkets of slight value, disposed of. The child was of small cost, but still her sordid protectress harped perpetually on her ill luck: she had a family of her own, and plenty of mouths to feed. Missy was but little, but she would get bigger—though for that matter it was worse now, as she wanted more taking care of—besides, she was getting quite a disgrace—her bonnet was so shabby, and her shoes worn out—and how could she afford to buy others for one who was not a bit of her flesh and blood, to the evident hurt of her own children? It was bad enough now; but, by-and-by, she saw nothing but the parish; though Missy was born for better than that, and her poor mamma would turn in her grave at the name of such a thing. For her part, she was to blame, she feared, and too generous—but she would wait yet a little longer before it came to that—for who could tell—and here Mrs. Baker's prudence dammed up the stream of her eloquence—to no living ear did she dare trust her dream of the coach and six that might one day come for her little charge—and the remuneration and presents that would be heaped upon her; she actually saved the child's best frock, though she had quite outgrown it, that on such a day her appearance might do her honour. But this was a secret—she hid these vague but splendid images deep in her heart, lest some neighbour might be seized with a noble emulation—and, through some artifice, share in her dreamy gains. It was these anticipations that prevented Mrs. Baker from taking any decisive step injurious to her charge—but they did not shed any rosy hues over her diurnal complaints—they grew more peevish and frequent as time passed away, and her visions attained no realization.

The little orphan grew, meanwhile, as a garden rose that accident has thrown amid briers and weeds—blooming with alien beauty, and unfolding its soft petals—and shedding its ambrosial odour beneath the airs of heaven, unharmed by its strange position. Lovely as a day of paradise, which, by some strange chance, visits this nether world to gladden every heart, she charmed even her selfish protectress; and, despite her shabby attire, her cherub smiles—the free and noble steps which her tiny feet could take even now, and the music of her voice, rendered her the object of respect and admiration, as well as love, to the whole village.

The loss of her father had acquainted the poor child with death. Her mother had explained the awful mystery as well as she could to her infantine intellects, and, indulging in her own womanish and tender fancies, had often spoken of the dead as hovering over and watching around his loved ones, even in the new state of existence to which he had been called. Yet she wept as she spoke: "He is happy," she exclaimed, "but he is not here! Why did he leave us? Ah, why desert those who loved him so well, who need him so dearly! How forlorn and cast away are we without him!"

These scenes made a deep impression upon the sensitive child—and when her mother died too, and was carried away and placed in the cold earth beside her husband, the orphan would sit for hours by the graves, now fancying that her mother must soon return, now exclaiming, "Why are you gone away? Come, dear mamma, come back—come quickly!" Young as she was, it was no wonder that such thoughts were familiar to her. The minds of children are often as intelligent as those of persons of maturer age—and differ only by containing fewer ideas—but these had so often been presented to her—and she so fixed her little heart on the idea that her mother was watching over her, that at last it became a part of her religion to visit, every evening, the two graves, and saying her prayers near them, to believe that her mother's spirit, which was obscurely associated with her mortal remains reposing below, listened to and blessed her on that spot.

At other times, neglected as she was, and left to wander at will, she conned her lesson, as she had been accustomed at her mother's feet, beside her grave. She took her picture-books there, and even her playthings. The villagers were affected by her childish notion of being "with mamma;" and Missy became something of an angel in their eyes, so that no one interfered with her visits, or tried to explain away her fancies. She was the nursling of love and nature: but the human hearts which could have felt the greatest tenderness for her beat no longer, and had become clods of the soil—

"Borne round in earth's diurnal course
With rocks, and stones, and trees."

There was no knee on which she could playfully climb—no neck round which she could fondly hang—no parent's cheek on which to print her happy kisses—these two graves were all of relationship she knew upon the earth—and she would kiss the ground and the flowers, not one of which she plucked—as she sat embracing the sod. "Mamma" was everywhere around. "Mamma" was there beneath, and still she could love and feel herself beloved.

At other times she played gayly with her young companions in the village—and sometimes she fancied that she loved some one among them—she made them presents of books and toys, the relics of happier days; for the desire to benefit, which springs up so naturally in a loving heart, was strong within her, even in that early age. But she never took any one with her in her churchyard visits—she needed none while she was with mamma. Once, indeed, a favourite kitten was carried to the sacred spot, and the little animal played amid the grass and flowers, and the child joined in its frolics—her solitary gay laugh might be heard among the tombs—she did not think it solitary; mamma was there to smile on her, as she sported with her tiny favourite.

# CHAPTER III

Towards the end of a hot, calm day of June, a stranger arrived at Treby. The variations of calm and wind are always remarkable at the seaside, and are more particularly to be noticed on this occasion; since it was the stillness of the elements that caused the arrival of the stranger. During the whole day several vessels had been observed in the offing, lying to for a wind, or making small way under press of sail. As evening came on, the water beyond the bay lay calmer than ever; but a slight breeze blew from shore, and these vessels, principally colliers, bore down close under it, endeavouring by short tacks to procure a long one, and at last to gain searoom to make the eastern headland of the bay. The fishermen on shore watched the manœuvres of the different craft; and even interchanged shouts with the sailors, as they lay lazily on the beach. At length they were put in motion by a hail for a boat from a small merchantman—the call was obeyed—the boat neared the vessel—a gentleman descended into it—his portmanteau was handed after him—a few strokes of the oar drove the boat on the beach, and the stranger leaped out upon the sands.

The new comer gave a brief order, directing his slight luggage to be carried to the best inn, and, paying the boatmen liberally, strolled away to a more solitary part of the beach. "A gentleman," all the spectators decided him to be—and such a designation served for a full description of the new arrival to the villagers of Treby. But it were better to say a few words to draw him from among a vast multitude who might be similarly named, and to bestow individuality on the person in question. It would be best so to present his appearance and manner to the "mind's eye" of the reader, that if any met him by chance, he might exclaim, "That is the man!" Yet there is no task more difficult than to convey to another, by mere words, an image, however distinctly it is impressed on our own minds. The individual expression and peculiar traits which cause a man to be recognised among ten thousand of his fellow-men, by one who has known him, though so palpable to the eye, escape when we would find words whereby to delineate them.

There was something in the stranger that at once arrested attention—a freedom, and a command of manner—self-possession joined to energy. It might be difficult to guess his age, for his face had been exposed to the bronzing influence of a tropical climate, and the smoothness of youth was exchanged for the deeper lines of maturity, without anything being as yet taken from the vigour of the limbs, or the perfection of those portions of the frame and face, which so soon show marks of decay. He might have reached the verge of thirty, but he could not be older—and might be younger. His figure was active, sinewy, and strong—upright as a soldier (indeed, a military air was diffused all over his person); he was tall, and, to a certain degree, handsome; his dark gray eyes were piercing as an eagle's, and his forehead high and expansive, though somewhat distorted by various lines that spoke more of passion than thought; yet his face was eminently intelligent; his mouth, rather too large in its proportions, yet grew into beauty when he smiled—indeed, the remarkable trait of his physiognomy was its great variation—restless, and even fierce; the expression was often that of passionate and unquiet thoughts; while at other times it was almost bland from the apparent smoothness and graceful undulation of the lines. It was singular, that when communing only with himself, storms appeared to shake his muscles and disfigure the harmony of his countenance—and that, when he addressed others, all was composed—full of meaning, and yet of repose. His complexion, naturally of an olive tint, had grown red and adust under the influence of climate—and often flushed from the inroads of vehement feeling. You could not doubt at the instant of seeing him, that many singular, perhaps tragical, incidents were attached to his history— but conviction was enforced that he reversed the line of Shakspeare, and was *less* sinned against than sinning—or, at least, that he had been the active machinator of his fate, not the passive recipient of disappointment and sorrow. When he believed himself to be unobserved, his face worked with a thousand contending emotions, fiery glances shot from his eyes— he appeared to wince from sudden anguish—to be transported by a rage that changed his beauty into utter deformity: was he spoken to, all these tokens vanished on the instant—dignified, calm, and even courteous; though cold, he would persuade those whom he addressed that he was one of themselves—and not a being transported by his own passions and actions into a sphere which every other human being would have trembled to approach. A superficial observer had pronounced him a good fellow, though a little too stately—a wise man had been pleased by the intelligence and information he displayed—the variety of his powers, and the ease with which he brought forward the stores of his intellect to enlighten any topic of discourse. An independent and a gallant spirit he surely had—what, then, had touched it with destruction—shaken it to ruin, and made him, while yet so young, abhorrent even to himself?

Such is an outline of the stranger of Treby; and his actions were in conformity with the incongruities of his appearance—outwardly unemployed and tranquil; inwardly torn by throes of the most tempestuous and agonizing feelings. After landing he had strolled away, and was soon out of sight; nor did he return till night, when he looked fatigued and depressed. For form's sake—or for the sake of the bill at the inn—he allowed food to be placed before him; but he neither ate nor drank—soon he hurried to the solitude of his chamber—not to bed—he paced the room for some hours; but as soon as all was still—when his watch and the quiet stars told him that it was midnight, he left the house—he wandered down to the beach—he threw himself upon the sands—and then again he started up and strode along the verge of the tide—and then sitting down, covering his face with his hands, remained motionless: early dawn found him thus—but, on the first appearance of a fisherman, he left the neighbourhood of the village, nor returned till the afternoon—and now, when food was placed before him, he ate like one half famished; but after the keen sensation of extreme hunger was satisfied, he left the table and retired to his own room.

Taking a case of pistols from his portmanteau, he examined the weapons with care, and, putting them in his pocket, walked out upon the sands. The sun was fast descending in the sky, and he looked, with varying glances, at it and at the blue sea, which slumbered peacefully, giving forth scarcely any sound as it receded from the shore. Now he seemed wistful— now impatient—now struck by bitterer pangs, that caused drops of agony to gather on his brow. He spoke no word; but these were the thoughts that hovered, though unexpressed, upon his lips: "Another day! Another sun! Oh, never, never more for me shall day or sun exist. Coward! Why fear to die? And do I fear? No! no! I fear nothing but this pain—this unutterable anguish—this image of fell despair! If I could feel secure that memory would cease when my brain lies scattered on the earth, I should again feel joy before I die. Yet that is false. While I live, and memory lives, and the knowledge of my crime still creeps through every particle of my frame, I have a hell around me, even to the last pulsation! For ever and for ever I see her, lost and dead at my feet—I the cause—the murderer! My death shall atone. And yet even in death the curse is on me—I cannot give back the breath of life to her sweet pale lips! Oh fool! Oh villain! Haste to the last act; linger no more, lest you grow mad, and fetters and stripes become your fitter punishment than the death you covet!"

"Yet"—after a pause, his thoughts thus continued:—"not here, nor now: there must be darkness on the earth before the deed is done! Hasten and hide thyself, oh sun! Thou wilt never be cursed by the sight of my living form again!"

Thus did the transport of passion embrace the universe in its grasp; and the very sunlight seemed to have a pulse responsive to his own. The bright orb sunk lower; and the little western promontory, with its crowning spire, was thrown into bold relief against the glowing sky. As if some new idea were awakened, the stranger proceeded along the sands, towards the extremity of the headland. A short time before, unobserved by him, the little orphan had tripped along, and, scaling the cliff, had seated herself, as usual, beside her mother's grave.

The stranger proceeded slowly, and with irregular steps. He was waiting till darkness should blind the eyes of day, which now appeared to gaze on him with intolerable scrutiny, and to read his very soul, that sickened and writhed with its burden of sin and sorrow. When out of the immediate neighbourhood of the village, he threw himself upon a fragment of rock, and—he could not be said to meditate—for that supposes some sort of voluntary action of the mind—while to him might be applied the figure of the poet, who represented himself as hunted by his own thoughts—pursued by memory, and torn to pieces, as Actæon by his own hounds. A troop of horrid recollections assailed his soul! there was no shelter, no escape! various passions, by turns, fastened themselves upon him—jealousy, disappointed love, rage, fear, and, last and worst, remorse and despair. No bodily torture, invented by revengeful tyrant, could produce agony equal to that which he had worked out for his own mind. His better nature, and the powers of his intellect, served but to sharpen and strike deeper the pangs of unavailing regret. Fool! He had foreseen nothing of all this! He had fancied that he could bend the course of fate to his own will; and that to desire with energy was to ensure success. And to what had the immutable resolve to accomplish his ends brought him? She was dead—the loveliest and best of created beings: torn from the affections and the pleasures of life! from her home, her child! He had seen her stretched dead at his feet: he had heaped the earth upon her clay-cold form; and he the cause! he the murderer!

Stung to intolerable anguish by these ideas, he felt hastily for his pistols, and rising, pursued his way. Evening was closing in; yet he could distinguish the winding path of the cliff; he ascended, opened the little gate, and entered the churchyard. Oh! how he envied the dead!—the guiltless dead, who had closed their eyes on this mortal scene, surrounded by weeping friends, cheered by religious hope. All that imaged innocence and repose appeared in his eyes so beautiful and desirable; and how could he, the criminal, hope to rest like one of these? A star or two came out in the heavens above, and the church spire seemed almost to reach them, as it pointed upward. The dim, silent sea was spread beneath: the dead slept around: scarcely did the tall grass bend its head to the summer air. Soft, balmy peace possessed the scene. With what thrilling sensations of self-enjoyment and gratitude to the Creator, might the mind at ease drink in the tranquil loveliness of such an hour. The stranger felt every nerve wakened to fresh anguish. His brow contracted convulsively. "Shall I ever die!" he cried; "will not the dead reject me!"

He looked round with the natural instinct that leads a human being, at the moment of dissolution, to withdraw into a cave or corner, where least to offend the eyes of the living by the loathsome form of death. The ivied wall and paling, overhung by trees, formed a nook, whose shadow at that hour was becoming deep. He approached the spot; for a moment he stood looking afar: he knew not at what; and drew forth his pistol, cocked it, and throwing himself on the grassy mound, raised the mouth of the fatal instrument to his forehead. "Oh, go away! go away from mamma!" were words that might have met his ear, but that every sense was absorbed. As he drew the trigger, his arm was pulled; the ball whizzed harmlessly by his ear: but the shock of the sound, the unconsciousness that he had been touched at that moment — the belief that the mortal wound was given, made him fall back; and, as he himself said afterward, he fancied that he had uttered the scream he heard, which had, indeed, proceeded from other lips.

In a few seconds he recovered himself. Yet so had he worked up his mind to die; so impossible did it appear that his aim should fail him, that in those few seconds the earth and all belonging to it had passed away — and his first exclamation, as he started up, was, "Where am I?" Something caught his gaze; a little white figure, which lay but a few paces distant, and two eyes that gleamed on him — the horrible thought darted into his head — had another instead of himself been the victim? and he exclaimed in agony, "Gracious God! who are you? — speak! What have I done!" Still more was he horror-struck when he saw that it was a little child who lay before him — he raised her — but her eyes had glared with terror, not death; she did not speak; but she was not wounded, and he endeavoured to comfort and reassure her, till she, a little restored, began to cry bitterly, and he felt, thankfully, that her tears were a pledge that the worst consequences of her fright had passed away. He lifted her from the ground, while she, in the midst of her tears, tried to get him away from the grave he desecrated. The twilight scarcely showed her features; but her surpassing fairness — her lovely countenance and silken hair, so betokened a child of love and care, that he was more the surprised to find her alone, at that hour, in the solitary churchyard.

He soothed her gently, and asked, "How came you here? what could you be doing so late so far from home?"

"I came to see mamma."

"To see mamma! Where? how? Your mother is not here."

"Yes she is; mamma is there;" and she pointed with her little finger to the grave.

The stranger started up—there was something awful in this childish simplicity and affection: he tried to read the inscription on the stone near—he could just make out the name of Edwin Raby. "That is not your mother's grave," he said.

"No; papa is there—mamma is here, next to him."

The man, just bent on self-destruction, with a conscience burning him to the heart's core—all concentrated in the omnipotence of his own sensations—shuddered at the tale of dereliction and misery these words conveyed; he looked earnestly on the child, and was fascinated by her angel look; she spoke with a pretty seriousness, shaking her head, her lips trembling—her large eyes shining in brimming tears. "My poor child," he said, "your name is Raby then?"

"Mamma used to call me Baby," she replied; "they call me Missy at home—my name is Elizabeth."

"Well, dear Elizabeth, let me take you home; you cannot stay all night with mamma."

"Oh, no; I was just going home when you frightened me."

"You must forget that; I will buy you a doll to make it up again, and all sorts of toys; see, here is a pretty thing for you!" and he took the chain of his watch, and threw it over her head; he wanted so to distract her attention as to make her forget what had passed, and not to tell a shocking story when she got home.

"But," she said, looking up into his face, "you will not be so naughty again, and sit down where mamma is lying."

The stranger promised, and kissed her; and, taking her hand, they walked together to the village; she prattled as she went, and he sometimes listened to her stories of mamma, and answered, and sometimes thought with wonder that he still lived—that the ocean's tide still broke at his feet—and the stars still shone above; he felt angry and impatient at the delay, as if it betokened a failing of purpose. They walked along the sands, and stopped at last at Mrs. Baker's door. She was standing at it, and exclaimed, "Here you are, Missy, at last! What have you been doing with yourself? I declare I was quite frightened—it is long past your bedtime."

"You must not scold her," said the stranger; "I detained her. But why do you let her go out alone? it is not right."

"Lord, sir," she replied, "there is none hereabouts to do her a harm—and she would not thank me if I kept her from going to see her mamma, as she calls it. I have no one to spare to go with her; it's hard enough on me to keep her on charity, as I do. But"—and her voice changed as a thought flashed across her—"I beg your pardon, sir, perhaps you come for Missy, and know all about her. I am sure I have done all I can; it's a long time since her mamma died; and, but for me, she must have gone to the parish. I hope you will judge that I have done my duty towards her."

"You mistake," said the stranger; "I know nothing of this young lady, nor of her parents, who, it would seem, are both dead. Of course she has other relations?"

"That she has, and rich ones too," replied Mrs. Baker, "if one could but find them out. It's hard upon me, who am a widow woman, with four children of my own, to have other people's upon me—very hard, sir, as you must allow; and often I think that I cannot answer it to myself, taking the bread from my own children and grandchildren, to feed a stranger. But, to be sure, Missy has rich relations, and some day they will inquire for her; though come the tenth of next August, and it's a year since her mother died, and no one has come to ask good or bad about her, or Missy."

"Her father died also in this village?" asked the stranger.

"True enough," said the woman; "both father and mother died in this very house, and lie up in the churchyard yonder. Come, Missy, don't cry; that's an old story now, and it's no use fretting."

The poor child, who had hitherto listened in simple ignorance, began to sob at this mention of her parents; and the stranger, shocked by the woman's unfeeling tone, said, "I should like to hear more of this sad story. Pray let the poor dear child be put to bed, and then, if you will relate what you know of her parents, I dare say I can give you some advice to enable you to discover her relations, and relieve you from the burden of her maintenance."

"These are the first comfortable words I have heard a long time," said Mrs. Baker. "Come, Missy, Nancy shall put you to bed; it's far past your hour. Don't cry, dear; this kind gentleman will take you along with him, to a fine house, among grand folks, and all our troubles will be over. Be pleased, sir, to step into the parlour, and I will show you a letter of the lady, and tell you all I know. I dare say, if you are going to London, you will find out that Missy ought to be riding in her coach at this very moment."

This was a golden idea of Mrs. Baker, and, in truth, went a little beyond her anticipations; but she had got tired of her first dreams of greatness, and feared that, in sad truth, the little orphan's relations would entirely disown her; but it struck her that, if she could persuade this strange gentleman that all she said was true, he might be induced to take the little girl with him when he went away, and undertake the task of restoring her to her father's family, by which means she at least would be released from all further care on her account:—"Upon this hint she spake."

She related how Mr. and Mrs. Raby had arrived with their almost infant child—death already streaked the brow of the dying man; each day threatened to be his last; yet he lived on. His sufferings were great; and night and day his wife was at his side, waiting on him, watching each turn of his eye, each change of complexion or of pulse. They were poor, and had only one servant, hired at the village soon after their arrival, when Mrs. Raby found herself unable to bestow adequate attention on both husband and child; yet she did so much as evidently to cause her to sink beneath her too great exertions. She was delicate and fragile in appearance; but she never owned to being fatigued, or relaxed in her attentions. Her voice was always attuned to cheerfulness, her eyes beaming with tenderness: she, doubtless, wept in secret; but when conversing with her husband, or playing with her child, a natural vivacity animated her, that looked like hope; indeed, it was certain that, in spite of every fatal symptom, she did not wholly despair. When her husband declared himself better, and resumed for a day his task of instructer to his little girl, she believed that his disorder had taken a favourable turn, and would say, "Oh, Mrs. Baker, please God, he is really better; doctors are not infallible; he may live!" And as she spoke, her eyes swam in tears, while a smile lay like a sunbeam on her features. She did not sink till her husband died, and even then struggled, both with her grief and the wasting malady already at work within her, with a fortitude a mother only could practise; for all her exertions were for her dear child; and she could smile on her, a wintry smile—yet sweet as if warmed by seraphic faith and love. She lingered thus, hovering on the very limits of life and death; her heart warm and affectionate, and hoping, and full of fire to the end, for her child's sake, while she herself pined for the freedom of the grave, and to soar from the cares and sorrows of a sordid world, to the heaven already open to receive her. In homely phrase, Mrs. Baker dwelt upon this touching mixture of maternal tenderness and soft languor, that would not mourn for him she was so soon to join. The woman then described her sudden death, and placed the fragment of her last letter before her auditor.

Deeply interested, the stranger began to read, when suddenly he became ghastly pale, and, trembling all over, he asked, "To whom was this letter addressed?"

"Ah, sir," replied Mrs. Baker, "would that I could tell, and all my troubles would be over. Read on, sir, and you will see that Mrs. Raby feels sure that the lady would have been a mother to poor Missy; but who, or where she is, is past all my guessing."

The stranger strove to read on; but violent emotion, and the struggle to hide what he felt, hindered him from taking in the meaning of a single word. At length he told Mrs. Baker that, with her leave, he would take the letter away, and read it at his leisure. He promised her his aid in discovering Mrs. Raby's relatives, and assured her that there would be small difficulty in so doing. He then retired, and Mrs. Baker exclaimed, "Please God, this will prove a good day's work."

A voice from the grave had spoken to the stranger. It was not the dead mother's voice—she, whatever her merits and sufferings had been, was to him an image of the mind only—he had never known her. But her benefactress, her hope and trust, who and where was she! Alithea! the warm-hearted friend—the incomparable mother! She to whom all hearts in distress turned, sure of relief—who went before the desires of the necessitous; whose generous and free spirit made her emperess of all hearts; who, while she lived, spread, as does the sun, radiance and warmth around—her pulses were stilled; her powers cribbed up in the grave. She was nothing now; and he had reduced to this nothing the living frame of this glorious being.

The stranger read the letter again and again; again he writhed, as her name appeared, traced by her friend's delicate hand, and the concluding hope seemed the acme of his despair. She would indeed have been a mother to the orphan—he remembered expressions that told him that she was making diligent inquiry for her friend, whose luckless fate had not reached her. Yes, it was his Alithea; he could not doubt. His? Fatal mistake—his she had never been; and the wild resolve to make her such had ended in death and ruin.

The stranger had taken the letter to his inn—but any roof seemed to imprison and oppress him—again he sought relief in the open air, and wandered far along the sands, with the speed of a misery that strove to escape from itself. The whole night he spent thus—sometimes climbing the jagged cliffs, then descending to the beach, and throwing himself his length upon the sands. The tide ebbed and flowed—the roar of ocean filled the lone night with sound—the owl flapped down from its home in the rock, and hooted. Hour after hour passed—and, driven by a thousand thoughts—tormented by the direst pangs of memory—still the stranger hurried along the winding shores. Morning found him many miles from Treby. He did not stop till the appearance of another village put a limit to solitude, and he returned upon his steps.

Those who could guess his crime, could alone divine the combat of life and death waging in his heart. He had, through accident and forgetfulness, left his pistols on the table of his chamber at the inn, or, in some of the wildest of the paroxysms of despair, they had ended all. To die, he fondly hoped, was to destroy memory and to defeat remorse; and yet there arose within his mind that feeling, mysterious and inexplicable to common reason, which generates a desire to expiate and to atone. Should he be the cause of good to the friendless orphan, bequeathed so vainly to his victim, would not that, in some sort, compensate for his crime? Would it not double it to have destroyed her, and also the good of which she would have been the author? The very finger of God pointed to this act, since the child's little hand had arrested his arm at the fatal moment when he believed that no interval of a second's duration intervened between him and the grave. Then, to aid those dim religious misgivings, came the manly wish to protect the oppressed and assist the helpless. The struggle was long and terrible. Now he made up his mind that it was cowardice to postpone his resolve—that to live was to stamp himself poltron and traitor. And now again, he felt that the true cowardice was to die—to fly from the consequences of his actions, and the burden of existence. He gazed upon the dim waste of waters, as if from its misty skirt some vision would arise to guide or to command. He cast his eyes upward to interrogate the silent stars—the roaring of the tide appeared to assume an inorganic voice, and to murmur hoarsely, "Live! miserable wretch! Dare you hope for the repose which your victim enjoys? Know that the guilty are unworthy to die—that is the reward of innocence!"

The cool air of morning chilled his brow, and the broad sun arose from the eastern sea, as, pale and haggard, he retrod many a weary step towards Treby. He was faint and weary. He had resolved to live yet a little longer— till he had fulfilled some portion of his duty towards the lovely orphan. So resolving, he felt as if he paid a part of the penalty due. A soothing feeling, which resembled repentance, stole over his heart, already rewarding him. How swiftly and audibly does the inner voice of our nature speak, telling us when we do right. Besides, he believed that to live was to suffer; to live, therefore, was in him a virtue: and the exultation, the balmy intoxication which always follows our first attempt to execute a virtuous resolve, crept over him, and elevated his spirits, though body and soul were alike weary. Arriving at Treby, he sought his bed. He slept peacefully; and it was the first slumber he had enjoyed since he had torn himself from the spot where she lay, whom he had loved so truly, even to the death to which he had brought her.

# CHAPTER IV

Two days after, the stranger and the orphan had departed for London. When it came to the point of decision, Mrs. Baker's conscience began to reproach her; and she doubted the propriety of intrusting her innocent charge to one totally unknown. But the stranger satisfied her doubts; he showed her papers betokening his name and station, as John Falkner, captain in the native cavalry of the East India Company, and moreover possessed of such an independence as looked like wealth in the eyes of Mrs. Baker, and at once commanded her respect.

His own care was to collect every testimony and relic that might prove the identity of the little Elizabeth. Her unfortunate mother's unfinished letter—her Bible and prayer-book—in the first of which was recorded the birth of her child—and a seal (which Mrs. Baker's prudence had saved, when her avarice caused her to sell the watch), with Mr. Raby's coat of arms and crest engraved—a small desk, containing a few immaterial papers, and letters from strangers, addressed to Edwin Raby—such was Elizabeth's inheritance. In looking over the desk, Mr. Falkner found a little foreign almanac, embellished with prints, and fancifully bound—on the first page of which was written, in a woman's elegant hand, *To dearest Isabella—from her A. R.*

Had Falkner wanted proof as to the reality of his suspicions with regard to the friend of Mrs. Raby, here was conviction; he was about to press the dear handwriting to his lips, when, feeling his own unworthiness, he shuddered through every limb, and thrusting the book into his bosom, he, by a strong effort, prevented every outward mark of the thrilling agony which the sight of his victim's writing occasioned. It gave, at the same time, fresh firmness to his resolve to do all that was requisite to restore the orphan daughter of her friend to her place in society. She was as a bequest, left him by whom he last saw pale and senseless at his feet—who had been the dream of his life from boyhood, and was now the phantom to haunt him with remorse to his latest hour. To replace the dead to the lovely child was impossible. He knew the incomparable virtues of her to whom her mother bequeathed her, while every thought that tended to recall her to his memory was armed with a double sting—regret at having lost—horror at the fate he had brought upon her.

By what strange, incalculable, and yet sure enchainment of events had he been brought to supply her place! She was dead—through his accursed machinations she no longer formed a portion of the breathing world—how marvellous that he, flying from memory and conscience, resolved to expiate his half involuntary guilt by his own death, should have landed at Treby! Still more wondrous were the motives—hair slight in appearance, yet on which so vast a weight of circumstance hung—that led him to the twilight churchyard, and had made Mrs. Raby's grave the scene of the projected tragedy—which had brought the orphan to guard that grave from pollution, caused her to stay his upraised hand, and gained for herself a protector by the very act.

Whoever has been the victim of a tragic event—whoever has experienced life and hope—the past and the future wrecked by one fatal catastrophe, must be at once dismayed and awestruck to trace the secret agency of a thousand foregone, disregarded, and trivial events, which all led to the deplored end, and served, as it were, as invisible meshes to envelop the victim in the fatal net. Had the meanest among these been turned aside, the progress of the destroying destiny had been stopped; but there is no voice to cry "Hold!" no prophesying eye to discern the unborn event—and the future inherits its whole portion of wo.

Awed by the mysteries that encompassed and directed his steps, which used no agency except the unseen, but not unfelt, power which surrounds us with motive as with an atmosphere, Falkner yielded his hitherto unbending mind to control. He was satisfied to be led, and not to command; his impatient spirit wondered at this new docility, while yet he felt some slight self-satisfaction steal over him; and the prospect of being useful to the helpless little being who stood before him, weak in all except her irresistible claim to his aid, imparted such pleasure as he was surprised to feel.

Once again he visited the churchyard of Treby, accompanied by the orphan. She was loath to quit the spot—she could with difficulty consent to leave mamma. But Mrs. Baker had made free use of a grown-up person's much abused privilege of deceit, and told her lies in abundance; sometimes promising that she should soon return; sometimes assuring her that she would find her mother alive and well at the grand place whither she was going: yet, despite the fallacious hopes, she cried and sobbed bitterly during her last visits to her parents' graves. Falkner tried to sooth her, saying, "We must leave papa and mamma, dearest; God has taken them from you; but I will be a new papa to you."

The child raised her head, which she had buried in his breast, and in infantine dialect and accent said, "Will you be good to her, and love Baby, as papa did?"

"Yes, dearest child, I promise always to love you: will you love me, and call me your papa?"

"Papa, dear papa," she cried, clinging round his neck—"my new, good papa!" And then, whispering in his ear, she softly, but seriously, added, "I can't have a new mamma—I won't have any but my own mamma."

"No, pretty one," said Falkner, with a sigh, "you will never have another mamma; she is gone who would have been a second mother, and you are wholly orphaned."

An hour after they were on the road to London; and, full of engrossing and torturing thoughts as Falkner was, still he was called out of himself, and forced to admire the winning ways, the enchanting innocence and loveliness of his little charge. We human beings are so unlike one to the other, that it is often difficult to make one person understand that there is any force in an impulse which is omnipotent with another. Children, to some, are mere animals, unendued with instinct, troublesome, and unsightly—with others they possess a charm that reaches to the heart's core, and stirs the purest and most generous portions of our nature. Falkner had always loved children. In the Indian wilds, which for many years he had inhabited, the sight of a young native mother with her babe had moved him to envious tears. The fair, fragile offspring of European women, with blooming faces and golden hair, had often attracted him to bestow kind offices on parents whom otherwise he would have disregarded; the fiery passions of his own heart caused him to feel a soothing repose while watching the innocent gambols of childhood, while his natural energy, which scarcely ever found sufficient scope for exercise, led him to delight in protecting the distressed. If the mere chance spectacle of infant helplessness was wont to excite his sympathy, this sentiment, by the natural workings of the human heart, became far more lively when so beautiful and perfect a creature as Elizabeth Raby was thrown upon his protection. No one could have regarded her unmoved; her silver-toned laugh went to the heart; her alternately serious or gay looks, each emanating from the spirit of love; her caresses, her little words of endearment; the soft pressure of her tiny hand and warm rosy lips—were all as charming as beauty and the absence of guile could make them. And he, the miserable man, was charmed, and pitied the mother who had been forced to desert so sweet a flower—leaving to the bleak elements a blossom which it had been paradise for her to have cherished and sheltered in her own bosom for ever.

At each moment Falkner became more enchanted with his companion. Sometimes they got out of the chaise to walk up a hill; then, taking the child in his arms, he plucked flowers for her from the hedges, or she ran on before and gathered them for herself—now pulling ineffectually at some stubborn parasite—now pricking herself with brier, when his help was necessary to assist and make all well again. When again in the carriage she climbed on his knee and stuck the flowers in his hair, "to make papa fine;" and as trifles affect the mind when rendered sensitive by suffering, so was he moved by her trying to remove the thorns of the wild roses before she decorated him with them; at other times she twisted them among her own ringlets, and laughed to see herself mirrored in the front glasses of the chaise. Sometimes her mood changed, and she prattled seriously about "mamma." Asked if he did not think that she was sorry at Baby's going so far—far away—or, remembering the fanciful talk of her mother when her father died, she asked whether she were not following them through the air. As evening closed in, she looked out to see whether she could not perceive her; "I cannot hear her; she does not speak to me," she said; "perhaps she is a long way off, in that tiny star; but then she can see us—Are you there, mamma?"

Artlessness and beauty are more truly imaged on the canvass than in the written page. Were we to see the lovely orphan thus pictured (and Italian artists, and our own Reynolds, have painted such) with uplifted finger; her large earnest eyes looking inquiringly and tenderly for the shadowy form of her mother, as she might fancy it descending towards her from the little star her childish fancy singled out, a half smile on her lips, contrasted with the seriousness of her baby brow—if we could see such visibly presented on the canvass, the world would crowd round to admire. This pen but feebly traces the living grace of the little angel; but it was before Falkner; it stirred him to pity first, and then to deeper regret: he strained the child to his breast, thinking, "Oh, yes, I might have been a better and a happy man! False Alithea! why, through your inconstancy, are such joys buried for ever in your grave!"

A few minutes after and the little girl fell asleep, nestled in his arms. Her attitude had all the inartificial grace of childhood; her face hushed to repose, yet breathed of affection. Falkner turned his eyes from her to the starry sky. His heart swelled impatiently—his past life lay as a map unrolled before him. He had desired a peaceful happiness—the happiness of love. His fond aspirations had been snakes to destroy others, and to sting his own soul to torture. He writhed under the consciousness of the remorse and horror which were henceforth to track his path of life. Yet, even while he shuddered, he felt that a revolution was operating within himself—he no longer contemplated suicide. That which had so lately appeared a mark of courage wore now the guise of cowardice. And yet, if he were to live, where and how should his life be passed? He recoiled from the solitude of the heart which had marked his early years—and yet he felt that he could never more link himself in love or friendship to any.

He looked upon the sleeping child, and began to conjecture whether he might not find in her the solace he needed. Should he not adopt her, mould her heart to affection, teach her to lean on him only, be all the world to her, while her gentleness and caresses would give life a charm—without which it were vain to attempt to endure existence?

He reflected what Elizabeth's probable fate would be if he restored her to her father's family. Personal experience had given him a horror for the forbidding, ostentatious kindness of distant relations. That hers resembled such as he had known, and were imperious and cold-hearted, their conduct not only to Mrs. Raby, but previously to a meritorious son, did not permit him to doubt. If he made the orphan over to them, their luxuries and station would ill stand instead of affection and heartfelt kindness. Soft, delicate, and fond, she would pine and die. With him, on the contrary, she would be happy—he would devote himself to her—every wish gratified—her gentle disposition carefully cultivated—no rebuke, no harshness; his arms ever open to receive her in grief—his hand to support her in danger. Was not this a fate her mother would have preferred? In bequeathing her to her friend, she showed how little she wished that her sweet girl should pass into the hands of her husband's relations. Could he not replace that friend of whom he had so cruelly robbed her—whose loss was to be attributed to him alone?

We all are apt to think that when we discard a motive we cure a fault, and foster the same error from a new cause with a safe conscience. Thus, even now, aching and sore from the tortures of remorse for past faults, Falkner indulged in the same propensity, which, apparently innocent in its commencement, had led to fatal results. He meditated doing rather what he wished than what was strictly just. He did not look forward to the evils his own course involved, while he saw in disproportionate magnitude those to be brought about if he gave up his favourite project. What ills might arise to the orphan from her interweaving her fate with his—he, a criminal, in act, if not in intention—who might be called upon hereafter to answer for his deeds, and who at least must fly and hide himself—of this he thought not; while he determined that, fostered and guarded by him, Elizabeth must be happy—and, under the tutelage of her relations, she would become the victim of hardhearted neglect. These ideas floated somewhat indistinctly in his mind—and it was half unconsciously that he was building from them a fabric for the future as deceitful as it was alluring.

After several days' travelling, Falkner found himself with his young charge in London, and then he began to wonder wherefore he had repaired thither, and to consider that he must form some settled scheme for the future. He had in England neither relation nor friend whom he cared for. Orphaned at an early age, neglected by those who supported him, at least as far as the affections were concerned, he had, even in boyhood, known intimately, and loved but one person only—she who had ruled his fate to this hour—and was now among the dead. Sent to India in early youth, he had there to make his way in defiance of poverty, of want of connexion, of his own overbearing disposition—and the sense of wrong early awakened that made him proud and reserved. At last, most unexpectedly, the death of several relations caused the family estate to devolve upon him—and he had sold his commission in India and hastened home—with his heart so set upon one object, that he scarcely reflected, or reflected only to congratulate himself, on how alone he stood. And now that his impetuosity and ill-regulated passions had driven the dear object of all his thoughts to destruction—still he was glad that there were none to question him—none to wonder at his resolves; to advise or to reproach.

Still a plan was necessary. The very act of his life which had been so big with ruin and remorse enjoined some forethought. It was probable that he was already suspected, if not known. Detection and punishment in a shape most loathsome would overtake him, did he not shape his measures with prudence; and, as hate as well as love had mixed strongly in his motives, he was in no humour to give his enemies the triumph of visiting his crime on him.

What is written in glaring character in our own consciousness we believe to be visible to the whole world; and Falkner, after arriving in London, after leaving Elizabeth at an hotel, and walking into the streets, felt as if discovery was already on him, when he was accosted by an acquaintance, who asked him where he had been—what he had been doing—and why he was looking so deusedly ill. He stammered some reply, and was hastening away, when his friend, passing his arm through his, said, "I must tell you the strangest occurrence I ever heard of—I have just parted from a man—do you remember a Mr. Neville, whom you dined with at my house, when last in town?"

Falkner at this moment exercised with success the wonderful mastery which he possessed over feature and voice, and coldly replied that he did remember.

"And do you remember our conversation after he left us?" said his friend, "and my praises of his wife, whom I exalted as the pattern of virtue? Who can know woman! I could have bet any sum that she would preserve her good name to the end—and she has eloped."

"Well!" said Falkner, "is that all? is that the most wonderful circumstance ever heard?"

"Had you known Mrs. Neville," replied his companion, "you would be as astonished as I: with all her charms—all her vivacity—never had the breath of scandal reached her—she seemed one of those whose hearts, though warm, are proof against the attacks of love; and with ardent affections yet turn away from passion, superior and unharmed. Yet she has eloped with a lover—there is no doubt of that fact, for he was seen—they were seen going off together, and she has not been heard of since."

"Did Mr. Neville pursue them?" asked Falkner.

"He is even now in full pursuit—vowing vengeance—more enraged than I ever beheld man. Unfortunately, he does not know who the seducer is; nor have the fugitives yet been traced. The whole affair is the most mysterious—a lover dropped from the clouds—an angel of virtue subdued, almost before she is sought. Still they must be found out—they cannot hide themselves for ever."

"And then there will be a duel to the death?" asked Falkner, in the same icy accents.

"No," replied the other; "Mrs. Neville has no brother to fight for her, and her husband breathes law only. Whatever vengeance the law will afford, that he will use to the utmost—he is too angry to fight."

"The poltron!" exclaimed Falkner; "and thus he loses his sole chance of revenge."

"I know not that," replied his companion; "he has formed a thousand schemes of chastisement for both offenders, more dread than the field of honour—there is, to be sure, a mean, as well as an indignant spirit in him, that revels rather in the thought of inflicting infamy than death. He utters a thousand mysterious threats—I do not see exactly what he can do—but when he discovers his injurer, as he must some day—and I believe there are letters that afford a clew—he will wreak all that a savage, and yet a sordid desire of vengeance can suggest. Poor Mrs. Neville! after all, she must have lived a sad life with such a fellow!"

"And here we part," said Falkner; "I am going another way. You have told me a strange story—it will be curious to mark the end. Farewell!"

Brave to rashness as Falkner was, yet there was much in what he had just heard that made him recoil, and almost tremble. What the vengeance was that Mr. Neville could take, he too well knew—and he resolved to defeat it. His plans, before vague, were formed on the instant. His lip curled with a disdainful smile when he recollected what his friend had said of the mystery that hung over the late occurrences—he would steep them all in tenfold obscurity. To grieve for the past was futile, or rather, nothing he could do would prevent or alleviate the piercing regret that tortured him—but that need not influence his conduct. To leave his arch enemy writhing from injury, yet powerless to revenge himself—blindly cursing he knew not who, and removing the object of his curses from all danger of being hurt by them, was an image not devoid of satisfaction. Acting in conformity with these ideas, the next morning saw him on the road to Dover—Elizabeth still his companion, resolved to seek oblivion in foreign countries and far climes—and happy, at the same time, to have her with him, whose infantine caresses already poured balm upon his rankling wounds.

# CHAPTER V

Paris was the next, but transient, resting-place of the travellers. Here Falkner made such arrangements with regard to remittances as he believed would best ensure his scheme of concealment. He laid the map of Europe before him, and traced a course with his pencil somewhat erratic, yet not without a plan. Paris, Hamburgh, Stockholm, St. Petersburgh, Moscow, Odessa, Constantinople, through Hungary to Vienna. How many thousand miles! miles which, while he traversed, he could possess his soul in freedom—fear no scrutiny—be asked no insidious questions. He could look each man in the face, and none trace his crime in his own.

It was a wild scheme to make so young a child as Elizabeth the companion of these devious and long wanderings, yet it was her idea that shed golden rays on the boundless prospect he contemplated. He could not have undertaken this long journey alone—memory and remorse his only companions. He was not one of those, unfortunately, whom a bright eye and kindly smile can light at once into a flame—soon burnt out, it is true, but warming and cheering, and yet harmless, while it lasted. He could not, among strangers, at once discern the points to admire, and make, himself the companion of the intelligent and good, through a sort of freemasonry some spirits possess. This was a great defect of character. He was proud and reserved. His esteem must be won—long habits of intimacy formed—his fastidious taste never wounded—his imagination never balked; without this he was silent and wrapped in himself. All his life he had cherished a secret and ardent passion, beyond whose bounds everything was steril—this had changed from the hopes of love to the gnawing pangs of remorse—but still his heart fed on itself—and unless that was interested, and by the force of affection he were called out of himself, he must be miserable. To arrive unwelcomed at an inn—to wander through unknown streets and cities without any stimulus of interest or curiosity—to traverse vast tracts of country, useless to others, a burden to himself, alone—this would have been intolerable. But Elizabeth was the cure; she was the animating soul of his project; her smiles—her caresses—the knowledge that he benefited her, was the life-blood of his design. He indulged, with a sort of rapture, in the feeling that he loved, and was beloved by an angel of innocence, who grew each day into a creature endowed with intelligence, sympathies, hopes, fears, and affections—all individually her own, and yet all modelled by him—centred in him—to whom he was necessary—who would be his; not, like the vain love of his youth, only in imagination, but in every thought and sensation, to the end of time.

Nor did he intend to pursue his journey in such a way as to overtask her strength or injure her health. He cared not how much time elapsed before its completion. It would certainly employ years; it mattered not how many. When winter rendered travelling painful, he could take up his abode in a metropolis abounding in luxuries. During the summer heats he might fix himself in some villa, where the season would be mitigated to pleasantness. If impelled by a capricious predilection, he could stay for months in any chance-selected spot; but his home was, with Elizabeth beside him, in his travelling carriage. Perpetual change would baffle pursuit if any were set on foot; while the restlessness of his life, the petty annoyances and fleeting pleasures of a traveller's existence, would serve to occupy his mind, and prevent its being mastered by those passions to which one victim had been immolated, and which rendered the remnant of his days loathsome to himself. "I have determined to live," he thought, "and I must therefore ensure the means of life. I must adopt a method by which I can secure for each day that stock of patience which is necessary to lead me to the end of it. In the plan I have laid down, every day will have a task to be fulfilled, and while I employ myself in executing it, I need look neither before nor behind; and each day added thus, one by one, to one another, will form months and years, and I shall grow old travelling post over Europe."

His resolution made, he was eager to enter on his travels, which, singular to say, he performed even in the very manner he had determined; for the slight changes in the exact route, introduced afterward from motives of convenience or pleasure, might be deemed rather as in accordance with, than deviating from, his original project.

Falkner was not a man ordinarily met with. He possessed wild and fierce passions, joined to extreme sensibility, beneficence, and generosity. His boyhood had been rendered miserable by the violence of a temper roused to anger even from trifles. Collision with his fellow-creatures, a sense of dignity with his equals, and of justice towards his inferiors, had subdued this; still his blood was apt to boil when roused by any impediment to his designs, or the sight of injury towards others, and it was with great difficulty that he kept down the outward marks of indignation or contempt. To tame the vehemence of his disposition, he had endeavoured to shackle his imagination, and to cultivate his reason—and perhaps he fancied that he succeeded best when, in fact, he entirely failed. As now, when he took the little orphan with him away from all the ties of blood—the manners and customs of her country—from the discipline of regular education, and the society of others of her sex—had not Elizabeth been the creature she was, with a character not to be disharmonized by any circumstances, this had been a fearful experiment.

Yet he fondly hoped to derive happiness from it. Traversing long tracts of country with vast speed, cut off from intercourse with every one but her, and she endearing herself more, daily, by extreme sweetness of disposition, he began almost to forget the worm gnawing at his bosom; and, feeling himself free, to fancy himself happy. Unfortunately, it was not so: he had passed the fatal Rubicon, placed by conscience between innocence and crime; and however much he might for a time deaden the stings of feeling or baffle the inevitable punishment hereafter to arise from the consequences of his guilt, still there was a burden on his soul that took all real zest from life, and made his attempts at enjoyment more like the experiments of a physician to dissipate sickness, than the buoyant sensations of one in health.

But then he thought not of himself—he did not live in himself, but in the joyous being at his side. Her happiness was exuberant. She might be compared to an exotic, lately pinched, and drooping from the effects of the wintry air, transported back, in the first opening of a balmy southern spring, to its native clime. The young and tender green leaves unfolded themselves in the pleasant air; blossoms appeared among the foliage, and sweet fruit might be anticipated. Nor was it only the kindness of her protector that endeared him to her: much of the warm sentiment of affection arose from their singular modes of life. Had they continued at a fixed residence, in town or country, in a civilized land, Elizabeth had seen her guardian at stated periods; have now and then taken a walk with him, or gambolled in the garden at his side; while, for the chief part, their occupation and pursuits being different, they had been little together. As it was, they were never apart: side by side in a travelling carriage—now arriving, now departing; now visiting the objects worthy of observation in various cities. They shared in all the pleasures and pains of travel, and each incident called forth her sense of dependance, and his desire to protect; or, changing places, even at that early age, she soothed his impatience, while he was beguiled of his irritability by her cheerful voice and smiling face. In all this, Elizabeth felt most strongly the tie that bound them. Sometimes benighted; sometimes delayed by swollen rivers; reduced to bear together the miseries of a bad inn, or, at times, of no inn at all; sometimes in danger—often worn by fatigue—Elizabeth found in her adopted parent a shelter, a support, and a preserver. Creeping close to him, her little hand clasped in his, or carried in his arms, she feared nothing, because he was there. During storms at sea, he had placed his own person between her and the bitter violence of the wind, and had often exposed himself to the inclemency of the weather to cover her, and save her from wet and cold. At all times he was on the alert to assist, and his assistance was like the coming of a superior being, sufficient to save her from harm, and inspire her with courage. Such circumstances had, perhaps, made a slight impression on many children; but Elizabeth had senses and sensibilities so delicately strung, as to be true to the slightest touch of harmony.

She had not forgotten the time when, neglected, and almost in rags, she only heard the voice of complaint or chiding; when she crept alone over the sands to her mother's grave, and, did a tempest overtake her, there was none to shield or be of comfort; she remembered little accidents that had at times befallen her, which, to her infantine feelings, seemed mighty dangers. But there had been none, as now, to pluck her from peril and ensure her safety. She recollected when, on one occasion, a thunder-storm had overtaken her in the churchyard; when, hurrying home, her foot slipped, as she attempted to descend the wet path of the cliff; frightened, she clambered up again, and, returning home by the upper road, had lost her way, and found night darkening round her—wet, tired, and shivering with fear and cold; and then, on her return, her welcome had been a scolding—well meant, perhaps, but vulgar, loud, and painful: and now the contrast! Her wishes guessed—her thoughts divined—ready succour and perpetual vigilance were for ever close at hand; and all this accompanied by a gentleness, kindness, and even by a respect, which the ardent yet refined feelings of her protector readily bestowed. Thus a physical gratitude—so to speak—sprung up in her child's heart, a precursor to the sense of moral obligation to be developed in after years. Every hour added strength to her affection, and habit generated fidelity, and an attachment not to be shaken by any circumstances.

Nor was kindness from him the only tie between them. Elizabeth discerned his sadness, and tried to cheer his gloom. Now and then the fierceness of his temper broke forth towards others; but she was never terrified, and grieved for the object of his indignation; or if she felt it to be unjust, she pleaded the cause of the injured, and, by her caresses, brought him back to himself. She early learned the power she had over him, and loved him the more fondly on that account. Thus there existed a perpetual interchange of benefit—of watchful care—of mutual forbearance—of tender pity and thankfulness. If all this seems beyond the orphan's years, it must be remembered that peculiar circumstances develop peculiar faculties; and that, besides, what is latent does not the less exist on that account. Elizabeth could not have expressed, and was, indeed, unconscious of the train of feeling here narrated. It was the microcosm of a plant folded up in its germe. Sometimes looking at a green, unformed bud, we wonder why a particular texture of leaves must inevitably spring from it, and why another sort of plant should not shoot out from the dark stem: but, as the tiny leaflet uncloses, it is there in all its peculiarity, and endowed with all the especial qualities of its kind. Thus with Elizabeth, however, in the thoughtlessness and inexperience of childhood, small outward show was made of the inner sense; yet in her heart, tenderness, fidelity, and unshaken truth were folded up, to be developed as her mind gained ideas, and sensation gradually verged into sentiment.

The course of years, also, is included in this sketch. She was six years old when she left Paris—she was nearly ten when, after many wanderings, and a vast tract of country overpassed, they arrived at Odessa. There had always been a singular mixture of childishness and reflection in her, and this continued even now. As far as her own pleasures were concerned, she might be thought behind her age: to chase a butterfly—to hunt for a flower—to play with a favourite animal—to listen with eagerness to the wildest fairy tales—such were her pleasures; but there was something more as she watched the turns of countenance in him she named her father— adapted herself to his gloomy or communicative mood—pressed near him when she thought he was annoyed—and restrained every appearance of discomfort when he was distressed by her being exposed to fatigue or the inclement sky.

When at St. Petersburgh he fell ill, she never left his bedside; and, remembering the death of her parents, she wasted away with terror and grief. At another time, in a wild district of Russia, she sickened of the measles. They were obliged to take refuge in a miserable hovel; and, despite all his care, the want of medical assistance endangered her life, while her convalescence was rendered tedious and painful by the absence of every comfort. Her sweet eyes grew dim; her little head drooped. No mother could have attended on her more assiduously than Falkner; and she long after remembered his sitting by her in the night to give her drink—her pillow smoothed by him—and, when she grew a little better, his carrying her in his arms under a shady grove, so to give her the benefit of the air, in a manner that would least incommode her. These incidents were never forgotten. They were as the colour and fragrance to the rose—the very beauty and delight of both their lives. Falkner felt a half remorse at the too great pleasure he derived from her society; while hers was a sort of rapturous, thrilling adoration, that dreamed not of the necessity of a check, and luxuriated in its boundless excess.

# CHAPTER VI

It was late in the autumn when the travellers arrived at Odessa, whence they were to embark for Constantinople, in the neighbourhood of which city they intended to pass the winter.

It must not be supposed that Falkner journeyed in the luxurious and troublesome style of a *Milord Anglais*. A calèche was his only carriage. He had no attendant for himself, and was often obliged to change the woman hired for the service of Elizabeth. The Parisian with whom they commenced their journey was reduced to despair by the time they arrived at Hamburgh. The German who replaced her was dismissed at Stockholm. The Swede next hired became homesick at Moscow, and they arrived at Odessa without any servant. Falkner scarcely knew what to do, being quite tired of the exactions, caprices, and repinings of each expatriated menial—yet it was necessary that Elizabeth should have a female attendant; and, on his arrival at Odessa, he immediately set on foot various inquiries to procure one. Several presented themselves, who proved wholly unfit; and Falkner was made angry by their extortionate demands and total incapacity.

At length a person was ushered in to him, who looked, who was, English. She was below the middle stature—spare, and upright in figure, with a composed countenance, and an appearance of tidiness and quiet that was quite novel, and by no means unpleasing, contrasted with the animated gestures, loud voices, and exaggerated protestations of the foreigners.

"I hear, sir," she began, "that you are inquiring for an attendant to wait on Miss Falkner during your journey to Vienna: I should be very glad if you would accept my services."

"Are you a lady's maid in any English family here?" asked Falkner.

"I beg your pardon, sir," continued the little woman, primly, "I am a governess. I lived many years with a Russian lady at St. Petersburgh; she brought me here, and is gone and left me."

"Indeed!" exclaimed Falkner; "that seems a very unjust proceeding—how did it happen?"

"On our arrival at Odessa, sir, the lady, who had no such notion before, insisted on converting me to her church; and because I refused, she used me, I may say, very ill; and hiring a Greek girl, left me here quite destitute."

"It seems that you have the spirit of a martyr," observed Falkner, smiling.

"I do not pretend to that," she replied; "but I was born and brought up a Protestant; and I did not like to pretend to believe what I could not."

Falkner was pleased with the answer, and looked more scrutinizingly on the applicant. She was not ugly—but slightly pitted with the smallpox—and with insignificant features; her mouth looked obstinate—and her light gray eyes, though very quick and intelligent, yet from their smallness, and the lids and brows being injured by the traces of the malady, did not redeem her countenance from an entirely commonplace appearance, which might not disgust, but could not attract.

"Do you understand," asked Falkner, "that I need a servant, and not a governess? I have no other attendant for my daughter; and you must not be above waiting on her as she has been accustomed."

"I can make no objection," she replied; "my first wish is to get away from this place, free from expense. At Vienna I can find a situation such as I have been accustomed to—now I shall be very glad to reach Germany safely in any creditable capacity—and I shall be grateful to you, sir, if you do not consider my being destitute against me, but be willing to help a countrywoman in distress."

There was a simplicity, though a hardiness in her manner, and an entire want of pretension or affectation that pleased Falkner. He inquired concerning her abilities as a governess, and began to feel that in that capacity also she might be useful to Elizabeth. He had been accustomed, on all convenient occasions, to hire a profusion of masters; but this desultory sort of teaching did not inculcate those habits of industry and daily application which it is the best aim of education to promote. At the same time he much feared an improper female companion for the child, and had suffered a good deal of anxiety on account of the many changes he had been forced to make. He observed the lady before him narrowly—there was nothing prepossessing, but all seemed plain and unassuming; though formal, she was direct—her words few—her voice quiet and low, without being soft or constrained. He asked her what remuneration she would expect; she said that her present aim was to get to Vienna free of expense, and she did not expect much beyond—she had been accustomed to receive eighty pounds a year as governess, but as she was to serve Miss Falkner as maid, she would only ask twenty.

"But as I wish you to act as both," said Falkner, "we must join the two sums, and I will pay you a hundred."

A ray of pleasure actually for a second illuminated the little woman's face: while with an unaltered tone of voice she replied, "I shall be very thankful, sir, if you think proper."

"You must, however, understand our conditions," said Falkner. "I talk of Vienna—but I travel for my pleasure, with no fixed bourn or time. I am not going direct to Germany—I spend the winter at Constantinople. It may be that I shall linger in those parts—it may be that from Greece I shall cross to Italy. You must not insist on my taking you to Vienna: it is enough for your purpose, I suppose, if you reach a civilized part of the world, and are comfortably situated, till you find some other family going whither you desire."

She was acquiescent. She insisted, however, with much formality, that he should make inquiries concerning her from several respectable families at Odessa; otherwise, she said, he could not fitly recommend her to any other situation. Falkner complied. Every one spoke of her in high terms, lauding her integrity and kindness of heart. "Miss Jervis is the best creature in the world," said the wife of the French consul; "only she is English to the core—so precise, and formal, and silent, and quiet, and cold. Nothing can persuade her to do what she does not think right. After being so shamefully deserted, she might have lived in my house, or four or five others, doing nothing; but she chose to have pupils, and to earn money by teaching. This might have been merely for the sake of paying for her journey; but, besides this, we discovered that she supports some poor relation in England, and, while cast away here, she still remembered and sent remittances to one whom she thought in want. She has a heart of gold, though it does not shine."

Pleased with this testimony, Falkner thought himself fortunate in securing her services, at the same time that he feared he should find her presence a considerable encumbrance. A servant was a cipher, but a governess must receive attention—she was an equal, who would perpetually form a third with him and Elizabeth. His reserve, his love of independence, and his regard for the feelings of another, would be perpetually at war. To be obliged to talk when he wished to be silent; to listen to, and answer frivolous remarks; to know that at all times a stranger was there—all this seemed to him a gigantic evil; but it vanished after a few days' trial of their new companion's qualities. Whatever Miss Jervis's latent virtues might be, she thought that the chief among them was to be

"Content to dwell in decencies for ever"—

her ambition was to be unimpeachably correct in conduct. It a little jarred with her notions to be in the house of a single gentleman—but her desolate situation at Odessa allowed her no choice; and she tried to counterbalance the evil by seeing as little of her employer as possible. Brought up from childhood to her present occupation, she was moulded to its very form; and her thoughts never strayed beyond her theory of a good governess. Her methods were all straightforward—pointing steadily to one undisguised aim—no freak of imagination ever led her out of one hard, defined, unerratic line. She had no pretension, even in the innermost recess of her heart, beyond her station. To be diligent and conscientious in her task of teaching was the sole virtue to which she pretended; and, possessed of much good sense, great integrity, and untiring industry, she succeeded beyond what could have been expected from one apparently so insignificant and taciturn.

She was, at the beginning, limited very narrowly in the exercise of any authority over her pupil. She was obliged, therefore, to exert herself in winning influence, instead of controlling by reprimands. She took great pains to excite Elizabeth to learn; and once having gained her consent to apply to any particular study, she kept her to it with patience and perseverance; and the very zeal and diligence she displayed in teaching made Elizabeth ashamed to repay her with an inattention that looked like ingratitude. Soon, also, curiosity and a love of knowledge developed themselves. Elizabeth's mind was of that high order which soon found something congenial in study. The acquirement of new ideas—the sense of order, and afterward of power—awoke a desire for improvement. Falkner was a man of no common intellect; but his education had been desultory; and he had never lived with the learned and well-informed. His mind was strong in its own elements, but these lay scattered, and somewhat chaotic. His observation was keen, and his imagination fervid; but it was inborn, uncultivated, and unenriched by any vast stores of reading. He was the very opposite of a pedant. Miss Jervis was much of the latter; but the two served to form Elizabeth to something better than either. She learned from Falkner the uses of learning: from Miss Jervis she acquired the thoughts and experience of other men. Like all young and ardent minds, which are capable of enthusiasm, she found infinite delight in the pages of ancient history: she read biography, and speedily found models for herself, whereby she measured her own thoughts and conduct, rectifying her defects, and aiming at that honour and generosity which made her heart beat and cheeks glow when narrated of others.

There was another very prominent distinction between Falkner and the governess: it made a part of the system of the latter never to praise. All that she tasked her pupil to do was a duty—when not done it was a deplorable fault—when executed, the duty was fulfilled, and she need not reproach herself—that was all. Falkner, on the contrary, fond and eager, soon looked upon her as a prodigy; and though reserved, as far as his own emotions were concerned, he made no secret of his almost adoration of Elizabeth. His praise was enthusiastic—it brought tears into her eyes—and yet, strange to say, it is doubtful whether she ever strived so eagerly, or felt so satisfied with it, as for the parsimonious expressions of bare satisfaction from Miss Jervis. They excited two distinct sensations. She loved her protector the more for his fervid approbation—it was the crown of all his gifts—she wept sometimes only to remember his ardent expressions of approbation; but Miss Jervis inspired self-diffidence, and with it a stronger desire for improvement. Thus the sensibility of her nature was cultivated, while her conceit was checked: to feel that to be meritorious with Miss Jervis was impossible—not to be faulty was an ambitious aim. She easily discovered that affection rather than discernment dictated the approbation of Falkner; and loved him better, but did not prize herself the more.

He, indeed, was transported by the progress she made. Like most self-educated, or uneducated men, he had a prodigious respect for learning, and was easily deceived into thinking much of what was little: he felt elated when he found Elizabeth eager to recite the wonders recorded in history, and to delineate the characters of ancient heroes—narrating their achievements, and quoting their sayings. His imagination and keen spirit of observation were, at the same time, of the utmost use. He analyzed with discrimination the actions of her favourites—brought the experience of a mind full of passion and reflection to comment upon every subject, and taught her to refer each maxim and boasted virtue to her own sentiments and situation; thus to form a store of principle by which to direct her future life.

Nor were these more masculine studies the only lessons of Miss Jervis—needlework entered into her plan of education, as well as the careful inculcation of habits of neatness and order; and thus Elizabeth escaped for ever the danger she had hitherto run of wanting those feminine qualities without which every woman must be unhappy—and, to a certain degree, unsexed. The governess, meanwhile, was the most unobtrusive of human beings. She never showed any propensity to incommode her employer by making him feel her presence. Seated in a corner of the carriage, with a book in her hand, she adopted the ghostly rule of never speaking except when spoken to. When stopping at inns, or when, on arriving at Constantinople, they became stationary, she was even less obtrusive. At first Falkner had deemed it proper to ask her to accompany them in their excursions and drives; but she was so alive to the impropriety of being seen with a gentleman, with only a young child for their companion, that she always preferred staying at home. After ranging a beautiful landscape, after enjoying the breezes of heaven and the sight of the finest views in the world, when Elizabeth returned she always found her governess sitting in the same place, away from the window (because, when in London, she had been told that it was not proper to look out of a window), even though the sublimest objects of nature were spread for her view; and employed on needlework, or the study of some language that might hereafter serve to raise her in the class of governesses. She had travelled over half the habitable globe, and part of the uninhabited—but she had never diverged from the prejudices and habits of home—no gleam of imagination shed its golden hue over her drab-coloured mind: whatever of sensibility existed to soften or dulcify, she sedulously hid; yet such was her serenity, her justice, her trustworthiness, and total absence of pretension, that it was impossible not to esteem, and almost to like her.

The trio, thus diverse in disposition, yet, by the force of a secret harmony, never fell into discord. Miss Jervis was valued, and by Elizabeth obeyed in all that concerned her vocation—she therefore was satisfied. Falkner felt her use, and gladly marked the good effects of application and knowledge on the character of his beloved ward—it was the moulding of a block of Parian marble into a muse; all corners—all superfluous surface—all roughness departed—the intelligent, noble brow—the serious, inquiring eye—the mouth—seat of sensibility—all these were developed with new beauty, as animated by the aspiring soul within. Her gentleness and sweetness increased with the cultivation of her mind. To be wise and good was her ambition—partly to please her beloved father—partly because her young mind perceived the uses and beauty of knowledge.

If anything could have cured the rankling wounds of Falkner's mind, it was the excellence of the young Elizabeth. Again and again he repeated to himself, that, brought up among the worldly and cold, her noblest qualities would either have been destroyed, or produced misery. In contributing to her happiness and goodness, he hoped to make some atonement for the past. There were many periods when remorse, and regret, and self-abhorrence held powerful sway over him: he was, indeed, during the larger portion of his time, in the fullest sense of the word—miserable. Yet there were gleams of sunshine he had never hoped to experience again—and he readily gave way to this relief; while he hoped that the worst of his pains were over.

In this idea he was egregiously mistaken. He was allowed to repose for a few years. But the cry of blood was yet unanswered—the evil he had committed unatoned; though they did not approach him, the consequences of his crime were full of venom and bitterness to others—and, unawares and unexpectedly, he was brought to view and feel the wretchedness of which he was the sole author.

# CHAPTER VII

Three more years passed thus over the head of the young Elizabeth; when, during the warm summer months, the wanderers established themselves for a season at Baden. They had hitherto lived in great seclusion—and Falkner continued to do so; but he was not sorry to find his adopted child noticed and courted by various noble ladies, who were charmed by the pure complexion—the golden hair, and spirited, though gentle, manners of the young English girl.

Elizabeth's characteristic was an enthusiastic affectionateness—every little act of kindness that she received excited her gratitude: she felt as if she never could—though she would constantly endeavour—repay the vast debt she owed her benefactor. She loved to repass in her mind those sad days when, under the care of the sordid Mrs. Baker, she ran every hazard of incurring the worst evils of poverty; ignorance and blunted sensibility. She had preserved her little well-worn shoes, full of holes, and slipping from her feet, as a sort of record of her neglected situation. She remembered how her hours had been spent loitering on the beach—sometimes with her little book, from which her mother had taught her—oftener in constructing sand castles, decorated with pebbles and broken shells. She recollected how she had thus built an imitation of the church and churchyard, with its shady corner and single stone marking two graves: she remembered the vulgar, loud voice that called her from her employment with, "Come, Missy, come to your dinner! The Lord help me! I wonder when anybody else will give you a dinner." She called to mind the boasts of Mrs. Baker's children, contrasting their Sunday frock with hers—the smallest portion of cake given to her last, and with a taunt that made her little heart swell and her throat feel choked, so that she could not eat it, but scattered it to the birds—on which she was beat for being wasteful; all this was contrasted with the vigilance, the tenderness, the respect of her protector. She brooded over these thoughts till he became sacred in her eyes; and, young as she was, her heart yearned and sickened for an occasion to demonstrate the deep and unutterable thankfulness that possessed her soul.

She was not aware of the services she rendered him in her turn. The very sight of her was the dearest—almost the only joy of his life. Devoured by disappointment, gloom, and remorse, he found no relief except in her artless prattle, or the consciousness of the good he did her. She perceived this, and was ever on the alert to watch his mood, and to try by every art to awaken complacent feelings. She did not know, it is true, the cause of his sufferings—the fatal memories that haunted him in the silence of night—and threw a dusky veil over the radiance of day. She did not see the fair, reproachful figure that was often before him to startle and appal—she did not hear the shrieks that rung in his ears—nor behold her floating away, lifeless, on the turbid waves, who, but a little before, had stood in all the glow of life and beauty before him. All these agonizing images haunted silently his miserable soul, and Elizabeth could only see the shadow they cast over him, and strive to dissipate it. When she could perceive the dark hour passing off, chased away by her endeavours, she felt proud and happy. And when he told her that she had saved his life, and was his only tie to it—that she alone prevented his perishing miserably, or lingering in anguish and despair, her fond heart swelled with rapture; and what soul-felt vows she made to remain for ever beside him, and pay back to the last the incalculable debt she owed! If it be true that the most perfect love subsists between unequals—no more entire attachment ever existed than that between this man of sorrows and the happy, innocent child. He, worn by passion, oppressed by a sense of guilt, his brow trenched by the struggles of many years—she, stepping pure and free into life, innocent as an angel, animated only by the most disinterested feelings. The link between them, of mutual benefit and mutual interest, had been cemented by time and habit—by each waking thought and nightly dream. What is so often a slothful, unapparent sense of parental and filial duty, was with them a living, active spirit, for ever manifesting itself in some new form. It woke with them, went abroad with them—attuned the voice, and shone brightly in the eyes.

    It is a singular law of human life, that the past, which apparently no longer forms a portion of our existence, never dies; new shoots, as it were, spring up at different intervals and places, all bearing the indelible characteristics of the parent stalk; the circular emblem of eternity is suggested by this meeting and recurrence of the broken ends of our life. Falkner had been many years absent from England. He had quitted it to get rid of the consequences of an act which he deeply deplored, but which he did not wish his enemies to have the triumph of avenging. So completely during this interval had he been cut off from any, even allusion to the past, that he often tried to deceive himself into thinking it a dream; often into the persuasion that, tragical as was the catastrophe he had brought about, it was in its result for the best. The remembrance of the young and lovely victim lying dead at his feet prevented his ever being really the dupe of these fond deceits—but still, memory and imagination alone ministered to remorse—it was brought home to him by none of the effects from which he had separated himself by a vast extent of sea and land.

The sight of the English at Baden was exceedingly painful to him. They seemed so many accusers and judges; he sedulously avoided their resorts, and turned away when he saw any approach. Yet he permitted Elizabeth to visit among them, and heard her accounts of what she saw and heard even with pleasure; for every word showed the favourable impression she made, and the simplicity of her own tastes and feelings. It was a new world to her, to find herself talked to, praised, and caressed by decrepit, painted, but courteous old princesses, dowagers, and all the tribe of German nobility and English fashionable wanderers. She was much amused, and her lively descriptions often made Falkner smile, and pleased him by proving that her firm and unsophisticated heart was not to be deluded by adulation.

Soon, however, she became more interested by a strange tale she brought home of a solitary boy. He was English—handsome and well-born—but savage, and secluded to a degree that admitted of no attention being paid him. She heard him spoken of at first at the house of some foreigners. They entered on a dissertation on the peculiar melancholy of the English, that could develop itself in a lad scarcely sixteen. He was a misanthrope. He was seen rambling the country either on foot, or on a pony—but he would accept no invitations—shunned the very aspect of his fellows—never appearing, by any chance, in the frequented walks about the baths. Was he deaf and dumb? Some replied in the affirmative, and yet this opinion gained no general belief. Elizabeth once saw him at a little distance, seated under a wide-spreading tree in a little dell—to her he seemed more handsome than anything she had ever seen, and more sad. One day she was in company with a gentleman, who, she was told, was his father; a man somewhat advanced in years—of a stern, saturnine aspect—whose smile was a sneer, and who spoke of his only child, calling him that "unhappy boy," in a tone that bespoke rather contempt than commiseration. It soon became rumoured that he was somewhat alienated in mind through the ill treatment of his parent—and Elizabeth could almost believe this—she was so struck by the unfeeling and disagreeable appearance of the stranger.

All this she related to Falkner with peculiar earnestness—"If you could only see him," she said, "if we could only get him here—we would cure his misery, and his wicked father should no longer torment him. If he is deranged, he is harmless, and I am sure he would love us. It is too sad to see one so gentle and so beautiful pining away without any to love him."

Falkner smiled at the desire to cure every evil that crossed her path, which is one of the sweetest illusions of youth, and asked, "Has he no mother?"

"No," replied Elizabeth, "he is an orphan like me, and his father is worse than dead, as he is so inhuman. Oh! how I wish you would save him as you saved me."

"That, I am afraid, would be out of my power," said Falkner; "yet, if you can make any acquaintance with him, and can bring him here, perhaps we may discover some method of serving him."

For Falkner had, with all his sufferings and his faults, much of the Don Quixote about him, and never heard a story of oppression without forming a scheme to relieve the victim. On this permission, Elizabeth watched for some opportunity to become acquainted with the poor boy. But it was vain. Sometimes she saw him at a distance; but if walking in the same path, he turned off as soon as he saw her; or, if sitting down, he got up, and disappeared, as if by magic. Miss Jervis thought her endeavours by no means proper, and would give her no assistance. "If any lady introduced him to you," she said, "it would be very well; but, to run after a young gentleman, only because he looks unhappy, is very odd, and even wrong."

Still Elizabeth persisted; she argued, that she did not want to know him herself, but that her father should be acquainted with him—and either induce his father to treat him better, or take him home to live with them.

They lived at some distance from the baths, in a shady dell, whose sides, a little farther on, were broken and abrupt. One afternoon they were lingering not far from their house, when they heard a noise among the underwood and shrubs above them, as if some one was breaking his way through. "It is he—look!" cried Elizabeth; and there emerged from the covert, on to a more open but still more precipitous path, the youth they had remarked: he was urging his horse, with wilful blindness to danger, down a declivity which the animal was unwilling to attempt. Falkner saw the danger, and was sure that the boy was unaware of how steep the path grew at the foot of the hill. He called out to him, but the lad did not heed his voice—in another minute the horse's feet slipped, the rider was thrown over his head, and the animal himself rolled over. With a scream, Elizabeth sprang to the side of the fallen youth, but he rose without any appearance of great injury, or any complaint, evidently displeased at being observed: his sullen look merged into one of anxiety as he approached his fallen horse, whom, together with Falkner, he assisted to rise—the poor thing had fallen on a sharp point of a rock, and his side was cut and bleeding. The lad was now all activity; he rushed to the stream that watered the little dell to procure water, which he brought in his hat to wash the wound; and as he did so, Elizabeth remarked to her father that, he used only one hand, and that the other arm was surely hurt. Meanwhile Falkner had gazed on the boy with a mixture of admiration and pain. He was wondrously handsome; large, deep-set hazel eyes, shaded by long dark lashes—full at once of fire and softness; a brow of extreme beauty, over which clustered a profusion of chestnut-coloured hair; an oval face; a person light and graceful as a sculptured image—all this, added to an expression of gloom that amounted to sullenness, with which, despite the extreme refinement of his features, a certain fierceness even was mingled, formed a study a painter would have selected for a kind of ideal poetic sort of bandit stripling; but, besides this, there was resemblance, strange and thrilling, that struck Falkner, and made him eye him with a painful curiosity. The lad spoke with fondness to his horse, and accepted the offer made that it should be taken to Falkner's stable, and looked to by his groom.

"And you, too," said Elizabeth, "you are in pain, you are hurt."

"That is nothing," said the youth; "let me see that I have not killed this poor fellow—and I am not hurt to signify."

Elizabeth felt by no means sure of this. And while the horse was carefully led home, and his wound visited, she sent a servant off for a surgeon, believing, in her own mind, that the stranger had broken his arm. She was not far wrong—he had dislocated his wrist. "It were better had it been my neck," he muttered, as he yielded his hand to the gripe of the surgeon, nor did he seem to wince during the painful operation; far more annoyed was he by the eyes fixed upon him and the questions asked—his manner, which had become mollified as he waited on his poor horse, resumed all its former repulsiveness; he looked like a young savage, surrounded by enemies whom he suspects, yet is unwilling to assail: and when his hand was bandaged, and his horse again and again recommended to the groom, he was about to take leave, with thanks that almost seemed reproaches, for having an obligation thrust on him, when Miss Jervis exclaimed, "Surely, I am not mistaken—are you not Master Neville?"

Falkner started as if a snake had glided across his path, while the youth, colouring to the very roots of his hair, and looking at her with a sort of rage at being thus in a matter detected, replied, "My name is Neville."

"I thought so," said the other; "I used to see you at Lady Glenfell's. How is your father, Sir Boyvill?"

But the youth would answer no more; he darted at the questioner a look of fury, and rushed away. "Poor fellow!" cried Miss Jervis, "he is wilder than ever—he is a very sad case. His mother was the Mrs. Neville talked of so much once—she deserted him, and his father hates him. The young gentleman is half crazed by ill treatment and neglect."

"Dearest father, are you ill?" cried Elizabeth—for Falkner had turned ashy pale—but he commanded his voice to say that he was well, and left the room; a few minutes afterward he had left the house, and, seeking the most secluded pathways, walked quickly on as if to escape from himself. It would not do—the form of *her* son was before him—a ghost to haunt him to madness. *Her* son, whom she had loved with passion inexpressible, crazed by neglect and unkindness. Crazed he was not—every word he spoke showed a perfect possession of acute faculties—but it was almost worse to see so much misery in one so young. In person, he was a model of beauty and grace—his mind seemed formed with equal perfection; a quick apprehension, a sensibility, all alive to every touch; but these were nursed in anguish and wrong, and strained from their true conclusions into resentment, suspicion, and a fierce disdain of all who injured, which seemed to his morbid feelings all who named or approached him. Falkner knew that he was the cause of this evil. How different a life he had led, if his mother had lived! The tenderness of her disposition, joined to her great talents and sweetness, rendered her unparalleled in the attention she paid to his happiness and education. No mother ever equalled her—for no woman ever possessed at once equal virtues and equal capacities. How tenderly she had reared him, how devotedly fond she was, Falkner too well knew; and tones and looks, half forgotten, were recalled vividly to his mind at the sight of this poor boy, wretched and desolate through his rashness. What availed it to hate, to curse the father!—he had never been delivered over to this father, had never been hated by him, had his mother survived. All these thoughts crowded into Falkner's mind, and awoke an anguish, which time had rendered, to a certain degree, torpid. He regarded himself with bitter contempt and abhorrence—he feared, with a kind of insane terror, to see the youth again, whose eyes, so like *hers*, he had robbed of all expression of happiness, and clouded by eternal sorrow. He wandered on—shrouded himself in the deepest thickets, and clambered abrupt hills, so that, by breathless fatigue of body, he might cheat his soul of its agony.

Night came on, and he did not return home. Elizabeth grew uneasy—till at last, on making more minute inquiry, she found that he had come back, and was retired to his room.

It was the custom of Falkner to ride every morning with his daughter soon after sunrise; and on the morrow, Elizabeth had just equipped herself, her thoughts full of the handsome boy—whose humanity to his horse, combined with fortitude in enduring great personal pain, rendered far more interesting than ever. She felt sure that, having once commenced, their acquaintance would go on, and that his savage shyness would be conquered by her father's kindness. To alleviate the sorrows of his lot—to win his confidence by affection, and to render him happy, was a project that was occupying her delightfully—when the tramp of a horse attracted her attention—and, looking from the window, she saw Falkner ride off at a quick pace. A few minutes afterward a note was brought to her from him. It said—

"DEAR ELIZABETH,

"Some intelligence which I received yesterday obliges me unexpectedly to leave Baden. You will find me at Mayence. Request Miss Jervis to have everything packed up as speedily as possible; and to send for the landlord, and give up the possession of our house. The rent is paid. Come in the carriage. I shall expect you this evening.

"Yours, dearest,

"J. FALKNER."

Nothing could be more disappointing than this note. Her first fairy dream beyond the limits of her home, to be thus brushed away at once. No word of young Neville—no hope held out of return! For a moment an emotion ruffled her mind, very like ill-humour. She read the note again—it seemed yet more unsatisfactory—but, in turning the page, she found a postscript. "Pardon me," it said, "for not seeing you last night; I was not well—nor am I now."

These few words instantly gave a new direction to her thoughts—her father not well, and she absent, was very painful—then she recurred to the beginning of the note. "Intelligence received yesterday"—some evil news, surely—since the result was to make him ill—at such a word the recollection of his sufferings rushed upon her, and she thought no more of the unhappy boy, but, hurrying to Miss Jervis, entreated her to use the utmost expedition that they might depart speedily. Once she visited Neville's horse; it was doing well, and she ordered it to be led carefully and slowly to Sir Boyvill's stables.

So great was her impatience, that by noon they were in the carriage—and in a few hours they joined Falkner at Mayence. Elizabeth gazed anxiously on him. He was an altered man—there was something wild and haggard in his looks, that bespoke a sleepless night, and a struggle of painful emotion by which the very elements of his being were convulsed:—"You are ill, dear father," cried Elizabeth; "you have heard some news that afflicts you very much."

"I have," he replied; "but do not regard me: I shall recover the shock soon, and then all will be as it was before. Do not ask questions—but we must return to England immediately."

To England! such a word Falkner had never before spoken—Miss Jervis looked almost surprised, and really pleased. A return to her native country, so long deserted, and almost forgotten, was an event to excite Elizabeth even to agitation—the very name was full of so many associations. Were they hereafter to reside there? Should they visit Treby? What was about to happen? She was bid ask no questions, and she obeyed—but her thoughts were the more busy. She remembered, also, that Neville was English, and she looked forward to meeting him, and renewing her projects for his welfare.

# CHAPTER VIII

In the human heart, and, if observation does not err, more particularly in the heart of man, the passions exert their influence fitfully. With some analogy to the laws which govern the elements, they now sleep in calm, and now arise with the violence of furious winds. Falkner had latterly attained a state of feeling approaching to equanimity. He displayed more cheerfulness—a readier interest in the daily course of events—a power to give himself up to any topic discussed in his presence; but this had now vanished. Gloom sat on his brow—he was inattentive even to Elizabeth. Sunk back in the carriage—his eyes bent on vacancy, he was the prey of thoughts, each of which had the power to wound.

It was a melancholy journey. And when they arrived in London, Falkner became still more absorbed and wretched. The action of remorse, which had been for some time suspended, renewed its attacks, and made him look upon himself as a creature at once hateful and accursed. We are such weak beings, that the senses have power to impress us with a vividness which no mere mental operation can produce. Falkner had been at various times haunted by the probable consequences of his guilt on the child of his victim. He recollected the selfish and arrogant character of his father; and conscience had led him to reproach himself with the conviction, that whatever virtues young Neville derived from his mother, or had been implanted by her care, must have been rooted out by the neglect or evil example of his surviving parent. The actual effect of her loss he had not anticipated. There was something heart-breaking to see a youth, nobly gifted by nature and fortune, delivered over to a sullen resentment for unmerited wrongs—to dejection, if not to despair. An uninterested observer must deeply compassionate him; Elizabeth had done so, child as she was, with a pity almost painful from its excess; what, then, must he feel who knew himself to be the cause of all his wo?

Falkner was not a man to sit quietly under these emotions. In their first onset they had driven him to suicide; preserved as by a miracle, he had exerted strong self-command, and, by dint of resolution, forced himself to live. Year after year had passed, and he abided by the sentence of life he had passed on himself—and, like the galley-slave, the iron which had eaten into the flesh galled less than when newly applied. But he was brought back from the patience engendered by custom at the sight of the unfortunate boy. He felt himself accursed—God-reprobated—mankind (though they knew it not) abhorred him. He would no longer live—for he deserved to die. He would not again raise his hand against himself—but there are many gates to the tomb; he found no difficulty in selecting one by which to enter. He resolved to enter upon a scene of desperate warfare in a distant country, and to seek a deliverance from the pains of life by the bullet or the sword on the field of battle. Above all, he resolved that Elizabeth's innocence should no longer be associated with his guilt. The catastrophe he meditated must be sought alone, and she, whom he had lived to protect and foster, must be guarded from the hardships and perils to which he was about to deliver himself up.

Meditation on this new course absorbed him for some days. At first he had been sunk in despondency; as the prospect opened before him of activity allied to peril, and sought for the sake of the destruction to which it unavoidably led, his spirits rose; like a war-horse dreaming of the sound of a trumpet, his heart beat high in the hope of forgetting the consciousness of remorse in all the turbulence of battle or the last forgetfulness of the grave. Still it was a difficult task to impart his plan to the orphan, and to prepare her for a separation. Several times he had tried to commence the subject, and felt his courage fail him. At length, being together one day, some weeks after their arrival in London—when, indeed, many steps had been already taken by him in furtherance of his project—at twilight, as they sat together near the window which looked upon one of the London squares—and they had been comparing this metropolis with many foreign cities—Falkner abruptly, fearful, if he lost this occasion, of not finding another so appropriate, said, "I must bid you good-by to-night, Elizabeth—to-morrow, early, I set out for the north of England."

"You mean to leave me behind?" she asked; "but you will not be away long?"

"I am going to visit your relations," he replied; "to disclose to them that you are under my care, and to prepare them to receive you. I hope soon to return, either to conduct you to them, or to bring one among them to welcome you here."

Elizabeth was startled. Many years had elapsed since Falkner had alluded to her alien parentage. She went by his name, she called him father; and the appellation scarcely seemed a fiction—he had been the kindest, fondest parent to her—nor had he ever hinted that he meant to forego the claim his adoption had given him, and to make her over to those who were worse than strangers in her eyes. If ever they had recurred to her real situation, he had not been chary of expressions of indignation against the Raby family. He had described with warm resentment the selfishness, the hardness of heart, and disdain of the well-being of those allied to them by blood, which too often subsists in aristocratic English families when the first bond has been broken by any act of disobedience. He grew angry as he spoke of the indignity with which her mother had been treated, and the barbarous proposition of separating her from her only child; and he had fondly assured her that it was his dearest pride to render her independent of these unworthy and inhuman relations. Why were his intentions changed? His voice and look were ominous. Elizabeth was hurt—she did not like to object; she was silent—but Falkner deciphered her wounded feelings in her ingenuous countenance, and he too was pained; he could not bear that she should think him ungrateful—mindless of her affection, her filial attentions, and endearing virtues; he felt that he must, to a certain degree, explain his views—difficult as it was to make a segment of his feelings in any way take a definite or satisfactory shape.

"Do not think hardly of me, my own dear girl," he began, "for wishing that we should separate. God knows that it is a blow that will visit me far more severely than you. You will find relations and friends who will be proud of you—whose affections you will win; wherever you are, you will meet with love and admiration—and your sweet disposition and excellent qualities will make life happy. I depart alone. You are my only tie—my only friend—I break it and leave you—never can I find another. Henceforth, alone, I shall wander into distant and uncivilized countries, enter on a new and perilous career, during which I may perish miserably. You cannot share these dangers with me."

"But why do you seek them?" exclaimed Elizabeth, alarmed by this sudden prophecy of ill.

"Do you remember the day when we first met?" replied Falkner; "when my hand was raised against my own life, because I knew myself unworthy to exist. It is the same now. It is cowardly to live, feeling that I have forfeited every right to enjoy the blessings of life. I go that I may die—not by my own hand—but where I can meet death by the hand of others."

Strangely and frightfully did these words fall on the ear of his appalled listener; he went on rapidly—for having once begun, the words he uttered relieved, in some degree, the misery that burdened his soul.

"This idea cannot astonish you, my love; you have seen too much of the secret of my heart; you have witnessed my fits of distress and anguish, and are not now told, for the first time, that grief and remorse weigh intolerably on me. I can endure the infliction no longer. May God forgive me in another world—the light of this I will see no more!"

Falkner saw the sort of astonished distress her countenance depicted; and, angry with himself for being its cause, was going on in a voice changed to one less expressive of misery, but Elizabeth, seized with dismay—the unbidden tears pouring from her eyes—her young—her child's heart bursting with a new sense of horror—cast herself at his feet, and, embracing his knees as he sat, exclaimed, "My dear, dear father!—my more than father, and only friend—you break my heart by speaking thus. If you are miserable, the more need that your child—the creature you preserved, and taught to love you—should be at your side to comfort—I had almost said to help you. You must not cast me off! Were you happy, you might desert me; but if you are miserable, I cannot leave you—you must not ask me—it kills me to think of it!"

The youthful, who have no experience of the changes of life, regard the present with far more awe and terror than those who have seen one turn in the hourglass suffice to change, and change again, the colour of their lives. To be divided from Falkner was to have the pillars of the earth shaken under her—and she clung to him, and looked up imploringly in his face, as if the next word he spoke were to decide all; he kissed her, and, seating her on his knee, said, "Let us talk of this more calmly, dearest—I was wrong to agitate you—or to mix the miserable thoughts forced on me by my wretchedness, with the prudent consideration of your future destiny. I feel it to be unjust to keep you from your relations. They are rich. We are ignorant of what changes and losses may have taken place among them, to soften their hearts—which, after all, were never shut against you. You may have become of importance in their eyes. Raby is a proud name, and we must not heedlessly forego the advantages that may belong to your right to it."

"My dear father," replied Elizabeth, "this talk is not for me. I have no wish to claim the kindness of those who treated my true parents ill. You are everything to me. I am little more than a child, and cannot find words to express all I mean; but my truest meaning is, to show my gratitude to you till my dying day; to remain with you for ever, while you love me; and to be the most miserable creature in the world if you drive me from you. Have we not lived together since I was a little thing, no higher than your knee? And all the time you have been kinder than any father. When we have been exposed to storms, you have wrapped me round in your arms so that no drop could fall on my head. Do you remember that dreadful evening, when our carriage broke down in the wide, dark steppe; and you, covering me up, carried me in your arms, while the wind howled and the freezing rain drove against you? You could hardly bear up; and when we arrived at the post-house, you, strong man as you are, fainted from exhaustion; while I, sheltered in your arms, was as warm and well as if it had been a summer's day. You have earned me—you have bought me by all this kindness, and you must not cast me away!"

She clung round his neck—her face bathed in tears, sobbing and speaking in broken accents. As she saw him soften, she implored him yet more earnestly, till his heart was quite subdued; and, clasping her to his heart, he showered kisses on her head and neck; while, to his surprise, forgotten tears sprung to his own eyes. "For worlds I would not desert you," he cried. "It is not casting you away that we should separate for a short time; for where I go, indeed, dearest, you cannot accompany me. I cannot go on living as I have done. For many years now my life has been spent in pleasantness and peace—I have no right to this—hardship, and toil, and death I ought to repay. I abhor myself for a coward, when I think of what others suffer through my deeds—while I am scathless. You can scarcely remember the hour when the touch of your little hand saved my life. My heart is not changed since then—I am unworthy to exist. Dear Elizabeth, you may one day hate me, when you know the misery I have caused to those who deserved better at my hands. The cry of my victim rings in my ears, and I am base to survive my crime. Let me, dearest, make my own the praise, that nothing graced my life more than the leaving it. To live a coward and a drone, suits vilely with my former acts of violence and ill. Let me gain peace of mind by exposing my life to danger. By advocating a just cause I may bring a blessing down upon my endeavours. I shall go to Greece. Theirs is a good cause—that of liberty and Christianity against tyranny and an evil faith. Let me die for it; and when it is known, as it will one day be, that the innocent perished through me, it will be added, that I died in the defence of the suffering and the brave. But you cannot go with me to Greece, dearest; you must await my return in this country."

"You go to die!" she exclaimed, "and I am to be far away. No, dear father, I am a little girl, but no harm can happen to me. The Ionian Isles are under the English government—there, at least, I may go. Athens too, I dare say, is safe. Dear Athens—we spent a happy winter there before the revolution began. You forget what a traveller I am—how accustomed to find my home among strangers in foreign and savage lands. No, dear father, you will not leave me behind. I am not unreasonable—I do not ask to follow you to the camp—but you must let me be near—in the same country as yourself."

"You force me to yield against my better reason," said Falkner. "This is not right—I feel that it is not so—one of your sex, and so young, ought not to be exposed to all I am about to encounter; and if I should die, and leave you there desolate?"

"There are good Christians everywhere to protect the orphan," persisted Elizabeth. "As if you could die when I am with you! And if you died while I was far, what would become of me? Am I to be left, like a poor sailor's wife—to get a shocking, black-sealed letter, to tell me that, while I was enjoying myself, and hoping that you had long been—It is wicked to speak of these things—but I shall go with my own dear, dear father, and he shall not die!"

Falkner yielded to her tears, her caresses, and persuasions. He was not convinced, but he could not withstand the excess of grief she displayed at the thought of parting. It was agreed that she should accompany him to the Ionian Isles, and take up her residence there while he joined the patriot band in Greece. This point being decided upon, he was anxious that their departure should not be delayed a single hour, for most earnest was he to go, to throw off the sense of the present—to forget his pangs in anticipated danger.

Falkner played no false part with himself. He longed to die; nor did the tenderness and fidelity of Elizabeth disarm his purpose. He was convinced that she must be happier and more prosperous when he was removed. His tortured mind found relief when he thought of sacrificing his life, and quitting it honourably on the field of battle. It was only by the prospect of such a fate that he shut his eyes to sterner duties. In his secret heart, he knew that the course demanded of him by honour and conscience was to stand forth, declare his crime, and reveal the mysterious tragedy, of which he was the occasion, to the world; but he dared not accuse himself, and live. It was this that urged him to the thoughts of death. "When I am no more," he told himself, "let all be declared—let my name be loaded with curses—but let it be added, that I died to expiate my guilt. I cannot be called upon to live with a brand upon my name; soon it will be all over, and then let them heap obloquy, pyramid-high, upon my grave! Poor Elizabeth will become a Raby; and, once cold beneath the sod, no more misery will spring from acts of mine!"

Actuated by these thoughts, Falkner drew up two narratives—both short. The tenour of one need not be mentioned in this place. The other stated how he had found Elizabeth and adopted her. He sealed up with this the few documents that proved her birth. He also made his will—dividing his property between his heir at law and adopted child—and smiled proudly to think, that, dowered thus by him, she would be gladly received into her father's family.

Every other arrangement for their voyage was quickly made, and it remained only to determine whether Miss Jervis should accompany them. Elizabeth's mind was divided. She was averse to parting with an unoffending and kind companion, and to forego her instructions—though, in truth, she had got beyond them. But she feared that the governess might hereafter shackle her conduct. Every word Falkner had let fall concerning his desire to die, she remembered and pondered upon. To watch over and to serve him was her aim in going with him. Child as she was, a thousand combinations of danger presented themselves to her imagination, when her resolution and fearlessness might bring safety. The narrow views and timid disposition of Miss Jervis might impede her grievously.

The governess herself was perplexed. She was startled when she heard of the new scheme. She was pleased to find herself once again in England, and repugnant to the idea of leaving so soon again for so distant a region, where a thousand perils of war and pestilence would beset every step. She was sorry to part with Elizabeth, but some day that time must come; and others, dearer from ties of relationship, lived in England from whom she had been too long divided. Weighing these things, she showed a degree of hesitation that caused Falkner to decide as his heart inclined, and to determine that she should not accompany him. She went with them as far as Plymouth, where they embarked. Elizabeth, so long a wanderer, felt no regret in leaving England. She was to remain with one who was far more than country—who was indeed her all. Falkner felt a load taken from his heart when his feet touched the deck of the vessel that was to bear them away—half his duty was accomplished—the course begun which would lead to the catastrophe he coveted. The sun shone brightly on the ocean, the breeze was fresh and favourable. Miss Jervis saw them push from shore with smiles and happy looks—she saw them on the deck of the vessel, which, with sails unfurled, had already begun its course over the sea. Elizabeth waved her handkerchief—all grew confused; the vessel itself was sinking beneath the horizon, and long before night no portion of her canvass could be perceived.

"I wonder," thought Miss Jervis, "whether I shall ever see them again!"

# CHAPTER IX

Three years from this time, Elizabeth found herself in the position she had vaguely anticipated at the outset, but which every day spent in Greece showed her as probable, if not inevitable. These three years brought Falkner to the verge of the death he had gone out to seek. He lay wounded, a prey of the Greek fever, to all appearance about to die; while she watched over him, striving, not only to avert the fatal consequences of disease, but also to combat the desire to die which destroyed him.

In describing Elizabeth's conduct during these three years, it may be thought that the type is presented of ideal and almost unnatural perfection. She was, it is true, a remarkable creature; and unless she had possessed rare and exalted qualities, her history had not afforded a topic for these pages. She was intelligent, warm-hearted, courageous, and sincere. Her lively sense of duty was perhaps her chief peculiarity. It was that which strung to such sweet harmony the other portions of her character. This had been fostered by the circumstances of her life. Her earliest recollection was of her dying parents. Their mutual consolations, the bereaved widow's lament, and her talk of another and a better world, where all would meet again who fulfilled their part virtuously in this world. She had been taught to remember her parents as inheriting the immortal life promised to the just, and to aspire to the same. She had learned, from her mother's example, that there is nothing so beautiful and praiseworthy as the sacrifice of life to the good and happiness of one beloved. She never forgot her debt to Falkner. She felt herself bound to him by stronger than filial ties. A father performs an imperious duty in cherishing his child; but all had been spontaneous benevolence in Falkner. His very faults and passions made his sacrifice the greater, and his generosity the more conspicuous. Elizabeth believed that she could never adequately repay the vast obligation which she was under to him.

Miss Jervis also had conduced to perfectionize her mind by adding to its harmony and justness. Miss Jervis, it is true, might be compared to the rough-handed gardener, whose labours are without elegance, and yet to whose waterings and vigilance the fragrant carnation owes its peculiar tint, and the wax-like camellia its especial variety. It was through her that she had methodised her mind—through her that she had learned to concentrate and prolong her attention, and to devote it to study. She had taught her order and industry—and, without knowing it, she had done more—she had inspired ardour for knowledge, delight in its acquisition, and a glad sense of self-approbation when difficulties were conquered by perseverance; and when, by dint of resolution, ignorance was exchanged for a clear perception of any portion of learning.

It has been said that every clever person is, to a certain degree, mad. By which it is to be understood, that every person whose mind soars above the vulgar, has some exalted and disinterested object in view to which they are ready to sacrifice the common blessings of life. Thus, from the moment that Elizabeth had brought Falkner to consent to her accompanying him to Greece, she had devoted herself to the task, first, of saving his life, if it should be in danger; and, secondly, of reconciling him in the end to prolonged existence. There were many difficulties which presented themselves, since she was unaware of the circumstances that drove him to seek death as a remedy and an atonement; nor had she any desire to pry into her benefactor's secrets: in her own heart, she suspected an overstrained delicacy or generosity of feeling, which exaggerated error, and gave the sting to remorse. But whatever was the occasion of his sufferings, she dedicated herself to their relief; and resolved to educate herself so as to fulfil the task of reconciling him to life, to the best of her ability.

Left at Zante, while he proceeded to join the patriot bands of Greece, she boarded in the house of a respectable family, but lived in the most retired manner possible. Her chief time was spent in study. She read to store her mind—to confirm its fortitude—to elevate its tone. She read, also, to acquire such precepts of philosophy and religion as might best apply to her peculiar task, and to learn those secrets of life and death which Falkner's desire to die had brought so home to her juvenile imagination.

If a time is to be named when the human heart is nearest moral perfection, most alive, and yet most innocent, aspiring to good, without a knowledge of evil, the period at which Elizabeth had arrived—from thirteen to sixteen—is it. Vague forebodings are awakened; a sense of the opening drama of life, unaccompanied with any longing to enter on it—that feeling is reserved for the years that follow; but at fourteen and fifteen we only feel that we are emerging from childhood, and we rejoice, having yet a sense that as yet it is not fitting that we should make one of the real actors on the world's stage. A dreamy, delicious period, when all is unknown; and yet we feel that all is soon to be unveiled. The first pang has not been felt; for we consider childhood's woes (real and frightful as those sometimes are) as puerile, and no longer belonging to us. We look upon the menaced evils of life as a fiction. How can care touch the soul which places its desires beyond low-minded thought? Ingratitude, deceit, treason—these have not yet engendered distrust of others, nor have our own weaknesses and errors planted the thorn of self-disapprobation and regret. Solitude is no evil, for the thoughts are rife with busy visions; and the shadows that flit around and people our reveries have almost the substance and vitality of the actual world.

Elizabeth was no dreamer. Though brought up abstracted from common worldly pursuits, there was something singularly practical about her. She aimed at being useful in all her reveries. This desire was rendered still more fervent by her affection for Falkner—by her fears on his account— by her ardent wish to make life dear to him. All her employments, all her pleasures, referred themselves, as it were, to this primary motive, and were entirely ruled by it.

She portioned out the hours of each day, and adhered steadily to her self-imposed rules. To the early morning's ride succeeded her various studies, of which music, for which she developed a true ear and delicate taste, formed one: one occupation relieved the other; from her dear books she had recourse to her needle, and, bending over her embroidery frame, she meditated on what she read; or, occupied by many conjectures and many airy dreams concerning Falkner, she became absorbed in revery. Sometimes, from the immediate object of these, her memory reverted to the melancholy boy she had seen at Baden. His wild eyes—his haughty glance—his lively solicitude about the animal he had hurt, and uncomplaining fortitude with which he had endured bodily pain, were often present to her. She wished that they had not quitted Baden so suddenly: if they had remained but a few days longer, he might have learned to love them; and even now he might be with Falkner, sharing his dangers, it is true, but also each guarding the other from that rash contempt of life in which they both indulged.

Her whole mind being filled by duties and affection, each day seemed short, yet each was varied. At dawn she rose lightly from her bed, and looked out over the blue sea and rocky shore; she prayed, as she gazed, for the safety of her benefactor; and her thoughts, soaring to her mother in heaven, asked her blessing to descend upon her child. Morning was not so fresh as her, as she met its first sweet breath; and, cantering along the beach, she thought of Falkner—his absence, his toils and dangers—with resignation, mingled with a hope that warmed into an ardent desire to see him again. Surely there is no object so sweet as the young in solitude. In after years—when death has bereaved us of the dearest—when cares, and regrets, and fears, and passions, evil either in their nature or their results, have stained our lives with black, solitude is too sadly peopled to be pleasing; and when we see one of mature years alone, we believe that sadness must be the companion. But the solitary thoughts of the young are glorious dreams—

"Their state,
Like to a lark at break of day arising
From sullen earth, sings hymns at heaven's gate."

To behold this young and lovely girl wandering by the lonely shore, her thoughts her only companions, love for her benefactor her only passion, no touch of earth and its sordid woes about her, it was as if a new Eve, watched over by angels, had been placed in the desecrated land, and the very ground she trod grew into paradise.

Sometimes the day was sadly checkered by bad news brought from the continent of Greece. Sometimes it was rendered joyous by the arrival of a letter from her adored father. Sometimes he was with her, and he, animated by the sense of danger, and the knowledge of his usefulness to the cause he espoused, was eloquent in his narrations, overflowing in his affection to her, and almost happy in the belief that he was atoning for the past. The idea that he should fall in the fields of Greece, and wash out with his heart's blood the dark blot on his name, gave an elevation to his thoughts, a strained and eager courage and fortitude that accorded with his fiery character. He was born to be a soldier; not the military man of modern days, but the hero who exposed his life without fear, and found joy in battle and hard-earned victory, when these were sought and won for a good cause, from the cruel oppressor.

# CHAPTER X

During Falkner's visits to Zante, Elizabeth had been led to remark the faithful attentions of his chief follower, an Albanian Greek. This man had complained to his young mistress of the recklessness with which Falkner exposed himself—of the incredible fatigue he underwent—and his belief that he must ere long fall a victim to his disdain of safety and repose; which, while it augmented the admiration his courage excited, was yet not called for by the circumstances of the times. He would have been termed rash and fool-hardy, but that he maintained a dignified composure throughout, joined to military skill and fertility of resource; and while contempt of life led him invariably to select the post of danger for himself, he was sedulous to preserve the lives of those under his command. His early life had familiarized him with the practices of war. He was a valuable officer; kind to his men, and careful to supply their wants, while he contended for no vain distinctions; and was ready, on all occasions, to undertake such duties as others shrunk from, as leading to certain death.

Elizabeth listened to Vasili's account of his hairbreadth escapes, his toils, and desperate valour, with tearful eyes and an aching heart. "Oh! that I could attach him to life!" she thought. She never complained to him, nor persuaded him to alter his desperate purpose, but redoubled her affectionate attentions. When he left her, after a hurried visit, she did not beseech him to preserve himself; but her tearful eyes, the agony with which she returned his parting embrace, her despondent attitude as his bark left the shore; and, when he returned, her eager joy—her eye lighted up with thankful love—all bespoke emotions that needed no other interpreter, and which often made him half shrink from acting up to the belief he had arrived at, that he ought to die, and that he could only escape worse and ignominious evils by a present and honourable death.

As time passed on—as by the arrival of the forces from Egypt the warfare grew more keen and perilous—as Vasili renewed the sad tale of his perils at each visit, with some added story of lately and narrowly escaped peril—fear began to make too large and engrossing a portion of her daily thoughts. She ceased to take in the ideas as she read—her needle dropped from her hand—and, as she played, the music brought streams of tears from her eyes, to think of the scene of desolation and suffering in which she felt that she should soon be called upon to take a part. There was no help or hope, and she must early learn the woman's first and hardest lesson, to bear in silence the advance of an evil which might be avoided, but for the unconquerable will of another. Almost she could have called her father cruel, had not the remembrance of the misery that drove him to desperation inspired pity, instead of selfish resentment.

He had passed a few days with her, and the intercourse they held had been more intimate and more affectionate than ever. As she grew older, her mind, enriched by cultivation, and developed by the ardour of her attachment, grew more on an equality with his experienced one, than could have been the case in mere childhood. They did not take the usual position of father and child—the instructer and instructed—the commander and the obedient—

"They talked with open heart, and tongue
Affectionate and true,
A pair of friends."

And the inequality which made her depend on him, and caused him to regard her as the creature who was to prolong his existence, as it were, beyond the grave, into which he believed himself to be descending, gave a touch of something melancholy to their sympathy, without which, in this shadowy world, nothing seems beautiful and enduring.

He left her; and his little bark, under press of sail, sped merrily through the waves. She stood to watch—her heart warmed by the recollection of his fervent affection—his attentive kindness. He had ever been brave and generous; but now he had become so sympathizing and gentle, that she hoped that the time was not far off when moral courage would spring from that personal hardihood which is at once so glorious and so fearful. "God shield you, my father!" she thought, "God preserve you, my more than father, for happier thoughts and better days! For the full enjoyment of, and control over, those splendid qualities with which Nature has gifted you!"

Such was the tenour of her thoughts. Enthusiasm mingled with fond solicitude—and thus she continued her anxious watchings. By every opportunity she received brief letters, breathing affection, yet containing no word of self. Sometimes a phrase occurred directing her what to do if anything fatal occurred to him, which startled and pained her; but there was nothing else that spoke of death—nor any allusion to his distaste for life. Autumn was far advanced—the sounds of war were somewhat lulled; and, except in small skirmishing parties, that met and fought under cover of the ravines and woods, all was quiet. Elizabeth felt less fearful than usual. She wrote to ask when Falkner would again visit her; and he, in reply, promised so to do immediately after a meditated attack on a small fortress, the carrying of which was of the first import to the safe quartering of his little troop during the winter. She read this with delight—she solaced herself with the prospect of a speedier and longer visit than usual; with childish thoughtlessness she forgot that the attack on the town was a work of war, and might bring with it the fatal results of mortal struggle.

A few days after, a small, ill-looking letter was put into her hands—it was written in Romaic, and the meaning of its illegible ciphers could only be guessed at by a Greek. It was from Vasili—to tell her, in a few words, that Falkner was lying in a small village, not far from the seacoast, opposite Zante. It mentioned that he had been long suffering from a Greek fever; and having been badly wounded in the late attack, the combined effects of wound and malady left little hopes of recovery; while the fatal moment was hastened by the absence of all medical assistance—the miserable state of the village where he was lying—and the bad air of the country around.

Elizabeth read as if in a dream—the moment, then, had come, the fatal moment which she had often contemplated with terror, and prayed Heaven to avert—she grew pale and trembling; but again in a moment she recalled her presence of mind, and summoned all the resolution she had endeavoured to store up to assist her at this extremity. She went herself to the chief English authority in the island, and obtained an order for a vessel to bring him off—instantly she embarked. She neither wept nor spoke; but sitting on the deck, tearless and pale, she prayed for speed, and that she might not find him dead. A few hours brought her to the desired port. Here a thousand difficulties awaited her—but she was not to be intimidated by all the threatened dangers—and only besought the people about her to admit of no excuses for delay. She was accompanied by an English surgeon and a few attendants. She longed to outspeed them all, and yet she commanded herself to direct everything that was done; nor did her heart quail when a few shot, and the cry of the men about her, spoke of the neighbourhood of the enemy. It proved a false alarm—the shots came from a straggling party of Greeks—salutations were exchanged, and still she pushed on—her only thought was—"Let me but find him alive—and then surely he will live!"

As she passed along, the sallow countenances and wasted figures of the peasants spoke of the frightful ravages of the epidemic by which Falkner was attacked—and the squalidness of the cabins and the filth of the villages were sights to make her heart ache; at length they drew near one which the guide told her was that named by Vasili. On inquiring, they were directed down a sort of lane to a wretched dilapidated dwelling—in the courtyard of which were a party of armed Greeks, gathered together in a sort of ominous silence. This was the abode of Falkner; she alighted—and in a few minutes Vasili presented himself—his face painted with every mark of apprehension and sorrow—he led her on. The house was desolate beyond expression—there was no furniture, no glass in the windows—no token of human habitation beyond the weather-stained walls. She entered the room where her father lay—some mattresses placed on the divan were all his bed; and there was nothing else in the room except a brazier to heat his food. Elizabeth drew near—and gazed in awe and grief. Already he was so changed that she could scarcely know him—his eyes sunk, his cheeks fallen, his brow streaked with pallid hues; a ghastly shadow lay upon his face, the apparent forerunner of death. He had scarcely strength sufficient to raise his hand, and his voice was hollow—yet he smiled when he saw her—and that smile, the last refuge of the soul that informs our clay, and even sometimes survives it, was all his own; it struck her to the heart—and her eyes were dimmed with tears while Vasili cast a wistful glance on her—as much as to say, "I have lost hope!"

"Thank you for coming—yet you ought not to be here," hoarsely murmured the sick man. Elizabeth kissed his hand and brow in answer—and, despite of all her endeavours, the tears fell from her eyes on his sunken cheek; again he smiled. "It is not so bad," he said; "do not weep, I am willing to die! I do not suffer very much, though I am weary of life."

The surgeon was now admitted. He examined the wound, which was of a musket bullet in his side. He dressed it, and administered some potion, from which the patient received instant relief; and then joined the anxious girl, who had retired to another room.

"He is in a very dangerous state," the surgeon remarked, in reply to her anxious looks. "Nothing certain can be pronounced yet. But our first care must be to remove him from this pestiferous place—the fever and wound combined must destroy him. Change of air may produce an amelioration in the former."

With all the energy which was her prominent characteristic, Elizabeth caused a litter to be prepared, horses hired, and everything arranged so that their journey might be commenced at daybreak. Every one went early to rest, to enjoy some repose before the morrow's journey, except Elizabeth; she spent the livelong night watching beside Falkner, marking each change, tortured by the groans that escaped him in his sleep, or the suppressed complaints that fell from his lips—by the restlessness and fever that rendered each moment full of fate. The glimmering and dreary light of the lamp increased even the squalid and bare appearance of the wretched chamber in which he lay; Elizabeth gazed for a moment from the casement to see how moved the stars—and there, without, nature asserted herself—and it was the lovely land of Greece that met her eyes; the southern night reigned in all its beauty—the stars hung refulgent lamps in the transparent ether: the fire-flies darted and wheeled among the olive groves, or rested in the myrtle hedges, flashing intermittingly, and filling for an instant a small space around them with fairy brightness; each form of tree, of rocky fragment, and broken upland, lay in calm and beautiful repose; she turned to the low couch on which lay all her hope—her idolized father; the streaked brow—the nerveless hand—half-open eye, and hard breathing betokened a frightful stage of weakness and suffering.

The scene brought unsought into her mind the lines of the English poet, which so touchingly describes the desolation of Greece—blending the idea of mortal suffering with the long-drawn calamities of that oppressed country. The words, the lines, crowded on her memory; and a chord was struck in her heart as she ejaculated, "No! no, not so! Not the first day of death—not now, or ever!" As she spoke, she dissolved in tears—and, weeping long and bitterly, she became afterward calmer—the rest of her watch passed more peacefully. Even the patient suffered less as night verged into morning.

At an early hour all was ready. Falkner was placed in the litter; and the little party, gladly leaving the precincts of the miserable village, proceeded slowly towards the seashore. Every step was replete with pain and danger. Elizabeth was again all herself. Self-possessed and vigilant, she seemed at once to attain years of experience. No one could remember that it was a girl of sixteen who directed them. Hovering round the litter of the wounded man, and pointing out how best to carry him, so that he might suffer least—as the inequalities of the ground, the heights to climb, and the ravines to cross, made it a task of difficulty. Now and then the report of a musket was heard; sometimes a Greek cap, not unoften mistaken for a turban, peered above the precipice that overlooked the road frequent alarms were given, but she was frightened by none. Her large eyes dilated and darkened as she looked towards the danger pointed out—and she drew nearer the litter, as a lonely mother might to the cradle of her child, when in the stillness of night some ravenous beast intruded on a savage solitude; but she never spoke, except to point out the mistakes she was the first to perceive—or to order the men to proceed lightly, but without fear—nor to allow their progress to be checked by vain alarms.

At length the seashore was gained, and Falkner at last placed on the deck of the vessel, reposing after the torture which, despite every care, the journey had inflicted. Already Elizabeth believed that he was saved—and yet, one glance at his wan face and emaciated figure reawakened every fear. He looked, and all around believed him to be, a dying man.

# CHAPTER XI

Arrived at Zante, placed in a cool and pleasant chamber, attended by a skilful surgeon, and watched over by the unsleeping vigilance of Elizabeth, Falkner slowly receded from the shadow of death, whose livid hue had sat upon his countenance. Still health was far. His wound was attended by bad symptoms, and the fever eluded every attempt to dislodge it from his frame. He was but half saved from the grave; emaciated and feeble, his disorder even tried to vanquish his mind; but that resisted with more energy than his prostrate body. The death he had gone out to seek he awaited with courage, yet he no longer expressed an impatience of existence, but struggled to support with manly fortitude at once the inroads of disease and the long-nourished sickness of his soul.

It had been a hard trial to Elizabeth to watch over him, while each day the surgeon's serious face gave no token of hope. But she would not despond, and in the end his recovery was attributed to her careful nursing. She never quitted his apartment except for a few hours' sleep; and, even then, her bed was placed in the chamber adjoining his. If he moved, she was roused and at his side, divining the cause of his uneasiness, and alleviating it. There were other nurses about him, and Vasili, the most faithful of all—but she directed them, and brought that discernment and tact of which a woman only is capable. Her little soft hand smoothed his pillow, or, placed upon his brow, cooled and refreshed him. She scarcely seemed to feel the effects of sleepless nights and watchful days—every minor sensation was merged in the hope and resolution to preserve him.

Several months were passed in a state of the utmost solicitude. At last he grew a little better—the fever intermitted—and the wound gave signs of healing. On the first day that he was moved to an open alcove, and felt some enjoyment from the soft air of evening, all that Elizabeth had gone through was repaid. She sat on a low cushion near; and his thin fingers, now resting on her head, now playing with the ringlets of her hair, gave token, by that caress, that though he was silent and his look abstracted, his thoughts were occupied upon her. At length he said—"Elizabeth, you have again saved my life."

She looked up with a quick, glad look, and her eyes brightened with pleasure.

"You have saved my life twice," he continued; "and through you, it seems, I am destined to live. I will not quarrel again with existence, since it is your gift; I will hope, prolonged as it has been by you, that it will prove beneficial to you. I have but one desire now—it is to be the source of happiness to you."

"Live! dear father, live! and I must be happy!" she exclaimed.

"God grant that it prove so!" he replied, pressing her hand to his lips. "The prayers of such as I too often turn to curses. But you, my own dearest, must be blessed; and as my life is preserved, I must hope that this is done for your sake, and that you will derive some advantage from it."

"Can you doubt it?" said Elizabeth. "Could I ever be consoled if I lost you? I have no other tie on earth—no other friend—nor do I wish for any. Only put aside your cruel thoughts of leaving me for ever, and every blessing is mine."

"Dear, generous, faithful girl! Yet the time will come when I shall not be all in all to you; and then, will not my name—my adoption—prove a stumbling-block to your wishes?"

"How could that happen?" she said. "But do not, dear father, perplex yourself with looking either forward or backward—repose on the present, which has nothing in it to annoy you; or rather, your gallantry—your devotion to the cause of an injured people, must inspire you with feelings of self-gratulation, and speak peace to your troubles. Let the rest of your life pass away as a dream; banish quite those thoughts that have hitherto made you wretched. Your life is saved, despite yourself. Accept existence as an immediate gift from Heaven; and begin life, from this moment, with new hopes, new resolves. Whatever your error was, which you so bitterly repent, it belonged to another state of being. Your remorse, your resignation, has effaced it; or if any evil results remain, you will rather exert yourself to repair them—than uselessly to lament."

"To repair my error—my crime!" cried Falkner, in an altered voice, while a cloud gathered over his face; "no, no! that is impossible! never, till we meet in another life, can I offer reparation to the dead. But I must not think of this now; it is too ungrateful to you to dwell upon thoughts which would deliver me over to the tomb. Yet one thing I would say. I left a short detail in England of the miserable event that must at last destroy me, but it is brief and unsatisfactory. During my midnight watchings in Greece, I prepared a longer account. You know that little rosewood box, which, even when dying, I asked for; it is now close to my bed; the key is here attached to my watch-chain. That box contains the narrative of my crime; when I die, you will read it and judge me."

"Never! never!" exclaimed Elizabeth, earnestly. "Dear father, how cruelly you have tormented yourself by dwelling upon and writing about the past! and do you think that I would ever read accusations against you, the guardian angel of my life, even though written by yourself? Let me bring the box—let me burn the papers—let no word remain to tell of misery you repent, and have atoned for."

Falkner detained her, as she would have gone to execute her purpose. "Not alone for you, my child," he said, "did I write, though hereafter, when you hear me accused, it may be satisfactory to learn the truth from my own hand. But there are others to satisfy—an injured angel to be vindicated—a frightful mystery to be unveiled to the world. I have waited till I should die to fulfil this duty, and still, for your sake, I will wait; for while you love me and bear my name, I will not cover it with obloquy. But if I die, this secret must not die with me. I will say no more now, nor ask any promises: when the time comes, you will understand and submit to the necessity that urged me to disclosure."

"You shall be obeyed, I promise you," she replied. "I will never set my reason above yours, except in asking you to live for the sake of the poor little thing you have preserved."

"Have I preserved you, dearest? I often fear I did wrong in not restoring you to your natural relations. In making you mine, and linking you to my blighted fortunes, I may have prepared unnumbered ills for you. Oh, how sad a riddle is life! we hear of the straight and narrow path of right in youth, and we disdain the precept; and now would I were sitting among the nameless crowd on the common road-side, instead of wandering blindly in this dark desolation; and you—I have brought you with me into the wilderness of error and suffering; it was wrong—it was mere selfishness; yet who could foresee?"

"Talk not of foreseeing," said Elizabeth, soothingly, as she pressed his thin hand to her warm young lips, "think only of the present; you have made me yours for ever—you cannot cast me off without inflicting real pangs of misery, instead of those dreamy ills you speak of. I am happy with you, attending on, being of use to you. What would you more?"

"Perhaps it is so," replied Falkner, "and your good and grateful heart will repay itself for all its sacrifices. I never can. Henceforth I will be guided by you, my Elizabeth. I will no longer think of what I have done, and what yet must be suffered, but wrap up my existence in you; live in your smiles, your hopes, your affections."

This interchange of heartfelt emotions did good to both. Perplexed, nay, tormented by conflicting duties, Falkner was led by her entreaties to dismiss the most painful of his thoughts, and to repose at last on those more healing. The evil and the good of the day he resolved should henceforth be sufficient; his duty towards Elizabeth was a primary one, and he would restrict himself to the performing it.

There is a magic in sympathy, and the heart's overflowing, that we feel as bliss, though we cannot explain it. This sort of joy Elizabeth felt after this conversation with her father. Their hearts had united; they had mingled thought and sensation, and the intimacy of affection that resulted was an ample reward to her for every suffering. She loved her benefactor with inexpressible truth and devotedness, and their entire and full interchange of confidence gave a vivacity to this sentiment, which of itself was happiness.

## CHAPTER XII

Though saved from immediate death, Falkner could hardly be called convalescent. His wound did not heal healthily, and the intermitting fever, returning again and again, laid him prostrate after he had acquired a little strength. After a winter full of danger, it was pronounced that the heats of a southern summer would probably prove fatal to him, and that he must be removed without delay to the bracing air of his native country.

Towards the end of the month of April they took their passage to Leghorn. It was a sad departure; the more so that they were obliged to part with their Greek servant, on whose attachment Elizabeth so much depended. Vasili had entered into Falkner's service at the instigation of the Protokleft, or chief of his clan; when the Englishman was obliged to abandon the cause of Greece, and return to his own country, Vasili, though loath and weeping, went back to his native master. The young girl, being left without any attendant on whom she could wholly rely, felt singularly desolate; for as her father lay on the deck, weak from the exertion of being removed, she felt that his life hung by a very slender thread, and she shrank half affrighted from what might ensue to her, friendless and alone.

Her presence of mind and apparent cheerfulness was never, however, diminished by these secret misgivings; and she sat by her father's low couch, and placed her hands in his, speaking encouragingly, while her eyes filled with tears as the rocky shores of Zante became indistinct and vanished.

Their voyage was without any ill accident, except that the warm southeast wind, which favoured their navigation, sensibly weakened the patient; and Elizabeth grew more and more eager to proceed northward. At Leghorn they were detained by a long and vexatious quarantine. The summer had commenced early, with great heats; and the detention of several weeks in the lazaretto nearly brought about what they had left Greece to escape. Falkner grew worse. The seabreezes a little mitigated his sufferings; but life was worn away by repeated struggles, and the most frightful debility threatened his frame with speedy dissolution. How could it be otherwise? He had wished to die. He sought death where it lurked insidiously in the balmy airs of Greece, or met it openly armed against him on the field of battle. Death wielded many weapons; and he was struck by many, and the most dangerous. Elizabeth hoped, in spite of despair; yet, if called away from him, her heart throbbed wildly as she re-entered his apartment; there was no moment when the fear did not assail her, that she might, on a sudden, hear and see that all was over.

An incident happened at this period, to which Elizabeth paid little attention at the time, engrossed as she was by mortal fears. They had been in quarantine about a fortnight, when, one day, there entered the gloomy precincts of the lazaretto a tribe of English people. Such a horde of men, women, and children, as gives foreigners a lively belief that we islanders are all mad, to migrate in this way, with the young and helpless, from comfortable homes, in search of the dangerous and comfortless. This roving band consisted of the eldest son of an English nobleman and his wife—four children, the eldest being six years old—a governess—three nursery-maids, two lady's maids, and a sufficient appendage of men-servants. They had all just arrived from viewing the pyramids of Egypt. The noise and bustle—the servants insisting on making everybody comfortable, where comfort was not—the spreading out of all their own camp apparatus—joined to the seeming indifference of the parties chiefly concerned, and the unconstrained astonishment of the Italians—was very amusing. Lord Cecil, a tall, thin, plain, quiet, aristocratic-looking man of middle age, dropped into the first chair—called for his writing-case—began a letter, and saw and heard nothing that was going on. Lady Cecil—who was not pretty, but lively and elegant—was surrounded by her children—*they* seemed so many little angels, with blooming cheeks and golden hair—the youngest cherub slept profoundly amid the din; the others were looking eagerly out for their dinner.

Elizabeth had seen their entrance—she saw them walking in the garden of the lazaretto—one figure, the governess, though disguised by a green shade over her eyes, she recognised—it was Miss Jervis. Desolate and sad as the poor girl was, a familiar face and voice was a cordial drop to comfort her; and Miss Jervis was infinitely delighted to meet her former pupil. She usually looked on those intrusted to her care as a part of the machinery that supported her life; but Elizabeth had become dear to her from the irresistible attraction that hovered round her—arising from her carelessness of self, and her touching sensibility to the sufferings of all around. She had often regretted having left her, and she now expressed this, and even her silence grew into something like talkativeness upon the unexpected meeting. "I am very unlucky," she said; "I would rather, if I could with propriety, live in the meanest lodging in London, than in the grandest tumbledown palace of the East, which people are pleased to call so fine—I am sure they are always dirty and out of order. Lady Glenfell recommended me to Lady Cecil—and, certainly, a more generous and sweet-tempered woman does not exist—and I was very comfortable, living at the Earl of G——'s seat in Hampshire, and having almost all my time to myself. One day, to my misfortune, Lady Cecil made a scheme to travel—to get out of her father-in-law's way, I believe— he is rather a tiresome old man. Lord Cecil does anything she likes. All was arranged, and I really thought I should leave them—I so hated the idea of going abroad again; but Lady Cecil said that I should be quite a treasure, having been everywhere, and knowing so many languages, and that she should have never thought of going, but from my being with her; so, in short, she was very generous, and I could not say no: accordingly, we set out on our travels, and went first to Portugal—where I had never been—and do not know a word of Portuguese; and then through Spain—and Spanish is Greek to me—and worse—for I do know a good deal of Romaic. I am sure I do not know scarcely where we went—but our last journey was to see the pyramids of Egypt—only, unfortunately, I caught the ophthalmia the moment we got to Alexandria, and could never bear to see a ray of light the whole time we were in that country."

As they talked, Lady Cecil came to join her children. She was struck by Elizabeth's beaming and noble countenance, which bore the impress of high thought and elevated sentiments. Her figure, too, had sprung up into womanhood—tall and graceful—there was an elasticity joined to much majesty in all her appearance; not the majesty of assumption, but the stamp of natural grandeur of soul, refined by education, and softened by sympathetic kindness for the meanest thing that breathed. Her dignity did not spring in the slightest degree from self-worship, but simply from a reliance on her own powers and a forgetfulness of every triviality which haunts the petty-minded. No one could chance to see her, without stopping to gaze; and her peculiar circumstances—the affectionate and anxious daughter of a dying man—without friend or support, except her own courage and patience— never daunted, yet always fearfully alive to his danger—rendered her infinitely interesting to one of her own sex. Lady Cecil was introduced to her by Miss Jervis, and was eager to show her kindness. She offered that they should travel together; but as Elizabeth's quarantine was out long before that of the new comers, and she was anxious to reach a more temperate climate, she refused; yet she was thankful, and charmed by the sweetness and cordiality of her new acquaintance.

Lady Cecil was not handsome, but there was something, not exactly amounting to fascination, but infinitely taking in her manner and appearance. Her cheerfulness, good-nature, and high-breeding diffused a grace and a pleasurable easiness over her manners that charmed everybody; good sense and vivacity, never loud nor ever dull, rendered her spirits agreeable. She was apparently the same to everybody; but she well knew how to regulate the inner spirit of her attentions while their surface looked so equal: no one ventured to go beyond her wishes—and where she wished, any one was astonished to find how far they could depend on her sincerity and friendliness. Had Elizabeth's spirit been more free, she had been delighted; as it was, she felt thankful, merely for a kindness that availed her nothing.

Lady Cecil viewed the dying Falkner and his devoted, affectionate daughter with the sincerest compassion; dying she thought him, for he was wasted to a shadow, his cheeks colourless, his hands yellow and thin—he could not stand upright—and when, in the cool of evening, he was carried into the open air, he seemed scarcely able to speak from very feebleness. Elizabeth's face bespoke continual anxiety: her vigilance, her patience, her grief, and her resignation formed a touching picture, which it was impossible to contemplate without admiration. Lady Cecil often tried to win her away from her father's couch, and to give herself a little repose from perpetual attendance; she yielded but for a minute; while she conversed, she assumed cheerfulness—but in a moment after she had glided back and taken her accustomed place at her father's pillow.

At length their prison-gates were opened, and Falkner was borne on board a felucca bound for Genoa. Elizabeth took leave of her new friend, and promised to write, but while she spoke she forgot what she said—for, dreading at each moment the death of her benefactor, she did not dare look forward, and had little heart to go beyond the circle of her immediate, though dreary sensations. A fair wind bore them to Genoa, and Falkner sustained the journey very well: at Genoa they transferred themselves to another vessel, and each mile they gained towards France lightened the fears of Elizabeth. But this portion of their voyage was not destined to be so prosperous They had embarked at night, and had made some way during the first hours; but by noon on the following day they were becalmed; the small vessel—the burning sun—the shocking smells—the want of all comfortable accommodation, combined to bring on a relapse—and again Falkner seemed dying. The very crew were struck with pity; while Elizabeth, wild almost with terror and the impotent wish to save, preserved an outward calm, more shocking almost than shrieks and cries. At evening she caused him to be carried on the deck, and placed on a couch, with a little sort of shed prepared for him there; he was too much debilitated to feel any great degree of relief—there was a ghastly hue settled on his face that seemed gradually sinking into death. Elizabeth's courage almost gave way; there was no physician, no friend; the servants were frightened, the crew pitying, but none could help.

As this sense of desertion grew strong, a despair she had never felt before invaded her; and it was as she thus hung over Falkner's couch, the tears fast gathering in her eyes, and striving to check the convulsive throb that rose in her throat, that a gentle voice said, "Let me place this pillow under your father's head, he will rest more quietly." The voice came as from a guardian angel; she looked up thankfully, the pillow was placed, some drink administered, a sail extended, so as to shield him from the evening sun, and a variety of little attentions paid, which evidently solaced the invalid; and the evening breeze rising as the sun went down, the air grew cool, and he sunk at last into a profound sleep. When night came on, the stranger conjured Elizabeth to take some repose, promising to watch by Falkner. She could not resist the entreaty, which was urged with sincere earnestness; going down, she found a couch had been prepared for her with almost a woman's care by the stranger; and before she slept he knocked at her door to tell her, Falkner having awoke, expressed himself as much easier, and very glad to hear that Elizabeth had retired to rest; after this he had dropped asleep again.

It was a new and pleasant sensation to the lone girl to feel that there was one sharing her task, on whom she might rely. She had scarcely looked at or attended to the stranger while on deck; she only perceived that he was English, and that he was young; but now, in the quiet that preceded her falling asleep, his low, melodious voice sounded sweetly in her ears, and the melancholy and earnest expression of his handsome countenance reminded her of some one she had seen before, probably a Greek; for there was something almost foreign in his olive complexion, his soft, dark eyes, and the air of sentiment mingled with a sort of poetic fervour, that characterized his countenance. With these thoughts Elizabeth fell asleep; and when early in the morning she rose, and made what haste she could to visit the little sort of hut erected for her father on deck, the first person she saw was the stranger, leaning on the bulwark, and looking on the sea with an air of softness and sadness that excited her sympathy. He greeted her with extreme kindness. "Your father is awake, and has inquired for you," he said. Elizabeth, after thanking him, took her accustomed post beside Falkner. He might be better, but he was too weak to make much sign, and one glance at his colourless face renewed all her half forgotten terrors.

Meanwhile the breeze freshened, and the vessel scudded through the blue sparkling waves. The heats of noon, though tempered by the gale, still had a bad effect on Falkner; and when, at about five in the evening—often in the south the hottest portion of the day, the air being thoroughly penetrated by the sun's rays—they arrived at Marseilles, it became a task of some difficulty to remove him. Elizabeth and the stranger had interchanged little talk during the day; but he now came forward to assist in removing him to the boat—acting without question, as if he had been her brother, guessing, as if by instinct, the best thing to be done, and performing all with activity and zeal. Poor Elizabeth, cast on these difficult circumstances, without relation or friend, looked on him as a guardian angel, consulted him freely, and witnessed his exertions in her behalf in a transport of gratitude. He did everything for her, and would sit for hours in the room at the hotel, next to that in which Falkner lay, waiting to hear how he was, and if there was anything to be done. Elizabeth joined him now and then; they were in a manner already intimate, though strangers; he took a lively interest in her anxieties, and she looked towards him for advice and help, relied on his counsels, and was encouraged by his consolations. It was the first time she had felt any friendship or confidence, except in Falkner; but it was impossible not to be won by her new friend's gentleness, and almost feminine delicacy of attention, joined to all a man's activity and readiness to do the thing that was necessary to be done. "I have an adopted father," thought Elizabeth, "and this seems a brother dropped from the clouds." He was of an age to be her brother, but few years older; in all the ardour and grace of early manhood, when developed in one of happy nature unsoiled by the world.

Elizabeth, however, remained but a few days at Marseilles—it was of the first necessity to escape the southern heats, and Falkner was pronounced able to bear the voyage up the Rhone. The stranger showed some sadness at the idea of being left behind. In truth, if Elizabeth was gladdened and comforted by her new friend, he felt double pleasure in the contemplation of her beauty and admirable qualities. No word of self ever passed her lips. All thought, all care, was spent on him she called her father—and the stranger was deeply touched by her demonstrations of filial affection— her total abnegation of every feeling that did not centre in his comfort and recovery. He had been present one evening, though standing apart, when Falkner, awakening from sleep, spoke with regret of the fatigue Elizabeth endured, and the worthlessness of his life compared with all that she went through for his sake. Elizabeth replied at once with such energy of affection, such touching representation of the comfort she derived from his returning health, and such earnest entreaties for him to love life, that the stranger listened as if an angel spoke. Falkner answered, but the remorse that burdened his heart gave something of bitterness to his reply. And her eloquent though gentle solicitations that he would look on life in a better and nobler light—not rashly to leave its duties here to encounter those he knew not of in an existence beyond—and kind intimations, which, exalting his repentance into a virtue, might reconcile him to himself—all this won the listener to a deep and wondering admiration. Not in human form had he ever seen imbodied so much wisdom, and so much, strong yet tender emotion—none but woman could feel thus, but it was beyond woman to speak and to endure as she did. She spoke only just so openly, remembering the stranger's presence, as to cast a veil over her actual relationship to Falkner, whom she called, and wished to have believed to be, her true father.

The fever of the sufferer being abated, a day was fixed for their departure from Marseilles. Their new friend appeared to show some inclination to accompany them in their river navigation as far as Lyons. Elizabeth thanked him with her gladdened eyes; she had felt the want of support, or rather she had experienced the inestimable benefit of being supported during the sad crisis now and then brought about by Falkner's changeful illness; there was something, too, in the stranger very attractive, not the less so for the melancholy which often quenched the latent fire of his nature. That his disposition was really ardent, and even vivacious, many little incidents, when he appeared to forget himself, evinced—nay, sometimes his very gloom merged into sullen savageness, that showed that coldness was not the secret of his frequent fits of abstraction. Once or twice, on these occasions, Elizabeth was reminded, she knew not of whom—but some one she had seen before—till one day it flashed across her; could it be the sullen, solitary boy of Baden! Singularly enough, she did not even know her new friend's name; to those accustomed to foreign servants this will not appear strange; he was their only visiter, and "le monsieur" was sufficient announcement when he arrived. But Elizabeth remembered well that the youth's name was Neville—and, on inquiry, she learned that this also was the appellation of her new acquaintance.

She now regarded him with greater interest. She recalled her girlish wish that he should reside with them, and benefit by the kindness of Falkner—hoping that his sullenness would be softened and his gloom dissipated by the affectionate attentions he would receive. She wished to discover in what degree time and other circumstances had operated to bring about the amelioration she had wished to be an instrument in achieving. He was altered—he was no longer fierce nor sullen—yet he was still melancholy, and still unhappy—and she could discern that as his former mood had been produced by the vehemence of his character fretting against the misfortunes of his lot, so it was by subduing every violence of temper that the change was operated—and she suspected that the causes that originally produced his unhappiness still remained. Yet violence of temper is not a right word to use; his temper was eminently sweet—he had a boiling ardour within—a fervent and a warm heart, which might produce vehemence of feeling, but never asperity of temper. All this Elizabeth remarked—and, as before, she longed to dissipate the melancholy that so evidently clouded his mind; and again she indulged fancies that, if he accompanied them, and was drawn near them, the affection he would receive must dissipate a sadness created by unfortunate circumstances in early youth—but not the growth of a saturnine disposition. She pitied him intensely, for she saw that he was often speechlessly wretched; but she reverenced his self-control, and the manner in which he threw off all his own engrossing feelings to sympathize with and assist her.

They were now soon to depart, and Elizabeth was not quite sure whether Neville was to accompany them—he had gone to the boat to look after some arrangements made for the patient's comfort—and she sat with the invalid, expecting his return. Falkner reclined near a window, clasping her hand, looking on her with fondness, and speaking of all he owed her; and how he would endeavour to repay, by living, and making life a blessing to her. "I shall live," he said; "I feel that this malady will pass away, and I shall live to devote myself to rewarding you for all your anxieties, to dissipating the cloud with which I have so cruelly overshadowed your young life, and to making all the rest sunshine. I will think only of you; all the rest, all that grieves me, and all that I repent, I cast even now into oblivion."

At this moment the stranger entered and drew near. Elizabeth saw him, and said, "And here, dearest father, is another to whom you owe more than you can guess—for kindness to me and the help to you. I do not think I should have preserved you without Mr. Neville."

The young man was standing near the couch, looking on the invalid, and rejoicing in the change for the better that appeared. Falkner turned his eyes on him as Elizabeth spoke, a tremour ran through all his limbs, he grew ghastly pale, and fainted.

An evil change from this time appeared in his state—and the physician was afraid of the journey, attributing his fainting to his inability to bear any excitement; while Falkner, who was before passive, grew eager to depart. "Change of scene and moving will do me good," he said, "so that no one comes near me, no one speaks to me, but Elizabeth."

At one time the idea of Neville's accompanying them was alluded to— he was greatly disturbed—and seriously implored Elizabeth not to allow it. It was rather hard on the poor girl, who found so much support and solace in her new friend's society—but Falkner's slightest wish was with her a law, and she submitted without a murmur, "Do not let me even see him before we go," said Falkner. "Act on this wish, dearest, without hurting his feelings—without betraying to him that I have formed it—it would be an ungracious return for the services he has rendered you—for which I would fain show gratitude; but that cannot be—you alone can repay—do so, as you best may, with thanks—but do not let me see him more."

Elizabeth wondered; and, as a last effort to vanquish his dislike, she said, "Do you know that he is the same boy who interested us so much at Baden?—he is no longer savage as he was then—but I fear that he is as unhappy as ever."

"Too well do I know it," replied Falkner; "do not question me—do not speak to me again of him." He spoke in disjointed sentences—a cold dew stood on his brow—and Elizabeth, who knew that a mysterious wound rankled in his heart, more painful than any physical injury, was eager to calm him. Something, she might wonder; but she thought more of sparing Falkner pain than of satisfying her curiosity, and she mentally resolved never to mention the name of Neville again.

They were to embark at sunrise; in the evening her new friend came to take leave, she having evaded the notion of his accompanying them, and insisted that he should not join them in the morning to assist at their departure. Though she had done this with sweetness, and so much cordiality of manner as prevented his feeling any sort of slight, yet in some sort he guessed that they wished to dismiss him, and this notion added to his melancholy, while some latent feeling made him readily acquiesce in it. Elizabeth was told that he had come, and left Falkner to join him. It was painful to her to take leave—to feel that she should see him no more—and to know that their separation was not merely casual, but occasioned by her father's choice, which hereafter might again and again interfere to separate them. As she entered the room he was leaning against the casement, and looking on the sea which glanced before their windows, still as a lake, blue as the twilight sky that bent over it. It was a July evening—soft, genial, and soothing; but no portion of the gladness of nature was reflected in the countenance of Neville. His large dark eyes seemed two wells of unfathomable sadness. The drooping lids gave them an expression of irresistible softness, which added interest to their melancholy earnestness. His complexion was olive, but so clear that each vein could be discerned. His full and finely-shaped lips bespoke the ardour and sensibility of his disposition; while his slim, youthful form appeared half bending with a weight of thought and sorrow. Elizabeth's heart beat as she came near and stood beside him. Neither spoke; but he took her hand—and they both felt that each regretted the moment of parting too deeply for the mere ceremony of thanks and leave-taking.

"I have grieved," said Neville, as if answering her, though no word had been said, "very much grieved at the idea of seeing you no more; and yet it is for the best, I feel—and am sure. You do not know the usual unhappy tenour of my thoughts, nor the cause I have to look on life as an unwelcome burden. This is no new sentiment—it has been my companion since I was nine years old. At one time, before I knew how to rein and manage it, it was more intolerable than now; as a boy, it drove me to solitude—to abhorrence of the sight of man—to anger against God for creating me. These feelings have passed away; nay, more—I live for a purpose—a sacred purpose, that shall be fulfilled despite of every obstacle—every seeming impossibility. Too often, indeed, the difficulties in my way have made me fear that I should never succeed, and I have desponded; but never, till I saw you, did I know pleasure unconnected with my ultimate object. With you I have been at times taken out of myself; and I have almost forgotten—this must not be. I must resume my burden, nor form one thought beyond the resolution I have made to die, if need be, to secure success."

"You must not speak thus," said Elizabeth, looking at once with pity and admiration on a face expressive of so much sensitive pride and sadness springing from a sense of injury. "If your purpose is a good one, as I must believe that it is, you will either succeed, or receive a compensation from your endeavours equivalent to success. We shall meet again, and I shall see you happier."

"When I am happier," he said, with more than his usual earnestness, "we shall indeed meet—for I will seek you at the farthest end of the globe. Till then, I shrink from seeing any one who interests me—or from renewing sentiments of friendship which had better end here. You are too good and kind not to be made unhappy by the sight of suffering, and I must suffer till my end is accomplished. Even now I regret that I ever saw you—though that feeling springs from a foolish pride. For hereafter you will hear my name—and if you already do not know—you will learn the miserable tale that hangs upon it—you will hear me commiserated; you will learn why—and share the feeling. I would even avoid your pity—judge, then, how loathsome it is to receive that of others; and yet I must bear it, or fly them as I do. This will change. I have the fullest confidence that one day I may throw back on others the slur now cast upon me. This confidence, this full and sanguine trust, has altered me from what I once was; it has changed the impatience, the almost ferocity I felt as a boy, into fortitude and resolution."

"Yes," said Elizabeth, "I remember once I saw you a long time since, when I was a mere girl, at Baden. Were you not there about four years ago? Do you not remember falling with your horse and dislocating your wrist?"

A tracery of strange wild thought came over the countenance of Neville. "Do I remember?" he cried—"yes—and I remember a beautiful girl—and I thought such would have been my sister, and I had not been alone—if fate, if cruel, inexorable, horrible destiny had not deprived me of her as well as all—all that made my childish existence paradise. It is so—and I see you again, whom then my heart called sister—it is strange."

"Did you give me that name?" said Elizabeth. "Ah, if you knew the strange ideas I then had of giving you my father for your friend, instead of one spoken harshly—perhaps unjustly of—"

As she spoke he grew gloomy again—his eyes drooped, and the expression of his face became at first despondent, then proud, and even fierce; it reminded her more forcibly than it had ever done before of the boy of Baden—"It is better as it is," he continued, "much better that you do not share the evil that pursues me; you ought not to be humiliated, pressed down—goaded to hatred and contempt.

"Farewell—I grieve to leave you—yet I feel deeply how it is for the best. Hereafter you will acknowledge your acquaintance with me, when we meet in a happier hour. God preserve you and your dear father, as he will for your sake! Twice we have met—the third time, if sibyls' tales are true, is the test of good or evil in our friendship—till then, farewell."

Thus they parted. Had Elizabeth been free from care with regard to Falkner, she had regretted the separation more, and pondered more over the mysterious wretchedness that darkened the lives of the only two beings, the inner emotions of whose souls had been opened to her. As it was, she returned to watch and fear beside her father's couch—and scarcely to remember that a few minutes before she had been interested by another—so entirely were her feelings absorbed by her affection and solicitude for him.

# CHAPTER XIII

From this time their homeward journey was more prosperous. They arrived safely at Lyons, and thence proceeded to Basle—to take advantage again of river navigation; the motion of a carriage being so inimical to the invalid. They proceeded down the Rhine to Rotterdam, and crossing the sea, returned at last to England, after an absence of four years.

This journey, though at first begun in terror and danger, grew less hazardous at each mile they traversed towards the North; and while going down the Rhine, Falkner and his adopted daughter spent several tranquil and happy hours—comparing the scenery they saw to other and distant landscapes—and recalling incidents that had occurred many years ago. Falkner exerted himself for Elizabeth's sake—she had suffered so much, and he had inflicted so much anguish upon her while endeavouring to free himself from the burden of life, that he felt remorse at having thus trifled with the deepest emotions of her heart—and anxious to recall the more pleasurable sensations adapted to her age. The listless, yet pleasing feelings attendant on convalescence influenced his mind also—and he enjoyed a peace to which he had long been a stranger.

Elizabeth, it is true, had another source of revery besides that ministered to her by her father. She often thought of Neville; and though he was sad, the remembrance of him was full of pleasure. He had been so kind, so sympathizing, so helpful; besides, there was a poetry in his very gloom that added a charm to every thought spent upon him. She did not only recall his conversation, but conjectured the causes of his sorrow, and felt deeply interested by the mystery that hung about him. So young and so unhappy! And he had been long so—he was more miserable when they saw him roving wildly among the Alsatian hills. What could it mean? She strove to recollect what Miss Jervis mentioned at that time; she remembered only that he had no mother, and that his father was severe and unkind.

Yet why, when nature is so full, of joyousness, when, at the summer season, vegetation basks in beauty and delight, and the very clouds seem to enjoy their aerial abode in upper sky, why should misery find a home in the mind of man? a misery which the balmy winds will not lull, nor the verdant landscape and its winding river dissipate. She thought thus as she saw Falkner reclining apart, a cloud gathered on his brow, his piercing eyes fixed in vacancy, as if it beheld there a heart-moving tragedy; but she was accustomed to his melancholy, she had ever known him as a man of sorrows; he had lived long before she knew him, and the bygone years were filled by events pregnant with wretchedness, nay, if he spoke truth, with guilt. But Neville, the young, the innocent, who had been struck in boyhood through no fault of his own, nor any act in which he bore a part; was there no remedy for him? and would not friendship, and kindness, and the elastic spirit of youth suffice to cure his wound? She remembered that he declared that he had an aim in view, in which he resolved to succeed, and, succeeding, he should be happy: a noble aim doubtless; for his soft eyes lighted joyously up, and his face expressed a glad pride when he prognosticated ultimate triumph. Her heart went with him in his efforts; she prayed earnestly for his success, and was as sure as he that Heaven would favour an object which she felt certain was generous and pure.

A sigh, a half groan from Falkner, called her to his side, while she meditated on these things. Both suffer, she thought; would that some link united them, so that both might find relief in the accomplishment of the same resolves! Little did she think of the real link that existed, mysterious, yet adamantine; that to pray for the success of one was to solicit destruction for the other. A dark veil was before her eyes, totally impervious; nor did she know that the withdrawing it, as was soon to be, would deliver her over to conflicting duties, sad struggles of feeling, and stain her life with the dark hues that now, missing her, blotted the existence of the two upon earth for whom she was most interested.

They arrived in London. Falkner's fever was gone, but his wound was rankling, painful, and even dangerous. The bullet had grazed the bone, and this, at first neglected, and afterward improperly treated, now betrayed symptoms of exfoliation; his sufferings were great—he bore them patiently; he looked on them as an atonement. He had gone out in his remorse to die— he was yet to live, broken and destroyed; and if suffered to live, was it not for Elizabeth's sake! and having bound her fate to his, what right had he to die? The air of London being injurious, and yet it being necessary to continue in the vicinity of the most celebrated surgeons, they took a pleasant villa on Wimbledon Common, situated in the midst of a garden, and presenting to the eye that mixture of neatness, seclusion, and comfort that renders some of our smaller English country-houses so delightful. Elizabeth, despite her wanderings, had a true feminine love of home. She busied herself in adding elegance to their dwelling, by a thousand little arts, which seem nothing, and are everything in giving grace and cheerfulness to an abode.

Their life became tranquil, and a confidence and Friendship existed between them, the source of a thousand pleasant conversations and happy hours. One subject, it is true, was forbidden; the name of Neville was never mentioned; perhaps, on that very account, it assumed more power over Elizabeth's imagination. A casual intercourse with one, however interesting, might have faded into the common light of day, had not the silence enjoined kept him in that indistinct, mysterious darkness so favourable to the processes of the imagination. On every other subject, the so called father and daughter talked with open heart, and Falkner was totally unaware of a secret growth of unspoken interest which had taken root in separation and secrecy.

Elizabeth, accustomed to fear death for one dearest to her, and to contemplate its near approaches so often, had something holy and solemn kneaded into the very elements of her mind, that gave sublimity to her thoughts, resignation to her disposition, and a stirring, inquiring spirit to her conversation, which, separated as they were from the busy and trivial duties of life, took from the monotony and stillness of their existence, by bringing thoughts beyond the world to people the commonplace of each day's routine. Falkner had not much of this; but he had a spirit of observation, a ready memory, and a liveliness of expression and description which corrected her wilder flights, and gave the interest of flesh and blood to her fairy dreams. When they read of the heroes of old, or the creations of the poets, she dwelt on the moral to be deduced, the theories of life and death, religion and virtue, therein displayed; while he compared them to his own experience, criticised their truth, and gave pictures of real human nature, either contrasting with, or resembling, those presented on the written page.

Their lives, thus spent, would have been equable and pleasant, but for the sufferings of Falkner; and as those diminished, another evil arose, in his eyes of far more awful magnitude. They had resided at Wimbledon about a year, when Elizabeth fell ill. Her medical advisers explained her malady as the effect of the extreme nervous excitement she had gone through during the last years, which, borne with a patience and fortitude almost superhuman, had meanwhile undermined her physical strength. This was a mortal blow to Falkner; while with self-absorbed, and, he now felt, criminal pertinacity, he had sought death, he had forgotten the results such acts of his might have on one so dear and innocent. He had thought that when she lost him, Elizabeth would feel a transitory sorrow; while new scenes, another family, and the absence of his griefs, would soon bring comfort. But he lived, and the consequences of his resolve to die fell upon her—she was his victim! there was something maddening in the thought. He looked at her dear face, grown so pale—viewed her wasting form—watched her loss of appetite and nervous tremours with an impatient agony that irritated his wound, and brought back malady on himself.

All that the physicians could order for Elizabeth, was change of air—added to an intimation that an entirely new scene, and a short separation from her father, would be of the utmost benefit. Where could she go? it was not now that she drooped—and trembled at every sound, that he could restore her to her father's family. No time ought to be lost, he was told, and the word consumption mentioned; the deaths of her parents gave a sting to that word, which filled him with terror. Something must be done immediately—what he knew not; and he gazed on his darling, whom he felt that by his own act he had destroyed, with an ardour to save that he felt was impotent, and he writhed beneath the thought.

One morning, while Falkner was brooding over these miserable ideas, and Elizabeth was vainly trying to assume a look of cheerfulness and health, which her languid step and pale cheek belied, a carriage entered their quiet grounds, and a visitor was announced. It was Lady Cecil. Elizabeth had nearly forgotten, nor ever expected to see her again—but that lady, whose mind was at ease at the period of their acquaintance, and who had been charmed by the beauty and virtues of the devoted daughter, had never ceased to determine at some time to seek her, and renew their acquaintance. She, indeed, never expected to see Falkner again, and she often wondered what would be his daughter's fate when he died; she and her family had remained abroad till the present spring, when, being in London, she, by Miss Jervis's assistance, learned that he still lived, and that they were both at Wimbledon.

Lady Cecil was a welcome visiter wherever she went, for there was an atmosphere of cheerful and kindly warmth around her, that never failed to communicate pleasure. Falkner, who had not seen her at Leghorn, and had scarcely heard her name mentioned, was won at once; and when she spoke with ardent praise of Elizabeth, and looked upon her altered appearance with undisguised distress, his heart warmed towards her, and he was ready to ask her assistance in his dilemma. That was offered, however, before it was asked—she heard that change of air was recommended—she guessed that too great anxiety for her father had produced her illness—she felt sure that her own pleasant residence and cheerful family was the best remedy that could be administered.

"I will not be denied," she said, after having made her invitation that both father and daughter should pay her a visit. "You must come to me: Lord Cecil is gone to Ireland for two months, to look after his estate there; and our little Julius being weakly, I could not accompany him. I have taken a house near Hastings—the air is salubrious, the place beautiful—I lead a domestic, quiet life, and I am sure Miss Falkner will soon be well with me."

As her invitation was urged with warmth and sincerity, Falkner did not hesitate to accept it. To a certain degree, he modified it, by begging that Elizabeth should accompany Lady Cecil, in the first place, alone. As the visit was to be for two months, he promised after the first was elapsed to join them. He alleged various reasons for this arrangement; his real one being, that he had gathered from the physicians that they considered a short separation from him as essential to the invalid's recovery. She acceded, for she was anxious to get well, and hoped that the change would restore her. Everything was therefore soon agreed upon; and, two days afterward, the two ladies were on their road to Hastings, where Lady Cecil's family already was—she having come to town with her husband only, who by this time had set out on his Irish tour.

"I feel convinced that three days of my nursing will make you quite well," said Lady Cecil, as they were together in her travelling carriage; "I wish you to look as you did in Italy. One so young, and naturally so healthy, will soon recover strength. You overtasked yourself—and your energetic mind is too strong for your body; but repose, and my care, will restore you. I am sure we shall be very happy—my children are dear little angels, and will entertain you when you like, and never be in your way. I shall be your head nurse—and Miss Jervis, dear odd soul! will act under my orders. The situation of my house is enchanting; and, to add to our family circle, I expect my brother Gerard, whom I am sure you will like. Did I ever mention him to you? perhaps not—but you must like Gerard—and you will delight him. He is serious—nay, to say the truth, sad—but it is a sadness a thousand times more interesting than the gayety of commonplace worldly men. It is a seriousness full of noble thoughts and affectionate feelings. I never knew, I never dreamed, that there was a creature resembling or to be compared to him in the world, till I saw you. You have the same freedom from worldliness—the same noble and elevated ideas—feeling for others, and thinking not of the petty circle of ideas that encompasses and presses down every other mind, so that they cannot see or feel beyond their Lilliputian selves.

"In one thing you do not resemble Gerard. You, though quiet, are cheerful; while he, naturally more vivacious, is melancholy. You look an inquiry, but I cannot tell you the cause of my brother's unhappiness; for his friendship for me, which I highly prize, depends upon my keeping sacredly the promise I have given never to make his sorrows a topic of conversation. All I can say is, that they result from a sensibility, and a delicate pride, which is overstrained, yet which makes me love him ten thousand times more dearly. He is better now than he used to be, and I hope that time and reason will altogether dissipate the vain regrets that imbitter his life. Some new, some strong feeling may one day spring up and scatter the clouds. I pray for this; for though I love him tenderly, and sympathize in his grief, yet I think it excessive and deplorable; and, alas! never to be remedied, though it may be forgotten."

Elizabeth listened with some surprise to hear of another so highly praised, and yet unhappy; while in her heart she thought, "Though this sound like one to be compared to Neville, yet, when I see him, how I shall scorn the very thought of finding another as high-minded, kind, and interesting as he!" She gave no utterance, however, to this reflection, and merely asked, "Is your brother older than you?"

"No, younger—he is only two-and-twenty; but passion and grief, endured almost since infancy, prevented him when a child from being childish; and now he has all that is beautiful in youth, with none of its follies. Pardon my enthusiasm; but you will grow enthusiastic also when you see Gerard."

"I doubt that," thought Elizabeth; "my enthusiasm is spent, and I should hate myself if I could think of another as of Neville." This latent thought made the excessive praises which Lady Cecil bestowed on her brother sound almost distastefully. Her thoughts flew back to Marseilles; to his sedulous attentions—their parting interview—and fixed at last upon the strange emotion Falkner had displayed when seeing him; and his desire that his name even should not be mentioned. Again she wondered what this meant, and her thoughts became abstracted; Lady Cecil conjectured that she was tired, and permitted her to indulge in her silent reveries.

# CHAPTER XIV

Lady Cecil's house was situated on the heights that overlook Fairlight Bay, near Hastings. Any one who has visited that coast knows the peculiar beauty of the rocks, downs, and groves of Fairlight. The oak, which clothes each dell, and, in a dwarf and clipped state, forms the hedges, imparts a richness not only to the wide landscape, but to each broken nook of ground and sequestered corner; the fern, which grows only in contiguity to the oak, giving a wild forest appearance to the glades. The mansion itself was large, convenient, and cheerful. The grounds were extensive; and from points of view you could see the wide sea—the more picturesque bay—and the undulating, varied shore that curves in towards Winchelsea. It was impossible to conceive a scene more adapted to revive the spirits, and give variety and amusement to the thoughts.

Elizabeth grew better, as by a miracle, the very day after her arrival; and within a week a sensible change had taken place in her appearance, as well as her health. The roses bloomed in her cheeks—her step regained its elasticity—her spirits rose even to gayety. All was new and animating. Lady Cecil's beautiful and spirited children delighted her. It was a domestic scene, adorned by elegance and warmed by affection. Elizabeth had, despite her attachment to her father, often felt the weight of loneliness when left by him at Zante; or when his illness threw her back entirely on herself. Now on each side there were sweet, kind faces—playful, tender caresses—and a laughing mirth, cheering in its perfect innocence.

The only annoyance she suffered arose from the great influx of visitors. Having lived a life disjoined from the crowd, she soon began to conceive the hermitess, delight in loneliness, and the vexation of being intruded upon by the frivolous and indifferent. She found that she loved friends, but hated acquaintance. Nor was this strange. Her mind was quite empty of conventional frivolities. She had not been at a ball twice in her life, and then only when a mere child; yet all had been interest and occupation. To unbend with her was to converse with a friend—to play with children—or to enjoy the scenes of nature with one who felt their beauties with her. "It was hard labour," she often said, "to talk with people with whom she had not one pursuit—one taste in common." Often when a barouche, crowded with gay bonnets, appeared, she stole away. Lady Cecil could not understand this. Brought up in the thick of fashionable life, no person of her clique was a stranger; and if any odd people called on her—still they were in some way entertaining; or if *bores*—bores are an integral portion of life, not to be shaken off with impunity, for, as oysters, they often retain the fairest pearls in close conjunction. "You are wrong," said Lady Cecil. "You must not be a savage—I cannot have mercy on you; this little jagged point in your character must be worn off—you must be as smooth and glossy in exterior as you are incalculably precious in the substance of your mind."

Elizabeth smiled; but not the less when a sleek, self-satisfied dowager, all smiles to those she knew—all impertinent scrutiny to the unknown—and a train of ugly old women in embryo—called, for the present, misses—followed, each honouring her with an insolent stare. "There was a spirit in her feet," and she could not stay, but hurried out into the woodland dells, and with a book, her own reveries, and the beautiful objects around her, as her companions; and feeling ecstatically happy, both at what she possessed, and what she had escaped from.

Thus it was one day that she deserted Lady Cecil, who was smiling sweetly on a red-faced gouty squire, and listening placidly to his angry wife, who was complaining that her name had been put too low down in some charity list. She stole out from the glass door that opened on the lawn, and, delighted that her escape was secure, hurried to join the little group of children whom she saw speeding beyond into the park.

"Without a bonnet, Miss Falkner!" cried Miss Jervis.

"Yes; and the sun is warm. You are not using your parasol, Miss Jervis; lend it me, and let us go into the shade." Then, taking her favourite child by the hand, she said, "Come, let us pay visits. Mamma has got some visitors; so we will go and seek for some. There is my Lord Deer and pretty Lady Doe. Ah! pretty Miss Fawn, what a nice dappled frock you have on!"

The child was enchanted; and they wandered on through the glades, among the fern, into a shady dell, quite at the other side of the park, and sat down beneath a spreading oak-tree. By this time they had got into a serious talk of where the clouds were going, and where the first tree came from, when a gentleman, who had entered the park gates unperceived, rode by, and pulling up his horse suddenly, with a start, and an exclamation of surprise, he and Elizabeth recognised each other.

"Mr. Neville!" she cried, and her heart was full in a moment of a thousand recollections—of the gratitude she owed—their parting scene—and the many conjectures she had formed about him since they separated. He looked more than pleased; and the expression of gloomy abstraction which his face too often wore was lighted up by a smile that went straight to the heart. He sprung from his horse, gave the rein to his groom, and joining Elizabeth and her little companion, walked towards the house.

Explanations and surprise followed. He was the praised, expected brother of Lady Cecil. How strange that Elizabeth had not discovered this relationship at Marseilles! and yet, at that time, she had scarcely a thought to spare beyond Falkner. His recovery surprised Neville, and he expressed the warmest pleasure. He looked with tenderness and admiration at the soft and beautiful creature beside him, whose courage and unwearied assiduity had preserved her father's life. It was a bewitching contrast to remember her face shadowed by fear—her vigilant, anxious eyes fixed on her father's wan countenance—her thoughts filled with one sad fear; and now to see it beaming in youthful beauty, animated by the happy, generous feelings which were her nature. Yet this very circumstance had a sad reaction upon Neville. His heart still bore the burden of its sorrow, and he felt more sure of the sympathy of the afflicted mourner, than of one who looked untouched by any adversity. The sentiment was transitory, for Elizabeth, with that delicate tact which is natural to a feeling mind, soon gave such a subdued tone to their conversation as made it accord with the mysterious unhappiness of her companion.

When near the house, they were met by Lady Cecil, who smiled at what she deemed a sudden intimacy naturally sprung between two who had so many qualities in common. Lady Cecil really believed them made for each other, and had been anxious to bring them together; for, being passionately attached to her brother, and grieving at the melancholy that darkened his existence, she thought she had found a cure in her new friend; and that the many charms of Elizabeth would cause him to forget the misfortunes on which he so vainly brooded. She was still more pleased when an explanation was given, and she found that they were already intimate—already acquainted with the claims each possessed to the other's admiration and interest; and each naturally drawn to seek in the other that mirror of their better nature, that touch of kindred soul, which showed that they were formed to share existence, or, separated, to pine eternally for a reunion.

Lady Cecil with playful curiosity questioned why they had concealed their being acquainted. Elizabeth could not well tell; she had thought much of Neville, but first the prohibition of Falkner, and then the excessive praises Lady Cecil bestowed upon her brother, chained her tongue. The one had accustomed her to preserve silence on a subject deeply interesting to her; the other jarred with any confidence, for there would have been a comparing Neville with the Gerard which was indeed himself; and Elizabeth neither wished to have her friend depreciated, nor to struggle against the enthusiasm felt by the lady for her brother. The forced silence of to-day on such a subject renders the silence of to-morrow almost a matter of necessity; and she was ashamed to mention one she had not already named. It may be remarked that this sort of shame arises in all dispositions; it is the seal and symbol of love. Shame of any kind was not akin to the sincere and ingenuous nature of Elizabeth; but love, though young and unacknowledged, will tyrannise from the first, and produce emotions never felt before.

Neville hoarded yet more avariciously the name of Elizabeth. There was delight in the very thought of her; but he shrunk from being questioned. He had resolved to avoid her; for, till his purpose was achieved, and the aim of his existence fulfilled, he would not yield to the charms of love, which he felt hovered round the beautiful Elizabeth. Sworn to a sacred duty, no self-centred or self-prodigal passion should come between him and its accomplishment. But, meeting her thus unawares, he could not continue guarded; his very soul drank in gladness at the sight of her. He remarked with joy the cheerfulness that had replaced her cares; he looked upon her open brow, her eyes of mingled tenderness and fire, her figure, free and graceful in every motion, and felt that she realized every idea he had formed of feminine beauty. He fancied, indeed, that he looked upon her as a picture; that his heart was too absorbed by its own griefs to catch a thought beyond; he was unmindful, while he gazed, of that emanation, that shadow of the shape, which the Latin poet tells us flows from every object, that impalpable impress of her form and being, which the air took and then folded round him, so that all he saw entered, as it were, into his own substance, and became mingled up for evermore with his identity.

# CHAPTER XV

Three or four days passed in great tranquillity; and Lady Cecil rejoiced that the great medicine acted so well on the rankling malady of her brother's soul. It was the leafy month of June, and nature was as beautiful as these lovely beings themselves, who enjoyed her sweets with enthusiastic and new-sprung delight. They sailed on the sunny sea—or lingered by the summer brooks, and among the rich woodlands—ignorant why all appeared robed in a brightness which before they had never observed. Elizabeth had little thought beyond the present hour—except to wish for the time when Falkner was to join them. Neville rebelled somewhat against the new law he obeyed, but it was a slothful rebellion—till on the day he was awakened from his dream of peace.

One morning, Elizabeth, on entering the breakfast-room, found Lady Cecil leaning discontentedly by the window, resting her cheek on her hand, and her brow overcast.

"He is gone," she exclaimed; "it is too provoking! Gerard is gone! A letter came, and I could not detain him—it will take him probably to the other end of the kingdom—and who knows when we shall see him again!"

They sat down to breakfast, but Lady Cecil was full of discontent. "It is not only that he is gone," she continued, "but the cause of his going is full of pain and care—and, unfortunately, you cannot sympathize with me, for I have not obtained his consent to confide his hapless story to you. Would that I might!—you would feel for him—for us all."

"He has been unhappy since childhood," observed Elizabeth.

"He has, it is true; but how did you learn that? has he ever told you anything?"

"I saw him, many years ago, at Baden. How wild, how sullen he was—unlike his present self! for then there was a violence and a savageness in his gloom, which has vanished."

"Poor boy!" said Lady Cecil; "I remember well—and it is a pleasure to think that I am, to a great degree, the cause of the change. He had no friend at that time—none to love—to listen to him, and foster hopes which, however vain, diminish his torments, and are all the cure he can obtain, till he forgets them. But what can this mean?" she continued, starting up; "what can bring him back? It is Gerard returned!"

She threw open the glass door, and went out to meet him as he rode up the avenue—he threw himself from his horse, and advanced, exclaiming, "Is my father here?"

"Sir Boyvill? No; is he coming?"

"Oh yes! we shall see him soon. I met a servant with a letter sent express—the post was too slow—he will be here soon; he left London last night—you know with what speed he travels."

"But why this sudden visit?"

"Can you not guess? He received a letter from the same person— containing the same account; he knew I was here—he comes to balk my purpose, to forbid, to storm, to reproach; to do all that he has done a thousand times before, with the same success."

Neville looked flushed and disturbed; his face, usually "more in sorrow than in anger," now expressed the latter emotion, mingled with scorn and resolution; he gave the letter he had received to Lady Cecil. "I am wrong, perhaps, in returning at his bidding, since I do not mean ultimately to obey—yet he charges me on my duty to hear him once again; so I am come to hear—to listen to the old war of his vanity with what he calls my pride—his vindictiveness with my sense of duty—his vituperation of her I worship—and I must bear this!"

Lady Cecil read the letter, and Neville pressed Elizabeth's hand, and besought her excuse, while she, much bewildered, was desirous to leave the room. At this moment the noise of a carriage was heard on the gravel. "He is here," said Neville; "see him first, Sophia, tell him how resolved I am—how right in my resolves. Try to prevent a struggle, as disgraceful as vain; and most so to my father, since he must suffer defeat."

With a look of much distress, Lady Cecil left the room to receive her new guest; while Elizabeth stole out by another door into the grove, and mused under the shady covert on what had passed. She felt curious, yet saddened. Concord, affection, and sympathy are so delightful, that all that disturbs the harmony is eminently distasteful. Family contentions are worst of all. Yet she would not prejudge Neville. He felt, in its full bitterness, the pain of disobeying his parent; and whatever motive led to such a mode of action, it hung like an eclipse over his life. What it might be she could not guess; but it was no ignoble, self-centred passion. Hope and joy were sacrificed to it. She remembered him as she first saw him, a boy driven to wildness by a sense of injury; she remembered him when reason and his better nature had subdued the selfish portion of his feeling—grown kind as a woman—active, friendly, and sympathizing, as few men are; she recollected him by Falkner's sick couch, and when he took leave of her, auguring that they should meet in a happier hour. That hour had not yet come, and she confessed to herself that she longed to know the cause of his unhappiness; and wondered whether, by counsel or sympathy, she could bring any cure.

She was plunged in revery, walking slowly beneath the forest trees, when she heard a quick step brushing the dead leaves and fern, and Neville joined her. "I have escaped," he cried, "and left poor Sophy to bear the scoldings of an unjust and angry man. I could not stay—it was not cowardice—but I have recollections joined to such contests, that make my heart sick. Besides, I should reply—and I would not willingly forget that he is my father."

"It must be indeed painful," said Elizabeth, "to quarrel with, to disobey a parent."

"Yet there are motives that might, that must excuse it. Do you remember the character of Hamlet, Miss Falkner?"

"Perfectly—it is the imbodying of the most refined, the most genuine, and yet the most harrowing feelings and situation, that the imagination ever conceived."

"I have read that play," said Neville, "till each word seems instinct with a message direct to my heart—as if my own emotions gave a conscious soul to every line. Hamlet was called upon to avenge a father—in execution of his task he did not spare a dearer, a far more sacred name—if he used no daggers with his mother, he spoke them; nor winced, though she writhed beneath his hand. Mine is a lighter, yet a holier duty. I would vindicate a mother—without judging my father—without any accusation against him, I would establish her innocence. Is this blameable? What would you do, Miss Falkner, if your father were accused of a crime?"

"My father and a crime! Impossible!" exclaimed Elizabeth; for, strange to say, all the self-accusations of Falkner fell empty on her ear. It was a virtue in him to be conscience-stricken for an error; of any real guilt she would have pledged her life that he was free.

"Yes—impossible!" cried Neville—"doubtless it is so; but did you hear his name stigmatized—shame attend your very kindred to him—what would you do?—defend him—prove his innocence—would you not?"

"A life were well sacrificed to such a duty."

"And to that very duty mine is devoted. In childhood I rebelled against the accusation with vain, but earnest indignation; now I am calmer because I am more resolved; but I will yield to no impediment—be stopped by no difficulty—not even by my father's blind commands. My mother! dear name—dearer for the ills attached to it—my angel mother shall find an unfaltering champion in her son.

"You must not be angry," he continued, in reply to her look of wonder, "that I mention circumstances which it is customary to slur over and conceal. It is shame for me to speak—for you to hear—my mother's name. That very thought gives a keener edge to my purpose. God knows what miserable truth is hidden by the veils which vanity, revenge, and selfishness have drawn around my mother's fate; but that truth—though it be a bleeding one—shall be disclosed, and her innocence be made as clear as the sun now shining above us.

"It is dreadful, very dreadful, to be told—to be persuaded that the idol of one's thoughts is corrupt and vile. It is no new story, it is true—wives have been false to their husbands ere now, and some have found excuses, and sometimes been justified; it is the manner makes the thing. That my mother should have left her happy home—which, under her guardian eye, was paradise—have deserted me, her child, whom she so fondly loved— and who, even in that unconscious age, adored her—and her poor little girl, who died neglected—that year after year she has never inquired after us— nor sent nor sought a word—while following a stranger's fortune through the world! That she whose nightly sleep was broken by her tender cares— whose voice so often lulled me, and whose every thought and act was pure as an angel's—that she, tempted by the arch fiend, strayed from hell for her destruction, should leave us all to misery, and her own name to obloquy. No! no! The earth is yet sheltered by heaven, and sweet and good things abide in it—and she was, and is, among them sweetest and best!"

Neville was carried away by his feelings—while Elizabeth, overpowered by his vehemence—astonished by the wild, strange tale he disclosed, listened in silence, yet an eloquent silence—for her eyes filled with tears— and her heart burned in her bosom with a desire to show how entirely she shared his deep emotion.

"I have made a vow," he continued—"it is registered in heaven; and each night as I lay my head on my pillow I renew it; and beside you—the best of earthly things now that my dear mother is gone, I repeat—that I devote my life to vindicate her who gave me life; and my selfish, revengeful father is here to impede—to forbid—but I trample on such obstacles, as on these dead leaves beneath our feet. You do not speak, Miss Falkner—did you ever hear of Mrs. Neville?"

"I have spent all my life out of England," replied Elizabeth, "yet I have some recollection."

"I do not doubt it—to the ends of the earth the base-minded love to carry the tale of slander and crime. You have heard of Mrs. Neville, who, for the sake of a stranger, deserted her home, her husband, her helpless children—and has never been heard of since; who, unheard and undefended, was divorced from her husband—whose miserable son was brought to witness against her. It is a story well fitted to raise vulgar wonder—vulgar abhorrence; do you wonder that I, who since I was nine years old have slept and waked on the thought, should have been filled with hate, rancour, and every evil passion, till the blessed thought dawned on my soul, that I would prove her innocence, and that she should be avenged—for this I live.

"And now I must leave you. I received yesterday a letter which promises a clew to guide me through this labyrinth; wherever it leads, there I follow. My father has come to impede me—but I have, after using unavailing remonstrance, told him that I will obey a sense of duty independent of parental authority. I do not mean to see him again—I now go—but I could not resist the temptation of seeing you before I went, and proving to you the justice of my resolves. If you wish for further explanation, ask Sophia—tell her that she may relate all; there is not a thought or act of my life with which I would have you unacquainted, if you will deign to listen."

"Thank you for this permission," said Elizabeth; "Lady Cecil is desirous, I know, of telling me the cause of a melancholy which, good and kind as you are, you ought not to suffer. Alas! this is a miserable world: and when I hear of your sorrows, and remember my dear father's, I think that I must be stone to feel no more than I do; and yet, I would give my life to assist you in your task."

"I know well how generous you are, though I cannot now express how my heart thanks you. I will return before you leave my sister; wherever fate and duty drives me, I will see you again."

They returned towards the house, and he left her; his horse was already saddled, and standing at the door; he was on it, and gone in a moment.

Elizabeth felt herself as in a dream when he was gone, yet her heart and wishes went with him; for she believed the truth of all he said, and revered the enthusiasm of affection that impelled his actions. There was something wild and proud in his manner, which forcibly reminded her of the boy of sixteen, who had so much interested her girlish mind; and his expressions, indignant and passionate as they were, yet vouched, by the very sentiment they conveyed, for the justice of his cause. "Gallant, noble-hearted being! God assist your endeavours! God and every good spirit that animates this world." Thus her soul spoke as she saw him ride off; and, turning into the house, a half involuntary feeling made her take up the volume of Shakspeare containing Hamlet; and she was soon buried, not only in the interest of the drama itself, but in the various emotions it excited by the association it now bore to one she loved more even than she knew. It was nothing strange that Neville, essentially a dreamer and a poet, should have identified himself with the Prince of Denmark; while the very idea that he took to himself, and acted on sentiments thus high-souled and pure, adorned him yet more in her eyes, endowing him in ample measure with that ideality which the young and noble love to bestow on the objects of their attachment.

After a short time, she was interrupted by Lady Cecil, who looked disturbed and vexed. She said little, except to repine at Gerard's going and Sir Boyvill's stay—he also was to depart the following morning: but Sir Boyvill was a man who made his presence felt disagreeably, even when it was limited to a few hours. Strangers acknowledged this; no one liked the scornful, morose old man; and a near connexion, who was open to so many attacks, and sincerely loved one whom Sir Boyvill pretended most to depreciate, was even more susceptible to the painful feelings he always contrived to spread round him. To despise everybody, to contradict everybody with marks of sarcasm and contempt, to set himself up for an idol, and yet to scorn his worshippers; these were the prominent traits of his character, added to a galled and sore spirit, which was for ever taking offence, which discerned an attack in every word, and was on the alert to repay these fancied injuries with real and undoubted insult. He had been a man of fashion, and retained as much good breeding as was compatible with a techy and revengeful temper; this was his only merit.

He was nearly seventy years of age, remarkably well preserved, but with strongly-marked features, and a countenance deeply lined, set off by a young-looking wig, which took all venerableness from his appearance, without bestowing juvenility; his lips were twisted into a sneer, and there was something in his evident vanity that might have provoked ridicule, but that traces of a violent, unforgiving temper prevented him from being merely despicable, while they destroyed every particle of compassion with which he might have been regarded; for he was a forlorn old man, separating himself from those allied to him by blood or connexion, excellent as they were. His only pleasure had been in society; secluding himself from that, or presenting himself only in crowds, where he writhed to find that he went for nothing, he was miserable, yet not to be comforted, for the torments he endured were integral portions of his own nature.

He looked surprised to see Elizabeth, and was at first very civil to her, with a sort of oldfashioned gallantry which, had it been good-humoured, might have amused, but, as it was, appeared forced, misplaced, and rendered its object very uncomfortable. Whatever Lady Cecil said, he contradicted. He made disagreeable remarks about her children, prophesying in them so much future torment; and when not personally impertinent, amused them by recapitulating all the most scandalous stories rife in London of unfaithful wives and divided families, absolutely gloating with delight, when he narrated anything peculiarly disgraceful. After half an hour, Elizabeth quite hated him; and he extended the same sentiment to her on her bestowing a meed of praise on his son. "Yes," he said, in reply, "Gerard is a very pleasant person; if I said he was half madman, half fool, I should certainly say too much, and appear an unkind father; but the sort of imbecility that characterizes his understanding is, I think, only equalled by his self-willed defiance of all laws which society has established; in conduct he very much resembles a lunatic armed with a weapon of offence, which he does not fear himself, and deals about on those unfortunately connected with him, with the same indifference to wounds."

On this speech, Lady Cecil coloured and rose from the table, and her friend gladly followed, leaving Sir Boyvill to his solitary wine. Never had Elizabeth experienced before the intolerable weight of an odious person's society—she was stunned. "We have but one resource," said Lady Cecil; "you must sit down to the piano. Sir Boyvill is too polite not to entreat you to play on, and too weary not to fall asleep; he is worse than ever."

"But he is your father!" cried Elizabeth, astonished.

"No, thank Heaven!" said Lady Cecil. "What could have put that into your head? Oh, I see—I call Gerard my brother. Sir Boyvill married my poor mother, who is since dead. We are only connected—I am happy to say—there is no drop of his blood in my veins. But I hear him coming. Do play something of Herz. The noise will drown every other sound, and even astonish my father-in-law."

The evening was quickly over, for Sir Boyvill retired early; the next morning he was gone, and the ladies breathed freely again. It is impossible to attempt to describe the sort of moral nightmare the presence of such a man produces. "Do you remember in Madame de Sévigné's Letters," said Lady Cecil, "where she observes that disagreeable society is better than good—because one is so pleased to get rid of it? In this sense, Sir Boyvill is the best company in the whole world. We will take a long drive to-day, to get rid of the last symptoms of the Sir Boyvill fever."

"And you will tell me what all this mystery means," said Elizabeth. "Mr. Neville gave some hints yesterday; but referred me to you. You may tell me all."

"Yes; I am aware," replied Lady Cecil. "This one good, at least, I have reaped from Sir Boyvill's angry visit. I am permitted to explain to you the causes of our discord, and of dear Gerard's sadness. I shall win your sympathy for him, and exculpate us both. It is a mournful tale—full of unexplainable mystery—shame—and dreaded ill. It fills me perpetually with wonder and regret; nor do I see any happy termination, except in the oblivion, in which I wish that it was buried. Here is the carriage. We will not take any of the children with us, that we may suffer no interruption."

Elizabeth's interest was deeply excited, and she was as eager to listen as her friend to tell. The story outlasted a long drive. It was ended in the dusky twilight—as they sat after dinner, looking out on the summer woods—while the stars came out twinkling amid the foliage of the trees—and the deer kept close to graze. The hour was still—and was rendered solemn by a tale as full of heartfelt sorrow and generous enthusiasm as ever won maiden's attention, and bespoke her favour for him who loved and suffered.

# CHAPTER XVI

Lady Cecil began:—

"I have already told you, that though I call Gerard my brother, and he possesses my sisterly affection, we are only connexions by marriage, and not the least related in blood. His father married my mother; but Gerard is the offspring of a former marriage, as I am also. Sir Boyvill's first wife is the unfortunate lady who is the heroine of my tale.

"Sir Boyvill, then Mr. Neville, for he inherited his baronetcy only a few years ago, had advanced beyond middle age when he first married. He was a man of the world, and of pleasure; and being also clever, handsome, and rich, had great success in the circles of fashion. He was often involved in liaisons with ladies, whose names were rife among the last generation for loving notoriety and amusement better than duty and honour. As he made a considerable figure, he conceived that he had a right to entertain a high opinion of himself, and not without some foundation; his good sayings were repeated; his songs were set to music, and sung with enthusiasm in his own set—he was courted and feared. Favoured by women, imitated by men, he reached the zenith of a system, any connexion with which is considered as enviable.

"He was some five-and-forty when he fell in love, and married. Like many dissipated men, he had a mean idea of female virtue—and especially disbelieved that any portion of it was to be found in London; so he married a country girl, without fortune, but with beauty and attractions sufficient to justify his choice. I never saw his lady; but several of her early friends have described her to me. She was something like Gerard—yet how unlike! In the colour of the eyes and hair, and the formation of the features, they resembled; but the expression was wholly different. Her clear complexion was tinged by a pure blood, that ebbed and flowed rapidly in her veins, driven by the pulsations of her soul, rather than of her body. Her large dark eyes were irresistibly brilliant; and opened their lids on the spectator with an effect such as the sun has, when it drops majestically below a heavy cloud, and dazzles the beholder with its unexpected beams. She was vivacious—nay, wild of spirit; but though raised far above the dull monotony of common life by her exuberant joyousness of soul, yet every thought and act was ruled by a pure unsullied heart. Her impulses were keen and imperative; her sensibility, true to the touch of nature, was tremblingly alive; but their more dangerous tendencies were guarded by excellent principles, and a truth never shadowed by a cloud. Her generous and confiding heart might be duped—might spring forward too eagerly—and she might be imprudent; but she was never false. An ingenuous confession of error, if ever she fell into it, purged away all suspicion that anything mysterious or forbidden lurked in her most thoughtless acts. Other women, who, like her, are keenly sensitive, and who are driven by ungovernable spirits to do what they afterward repent, and are endowed, as she was, with an aptitude to shame when rebuked, guard their dignity or their fears by falsehood; and while their conduct is essentially innocent, immesh themselves in such a web of deceit, as not only renders them absolutely criminal in the eyes of those who detect them, but in the end hardens and perverts their better nature. Alithea Neville never sheltered herself from the consequences of her faults; rather she met them too eagerly, acknowledged a venial error with too much contrition, and never rested till she had laid her heart bare to her friend and judge, and vindicated its every impulse. To this admirable frankness, soft tenderness, and heart-cheering gayety was added a great store of common sense. Her fault, if fault it could be called, was a too earnest craving for the sympathy and affection of those she loved; to obtain this, she was unwearied, nay, prodigal, in her endeavours to please and serve. Her generosity was a ready prompter, while her sensibility enlightened her. She sought love, and not applause; and she obtained both from all who knew her. To sum up all with the mention of a defect—though she could feel the dignity which an adherence to the dictates of duty imparts, yet sometimes going wrong—sometimes wounded by censure, and always keenly alive to blame, she had a good deal of timidity in her character. She was so susceptible to pain, that she feared it too much, too agonizingly; and this terror of meeting anything harsh or grating in her path rendered her too diffident of herself—too submissive to authority—too miserable, and too yielding, when anything disturbed the harmony with which she desired to be surrounded.

"It was these last qualities, probably, that led her to accept Mr. Neville's offer. Her father wished it, and she obeyed. He was a retired lieutenant in the navy. Sir Boyvill got him raised to the rank of post captain; and what naval officer but would feel unbounded gratitude for such a favour! He was appointed to a ship—sailed—and fell in an engagement not many months after his daughter's marriage—grateful, even in his last moments, that he died commanding the deck of a man-of-war. Meanwhile his daughter bore the effects of his promotion in a less gratifying way. Yet, at first, she loved and esteemed her husband. He was not then what he is now. He was handsome; and his good breeding had the polish of the day. He was popular, through a sort of liveliness which passes for wit, though it was rather a conventional ease in conversation than the sparkle of real intellect. Besides, he loved her to idolatry. Whatever he is now, still vehemence of passion forms his characteristic; and though the selfishness of his disposition gave an evil bias even to his love, yet it was there, and for a time it shed its delusions over his real character. While her artless and sweet caresses could create smiles — while he played the slave at her feet, or folded her in his arms with genuine and undisguised transport, even his darker nature was adorned by the, to him, alien and transitory magic of love.

"But marriage too soon changed Sir Boyvill for the worse. Close intimacy disclosed the distortions of his character. He was a vain and a selfish man. Both qualities rendered him exacting in the extreme; and the first gave birth to the most outrageous jealousy. Alithea was too ingenuous for him to be able to entertain suspicions; but his jealousy was nourished by the difference of their age and temper. She was nineteen—in the first bloom of loveliness—in the freshest spring of youthful spirits—too innocent to suspect his doubts—too kind in her most joyous hour to fancy that she could offend. He was a man of the world—a thousand times had seen men duped and women deceive. He did not know of the existence of a truth as spotless and uncompromising as existed in Alithea's bosom. He imagined that he was marked out as the old husband of a young wife; he feared that she would learn that she might have married more happily; and, desirous of engrossing her all to himself, a smile spent on another was treason to the absolute nature of his rights. At first she was blind to his bad qualities. A thousand times he frowned when she was gay—a thousand times ill-humour and cutting reproofs were the results of her appearing charming to others, before she discovered the selfish and contemptible nature of his passion, and became aware that, to please him, she must blight and uproot all her accomplishments, all her fascinations; that she must for ever curb her wish to spread happiness around; that she, the very soul of generous, unsuspecting goodness, must become cramped in a sort of bed of Procrustes, now having one portion lopped off, and then another, till the maimed and half-alive remnant should resemble the soulless, niggard tyrant, whose every thought and feeling centred in his Lilliputian self. That she did at last make this discovery, cannot be doubted; though she never disclosed her disappointment, nor complained of the tyranny from which she suffered. She grew heedful not to displease, guarded in her behaviour to others, and so accommodated her manner to his wishes, as showed that she feared, but concealed that she no longer esteemed him. A new reserve sprang up in her character, which, after all, was not reserve; for it was only the result of her fear to give pain, and of her unalterable principles. Had she spoken of her husband's faults, it would have been to himself—but she had no spirit of governing—and quarrelling and contention were the antipodes of her nature. If, indeed, this silent yielding to her husband's despotism was contrary to her original frankness, it was a sacrifice made to what she esteemed her duty, and never went beyond the silence which best becomes the injured.

"It cannot be doubted that she was alive to her husband's faults. Generous, she was restrained by his selfishness; enthusiastic, she was chilled by his worldly wisdom; sympathetic, she was rebuked by a jealousy that demanded every feeling. She was like a poor bird, that with untired wing would mount gayly to the skies, when on each side the wires of the aviary impede its flight. Still it was her principle that we ought not to endeavour to form a destiny for ourselves, but to act well our part on the scene where Providence has placed us. She reflected seriously, and perhaps sadly, for the first time in her life; and she formed a system for herself, which would give the largest extent to the exercise of her natural benevolence, and yet obviate the suspicions and cure the fears of her narrow-minded, self-engrossed husband.

"In pursuance of her scheme, she made it her request that they should take up their residence entirely at their seat in the north of England; giving up London society, and transforming herself altogether into a country lady. In her benevolent schemes, in the good she could there do, and in the few friends she could gather round her, against whom her husband could form no possible objection, she felt certain of possessing a considerable share of rational happiness—exempt from the hurry and excitement of town, for which her sensitive and ardent mind rendered her very unfit, under the guidance of a man who at once desired that she should hold a foremost place, and was yet disturbed by the admiration which she elicited. Sir Boyvill complied with seeming reluctance, but real exultation. He possesses a delightful seat in the southern part of Cumberland. Here, amid a simple-hearted peasantry, and in a neighbourhood where she could cultivate many social pleasures, she gave herself up to a life which would have been one of extreme happiness, had not the exactions, the selfishness, the uncongenial mind of Sir Boyvill debarred her from the dearest blessings of all—sympathy and friendship with the partner of her life.

"Still she was contented. Her temper was sweet and yielding. She did not look on each cross in circumstance as an injury or a misfortune; but rather as a call on her philosophy, which it was her duty to meet cheerfully. Her heart was too warm not to shrink with pain from her husband's ungenerous nature, but she had a resource, to which she gave herself up with ardour. She turned the full but checked tide of affections from her husband to her son. Gerard was all in all to her—her hope, her joy, her idol, and he returned her love with more than a child's affection. His sensibility developed early, and she cultivated it perhaps too much. She wished to secure a friend—and the temptation afforded by the singular affectionateness of his disposition and his great intelligence was too strong. Mr. Neville strongly objected to the excess to which she carried her maternal cares, and augured ill of the boy's devotion to her; but here his interference was vain, the mother could not alter; and the child, standing at her side, eyed his father even then with a sort of proud indignation, on his daring to step in between them.

"To Mrs. Neville, this boy was as an angel sent to comfort her. She could not bear that any one should attend on him except herself—she was his playmate and instructress. When he opened his eyes from sleep, his mother's face was the first he saw; she hushed him to rest at night—did he hurt himself, she flew to his side in agony—did she utter one word of tender reproach, it curbed his childish passions on the instant—he seldom left her side, but she was young enough to share his pastimes—her heart overflowed with its excess of love, and he, even as a mere child, regarded her as something to protect, as well as worship.

"Mr. Neville was angry, and often reproved her too great partiality, though by degrees it won some favour in his eyes. Gerard was his son and heir, and he might be supposed to have a share in the affection lavished on him. He respected, also, the absence of frivolous vanity that led her to be happy with her child—contented away from London—satisfied in fulfilling the duties of her station, though his eyes only were there to admire. He persuaded himself that there must exist much latent attachment towards himself, to reconcile her to this sort of exile; and her disinterestedness received the reward of his confidence—he who never before believed or respected woman. He began to yield to her more than he was wont, and to consider that he ought now and then to show some approbation of her conduct.

"When Gerard was about six years old, they went abroad on a tour. Travelling was a mode of passing the time that accorded well with Mr. Neville's matrimonial view of keeping his wife to himself. In the travelling carriage, he only was beside her; in seeing sights, he, who had visited Italy before, and had some taste, could guide and instruct her; and short as their stay in each town was, there was no possibility of forming serious attachments or lasting friendships; at the same time, his vanity was gratified by seeing his wife and son admired by strangers and natives. While abroad, Mrs. Neville bore another child, a little girl. This added greatly to her domestic happiness. Her husband grew extremely fond of his baby daughter; there was too much difference of age to set her up as a rival to Gerard; she was by contradistinction the father's darling, it is true; but this rather produced harmony than discord—for the mother loved both children too well to feel hurt by the preference; and, softened by having an object he really loved to lavish his favour on, Sir Boyvill grew much more of a tender father and indulgent husband than he had hitherto shown himself."

# CHAPTER XVII

"It was not until a year after their return from abroad that the events happened which terminated so disastrously Mrs. Neville's career in her own family. I am perplexed how to begin the narration, the story is so confused and obscure; the mystery that envelops the catastrophe so impenetrable; the circumstances that we really know so few, and these gleaned, as it were, ear by ear, as dropped in the passage of the event; so making, if you will excuse my rustic metaphor, a meager, ill-assorted sheaf. Mrs. Neville had been a wife nearly ten years; never had she done one act that could be disapproved by the most circumspect; never had she swerved from that veracity and open line of conduct which was a safeguard against the mingled ardour and timidity of her disposition. It required extraordinary circumstances to taint her reputation, as, to say the least, it is tainted; and we are still in the dark as to the main instrument by which these circumstances were brought about. Their result is too obvious. At one moment Mrs. Neville was an honoured and beloved wife; a mother, whose heart's pulsations depended on the well-being of her children; and whose fond affection was to them as the sun's warmth to the opening flower. At the next, where is she? Silence and mystery wrap her from us; and surmise is busy in tracing shapes of infamy from the fragments of truth that we can gather.

"On the return of the family from abroad, they again repaired to their seat of Dromore; and, at the time to which I allude, Mr. Neville had left them there, to go to London on business. He went for a week; but his stay was prolonged to nearly two months. He heard regularly from his wife. Her letters were more full of her children and household than herself; but they were kind; and her maternal heart warmed, as she wrote, into anticipations of future happiness in her children, greater even than she now enjoyed. Every line breathed of home and peace; every word seemed to emanate from a mind in which lurked no concealed feeling, no one thought unconfessed or unapproved. To such a home, cheered by so much beauty and excellence, Sir Boyvill returned, as he declares, with eager and grateful affection. The time came when he was expected at home; and true, both to the day and to the hour, he arrived. It was at eleven at night. His carriage drove through the grounds; the doors of the house were thrown open; several eager faces were thrust forward with more of curiosity and anxiety than is at all usual in an English household; and as he alighted, the servants looked aghast, and exchanged glances of terror. The truth was soon divulged. At about six in the evening, Mrs. Neville, who dined early in the absence of her husband, had gone to walk in the park with Gerard; since then, neither had returned.

"When the darkness, which closed in with a furious wind and thunderstorm, rendered her prolonged absence a matter of solicitude, the servants had gone to seek her in the grounds. They found their mistress's key in the lock of a small masked gate that opened on a green lane. They went one way up the lane to meet her; but found no trace. They followed the other, with like ill success. Again they searched the park with more care; and again resorted to the lanes and fields; but in vain. The obvious idea was, that she had taken shelter from the storm; and a horrible fear presented itself, that she might have found no better retreat than a tree or hay-rick, and that she had been struck by the lightning. A slight hope remained, that she had gone along the high-road to meet her husband, and would return with him. His arrival alone took from them this last hope.

"The country was now raised. Servants and tenants were sent divers ways; some on horseback, some on foot. Though summer-time, the night was inclement and tempestuous; a furious west wind swept the earth; high trees were bowed to the ground; and the blast howled and roared, at once baffling and braving every attempt to hear cries or distinguish sounds.

"Dromore is situated in a beautiful, but wild and thinly—inhabited part of Cumberland, on the verge of the plain that forms the coast where it first breaks into uplands, dingles, and ravines; there is no high-road towards the sea—but as they took the one that led to Lancaster, they approached the ocean, and the distant roar of its breakers filled up the pauses of the gale. It was on this road, at the distance of some five miles from the house, that Gerard was found. He was lying on the road in a sort of stupor—which could be hardly called sleep—his clothes were drenched by the storm, and his limbs stiff from cold. When first found, and disturbed, he looked wildly around; and his cry was for his mother—terror was painted in his face—and his intellects seemed deranged by a sudden and terrific shock. He was taken home. His father hurried to him, questioning him eagerly—but the child only raved that his mother was being carried from him; and his pathetic cry of 'Come back, mamma—stop—stop for me!' filled every one with terror and amazement. As speedily as possible, medical assistance was sent for; the physician found the boy in a high fever, the result of fright, exposure to the storm, and subsequent sleep in his wet clothes in the open air. It was many days before his life could be answered for—or the delirium left him—

and still he raved that his mother was being carried off, and would not stop for him, and often he tried to rise from his bed under the notion of pursuing her.

"At length consciousness returned—consciousness of the actual objects around him, mingled with an indistinct recollection of the events that immediately preceded his illness. His pulse was calm; his reason restored; and he lay quietly with open eyes fixed on the door of his chamber. At last he showed symptoms of uneasiness, and asked for his mother. Mr. Neville was called, as he had desired he might be the moment his son showed signs of being rational. Gerard looked up in his father's face with an expression of disappointment, and again murmured, 'Send mamma to me.'

"Fearful of renewing his fever by awakening his disquietude, his father told him that mamma was tired and asleep, and could not be disturbed.

"'Then she has come back?' he cried; 'that man did not take her quite away? The carriage drove here at last.'

"Such words renewed all their consternation. Afraid of questioning the child himself, lest he should terrify him, Mr. Neville sent the nurse who had been with him from infancy, to extract information. His story was wild and strange; and here I must remark, that the account drawn from him by the woman's questions differs somewhat from that to which he afterward adhered; though not so much in actual circumstances as in the colouring given. This his father attributes to his subsequent endeavours to clear his mother from blame; while he asserts, and I believe with truth, that time and knowledge, by giving him an insight into motives, threw a new light on the words and actions which he remembered; and that circumstances which bore one aspect to his ignorance, became clearly visible in another, when he was able to understand the real meaning of several fragments of conversation which had at first been devoid of sense.

"All that he could tell during this first stage of inquiry was, that his mother had taken him to walk with her in the grounds, that she had unlocked the gate that opened out on the lane with her own key, and that a gentleman was without waiting.

"Had he ever seen the gentleman before?

"Never; he did not know him, and the stranger took no notice of him; he heard his mamma call him Rupert.

"His mother took the stranger's arm, and walked on through the lane, while he sometimes ran on before, and sometimes remained at her side. They conversed earnestly, and his mother at one time cried; he, Gerard, felt very angry with the gentleman for making her cry, and took her hand, and begged her to leave him and come away; but she kissed the boy, told him to run on, and they would return very soon.

"Yet they did not return, but walked on to where the lane was intersected by the high-road. Here they stopped, and continued to converse; but it seemed as if she were saying good-by to the stranger, when a carriage, driven at full speed, was seen approaching; it stopped close to them; it was an open carriage, a sort of calèche, with the head pulled forward low down; as it stopped his mother went up to it, when the stranger, pulling the child's hand from hers, hurried her into the carriage, and sprang in after, crying out to him, 'Jump in, my boy!' but, before he could do so, the postillion whipped the horses, who started forward almost with a bound, and were in a gallop on the instant; he heard his mother scream; the words 'My child! my son!' reached his ears, shrieked in agony. He ran wildly after the carriage; it disappeared, but still he ran on. It must stop somewhere, and he would reach it—his mother had called for him; and thus, crying, breathless, panting, he ran along the high-road; the carriage had long been out of sight, the sun had set; the wind, rising in gusts, brought on the thunder-storm; yet still he pursued, till nature and his boyish strength gave way, and he threw himself on the ground to gain breath. At every sound which he fancied might be that of carriage-wheels, he started up; but it was only the howling of the blast in the trees, and the hoarse muttering of the now distant thunder; twice and thrice he rose from the earth and ran forward; till, wet through and utterly exhausted, he lay on the ground, weeping bitterly, and expecting to die.

"This was all his story. It produced a strict inquiry among the servants, and then circumstances scarcely adverted to were remembered, and some sort of information gained. About a week or ten days before, a gentleman on horseback, unattended by any servant, had called. He asked for Mrs. Neville; the servant requested his name, but he muttered that it was no matter. He was ushered into the room where their mistress was sitting; he stayed at least two hours; and, when he was gone, they remarked that her eyes were red, as if she had been weeping. The stranger called again, and Mrs. Neville was denied to him.

"Inquiries were now instituted in the neighbourhood. One or two persons remembered something of a stranger gentleman who had been seen riding about the country, mounted on a fine bay horse. One evening he was seen coming from the masked gate in the park, which caused it to be believed that he was on a visit at Dromore. Nothing more was known of him.

"The servants tasked themselves to remember more particularly the actions of their lady, and it was remembered that one evening she went to walk alone in the grounds, some accident having prevented Gerard from accompanying her. She returned very late, at ten o'clock; and there was, her maid declared, a good deal of confusion in her manner. She threw herself on a sofa, ordered the lights to be taken away, and remained alone for two hours past her usual time for retiring for the night, till, at last, her maid ventured in to ask her if she needed anything. She was awake, and, when lights were brought, had evidently been weeping. After this she only went out in the carriage with the children, until the fatal night of her disappearance. It was remembered, also, that she received several letters, brought by a strange man, who left them without waiting for any answer. She received one the very morning of the day when she left her home, and this last note was found; it threw some light on the fatal mystery. It was only dated with the day of the week, and began abruptly:—

> "'On one condition I will obey you; I will never see you more—I will leave the country—I will forget my threats against the most hated life in the world; he is safe on one condition. You must meet me this evening; I desire to see you for the last time. Come to the gate of your park that opens on the lane, which you opened for me a few nights ago; you will find me waiting outside. I will not detain you long. A farewell to you and to my just revenge shall be breathed at once. If you do not come I will wait till night, till I am past hope, and then enter your grounds, wait till he returns, and—oh, do not force me to say what you will call wicked and worse than unkind, but come, come, and prevent all ill. I charge you come, and hereafter you shall, if you please, be for ever delivered from your
>
> "'RUPERT.

"On this letter she went; yet in innocence, for she took her child with her. Could any one doubt that she was betrayed, carried off, the victim of the foulest treachery? No one did doubt it. Police were sent from London, the country searched, the most minute inquiries set on foot. Sometimes it was supposed that a clew was found, but in the end all failed. Month after month passed; hope became despair; pity merged into surmise; and condemnation quickly followed. If she had been carried forcibly from her home, still she could not forever be imprisoned and debarred from all possibility at least of writing. She might have sent tidings from the ends of the earth, nay, it was madness to think that she could be carried far against her own will. In any town, in any village, she might appeal to the justice and humanity of her fellow-creatures, and be set free. She would not have remained with the man of violence who had torn her away, unless she had at last become a party in his act, and lost all right to return to her husband's roof.

"Such suspicions began to creep about—rather felt in men's minds than inferred in their speech—till her husband first, uttered the fatal word; and then, as if set free from a spell, each one was full of indignation at her dereliction and his injuries. Sir Boyvill was beyond all men vain— vanity rendered him liable to jealousy—and, when jealous, full of sore and angry feelings. His selfishness and unforgiving nature, which had been neutralized by his wife's virtues, now, quickened by the idea of her guilt, burst forth and engrossed every other emotion. He was injured there where the pride of man is most accessible—branded by pity—the tale of the world. He had feared such a catastrophe during the first years of his wedded life, being conscious of the difference which age and nature had placed between him and his wife. In the recesses of his heart he had felt deeply grateful to her for having dissipated these fears. From the moment that her prudent conduct had made him secure, he had become another man—as far as his defective nature and narrow mind permitted—he had grown virtuous and disinterested; but this fabric of good qualities was the result of her influence; and it was swept away and utterly erased from the moment she left him, and that love and esteem were exchanged for contempt and hatred.

"Soon, very soon, had doubts of his wife's allegiance and a suspicion of her connivance insinuated themselves. Like all evilly-inclined persons, he jumped at once into a belief of the worst; her taking her son with her was a mere contrivance, or worse, since her design had probably been to carry him with her—a design frustrated by accident, and the lukewarmness of her lover on that point; the letter left behind he looked on as a fabrication, left there to gloss over her conduct. He forgot her patient goodness—her purity of soul—her devoted attachment to her children—her truth; and attributed at once the basest artifice—the grossest want of feeling. Want of feeling in her! She whose pulses quickened and whose blushes were called up at a word; she who idolized her child even to a fault, and whose tender sympathy was alive to every call; but these demonstrations of sensibility grew into accusations. Her very goodness and guarded propriety were against her. Why appear so perfect, except to blind? Why seclude herself, except from fears which real virtue need never entertain? Why foster the morbid sensibility of her child, except from a craving for that excitement which is a token of depravity? In this bad world we are apt to consider every deviation from stony apathy as tending at last to the indulgence of passions against which society has declared a ban; and thus with poor Alithea, all could see, it was said, that a nature so sensitive must end in ill at last; and that, if tempted, she must yield to an influence which few, even of the coldest natures, can resist.

"While Sir Boyvill revolved these thoughts, he grew gloomy and sullen. At first his increased unhappiness was attributed to sorrow; but a little word betrayed the real source—a little word that named his wife with scorn. That word turned the tide of public feeling; and she, who had been pitied and wept as dead, was now regarded as a voluntary deserter from her home. Her virtues were remembered against her; and surmises, which before would have been reprobated almost as blasphemy, became current— as undoubted truths.

"It was long before Gerard became aware of this altered feeling. The minds of children are such a mystery to us! They are so blank, yet so susceptible of impression, that the point where ignorance ends and knowledge is perfected is an enigma often impossible to solve. From the time that he rose from his sick-bed, the boy was perpetually on the watch for intelligence—eagerly inquiring what discoveries were made—what means were used for, what hopes entertained of, his mother's rescue. He had asked his father whether he should not be justified in shooting the villain who had stolen her if ever he met him. He had shed tears of sorrow and pity until indignation swallowed up each softer feeling, and a desire to succour and to avenge became paramount. His dear, dear mother! that she should be away—kept from him by force—that he could not find— not get at her, were ideas to incense his young heart to its very height of impatience and rage. Every one seemed too tame—too devoid of expedients and energy. It appeared an easy thing to measure the whole earth, step by step, and inch by inch, leaving no portion uninspected till she was found and liberated. He longed to set off on such an expedition; it was his dream by night and day; and he communicated these bursting feelings to every one, with an overflowing eloquence, inexpressibly touching from its truth and earnestness.

"Suddenly he felt the change. Perhaps some officious domestic suggested the idea. He says himself, it came on him as infection may be caught by one who enters an hospital. He saw it in the eyes—he felt it in the air and manner of all: his mother was believed to be a voluntary fugitive; of her own accord she went, and never would return. At the thought his heart grew sick within him:—

"'To see his nobleness!
Conceiving the dishonour of his mother,
He straight declined upon't, drooped, took it deeply;

Fastened and fixed the shame on't in himself;
Threw off his spirit, his appetite, his sleep,
And downright languished.'

"He refused food, and turned in disgust from every former pursuit. Hitherto he had ardently longed for the return of his mother; and it seemed to him that, give his limbs but a manlier growth, let a few years go over, and he should find and bring her back in triumph. But that contumely and disgrace should fall on that dear mother's head—how could he avert that? The evil was remediless, and death was slight in comparison. One day he walked up to his father, and fixing his clear young eyes upon him, said, 'I know what you think, but it is not true. Mamma would come back if she could. When I am a man I will find and bring her back, and you will be sorry then!'

"What more he would have said was lost in sobs. His heart had beat impetuously as he had worked on himself to address his father, and assert his mother's truth; but the consciousness that she was indeed gone, and that for years there was no hope of seeing her, broke in—his throat swelled, he felt suffocated, and fell down in a fit."

# CHAPTER XVIII

Lady Cecil had broken off her tale on their return from their morning drive. She resumed it in the evening, as she and Elizabeth sat looking on the summer woods; and the soft but dim twilight better accorded with her melancholy story.

"Poor Gerard! His young heart was almost broken by struggling passions, and the want of tenderness in those about him. After this scene with his father, his life was again in the greatest danger for some days, but at last health of body returned. He lay on his little couch, pale and wasted, an altered child—but his heart was the same, and he adhered tenaciously to one idea. 'Nurse,' he said, one day, to the woman who had attended him from his birth, 'I wish you would take pen and paper, and write down what I am going to say. Or, if that is too much trouble, I wish you would remember every word, and repeat it to my father. I cannot speak to him. He does not love mamma as he used; he is unjust, and I cannot speak to him—but I wish to tell every little thing that happened, that people may see that what I say is true, and be as sure as I am that mamma never meant to go away.

"'When we met the strange gentleman first, we walked along the lane, and I ran about gathering flowers—yet I remember I kept thinking, why is mamma offended with that gentleman?—what right has he to displease her? and I came back with it in my mind to tell him that he should not say anything to annoy mamma; but when I took her hand she seemed no longer angry, but very, very sorry. I remember she said, "I grieve deeply for you, Rupert"—and then she added, "My good wishes are all I have to give." I remember the words, for they made me fancy, in a most childish manner, mamma must have left her purse at home—and I began to think of my own—but seeing him so well dressed, I felt a few shillings would do him no good. Mamma talked on very softly, looking up in the stranger's face; he was tall—taller, younger—and better looking than papa: and I ran on again, for I did not know what they were talking about. At one time mamma called me and said she would go back, and I was very glad, for it was growing late, and I felt hungry—but the stranger said, "Only a little farther—to the end of the lane only"—so we walked on, and he talked about her forgetting him, and she said something that was best, and he ought to forget her. On this he burst forth very angrily, and I grew angry too—but he changed, and asked her to forgive him—and so we reached the end of the lane.

"'We stopped there, and mamma held out her hand, and said—"Farewell!"—and something more—when suddenly we heard the sound of wheels, and a carriage came at full speed round from a turn in the road; it stopped close to us—her hand trembled which held mine—and the stranger said—"You see I said true—I am going—and shall soon be far distant: I ask but for one half hour—sit in the carriage, it is getting cold." Mamma said, "No, no—it is late—farewell" but as she spoke the stranger as it were led her forward, and in a moment lifted her up; he seemed stronger than any two men—and put her in the carriage—and got in himself, crying to me to jump after, which I would have done, but the postillion whipped the horses. I was thrown almost under the wheel by the sudden motion—I heard mamma scream; but when I got up the carriage was already a long way off—and though I called as loud as I could—and ran after it—it never stopped, and the horses were going at full gallop. I ran on—thinking it would stop or turn back—and I cried out on mamma—while I ran so fast that I was soon breathless—and she was out of hearing—and then I shrieked and cried, and threw myself on the ground—till I thought I heard wheels, and I got up and ran again—but it was only the thunder—and that pealed and the wind roared, and the rain came down—and I could keep my feet no longer, but fell on the ground and forgot everything, except that mamma must come back and I was watching for her. And this, nurse, is my story—every word is true—and is it not plain that mamma was carried away by force?'

"'Yes,' said the woman, 'no one doubts that, Master Gerard—but why does she not come back!—no man could keep her against her will in a Christian country like this.'

"'Because she is dead or in prison,' cried the boy, bursting into tears—'but I see you are as wicked as everybody else—and have wicked thoughts too—and I hate you and everybody—except mamma.'

"From that time Gerard was entirely altered; his boyish spirit was dashed—he brooded perpetually over the wrong done his mother—and was irritated to madness, by feeling that by a look and a word he could not make others share his belief in her spotless innocence. He became sullen, shy—shut up in himself—above all, he shunned his father. Months passed away: requisitions, set on foot at first from a desire to succour, were continued from a resolve to revenge; no pains or expense were spared to discover the fugitives, and all in vain. The opinion took root that they had fled to America—and who on that vast continent could find two beings resolved on concealment? Inquiries were made at New-York and other principal towns; but all in vain.

"The strangest and most baffling circumstance in this mystery was, that no guess could be formed as to who the stranger was. Though he seemed to have dropped from the clouds, he had evidently been known long before to Mrs. Neville. His name, it appeared, was Rupert—no one knew of any bearing that name. Had Alithea loved before her marriage? such a circumstance must have been carefully hidden, for her husband had never suspected it. Her childhood had been spent with her mother, her father being mostly at sea. When sixteen, she lost her mother, and after a short interval resided with her father, then retired from service. He had assured Sir Boyvill that his daughter had never loved; and the husband, jealous as he was, had never seen cause to doubt the truth of this statement. Had she formed any attachment during the first years of her married life! Was it to escape the temptation so held out that she secluded herself in the country? Rupert was probably a feigned name; and Sir Boyvill tried to recollect who her favourites were, so to find a clew by their actions to her disappearance. It was in vain that he called to mind every minute circumstance, and pondered over the name of each visiter: he could remember nothing that helped discovery. Yet the idea that she had, several years ago, conceived a partiality for some man, who, as it proved, loved her to distraction, became fixed in Sir Boyvill's mind. The thought poured venom on the time gone by. It might have been a virtue in her to banish him she loved and to seclude herself; but this mystery, where all seemed so frank and open, this defalcation of the heart, this inward thought which made no sign, yet ruled every action, was gall and wormwood to her proud, susceptible husband. That in her secret soul she loved this other, was manifest—for though it might be admitted that he used art and violence to tear her from her home, yet in the end she was vanquished; and even maternal duties and affections sacrificed to irresistible passion.

"Can you wonder that such a man as Sir Boyvill, ever engrossed by the mighty idea of self—yet fearful that that self should receive the minutest wound; proud of his wife—because, being so lovely and so admired, she was all his—grateful to her, for being so glorious and enviable a possession— can you wonder that this vain but sensitive man should be wound up to the height of jealous rage by the loss of such a good, accompanied by circumstances of deception and dishonour? He had been fond of his wife in return for her affection, while she in reality loved another; he had respected the perfection of her truth, and there was falsehood at the core. Had she avowed the traitor passion; declared her struggles, and, laying bare her heart, confessed that, while she preferred his honour and happiness, yet in the weakness of her nature another had stolen a portion of that sentiment which she desired to consecrate to him—then with what tenderness he had forgiven her—with what soothing forbearance he had borne her fault—how magnanimous and merciful he had shown himself! But she had acted the generous part; thanks had come from him—the shows of obligation from her. He fancied that he held a flower in his hand, from which the sweetest perfume alone could be extracted—but the germe was blighted, and the very core turned to bitter ashes and dust.

"Such a theme is painful; howsoever we view it, it is scarcely possible to imagine any event in life more desolating. To be happy is to attain one's wishes, and to look forward to the lastingness of their possession. Sir Boyvill had long been skeptical and distrusting; but at last he was brought to believe that he had drawn the fortunate ticket; that his wife's faith was a pure and perfect chrysolite—and if in his heart he deemed that she did not regard him with all the reverence that was his due; if she did not nurture all the pride of place, and disdain of her fellow-creatures which he thought that his wife ought to feel—yet her many charms and virtues left him no room for complaint. Her sensibility, her vivacity, her wit, her accomplishments, her exceeding loveliness—they were all undeniably his—and all made her a piece of enchantment. This merit was laid low—deprived of its crown—her fidelity to him; and the selfish, the heartless, and the cold whom she reproved and disliked, were lifted to the eminence of virtue, while she lay fallen, degraded, worthless.

"Sir Boyvill was, in his own conceit, for ever placed on a pedestal; and he loved to imagine that he could say, 'Look at me, you can see no defect! I am a wealthy and a well-born man. I have a wife the envy of all—children who promise to inherit all our virtues. I am prosperous—no harm can reach me—look at me!' He was still on his pedestal, but had become a mark for scorn, for pity! Oh, how he loathed himself—how he abhorred her who had brought him to this pass! He had, in her best days, often fancied that he loved her too well, yielded too often his pride—nurtured schemes to her soft persuasions. He had indeed believed that Providence had created this exquisite and most beautiful being, that life might be made perfect to him. Besides, his months, and days, and hours had been replete with her image; her very admirable qualities, accompanied as they were by the trembling delicacy that droops at a touch, and then revives at a word; her quickness, not of temper, but of feeling, which received such sudden and powerful impression, formed her to be at once admired and cherished with the care a sweet exotic needs, when transplanted from its sunny, native clime, to the ungenial temperature of a northern land. It was madness to recollect all the fears he had wasted on her. *He* had foregone the dignity of manhood to wait on her—he had often feared to pursue his projects, lest they should jar some delicate chord in her frame; to his own recollection, it seemed that he had become but the lackey to her behests—and all for the sake of a love which she bestowed on another—to preserve that honour which she blasted without pity.

"It were in vain to attempt to delineate the full force of jealousy; natural sorrow at losing a thing so sweet and dear was blended with anger that he should be thrown off by her; the misery of knowing that he should never see her more was mingled with a ferocious desire to learn that every disaster was heaped on one whom, hitherto, he had, as well as he could, guarded from every ill. To this we may add, commiseration for his deserted children. His son, late so animated, so free—spirited and joyous, a more promising child had never blessed a father's hopes, was changed into a brooding, grief-struck, blighted visionary. His little girl, the fairy thing he loved best of all, she was taken from him; the carelessness of a nurse during a childish illness caused her death, within a year after her mother's flight. Had that mother remained, such carelessness had been impossible. Sir Boyvill felt that all good fell from him—the only remaining golden fruit dropped from the tree—calamity encompassed him; with his whole soul he abhorred and desired to wreak vengeance on her who caused the ill.

"After two years were passed, and no tidings were received of the fugitives, it seemed plain that there could be but one solution to the mystery. No doubt she and her lover concealed themselves in some far land, under a feigned name. If, indeed, it were—if it be so, it might move any heart to imagine poor Alithea's misery—the obloquy that mantles over her remembrance at home, while she broods over the desolation of the hearth she so long adorned, and the pining, impatient anguish of her beloved boy. What could or can keep her away, is matter of fearful conjecture; but this much is certain, that, at that time at least, and now, if she survives, she must be miserable. Sir Boyvill, if he deigned to recollect these things, enjoyed the idea of her anguish. But, without adverting to her state and feelings, he was desirous of obtaining what reparation he could, and to dispossess her of his name. Endeavours to find the fugitives in America, and false hopes held out, had delayed the process. He at last entered on it with eagerness. A thousand obvious reasons rendered a divorce desirable; and to him, with all his pride, then only would his pillow be without a thorn, when she lost his name, and every right or tie that bound them together. Under the singular circumstances of the case, he could only obtain a divorce by a bill in parliament, and to this measure he resorted.

"There was nothing reprehensible in this step; self-defence, as well as revenge, suggested its expediency. Besides this, it may be said, that he was glad of the publicity that would ensue, that he might be proved blameless to all the world. He accused his wife of a fault so great as tarnished irrecoverably her golden name. He accused her of being a false wife and an unnatural mother, under circumstances of no common delinquency. But he might be mistaken; he might view his injuries with the eye of passion, and others, more disinterested, might pronounce that she was unfortunate, but not guilty. By means of the bill for divorce, the truth would be investigated and judged by several hundred of the best born and best educated of his countrymen. The publicity, also, might induce discovery. It was fair and just; and though his pride rebelled against becoming the tale of the day, he saw no alternative. Indeed, it was reported to him by some officious friend that many had observed that it was strange that he had not sought this remedy before. Something of wonder, or blame, or both, was attached to his passiveness. Such hints galled him to the quick, and he pursued his purpose with all the obstinacy and imperious haste peculiar to him.

"When every other preliminary had been gone through, it was deemed necessary that Gerard should give his evidence at the bar of the House of Lords. Sir Boyvill looked upon his lost wife as a criminal, so steeped in deserved infamy, so odious, and so justly condemned, that none could hesitate in siding with him to free him from the bondage of those laws, which, while she bore his name, might be productive of incalculable injury. His honour, too, was wounded. His honour, which he would have sacrificed his life to have preserved untainted, he had intrusted to Alithea, and loved her the more fervently that she regarded the trust with reverence. She had foully betrayed it; and must not all who respected the world's customs and the laws of social life; above all, must not any who loved him be forward to cast her out from any inheritance of good that could reach her through him?

"Above all, must not their son—his son, share his indignation, and assist his revenge? Gerard was but a boy; but his mother's tenderness, his own quick nature and lastly, the sufferings he had endured through her flight, had early developed a knowledge of the realities of life, and so keen a sense of right and justice, as made his father regard him as capable of forming opinions, and acting from such motives, as usually are little understood by one so young. And true it was that Gerard fostered sentiments independent of any teaching; and cherished ideas the more obstinately, because they were confined to his single breast. He understood the pity with which his father was regarded—the stigma cast upon his mother—the suppressed voice— the wink of the eye—the covert hint. He understood it all; and, like the poet, longed for a word, sharp as a sword, to pierce the falsehood through and through.

"For many months he and his father had seen little of each other. Sir Boyvill had not a mind that takes pleasure in watching the ingenuous sallies of childhood, or the development of the youthful mind; the idea of making a friend of his child, which had been Alithea's fond and earnest aim, could never occur to his self-engrossed heart. Since his illness, Gerard had been weakly, or he would have been sent to school. As it was, a tutor resided in the house. This person was written to by Sir Boyvill's man of business, and directed to break the matter to his pupil; to explain the formalities, to sooth and encourage any timidity he might show, and to incite him, if need were, to a desire to assist in a measure, whose operation was to render justice to his father.

"The first allusion to his mother made by Mr. Carter caused the blood to rush from the boy's heart, and to die crimson his cheeks, his temples, his throat; then he grew deadly pale, and, without uttering a word, listened to his preceptor, till suddenly taking in the nature of the task assigned to him, every limb shook, and he answered by a simple request to be left alone, and he would consider. No more was thought by the unapprehensive people about, than that he was shy of being spoken to on the subject—that he would make up his mind in his own way—and Mr. Carter at once yielded to his request; the reserve which had shrouded him since he lost his mother had accustomed those about him to habitual silence. None—no one watchful, attached, intelligent eye marked the struggles which shook his delicate frame, blanched his cheek, took the flesh from his bones, and quickened his pulse into fever. None marked him as he lay in bed the livelong night, with open eyes and beating heart a prey to contending emotion. He was passed carelessly by as he lay on the dewy grass from morn to evening, his soul torn by grief—uttering his mother's name in accents of despair, and shedding floods of tears.

"I said that these signs of intense feeling were not remarked—and yet they were, in a vulgar way, by the menials, who said it would be well when the affair was over, Master Neville took it so to heart, and was sadly frightened. Frightened! such a coarse undistinguishing name was given to the sacred terror of doing his still loved mother an injury, which heaved his breast with convulsive sobs and filled his veins with fire.

"The thought of what he was called upon to do haunted him day and night with agony. He, her nursling, her idol, her child—he who could not think of her name without tears, and dreamed often that she kissed him in his sleep, and woke to weep over the delusion—he was to accuse her before an assembled multitude—to give support to the most infamous falsehoods—to lend his voice to stigmatize her name: and wherever she was, kept from him by some irresistible power, but innocent as an angel, and still loving him, she was to hear of him as her enemy, and receive a last wound from his hand. Such appeared the task assigned to him in his eyes, for his blunt—witted tutor had spoken of the justice to be rendered his father, by freeing him from his fugitive wife, without regarding the inner heart of his pupil, or being aware that his mother sat throned there, an angel of light and goodness, the victim of ill, but doing none.

"Soon after Mrs. Neville's flight, the family had abandoned the seat in Cumberland, and inhabited a house taken near the Thames, in Buckinghamshire. Here Gerard resided, while his father was in town watching the progress of the bill. At last the day drew near when Gerard's presence was required. The peers showed a disposition, either from curiosity or a love of justice, to sift the affair to the uttermost, and the boy's testimony was declared absolutely necessary. Mr. Carter told Gerard that on the following morning they were to proceed to London, in pursuance of the circumstances which he had explained to him a few days before.

"'Is it then true,' said the boy, 'that I am to be called upon to give evidence, as you call it, against my mother?'

"'You are called upon by every feeling of duty,' replied the sapient preceptor, 'to speak the truth to those whose decision will render justice to your father. If the truth injure Mrs. Neville, that is her affair.'

"Again Gerard's cheeks burned with blushes, and his eyes, dimmed as they were with tears, flashed fire. 'In that case,' he said, 'I beg to see my father.'

"'You will see him when in town,' replied Mr. Carter. 'Come, Neville, you must not take the matter in this girlish style; show yourself a man. Your mother is unworthy—'

"'If you please, sir,' said Gerard, half choked, yet restraining himself, 'I will speak to my father; I do not like any one else to talk to me about these things.'

"'As you please, sir,' said Mr. Carter, much offended.

"No more was said—it was evening. The next morning they set out for London. The poor boy had lain awake the whole night; but no one knew or cared for his painful vigils."

# CHAPTER XIX

"On the following day the journey was performed; and it had been arranged that Gerard should rest on the subsequent one; the third being fixed for his attendance in the House of Lords. Sir Boyvill had been informed how sullenly (that was the word they used) the boy had received the information conveyed him by his tutor. He would rather have been excused saying a word himself to his son on the subject; but this account, and the boy's request to see him, forced him to change his purpose. He did not expect opposition; but he wished to give a right turn to Gerard's expressions. The sort of cold distance that separation and variance of feeling produced, rendered their intercourse little like the tender interchange of parental and filial love.

"'Gerard, my boy,' Sir Boyvill began, 'we are both sufferers; and you, like me, are not of a race tamely to endure injury. I would willingly have risked my life to revenge the ruin brought on us; so I believe would you, child as you are; but the skulking villain is safe from my arm. The laws of his country cannot even pursue him; yet, what reparation is left, I must endeavour to get.'

"Sir Boyvill showed tact in thus bringing forward only that party, whose act none could do other than reprobate, and who was the object of Gerard's liveliest hatred. His face lightened up with something of pleasure—his eye flashed fire; to prove to the world the guilt and violence of the wretch who had torn his mother from him was indeed a task of duty and justice. A little more forbearance on his father's part had wound him easily to his will: but the policy Sir Boyvill displayed was involuntary, and his next words overturned all. 'Your miserable mother,' he continued, 'must bear her share of infamy; and if she be not wholly hardened, it will prove a sufficient punishment. When the events of to-morrow reach her, she will begin to taste of the bitter cup she has dealt out so largely to, others. It were folly to pretend to regret that—I own that I rejoice.'

"Every idea now suffered revulsion, and the stream of feeling flowed again in its old channels. What right had his father to speak thus of the beloved and honoured parent he had so cruelly lost? His blood boiled within him, and, despite childish fear and reverence, he said, 'If my mother will grieve or be injured by my appearing to-morrow, I will not go—I cannot.'

"'You are a fool to speak thus,' said his father, 'a galless animal, without sense of pride or duty. Come, sir, no more of this. You owe me obedience, and you must pay it on this occasion. You are only bid speak the truth, and that you must speak. I had thought, notwithstanding your youth, higher and more generous motives might be urged—a father's honour vindicated—a mother's vileness punished.'

"'My mother is not vile!' cried Gerard, and there stopped; for a thousand things restrain a child's tongue; inexperience, reverence, ignorance of the effect his words may produce, terror at the mightiness of the power with which he has to contend. After a pause, he muttered, 'I honour my mother; I will tell the whole world that she deserves honour.'

"'Now, Gerard, on my soul,' cried Sir Boyvill, roused to anger, as parents too easily are against their offspring when they show any will of their own, while they expect to move them like puppets; 'on my soul, my fine fellow, I could find it in my heart to knock you down. Enough of this; I don't want to terrify you: be a good boy to-morrow, and I will forgive all.'

"'Forgive me now, father,' cried the youth, bursting into tears; 'forgive me and spare me! I cannot obey you; I cannot do anything that will grieve my mother; she loved me so much—I am sure she loves me still—that I cannot do her a harm. I will not go to-morrow.'

"'This is most extraordinary,' said Sir Boyvill, controlling, as well as he could, the rage swelling within him. 'And are you such an idiot as not to know that your wretched mother has forfeited all claim to your affection? and am I of so little worth in your eyes, I, your father, who have a right to your obedience from the justice of my cause, not to speak of parental authority, am I nothing? to receive no duty, expect no service? I was, indeed, mistaken; I thought you were older than your years, and had that touch of gentlemanly pride about you that would have made you eager to avenge my injuries, to stand by me as a friend and ally, compensating, as well as you could, for the wrongs done me by your mother. I thought I had a son in whose veins my own blood flowed, who would be ready to prove his true birth by siding with me. Are you stone, or a baseborn thing, that you cannot even conceive what thing honour is?'

"Gerard listened, he wept; the tears poured in torrents from his eyes; but, as his father continued, and heaped many an opprobrious epithet on him, a proud and sullen spirit was indeed awakened; he longed to say—'Abuse me, strike me, but I will not yield!' Yet he did not speak; he dried his eyes, and stood in silence before his parent, his face darkening, and something ferocious gleaming in eyes hitherto so soft and sorrowing. Sir Boyvill saw that he was far from making the impression he desired; but he wished to avoid reiterated refusals to obey, and he summed up at last with vague but violent threats of what would ensue—exile from his home, penury, nay, starvation, the abhorrence of the world, his own malediction; and, after having worked himself up into a towering rage, and real detestation of the shivering, feeble, yet determined child before him, he left him to consider and to be vanquished.

"Far other thoughts occupied Gerard. 'I had thought,' he has told me, 'once or twice to throw myself into his arms, and pray for mercy; to kneel at his feet and implore him to spare me; one kind word had made the struggle intolerable, but no kind word did he say; and while he stormed, it seemed to me as if my dear mother were singing as she was used, while I gathered flowers and played beside her in the park, and I thought of her, not of him; the words, "kick me out of doors," suggested but the idea, "I shall be free, and I will find my mother." I feel intensely now; but surely a boy's feelings are far wilder, far more vehement than a man's; for I cannot now, violent as you think me, call up one sensation so whirlwind-like as those that possessed me while my father spoke!'

"Thus has Gerard described his emotions; his father ordered him to quit the room, and he went to brood upon the fate impending over him. On the morrow early he was bid prepare to attend the House of Lords. His father did not appear; he thought that the boy was terrified, and would make no further resistance. Gerard, indeed, obeyed in silence. He disdained to argue with strangers and hirelings; he had an idea that if he openly rebelled he might be carried by force, and his proud heart swelled at the idea of compulsion. He got into the carriage, and, as he went, Mr. Carter, who was with him, thought it advisable to explain the forms, and give some instructions. Gerard listened with composure, nay, asked a question or two concerning the preliminaries; he was told of the oath that would be administered; and how the words he spoke after taking that oath would be implicitly believed, and that he must be careful to say nothing that was not strictly true. The colour, not an indignant blush, but a suffusion as of pleasure, mantled over his cheeks as this was explained.

"They arrived; they were conducted into some outer room to await the call of the peers. What tortures the boy felt as strangers came up, some to speak, and others to gaze; all of indignation, resolution, grief, and more than manhood's struggles that tore his bosom during the annoying delays that always protract this sort of scenes, none cared to scan. He was there unresisting, apparently composed; if now his cheek flushed, and now his lips withered into paleness; if now the sense of suffocation rose in his throat, and now tears rushed into his eyes, as the image of his sweet mother passed across his memory, none regarded, none cared. When I have thought of the spasms and throes which his tender and highwrought soul endured during this interval, I often wonder his heart-strings did not crack, or his reason for ever unsettle; as it is, he has not yet escaped the influence of that hour; it shadows his life with eclipse, it comes whispering agony to him, when otherwise he might forget. Some author has described the effect of misfortune on the virtuous as the crushing of perfumes, so to force them to give forth their fragrance. Gerard is all nobleness, all virtue, all tenderness; do we owe any part of his excellence to this hour of anguish? If so, I may be consoled; but I can never think of it without pain. He says himself, 'Yes! without these sharp goadings, I had not devoted my whole life to clearing my mother's fame.' Is this devotion a good? As yet no apparent benefit has sprung from it.

"At length he was addressed: 'Young gentleman, are you ready?' and he was led into that stately chamber—fit for solemn and high debate—thronged with the judges of his mother's cause. There was a dimness in his eye—a tumult in his heart that confused him, while on his appearance there was first a murmur, then a general hush. Each regarded him with compassion as they discerned the marks of suffering in his countenance. A few moments passed before he was addressed; and when it was supposed that he had had time to collect himself, the proper officer administered the oath, and then the barrister asked him some slight questions, not to startle, but to lead back his memory by insensible degrees to the necessary facts. The boy looked at him with scorn—he tried to be calm, to elevate his voice; twice it faltered—the third time he spoke slowly but distinctly: 'I have sworn to speak the truth, and I am to be believed. My mother is innocent.'

"'But this is not the point, young gentleman,' interrupted his interrogator; 'I only asked if you remembered your father's house in Cumberland.'

"The boy replied more loudly, but with broken accents—'I have said all I mean to say—you may murder me, but I will say no more—how dare you entice me into injuring my mother?'

"At the word, uncontrollable tears burst forth, pouring in torrents down his burning cheeks. He told me that he well remembers the feeling that rose to his tongue, instigating him to cry shame on all present—but his voice failed, his purpose was too mighty for his young heart; he sobbed and wept; the more he tried to control the impulse, the more hysterical the fit grew—he was taken from the bar, and the peers, moved by his distress, came to a resolve that they would dispense with his attendance, and be satisfied by hearing his account of the transaction from those persons to whom he made it at the period when it occurred. I will now mention, that the result of this judicial inquiry was, a decree of divorce in Sir Boyvill's favour.

"Gerard, removed from the bar, and carried home, recovered his composure—but he was silent—revolving the consequences which he expected would ensue from disobedience. His father had menaced to turn him out of doors, and he did not doubt but that this threat would be put into execution, so that he was somewhat surprised that he was taken home at all; perhaps they meant to send him to a place of exile of their own choosing, perhaps to make the expulsion public and ignominious. The powers of grown-up people appear so illimitable in a child's eyes, who have no data whereby to discover the probable from the improbable. At length the fear of confinement became paramount; he revolted from it; his notion was to go and seek his mother—and his mind was quickly made up to forestall their violence, and to run away.

"He was ordered to confine himself to his own room—his food was brought to him—this looked like the confirmation of his fears. His heart swelled high: 'They think to treat me like a child, but I will show myself independent—wherever my mother is, she is better than they all—if she is imprisoned, I will free her, or I will remain with her; how glad she will be to see me—how happy shall we be again together! My father may have all the rest of the world to himself, when I am with my mother, in a cavern or a dungeon, I care not where.'

"Night came on—he went to bed—he even slept, and awoke terrified to think that the opportune hour might be overpassed—daylight was dawning faintly in the east; the clocks of London struck four—he was still in time—every one in the house slept; he rose and dressed—he had nearly ten guineas of his own, this was all his possession, he had counted them the night before—he opened the door of his chamber—daylight was struggling with darkness, and all was very still—he stepped out, he descended the stairs, he got into the hall—every accustomed object seemed new and strange at that early hour, and he looked with some dismay at the bars and bolts of the house door—he feared making a noise, and rousing some servant, still the thing must be attempted; slowly and cautiously he pushed back the bolts, he lifted up the chain—it fell from his hands with terrific clatter on the stone pavement—his heart was in his mouth—he did not fear punishment, but he feared ill success; he listened as well as his throbbing pulses permitted—all was still—the key of the door was in the lock, it turned easily at his touch, and in another moment the door was open; the fresh air blew upon his cheeks—the deserted street was before him. He closed the door after him, and with a sort of extra caution locked it on the outside, and then took to his heels, throwing the key down a neighbouring street. When out of sight of his home, he walked more slowly, and began to think seriously of the course to pursue. To find his mother!—all the world had been trying to find her, and had not succeeded—but he believed that by some means she would hear of his escape and come to him—but whither go in the first instance?—his heart replied, to Cumberland, to Dromore—there he had lived with his mother—there had he lost her—he felt assured that in its neighbourhood he should again be restored to her.

"Travelling had given him some idea of distance, and of the modes of getting from one place to another—he felt that it would be a task of too great difficulty to attempt walking across England—he had no carriage, he knew of no ship to take him, some conveyance he must get, so he applied to a hackney coach. It was standing solitary in the middle of the street, the driver asleep on the steps—the skeleton horses hanging down their heads—with the peculiarly disconsolate look these poor hacked animals have. Gerard, as the son of a wealthy man, was accustomed to consider that he had a right to command those whom he could pay—yet fear of discovery and being sent back to his father filled him with unusual fears; he looked at the horses and the man—he advanced nearer, but he was afraid to take the decisive step, till the driver awaking, started up and shook himself, stared at the boy, and seeing him well dressed—and he looked, too, older than his years, from being tall—he asked, 'Do you want me, sir?'

"'Yes,' said Gerard, 'I want you to drive me.'

"'Get in, then. Where are you going?'

"'I am going a long way—to Dromore, that is in Cumberland—'

"The boy hesitated; it struck him that those miserable horses could not carry him far. 'Then you want me to take you to the stage,' said the man. 'It goes from Piccadilly—at five—we have no time to lose.'

"Gerard got in—on they jumbled—and arriving at the coach-office, saw some half dozen stages ready to start. The name of Liverpool on one struck the boy, by the familiar name. If he could get to Liverpool, it were easy afterward even to walk to Dromore; so getting out of the hackney coach, he went up to the coachman, who was mounting his box, and asked, 'Will you take me to Liverpool?'

"'Yes, my fine fellow, if you can pay the fare.'

"'How much is it?' drawing out his purse.

"'Inside or outside?'

"From the moment he had addressed these men, and they began to talk of money, Gerard, calling to mind the vast disbursements of gold coin he had seen made by his father and the courier on their travels, began to fear that his little stock would ill suffice to carry him so far; and the first suggestion of prudence the little fellow ever experienced made him now answer, 'Whichever costs least.'

"'Outside, then.'

"'Oh, I have that—I can pay you.'

"'Jump up, then, my lad—lend me your hand—here, by me—that's right—all's well, you're just in the nick, we are off directly.'

"He cracked his whip, and away they flew; and as they went, Gerard felt free, and going to his mother.

"Such, in these civilized times, are the facilities offered to the execution of our wildest wishes! the consequences, the moral consequences, are still the same, still require the same exertions to overcome them; but we have no longer to fight with physical impediments. If Gerard had begun his expedition from any other town, curiosity had perhaps been excited; but in the vast, busy metropolis each one takes care of himself, and few scrutinize the motives or means of others. Perched up on the coach-box, Gerard had a few questions to answer—Was he going home? did he live in Liverpool? but the name of Dromore was a sufficing answer. The coachman had never heard of such a place; but it was a gentleman's seat, and it was Gerard's home, and that was enough.

"Some day you must ask Gerard to relate to you his adventures during this journey. They will come warmly and vividly from him; while mine, as a mere reflex, must be tame. It is his mind I would describe; and I will not pause to narrate the tantalizing cross-questioning that he underwent from a Scotchman—nor the heart-heavings with which he heard allusions made to the divorce case before the lords. A newspaper describing his own conduct was in the hands of one of the passengers; he heard his mother lightly alluded to. He would have leaped from the coach; but that was to give up all. He pressed his hands to his ears—he scowled on those around—his heart was on fire. Yet he had one consolation. He was free. He was going to her—he resolved never to mingle with his fellow-creatures more. Buried in some rural retreat with his mother, it mattered little what the vulgar and the indifferent said about either.

"Some qualms did assail him. Should he find his dear mother? Where was she? his childish imagination refused to paint her distant from Dromore—his own removal from that mansion so soon after losing her, associated her indelibly with the mountains, the ravines, the brawling streams, and clustering woods of his natal county. She must be there. He would drive away the man of violence who took her from him, and they would be happy together.

"A day and a night brought him to Liverpool, and the coachman, hearing whither he wished to go, deposited him in the stage for Lancaster on his arrival. He went inside this time, and slept all the way. At Lancaster he was recognised by several persons, and they wondered to see him alone. He was annoyed at their recognition and questionings; and, though it was night when he arrived, instantly set off to walk to Dromore.

"For two months from this time he lived wandering from cottage to cottage, seeking his mother. The journey from Lancaster to Dromore he performed as speedily as he well could. He did not enter the house—that would be delivering himself up as a prisoner. By night he clambered the park railings, and entered like a thief the demesnes where he had spent his childhood. Each path was known to him, and almost every tree. Here he sat with his mother; there they found the first violet of spring. His pilgrimage was achieved; but where was she? His heart beat as he reached the little gate whence they had issued on that fatal night. All the grounds bore marks of neglect and the master's absence; and the lock of this gate was spoiled; a sort of rough bolt had been substituted. Gerard pushed it back. The rank grass had gathered thick on the threshold; but it was the same spot. How well he remembered it!

"Two years only had since passed, he was still a child; yet to his own fancy how much taller, how much more of a man he had become! Besides, he now fancied himself master of his own actions—he had escaped from his father; and he—who had threatened to turn him out of doors—would not seek to possess himself of him again. He belonged to no one—he was cared for by no one—by none but her whom he sought with firm, yet anxious expectation. There he had seen her last—he stepped forward; he followed the course of the lane—he came to where the road crossed it—where the carriage drove up, where she had been torn from him.

"It was daybreak—a June morning; all was golden and still—a few birds twittered, but the breeze was hushed, and he looked out on the extent of country commanded from the spot where he stood, and saw only nature, the rugged hills, the green corn-fields, the flowery meads, and the umbrageous trees in deep repose. How different from the wild, tempestuous night when she whom he sought was torn away; he could then see only a few yards before him, now he could mark the devious windings of the road, and, afar off, distinguish the hazy line of the ocean. He sat down to reflect—what was he to do? in what nook of the wide expanse was his mother hid? that some portion of the landscape he viewed harboured her, was his fixed belief; a belief founded in inexperience and fancy, but not the less deep-rooted. He meditated for some time, and then walked forward—he remembered when he ran panting and screaming along that road; he was a mere child then, and what was he now? a boy of eleven; yet he looked back with disdain to the endeavours of two years before.

"He walked along in the same direction that he had at that time pursued, and soon found that he reached the turnpike-road to Lancaster. He turned off, and went by the cross-road that leads to the wild and dreary plains that form the coast. The inner range of picturesque hills, on the declivity of which Dromore is situated, is not more than five miles from the sea; but the shore itself is singularly blank and uninteresting, varied only by sand-hills thrown up to the height of thirty or forty feet, intersected by rivers, which at low water are fordable even on foot; but which, when the tide is up, are dangerous to those who do not know the right track, from the holes and ruts which render the bed of the river uneven. In winter, indeed, at the period of spring tides, or in stormy weather, with a west wind which drives the ocean towards the shore, the passage is often exceedingly dangerous, and, except under the direction of an experienced guide, fatal accidents occur.

"Gerard reached the borders of the ocean near one of these streams; behind him rose his native mountains, range above range, divided by tremendous gulfs, varied by the shadows of the clouds, and the gleams of sunlight; close to him was the waste seashore; the ebbing tide gave a dreary sluggish appearance to the ocean, and the river—a shallow, rapid stream—emptied its slender pittance of mountain water noiselessly into the lazy deep. It was a scene of singular desolation. On the other side of the river, not far from the mouth, was a rude hut, unroofed, and fallen to decay—erected, perhaps, as the abode of a guide; near it grew a stunted tree, withered, moss-covered, spectre-like—the sand-hills lay scattered around—the seagull screamed above, and skimmed over the waste. Gerard sat down and wept—motherless—escaped from his angry father; even to his young imagination, his fate seemed as drear and gloomy as the scene around."

# CHAPTER XX

"I do not know why I have dwelt on these circumstances so long. Let me hasten to finish. For two months Gerard wandered in the neighbourhood of Dromore. If he saw a lone cottage, imbowered in trees, hidden in some green recess of the hills, sequestered and peaceful, he thought, Perhaps my mother is there! and he clambered towards it, finding it at last, probably, a mere shepherd's hut, poverty-stricken, and tenanted by a noisy family. His money was exhausted—he made a journey to Lancaster to sell his watch, and then returned to Cumberland—his clothes, his shoes were worn out— often he slept in the open air—ewes' milk cheese and black bread were his fare—his hope was to find his mother—his fear to fall again into his father's hands. But as the first sentiment failed, his friendless condition grew more sad; he began to feel that he was indeed a feeble, helpless boy—abandoned by all—he thought nothing was left for him but to lie down and die.

"Meanwhile he was noticed, and at last recognised, by some of the tenants; and information reached his father of where he was. Unfortunately, the circumstance of his disappearance became public. It was put into the newspapers as a mysterious occurrence; and the proud Sir Boyvill found himself not only pitied on account of his wife's conduct, but suspected of cruelty towards his only child. At first he was himself frightened and miserable; but when he heard where Gerard was, and that he could be recovered at any time, these softer feelings were replaced by fury. He sent the tutor to possess himself of his son's person. He was seized with the help of a constable; treated more like a criminal than an unfortunate, erring child; carried back to Buckinghamshire; shut up in a barricadoed room; debarred from air and exercise; lectured; menaced; treated with indignity. The boy, hitherto accustomed to more than usual indulgence and freedom, was at first astonished, and then wildly indignant at the treatment he suffered. He was told that he should not be set free till he submitted. He believed that to mean, until he could give testimony against his mother. He resolved rather to die. Several times he endeavoured to escape, and was brought back and treated with fresh barbarity—his hands bound, and stripes inflicted by menials; till, driven to despair, he at one time determined to starve himself, and at another tried to bribe a servant to bring him poison. The trusting piety inculcated by his gentle mother was destroyed by the ill-judged cruelty of his father and his doltish substitute. It is painful to dwell on such circumstances; to think of a sensitive, helpless child treated with the brutality exercised towards a galley-slave. Under this restraint, Gerard grew such as you saw him at Baden—sullen, ferocious, plunged in melancholy, delivered up to despair.

"It was some time before he discovered that the submission demanded of him was not to run away again. On learning this, he wrote to his father. He spoke with horror of the personal indignities he had endured; of his imprisonment; of the conduct of Mr. Carter. He did not mean it as such, but his letter grew into an affecting, irresistible appeal that even moved Sir Boyvill. His stupid pride prevented him from showing the regret he felt. He still used the language of reproof and conditional pardon; but the tutor was dismissed, and Gerard restored to liberty. Had his father been generous or just enough to show his regret, he might probably have obliterated the effects of his harshness; as it was, Gerard gave no thanks for a boon which saved his life, but restored him to none of its social blessings. He was still friendless—still orphaned in his affections—still the memory of intolerable tyranny, the recurrence of which was threatened if he made an ill use of the freedom accorded him, clung like the shirt of Nessus—and his noble, ardent nature was lacerated by the intolerable recollection of slavish terrors.

"You saw him at Baden, and it was at Baden that I also first knew him. You had left the baths when my mother and I arrived. We became acquainted with Sir Boyvill. He was still handsome—he was rich—and those qualities of mind which ill agreed with Alithea's finer nature did not displease a fashionable woman of the world. Such was my mother. Something that was called an attachment sprang up, and they married. She preferred the situation of wife to that of widow; and he, having been accustomed to the social comforts of a domestic circle, despite his disasters, disliked his bachelor state. They married; and I, just then eighteen—just out, as it is called—became the sister of my beloved Gerard.

"I feel pride when I think of the services that I have rendered him. He had another fall from his horse not long after, or rather, again urging the animal down a precipice, it fell. He was underneath, and his leg was broken. During the long confinement that ensued, I was his faithful nurse and companion. Naturally lively, yet I could sympathize in his sorrows. By degrees I won his confidence. He told me all his story—all his feelings. He grew mild and soft under my influence. He grew to regret that he had been vanquished by adversity so as to become almost what he was accused of being, a frantic idiot. As he talked of his mother, and the care she bestowed on his early years, he wept to think how unlike he was to the creature she had wished him to become. A desire to reform, to repair past faults, to school himself, grew out of such talk. He threw off his sullenness and gloom. He became studious at the same time that he grew gentle. His education, which had proceeded but badly while he refused to lend his mind to improvement, was now the object of his own thoughts and exertions. Instead of careering wildly over the hills, or being thrown under some tree delivered up to miserable revery, he asked for masters, and was continually seen with a book in his hands.

"The passion of his soul still subsisted, modulated by his new feelings. He continued to believe in the innocence of his mother, though he often doubted her existence. He longed inexpressibly to unveil the mystery that shrouded her fate. He devoted himself in his heart to discovering the truth. He resolved to occupy his whole life in the dear task of reinstating her in that cloudless purity of reputation which he intimately felt she had never deserved to forfeit. He considered the promise exacted from him by his father as preventing him from following up his design, and as binding him till he was twenty-one. Till then he deferred his endeavours. No young spendthrift ever aspired for the attainment of the age of freedom and the possession of an estate as vehemently as did Gerard for the hour which was to permit him to deliver himself wholly up to this task.

"Before that time arrived I married. I wished to take him abroad with us; but the unfounded (as I believe) notion that the secret of his mother's fate is linked to the English shores made him dislike to leave his native country. It was only on our return that he consented to come as far as Marseilles to meet us.

"When he had reached the age of twenty-one he announced to his father his resolve to discover his mother's fate. Sir Boyvill was highly indignant. The only circumstance that at all mitigated the disgrace of his wife's flight was the oblivion into which she and all concerning her had sunk. To have new inquiries set on foot, and the forgotten shame recalled to the memories of men, appeared not less wicked than insane. He remonstrated, he grew angry, he stormed, he forbade; but Gerard considered that time had set a limit to his authority, and only withdrew in silence, not the less determined to pursue his own course.

"I need not say that he met with no success; a mystery so impenetrable at first, does not acquire clearness after time has obscured the little ever known. Whatever were the real circumstances and feelings that occasioned her flight, however innocent she might then be, time has cemented his mother's union with another, and made her forget those she left behind. Or may I not say, what I am inclined to believe, that though the violence of another was the cause at last of guilt in her, yet she pined for those she deserted—that her heart was soon broken—that the sod has long since covered her form—while the miserable man who caused all this evil is but too eager to observe a silence which prevents his name from being loaded with the execrations he deserves? I cannot help, therefore, regretting that Gerard insists upon discovering the obscure grave of his miserable mother—while he, who, whether living or dead, believes her to have been always innocent, is to be dissuaded by no arguments, still less by the angry denunciations of Sir Boyvill, whose conduct throughout he looks on as being the primal cause of his mother's misfortunes.

"I have told you the tale, as nearly as I can, in the spirit in which Gerard himself would have communicated it—such was my tacit pledge to him; nor do I wish, by my suspicions or conjectures, to deprive him of your sympathy, and the belief he wishes you to entertain of his mother's innocence; but truth will force its way, and who can think her wholly guiltless? Would to God! oh, how often and how fervently have I prayed that Gerard were cured of the madness which renders his life a wild, unprofitable dream; and, looking soberly on the past, consent to bury in oblivion misfortunes and errors which are beyond all cure, and which it is worse than vain to remember."

# CHAPTER XXI

There was to Elizabeth a fascinating interest in the story related by Lady Cecil. Elizabeth had no wild fairy-like imagination. Her talents, which were remarkable, her serious, thoughtful mind, was warmed by the vital heat emanating from her affections—whatever regarded these, moved her deeply.

Here was a tale full of human interest, of love, error, of filial tenderness, and deep-rooted, uneradicable fidelity. Elizabeth, who knew little of life, except through such experience as she gathered from the emotions of her own heart, and the struggling passions of Falkner, could not regard the story in the same worldly light as Lady Cecil. There was an unfathomable mystery; but, was there guilt as far as regarded Mrs. Neville? Elizabeth could not believe it. She believed, that in a nature as finely formed as hers was described to have been, maternal love, and love for such a child as Gerard, must have risen paramount to every other feeling. Philosophers have said that the most exalted natures are endowed with the strongest and deepest-seated passions. It is by combating and purifying them that the human being rises into excellence; and the combat is assisted by setting the good in opposition to the evil. Perhaps Mrs. Neville had loved—though even that seemed strange—but her devoted affection to her child must have been more powerful than a love which, did it exist, appeared unaccompanied by one sanctifying or extenuating circumstance.

Thus thought Elizabeth. Gerard appeared in a beautiful and heroic light, bent on his holy mission of redeeming his mother's name from the stigma accumulated on it. Her heart warmed within her at the thought, that such a task assimilated to hers. She was endeavouring to reconcile her benefactor to life, and to remove from his existence the stings of unavailing remorse. She tried to fancy that some secret tie existed between their two distinct tasks; and that a united happy end would spring up for both.

After musing for some time in silence, at length she said, "But you do not tell me whither Mr. Neville is now gone, and what it is that has so newly awakened his hopes."

"You remind me," replied Lady Cecil, "of what I had nearly forgotten. It is a provoking and painful circumstance; the artifice of cupidity to dupe enthusiasm. You must know that Gerard, in furtherance of his wild project, has left an intimation among the cottages and villages near Dromore, and in Lancaster itself, that he will give two hundred pounds to any one who shall bring any information that will conduce to the discovery of Mrs. Neville's fate. This is a large bribe to falsehood, and yet, until now, no one has pretended to have anything to tell. But the other day he received a letter, and the person who wrote it was so earnest, that he sent a duplicate to Sir Boyvill. This letter stated that the writer, Gregory Hoskins, believed himself to be in possession of some facts connected with Mrs. Neville of Dromore, and on the two hundred pounds being properly secured to him by a written bond he would communicate them. This letter was dated Lancaster—thither Gerard is gone."

"Does it speak of Mrs. Neville as still alive?" asked Elizabeth.

"It says barely the words which I have repeated," Lady Cecil replied. "Sir Boyvill, knowing his son's impetuosity, hurried down here, to stop, if he could, his reviving, through such means, the recollection of his unfortunate lady—with what success you have seen; Gerard is gone, nor can any one guess what tale will be trumped up to deceive and rob him."

Elizabeth could not feel as secure as her friend, that nothing would come of the promised information. This was not strange; besides, the different view taken by a worldly and an experienced person, the tale, with all its mystery, was an old one to Lady Cecil; while, to her friend, it bore the freshness of novelty: to the one, it was a story of the dead and the forgotten; to the other, it was replete with living interest; the enthusiasm of Gerard communicated itself to her, and she felt that his present, journey was full of event, the first step in a discovery of all that hitherto had been inscrutable.

A few days brought a letter from Gerard. Lady Cecil read it, and then gave it to her young friend to peruse. It was dated Lancaster; it said, "My journey has hitherto been fruitless; this man Hoskins has gone from Lancaster, leaving word that I should find him in London, but in so negligent a way as to lower my hopes considerably. His chief aim must be to earn the promised reward, and I feel sure that he would take more pains to obtain it, did he think that it was really within his grasp.

"He arrived but a few weeks since, it seems, from America, whither he migrated, some twenty years ago, from Ravenglass. How can he bring news of her I seek from across the Atlantic? The very idea fills me with disturbance. Has he seen her? Great God! does she yet live? Did she commission him to make inquiries concerning her abandoned child? No, Sophia, my life on it, it is not so; she is dead! My heart too truly reveals the sad truth to me.

"Can I then wish to hear that she is no more? My dear, dear mother! Were all the accusations true which are brought against you, still would I seek your retreat, endeavour to assuage your sorrows; wherever, whatever you are, you are of more worth to me—methinks that you must still be more worthy of affection than all else that the earth contains! But it is not so. I feel it—I know it—she is dead. Yet when, where, how? Oh, my father's vain commands! I would walk barefoot to the summit of the Andes to have these questions answered. The interval that must elapse before I reach London, and see this man, is hard to bear. What will he tell? Nothing! often, in my lucid intervals, as my father would call them, in my hours of despondency, I fear—nothing!

"You have not played me false, dearest Sophy? In telling your lovely friend the strange story of my woes, you have taught her to mourn my mother's fate, not to suspect her goodness? I am half angry with myself for devolving the task upon you. For, despite your kind endeavours, I read your heart, my worldly-wise sister, and know its unbelief. I forgive you, for you never saw my mother's face, nor heard her voice. Had you ever beheld the purity and integrity that sat upon her brow, and listened to her sweet tones, she would visit your dreams by day and night, as she does mine, in the guise of an angel robed in perfect innocence. I cannot forgive my father for his accusations; his own heart must be bad, or he could not credit that any evil inhabited hers. For how many years that guileless heart was laid bare to him! and if it was not so fond and admiring towards himself as he could have wished, still there was no concealment, no tortuosity; he saw it all, though now he discredits the evidence of his senses—shuts his eyes,

'And hooting at the glorious sun in Heaven,
Cries out, "Where is it?"'

For truth was her attribute; the open heart, which made the brow, the eyes, the cheerful mien, the sweet, loving smile and thrilling voice, all transcripts of its pure emotions. It was this that rendered her the adorable being, which all who knew her acknowledge that she was.

"I am solicitous beyond measure that Miss Falkner should receive no false impression. Her image is before me, when I saw her first, pale in the agony of fear, bending over her dying father; by day and by night she forgot herself to attend on him. She who loves a parent so well can understand me better than any other. She, I am convinced, will form a true judgment. She will approve my perseverance, and share my doubts and fears; will she not? ask her—or am I too vain, too credulous? Is there in the whole world one creature who will join with me in my faith and my labours? You do not, Sophia; that I have long known, and the feeling of disappointment is already blunted; but it will revive, it will be barbed with a new sting, if I am deceived in my belief that Elizabeth Falkner shares my convictions, and appreciates the utility, the necessity of my endeavours. I do not desire her pity, that you give me; but at this moment I am blessed by the hope that she feels with me. I cannot tell you the good this idea does me. It spurs me to double energy in my pursuit, and it sustains me during the uncertainty that attends it: it makes me inexpressibly more anxious to clear my mother's name in her eyes; since she deigns to partake my griefs. I desire that she should hereafter share in the triumph of my success.

"My success! the word throws me ten thousand fathoms deep, from the thoughts of innocence and goodness, to those of wrongs, death, or living misery. Farewell, dearest Sophia. This letter is written at night; to-morrow, early, I set out by a fast coach to London. I shall write again, or you will see me soon. Keep Miss Falkner with you till I return, and write me a few words of encouragement."

Not a line in this letter but interested and gratified Elizabeth—and Lady Cecil saw the blush of pleasure mantle over her speaking countenance; she was half glad, half sorry—she looked on Elizabeth as she who could cure Gerard of his Quixotic devotion, by inspiring him with feelings which, while they had all the enthusiasm natural to his disposition, would detach him from his vain endeavours, and centre his views and happiness in the living instead of the dead. Lady Cecil knew that Gerard already loved her friend—he had never loved before—and the tenderness of his manner, and the admiration that lighted up his eyes whenever he looked on her, revealed the birth of passion. Elizabeth, less quick to feel, or at least more tranquil in the display of feeling, yet sympathized too warmly with him—felt too deeply interested in all he said and did, not to betray that she was touched by the divine fire that smooths the ruggedness of life, and fills with peace and smiles a darkling, stormy world. But instead of weaning Gerard from his madness, she encouraged him in it—as she well knew; for when she wrote to Gerard, she asked Elizabeth to add a few lines, and thus she wrote:

"I thank you for the confidence you repose in me, and more than that, I must express how deeply I feel for you, the more that I think that justice and truth are on your side. Whether you succeed or not, I confess that I think you are right in your endeavours—your aim is a noble and a sacred one—and, like you, I cherish the hope that it will end in the exculpation of one deeply injured—and your being rewarded for your fidelity to her memory. God bless you with all the happiness you deserve."

No subsequent letter arrived from Gerard. Lady Cecil wondered and conjectured, and expected impatiently. She and her friend could talk of nothing else. The strange fact that a traveller from America proclaimed that he had tidings of the lost one, offered a fertile field for suppositions. Had Mrs. Neville been carried across the Atlantic? How impossible was this, against her own consent! No pirate's bark was there, with a crew experienced in crime, ready to acquiesce in a deed of violence; no fortalice existed, in whose impenetrable walls she could have been immured; yet so much of strange and fearful must belong to her fate, which the imagination mourned to think of! Love, though in these days it carries on its tragedies more covertly—and kills by the slow, untold pang—by the worm in the bosom—and exerts its influence rather by teaching deceit than instigating to acts of violence, yet love reigns in the hearts of men as tyrannically and fiercely—and causes as much evil, as much ruin, and as many tears, as when, in the younger world, hecatombs were slain in his honour. In former days mortals wasted rather life than feeling, and every blow was a physical one; now the heart dies, though the body lives—and a miserable existence is dragged out, after hope and joy have ceased to adorn it; yet love is still, despite the schoolmaster and the legislator, the prime law of human life, and Alithea Neville was well fitted to inspire an ardent passion. She had a sensibility which, while it gave strength to her affections, yet diffused a certain weakness over the mechanism of her being, that made those around her tremble; she had genius which added lustre to her eye, and shed around her a fascination of manner, which no man could witness without desiring to dedicate himself to her service. She seemed the very object whom Sheridan addressed when he said—

"For friends in every age you'll meet,
And lovers in the young."

That she should be loved to desperation could excite no wonder—but what had been the effects of this love? a distant home across the ocean—a home of privation and sorrow—the yearning for her lost children—the slow breaking of the contrite heart; a life dragged on despite the pangs of memory—or a nameless grave. Such were the conjectures caused by the letter of the American.

At length Neville returned. Each turned her eye on his face, to read the intelligence he had acquired in his speaking countenance. It was sad. "She lives and is lost," thought Lady Cecil; "He mourns her dead!" was the supposition of the single-minded Elizabeth. At first he avoided the subject of his inquiry, and his companions did not question him; till at last he suddenly exclaimed, "Do you not wish to learn something, Sophia? Have you forgotten the object of my journey?"

"Dear Gerard," replied Lady Cecil, "these walls and woods, had they a voice, could tell you that we have thought and spoken of nothing else."

"She is dead!" he answered, abruptly.

A start—an exclamation was the reply. He continued: "If there be any truth in the tale I have heard, my dear, injured mother is dead; that is, if what I have heard concern her—mean anything, or is not a mere fabrication. You shall hear all by-and-by; I will relate all I have been told. It is a sad story if it be hers, if it be a true story at all."

These disjointed expressions raised the curiosity and interest of his auditors to their height. It was evening; instead of going on with his account, he passed into the adjoining room, opened the glass door, and stepped out into the open air. It was dark, scarcely could you see the dim outline of the woods—yet, far on the horizon where sky and sea met, there was a streak of light. Sophia and Elizabeth followed to the room whence he had gone, and drew their chairs near the open window and pressed each other's hands.

"What can it all mean?" at length said Lady Cecil.

"Hush!" whispered Elizabeth—"he is here, I saw him cross the streak of light."

"True," said Gerard's voice—his person they could not distinguish, for they were in darkness; "I am here, and I will tell you now all I have heard. I will sit at your feet; give me your hand, Sophy, that I may feel that you are really present—it is too dark to see anything."

He did not ask for Elizabeth's hand, but he took it, and placing it on Lady Cecil's, gently clasped both: "I cannot see either of you—but indulge my wayward humour; so much of coarse and commonplace has been thrown on the most sacred subject in the world, that I want to bathe my soul in darkness—a darkness as profound as that which wraps my mother's fate. Now for my story."

# CHAPTER XXII

"You know that I did not find this man, this Hoskins, at Lancaster. By his direction I sought him in London, and, after some trouble, found him. He was busy in his own affairs, and it was difficult to get at him; but, by perseverance, and asking him to dine with me at a coffee-house, I at last succeeded. He is a native of Ravenglass, a miserable town on the seashore of Cumberland, with which I am well acquainted, for it is not far from Dromore. He semigrated to America before I was born; and after various speculations, is at last settled at Boston, in some sort of trade, the exigences of which brought him over here, and he seized the opportunity to visit his family. There they were, still inhabiting the forlorn town of Ravenglass; their cottage still looking out on a dreary extent of sand, mud, and marsh; and the far mountains, which would seem to invite the miserable dwellers of the flats to shelter themselves in their green recesses, but they invite in vain.

"Hoskins found his mother, a woman nearly a hundred years of age, alive; and a widowed sister living with her, surrounded by a dozen children of all ages. He passed two days with them, and naturally recurred to the changes that had taken place in the neighbourhood. He had at one time had dealings with the steward of Dromore, and had seen my father. When he emigrated, Sir Boyvill had just married. Hoskins asked how it went on with him and his bride. It is our glorious fate to be in the mouths of the vulgar, so he heard the story of my mother's mysterious flight; and, in addition to this, he was told of my boyish wanderings, my search for my mother, and my declaration that I would give two hundred pounds to any one through whose means I should discover her fate.

"The words fell at first upon a heedless ear, but the next morning it all at once struck him that he might gain the reward, and he wrote to me; and as I was described as a wanderer without a home, he wrote also to my father. When I saw him in town, he seemed ashamed of the trouble I had taken. 'It is I who am to get the two hundred pounds,' he said, 'not you; the chance was worth wasting a little breath; but you may not think the little I have to tell worth your long journey.'

"At length I brought him to the point. At one period, a good many years ago, he was a settler in New-York, and by some chance he fell in with a man lately arrived from England, who asked his advice as to obtaining employment: he had some little money—some few hundred pounds, but he did not wish to sink it in trade or the purchase of land, but to get some situation with a tolerable salary, and keep his little capital at command. A strange way of using money and time in America! but such was the fancy of the stranger; he said he should not be easy unless he could draw out his money at any time, and emigrate at an hour's notice. This man's name was Osborne; he was shrewd, ready-witted, and good-natured, but idle, and even unprincipled. 'He did me a good turn once,' said Hoskins, 'which makes me unwilling to do him a bad one; but you cannot injure him, I think, in America. He has risen in the world since the time I mention, and has an employment under our minister at Mexico. After all, he did not tell me much, and what I learned came out in long talks by degrees, during a journey or two we took together to the West. He had been a traveller, a soldier in the East. Indies, and unlucky everywhere; and it had gone hard with him at one time in Bengal, but for the kindness of a friend. He was a gentleman far above him in station who got him out of trouble, and paid his passage to England; and afterward, when this gentleman returned himself to the island, he found Osborne in trouble again, and again he assisted him. In short, sir, it came out, that if this gentleman (Osborne would never tell his name) stood his friend, it was not for nothing this time. There was a lady to be carried off. Osborne swore he did not know who—he thought it a runaway match; but it turned out something worse, for never did girl take on so for leaving her home with a lover. I tell the story badly, for I never got the rights of it. It ended tragically—the lady died—was drowned, as well as I could make out, in some river. You know how dangerous the streams are on our coast.

"'It was the naming Cumberland and our estuaries that set me asking questions, which frightened Osborne. When he found that I was a native of that part of the world, he grew as mute as a fish, and never a word more of lady or friend did I get from him; except, as I guessed, he was well rewarded, and sent over the water out of the way; and he swore he believed that the gentleman was dead too. It was no murder—that he averred, but a sad tragic accident that might look like one; and he grew as white as a sheet if ever I tried to bring him to speak of it again. It haunted his thoughts nevertheless: and he would talk in his sleep, and dream of being hanged—and mutter about a grave dug in the sands, and there being no parson; and the dark breakers of the ocean—and horses scampering away, and the lady's wet hair—nothing regular, but such as often made me waken him; for in wild nights, such mutterings were no lullaby.

"'Now, sir, whether the lady he spoke of were your lady mother, is more than I can say; but the time and place tally. It is twelve years this summer since he came out; and it had just happened, for his heart and head were full of horrors, and he feared every vessel from Europe brought out a warrant to arrest him, or the like. He was a chicken-hearted fellow; and I have known him hide himself for a week when a packet came from Liverpool. But he got courage as time went on; when I saw him last, he had forgotten all about it; and when I jeered him about his terrors, he laughed, and said all was well, and he should not care going to England; for that the story was blown over, and neither he nor his friend even so much as suspected.

"'This, sir, is my story; and I don't think he ever told me any more, or that I can remember anything else; but such as I tell it, I can swear to it. There was a lady run off with, and she died, by fair means or foul, before she quitted the coast; and was buried, as we might bury in the far West, without bell or prayer-book. And Osborne does not know the name of the lady; but the gentleman he knew, though he has never since heard of him, and believes him to be dead. You best know whether my story is worth the two hundred pounds.'

"Such, Sophia, is the tale I heard. Such is the coarse hand and vulgar tongue that first touches the veil that conceals my mother's fate."

"It is a strange story," said Lady Cecil, shuddering.

"But, on my life, a true one," cried Neville, "as I will prove. Osborne is now at Mexico. I have inquired at the American consul's. He is expected back to Washington at the end of this summer. In a few weeks I shall embark and see this man, who now bears a creditable character, and learn if there is any foundation for Hoskins's conjectures. If there is—and can I doubt it? if my mother died as he says, I shall learn the manner of her death, and who is the murderer."

"Murderer!" echoed both his auditors.

"Yes; I cannot retract the word. Murderer in effect, if not in deed. Remember, I witnessed the act of violence which tore my mother from me. He who carried her away is, in all justice, an assassin, even if his hands be not imbrued with blood. Blood! did I say? Nay, none was shed. I know the spot; I have viewed the very scene. Our waste and desolate coast—the perilous, deceitful rivers, in one of which she perished—the very night, so tempestuous—the wild west wind bearing the tide with irresistible impetuosity up the estuaries—he seeking the solitary sands—perhaps some smuggling vessel lying in wait to carry her off unseen, unheard. To me it is as if I knew each act of the tragedy, and heard her last sigh beneath the waves breathed for me. She was dragged out by these men; buried without friend; without decent rites; her tomb the evil report her enemy raised above her; her grave the sands of that dreary shore. Oh, what wild, what miserable thoughts are these! This tale, instead of alleviating my anxious doubts, has taken the sleep out from my eyes. Images of death are for ever passing before me; I think of the murderer with a heart that pants for revenge, and of my beloved mother with such pity, such religious wo, that I would spend my life on that shore seeking her remains, so that at last I might shed my tears above them, and bear them to a more sacred spot. There is an easier way to gain both ends."

"It is a sad, but a wild and uncertain story," remarked Lady Cecil, "and not sufficiently plain, I think, to take you away from us all across the Atlantic."

"A far slighter clew would take me so far," replied Gerard, "as you well know. It is not for a traveller to Egypt to measure miles with such timidity. My dear Sophy, you would indeed think me mad if, after devoting my life to one pursuit, I were now to permit a voyage across the Atlantic to stand between me and the slightest chance of having my doubts cleared up. It is a voyage which thousands take every week for their interest or their pleasure. I do much, I think, in postponing my journey till this man returns to Washington. At first I had thought of taking my passage on the instant, and meeting him on his journey homeward from Mexico; but I might miss him. Yet I long to be on the spot, in America; for, if anything should happen to him; if he should die, and his secret die with him, how for ever after I should be stung by self-reproach!"

"But there seems to me so little foundation," Lady Cecil began. Neville made an impatient gesture, exclaiming, "Are you not unreasonable, Sophy? my father has made a complete convert of you."

Elizabeth interposed, and asked, "You saw this man more than once?"

"Who? Hoskins? Yes, three times, and he always told the same story. He persisted in the main points. That the scene of the carrying off of the lady was his native shore, the coast of Cumberland; that the act immediately preceded Osborne's arrival in America, twelve years ago; and that she died miserably, the victim of her wretched lover. He knew Osborne immediately on his coming to New-York, when he was still suffering from the panic of such a tragedy, dreading the arrival of every vessel from England. At that time he concealed carefully from his new friend what he afterward, in the overflow of his heart, communicated so freely; and, in after times, he reminded him how, when an emissary of the police came from London to seek after some fraudulent defaulter, he, only hearing vaguely that there was search made for a criminal, hid himself for several days. That Osborne was privy to, was participator in a frightful tragedy, which, to my eyes, bears the aspect of murder, seems certain. I do not, I cannot doubt that my mother died then and there. How? the blood curdles to ask; but I would compass the earth to learn, to vindicate her name, to avenge her death."

Elizabeth felt Gerard's hand tremble and grow cold. He rose, and led the way into the drawing-room, while Lady Cecil whispered to her friend, "I am so very, very sorry! To go to America on such a story as this, a story which, if it bear any semblance to the truth, had better be for ever buried in oblivion. Dear Elizabeth, dissuade him, I entreat you."

"Do you think Mr. Neville so easy of persuasion, or that he ought to be?" replied her companion. "Certainly, all that he has heard is vague, coming, as it does, from a third, and an interested person. But his whole life has been devoted to the exculpation of his mother; and, if he believes that this tale affords a clew to lead to discovery, he is a son, and the nature that stirs within him may gift him with a clearer vision and a truer instinct than we can pretend to. Who can say but that a mysterious yet powerful hand is at last held out to guide him to the completion of his task? Oh, dear Lady Cecil, there are secrets in the moral, sentient world, of which we know nothing: such as brought Hamlet's father before his eyes; such as now may be stirring in your brother's heart, revealing to him the truth, almost without his own knowledge."

"You are as mad as he," said Lady Cecil, peevishly.

"I thought you a calm and reasonable being, who would co-operate with me in weaning Gerard from his wild fancies, and in reconciling him to the world as it is; but you indulge in metaphysical sallies and sublime flights, which my commonplace mind can only regard as a sort of intellectual will-o'-the-wisp. You betray, instead of assisting me. Peace be with Mrs. Neville, whether in her grave, or, in some obscure retreat, she grieves over the follies of her youth. She has been mourned for, as never mother was mourned before; but be reasonable, dear Elizabeth, and aid me in putting a stop to Gerard's insane career. You can, if you will; he reveres you—he would listen to you. Do not talk of mysterious hands, and Hamlet's ghost, and all that is to carry us away to Fairyland; but of the rational duties of life, and the proper aim of a man, to be useful to the living, and not spend the best years of his life in dreams of the dead."

"What can I say?" replied Elizabeth: "you will be angry, but I sympathize with Mr. Neville; and I cannot help saying, though you scoff at me, that I think that, in all he is doing, he is obeying the most sacred law of our nature—exculpating the innocent, and rendering duty to her who has a right, living or dead, to demand all his love."

"Well," said Lady Cecil, "I have managed very ill; I had meant to make you my ally, and have failed. I do not oppose Gerard in Sir Boyvill's open, angry manner; but it has been my endeavour throughout to mitigate his zeal, and to change him, from a wild sort of visionary, into a man of this world. He has talents, he is the heir to large possessions, his father would gladly assist any rational pursuit; he might make a figure in his country, he might be anything he pleased; and, instead of this, all is wasted on the unhappy dead. You do wrong to encourage him; think of what I say, and use your influence in a more beneficial manner."

During the following days, this sort of argument was several times renewed. Lady Cecil, who had heretofore opposed Neville covertly, with some show of sympathy, the fallacy of which he easily detected, and who had striven rather to lead him to forget, than to argue against his views, now openly opposed his voyage to America. Gerard heard in silence. He would not reply. Nothing she said carried the slightest weight with him, and he had long been accustomed to opposition, and to take his own way in spite of it. He was satisfied to do so now, without making an effort to convince her. Yet he was hurt, and turned gladly to Elizabeth for consolation. Her avowed and warm approval, her anxious sympathy, the certainty she expressed that in the end he would succeed, and that his enthusiasm and zeal were implanted in his heart for the express purpose of his mother's vindication, and that he would fail in every higher duty if he now held back; all this echoed so faithfully his own thoughts, that she already appeared a portion of his existence that he could never part from, the dear and promised reward of all his exertions.

In the ardour of her sympathy, Elizabeth wrote to Falkner. She had before written to tell him that she had seen again her friend of Marseilles; she wrote trembling, fearful of being recalled home; for she remembered the mysterious shrinking of her father from the name of Neville. His replies, however, only spoke of a short journey he was making, and a delay in his own joining her. Now again she wrote to speak of Neville's filial piety, his mother's death, her alleged dishonour, his sufferings and heroism; she dilated on this subject with fond approval, and expressed her wishes for his success in warm and eager terms; for many days she had no reply; a letter came at last—it was short. It besought her instantly to return. "This is the last act of duty, of affection, I shall ever ask," Falkner wrote: "comply without demurring, come at once; come, and hear the fatal secret that will divide us for ever. Come! I ask but for a day; the eternal future you may, you will, pass with your new friends."

Had the writing not been firm and clear, such words had seemed to portend her benefactor's death; wondering, struck by fear, inexpressibly anxious to comply with his wishes, pale and trembling, she besought Lady Cecil to arrange for her instant return. Gerard heard with sorrow, but without surprise; he knew, if her father demanded her presence, her first act would be obedience. But he grieved to see her suffer, and he began also to wonder by what strange coincidence they should both be doomed to sorrow, through the disasters of their parents.

# CHAPTER XXIII

Falkner had parted with his dear adopted child under a strong excitement of fear concerning her health. The change of air and scene restored her so speedily, that his anxieties were of short duration. He was, however, in no hurry to rejoin her, as he was taught to consider a temporary separation from him as important to her convalescence.

For the first time, after many years, Falkner was alone. True, he was so in Greece; but there he had an object. In Greece, also, it is true that he had dwelt on the past, writing even a narrative of his actions, and that remorse sat heavy at his heart, while he pursued this task. Yet he went to Greece to assist in a glorious cause, and to redeem his name from the obloquy his confession would throw on it, by his gallantry and death. There was something animating in these reflections. Then also disease had not attacked him, nor pain made him its prey—his sensations were healthful—and if his reflections were melancholy and self-condemning, yet they were attended by grandeur, and even by sublimity, the result of the danger that surrounded him, and the courage with which he met it.

Now he was left alone—broken in health—dashed in spirit; consenting to live—wishing to live for Elizabeth's sake—yet haunted still by one pale ghost, and the knowledge that his bosom contained a secret which, if divulged, would acquire for him universal detestation. He did not fear discovery; but little do they know the human heart who are not aware of the throes of shame and anguish that attend the knowledge that we are in reality a cheat, that we disguise our own real selves, and that truth is our worst enemy. Left to himself, Falkner thought of these things with bitterness; he loathed the burden that sat upon his soul; he longed to cast it off; yet, when he thought of Elizabeth; her devoted affection and earnest entreaties, he was again a coward; how could he consent to give her up, and plant a dagger in her heart!

There was but one cure to the irritation that his spirit endured, which was—to take refuge in her society; and he was about to join her, when a letter came, speaking of Gerard Neville—the same wild boy they had seen at Baden—the kind friend of Marseilles, still melancholy, still stricken by adversity; but endowed with a thousand qualities to attract love and admiration: full of sentiment and poetry—kind and tender as woman—resolute and independent as a man. Elizabeth said little, remembering Falkner's previous restriction upon his name—but she considered it her duty to mention him to her benefactor; and that being her duty to him, it became another to her new friend to assert his excellence, lest by some chance Falkner had mistaken, and attributed qualities that did not belong to him.

Falkner's thoughts became busy on this with new ideas. It was at once pleasing and painful to hear of the virtues of Gerard Neville. The pleasure was derived from the better portion of human nature—the pain from the worst; a lurking envy, and dislike to excellence derived in any degree from one he hated, and with such sentiment he regarded the father of Gerard. Still he was the son of the angel he worshipped and had destroyed; she had loved her child to adoration, and to know that he grew up all she would have wished would console her wandering, unappeased spirit. He remembered his likeness to her, and that softened him even more. Yet he thought of the past—and what he had done; and the very idea of her son lamenting for ever his lost mother filled him with renewed and racking remorse.

That Elizabeth should now for the third time be thrown in his way, was strange, and his first impulse was to recall her. It was well that Gerard should be noble-minded, endowed with talent, a rare and exalted being—but that she should be brought into near contact with him was evil: between Falkner and Gerard Neville there existed a gulf unfathomable, horrific, deadly; and any friendship between him and his adopted child must cause disunion between her and Falkner. He had suffered much, but this last blow, a cause for disuniting them, would tax his fortitude too much.

Yet thus it was to be taxed. He received a letter from Lady Cecil, of which Elizabeth was ignorant. Its ostensible object was to give good tidings of her fair guest's health, and to renew her invitation to him. But there was a covert meaning which Falkner detected. Lady Cecil, though too young to be an inveterate matchmaker, yet conceived and cherished the idea of the marriage of Neville and Elizabeth. In common parlance, Gerard might look higher; but so also might Elizabeth, apparently the only daughter and heiress of a man of good birth and easy fortune. But this went for little with Lady Cecil; Gerard's peculiar disposition—his devotion to his dead mother—his distaste to all society—the coldness he had hitherto manifested to feminine attractions, made the choice of a wife difficult for him. Elizabeth's heroic and congenial character; her total inexperience in the world, and readiness to sympathize with sentiments which, to the ordinary class of women, would appear extravagant and foolish; all this suited them for each other. Lady Cecil saw them together, and felt that intimacy would produce love.

She was delighted; but thinking it right that the father should have a voice, she wrote to Falkner, scarcely alluding to these things, but with a delicate tact that enabled her to convey her meaning, and Falkner, jumping at once to the conclusion, saw that his child was lost to him for ever.

There arose from this idea a convulsion of feeling, that shook him as an earthquake shakes the firm land, making the most stable edifices totter. A chill horror ran through his veins, a cold dew broke out on his forehead; it was unnatural—it was fatal—it must bring on all their heads tenfold ruin.

Yet wherefore? Elizabeth was no child of his—Elizabeth Falkner could never wed Gerard Neville—but between him and Elizabeth Raby there existed no obstacle. Nay, how better could he repay the injury he had done him in depriving him of his mother, than by bestowing on him a creature, perhaps more perfect, to be his solace and delight to the end of his life? So must it be—here Falkner's punishment would begin; to exile himself for ever from her, who was the child of his heart, the prop of his existence. It was dreadful to think of, but it must be done.

And how was the sacrifice to be fulfilled? by restoring Elizabeth to her father's family, and then withdrawing himself to a distant land. He need not add to this the confession of his crime. No! thus should he compensate to Gerard for the injury done him; and burning his papers, leaving still in mystery the unknown past, die, without its ever being known to Elizabeth that he was the cause of her husband's sorrows. It was travelling fast, to arrange this future for all three; but there are moments when the future, with all its contingences and possibilities, becomes glaringly distinct to our foreseeing eye; and we act as if that was, which we believe must be. He would become a soldier once again—and the boon of death would not be for ever denied to him.

To restore Elizabeth to her family was at any rate but doing her a long-withheld justice. The child of honour and faithful affection—who bore a proud name—whose loveliness of person and mind would make her a welcome treasure in any family; she, despite her generous sacrifices, should follow his broken fortunes no longer. If the notion of her marrying Neville were a mere dream, still to give back to her name and station, was a benefit which it was unjust any longer to withhold; nor should it be a question between them. They were now divided, so should they remain. He would reveal her existence to her family, claim their protection, and then withdraw himself; while she, occupied by a new and engrossing sentiment, would easily get reconciled to his absence.

The first step he took in furtherance of this new resolution, was to make inquiries concerning the present state of Elizabeth's family—of which hitherto he knew no more than what he gathered from her mother's unfinished letter, and this was limited to their being a wealthy Catholic family, proud of their ancestry, and devoted to their faith. Through his solicitor he gained intelligence of their exact situation. He heard that there was a family of that name in Northumberland; it was Roman Catholic, and exceedingly rich. The present head of the family was an old man; he had long been a widower; left with a family of six sons. The eldest had married early, and was dead, leaving his widow with four daughters and one son, yet a child, who was the heir of the family honours and estates, and resided with his mother, for the most part, at the mansion of his grandfather. Of the remaining sons little account could be gained. It was the family custom to concentrate all its prosperity and wealth on the head of the eldest son; and the younger, precluded by their religion, at that time, from advancement in their own country, entered foreign service. One only had exempted himself from the common lot, and become an outcast, and, in the eyes of his family, a reprobate. Edwin Raby had apostatized from the Catholic faith; he had married a portionless girl of inferior birth, and entered the profession of the law. His parents looked with indignation on the dishonour entailed on their name through his falling off; but his death relieved their terrors—he died, leaving a widow and an infant daughter. As the marriage had never been acknowledged, and female offspring were held supernumerary, and an encumbrance in the Raby family, they had refused to receive her, and never heard of her more; she was, it was conjectured, living in obscurity among her own relations. Falkner at once detected the truth. The despised, deserted widow had died in her youth; and the daughter of Edwin Raby was the child of his adoption. On this information Falkner regulated his conduct; and finding that Elizabeth's grandfather, old Oswi Raby, resided habitually at his seat in the north of England, he—his health now restored sufficiently to make the journey without inconvenience—set out for Northumberland, to communicate the existence, and claim his acknowledgment, of his granddaughter.

There are periods in our lives when we seem to run away from ourselves and our afflictions; to commence a new course of existence, upon fresh ground, towards a happier goal. Sometimes, on the contrary, the stream of life doubles—runs back to old scenes, and we are constrained to linger amid the desolation we had hoped to leave far behind. Thus was it with Falkner; the past clung to him inextricably. What had he to do with those who had suffered through his misdeed? He had fled from them—he had traversed a quarter of the earth—he had placed a series of years between them; but there he was again—in the same spot—the same forms before him—the same names sounding in his ears—the effects of his actions impending darkly and portentously over him; seeing no escape but by casting away the only treasure of his life—his adopted child—and becoming again a solitary, miserable wanderer.

No man ever suffered more keenly than Falkner the stings of remorse; no man ever resolved more firmly to meet the consequences of his actions systematically, and without outward flinching. It was perseverance to one goal that had occasioned all his sin and wo; it followed him in his repentance; and though misery set a visible mark on his brow, he did not hesitate nor delay. The journey to Northumberland was long, for he could only proceed by short stages; and all the time miserable reflection doubled every mile, and stretched each hour into twice its duration. He was alone. To look back was wretchedness—to think of Elizabeth was no solace; hereafter they were to be divided—hereafter no voice of love or gentle caress would chase the darkness from his brow—he was to be for ever alone.

At length he arrived at his destination, and reached the entrance to Belleforest. The mansion, a fine old Gothic building, adorned by the ruins of an ancient abbey, was in itself venerable and extensive, and surrounded by a princely demesne. This was the residence of Elizabeth's ancestors—of her nearest relations. Here her childhood would have been spent—under these venerable oaks—within these ancestral walls. Falkner was glad to think that, in being forced to withdraw from her his own protection, she would take a higher station, and in the world's eye become more on an equality with Gerard Neville. Everything around denoted grandeur and wealth; the very circumstance that the family adhered to the ancient faith of the land—to a form of worship which, though evil in its effects on the human mind, is to the eye imposing and magnificent, shed a greater lustre round the place. On inquiry, Falkner heard that the old gentleman was at Belleforest; indeed, he never quitted it; but that his daughter-in-law, with her family, were in the south of England. Mr. Raby was very accessible; on asking for him, Falkner was instantly ushered in.

He entered a library of vast dimensions, and fitted up with a sort of heavy splendour; very imposing, but very sombre. The high windows, painted ceiling, and massy furniture bespoke an oldfashioned, but almost regal taste. Falkner, for a moment, thought himself alone, when a slight noise attracted his attention to a diminutive and very white old gentleman, who advanced towards him. The mansion looked built for a giant race; and Falkner, expecting the majesty of size, could hardly contract his view to the slender and insignificant figure of the present possessor. Oswi Raby looked shrivelled, not so much by age as the narrowness of his mind; to whose dimensions his outward figure had contracted itself. His face was pale and thin; his light blue eyes grown dim; you might have thought that he was drying up and vanishing from the earth by degrees. Contrasted with this slight shadow of a man, was a mind that saw the whole world almost concentrated in himself. He, Oswi Raby, he, head of the oldest family in England, was first of created beings. Without being assuming in manner, he was self-important in heart; and there was an obstinacy and an incapacity to understand that anything was of consequence except himself, or rather, except the house he represented, that gave extreme repulsion to his manners.

It is always awkward to disclose an errand such as Falkner's; it was only by plunging at once into it, and warming himself by his own words, that he contrived to throw grace round his subject. A cloud gathered over the old man's features; he grew whiter, and his thin lips closed, as if they had never opened except with a refusal.

"You speak of very painful circumstances," he said; "I have sometimes feared that I should be intruded upon in behalf of this person; yet, after so many years, there is less pretence than ever for encroaching upon an injured family. Edwin himself broke the tie. He was rebellious and apostate. He had talents, and might have distinguished himself to his honour; he preferred irreparable disgrace. He abandoned the religion which we consider as the most precious part of our inheritance; and he added imprudence to guilt, by, he being himself unprovided for, marrying a portionless, low-born girl. He never hoped for my forgiveness; he never even asked it. His death—it is hard for a father to feel thus—but his death was a relief. We were applied to by his widow; but with her we could have nothing to do. She was the partner of his rebellion—nay, we looked upon her as its primal cause. I was willing to take charge of my grandchild, if delivered entirely up to me. She did not even think proper to reply to the letter making this concession. I had, indeed, come to the determination of continuing to her a portion of the allowance I made to my son, despite his disobedience; but from that time to this no tidings of either mother or daughter have reached us."

"Death must bear the blame of that negligence," said Falkner, mastering his rising disgust. "Mrs. Raby was hurried to the grave but a few months after your son's death, the victim of her devoted affection to her husband. Their innocent daughter was left among strangers, who did not know to whom to apply. She, at least, is free from all fault, and has every claim on her father's family."

"She is nothing, and has no claim," interrupted Mr. Raby, peevishly, "beyond a bare maintenance, even if she be the person you represent. I beg your pardon, sir, but you may be deceived yourself on this subject; but taking it for granted that this young person is the daughter of my son, what is she to me?"

"A granddaughter is a relation," Falkner began; "a near and dear one—"

"Under such circumstances," interrupted Mr. Raby, "under the circumstances of a marriage to which I gave no consent, and her being brought up at a distance from us all, I should rather call her a connexion than a relation. We cannot look with favour on the child of an apostate; educated in a faith which we consider pernicious. I am an oldfashioned man, accustomed only to the society of those whose feelings coincide with mine; and I must apologize, sir, if I say anything to shock you; but the truth is self-evident, a child of a discarded son may have a slender claim for support, none for favour or countenance. This young person has no right to raise her eyes to us; she must regulate her expectations by the condition of her mother, who was a sort of servant, a humble companion or governess, in the house of Mrs. Neville of Dromore—"

Falkner grew pale at the name, but, commanding himself, replied, "I believe she was a friend of that lady! I have said I was unacquainted with the parents of Miss Raby; I found her an orphan, subsisting on precarious charity. Her few years—her forlorn situation—her beauty and sweetness, claimed my compassion—I adopted her—"

"And would now throw her off," again interrupted the ill-tempered old man. "Had you restored her to us in her childhood—had she been brought up in our religion among us—she would have shared this home with her cousins. As it is, you must yourself be aware that it will be impossible to admit, as an inmate, a stranger—a person ignorant of our peculiar systems—an alien from our religion. Mrs. Raby would never consent to it; and I would on no account annoy her who, as the mother and guardian of my heir, merits every deference. I will, however, consult with her, and with the gentleman who has the conduct of my affairs; and as you wish to get rid of an embarrassment, which, pardon me if I say you entirely brought on yourself, we will do what we judge due to the honour of the family; but I cannot hold out any hopes beyond a maintenance—unless this young person, whom I should then regard as my granddaughter, felt a vocation for a religion, out of whose pale I will never acknowledge a relation."

At every word Falkner grew more angry. He always repressed any manifestation of passion, and only grew pale, and spoke in a lower, calmer voice. There was a pause; he glanced at the white hair and attenuated form of the old man, so to acquire a sufficient portion of forbearance, and then replied: "It is enough—forget this visit; you shall never hear again of the existence of your outraged grandchild. Could you for a moment comprehend her worth, you might feel regret at casting from you one whose qualities render her the admiration of all who know her. Some day, when the infirmities of age increase upon you, you may remember that you might have had a being near, the most compassionate and kind that breathes. If ever you feel the want of an affectionate hand to smooth your pillow, you may remember that you have shut your heart to one who would have been a daily blessing. I do not wish to disembarrass myself of Miss Raby—Miss Falkner, rather, let me call her; she has borne my name as my daughter for many years, and shall continue to retain it, together with my paternal guardianship, while I live. I have the honour to wish you a good-morning."

Falkner hastily departed; and, as he threw himself on his horse, and at a quick pace traversed the long avenues of Belleforest, he felt that boiling of the blood, that inexpressible bursting and tumult of the heart, that accompanies fierce indignation and disdain. A vehement desire to pour out the cataract of his contempt and anger on the offender, was mingled with redoubled tenderness for Elizabeth, with renewed gratitude for all he owed her, and a yearning, heart-warming desire to take her again to the shelter of his love, from whence she should never more depart.

# CHAPTER XXIV

Falkner's mind had undergone a total change; he had gone to Belleforest, believing it to be his duty to restore to its possessors a dearer treasure than any held by them; he left it, resolved never to part from his adopted child. "Get rid of an embarrassment!" he repeated to himself; "get rid of Elizabeth, of tender affection, truth, and fidelity! of the heart's fondest ties, my soul's only solace! How often has my life been saved and cheered by her only! And when I would sacrifice blessings of which I hold myself unworthy, I hear the noblest and most generous being in the world degraded by the vulgar, sordid prejudices of that narrow-minded bigot! How paltry seems the pomp of wealth, or the majesty of these ancient woods, when it is recollected that they are lorded over by such a thing as that!"

Falkner's reflections were all painful; his heavily-burdened conscience weighed him to the earth. He felt that there was justice in a part of Mr. Raby's representations; that if Elizabeth had been brought up under his care, in a religion which, because it was persecuted, was the more valuable in their eyes; participating in their prejudices, and endeared to them by habit, she would have had claims, which, as she was, unseen, unknown, and totally disjoined from them in opinions and feelings, she could never possess. He was the cause of this, having, in her infancy, chosen to take her to himself, to link his desolate fate to her brighter one; and now he could only repent for her sake; yet, for her sake, he did repent, when, looking forward, he thought of the growing attachment between her and the son of his victim.

What could he do? recall her? forbid her again to see Gerard Neville? Unexplained commands are ever unjust, and had any strong feeling sprung up in either of their hearts, they could not be obeyed. Should he tell her all, and throw himself on her mercy? He would thus inflict deep, irreparable pangs, and, besides, place her in a painful situation, where duty would struggle with inclination; and pride and affection both made it detestable to him to create such a combat in her heart, and cause her to feel pangs and make sacrifices for him. What other part was there to take? to remain neuter? let events take their course? If it ended as he foresaw, when a marriage was mentioned, he could reveal her real birth. Married to Gerard Neville, her relations would gladly acknowledge her, and then he could withdraw for ever. He should have much to endure meanwhile; to hear a name perpetually repeated that thrilled to the very marrow of his bones; perhaps to see the husband and son of her he had destroyed: he felt sick at heart at such a thought; he put it aside. It was not to-day, it could not be to-morrow, that he should be called upon to encounter these evils; meanwhile, he would shut his eyes upon them.

Returning homeward, he felt impelled to prolong his tour, he visited some of the lakes of Westmoreland, and the mountain scenery of Derbyshire. The thought of return was painful, so he lingered on the way, and wrote for his letters to be forwarded to him. He had been some weeks without receiving any from Elizabeth, and he felt extreme impatience again to be blessed with the sight of her handwriting—he felt how passionately he loved her—how to part from her was to part from every joy of life; he called himself her father—his heart acknowledged the tie in every pulsation; no father ever worshipped a child so fervently; her voice, her smile—and dear loving eyes, where were they?—they were far, but here was something—a little packet of letters, that must for the present stand in lieu of the dearer blessing of her presence. He looked at the papers with delight—he pressed them to his lips—he delayed to open them, as if he did not deserve the joy they would communicate—as if its excess would overpower him. "I purpose parting from her," he thought; "but still she is mine, mine when she traced those lines—mine as I read the expressions of her affection; there are hours of delight garnered for me in those little sealed talismans that nothing future or past can tarnish, and yet the name of Neville will be there!" The thought brought a cold chill with it, and he opened the letters hastily to know the worst.

Elizabeth had half forgotten the pain with which Falkner had at one time shrunk from a name become so dear to her; when she wrote, her heart was full of Gerard's story—and, besides, she had had letters from her father speaking of him with kindness, so that she indulged herself by alluding to it—to the disappearance of his mother and Gerard's misery; the trial— the brutality of Sir Boyvill; and last, to the resolution formed in childhood, brooded over through youth, now acted upon, to discover his mother's destroyer. "Nor is it," she wrote, "any vulgar feeling of vengeance that influences him—but the purest and noblest motives. She is stigmatized as unworthy—he would vindicate her fame. When I hear the surmises, the accusations cast on her, I feel with him. To hear a beloved parent accused of guilt, must indeed be the most bitter wo; to believe her innocent, and to prove her such, the only alleviation. God grant that he may succeed!—and though I wish no ill to any human being, yet rather may the height of evil fall on the head of the true criminal, than continue to cloud the days of a being whose soul is moulded in sensibility and honour!"

"Thus do you pray, heedless Elizabeth! May the true criminal feel the height of evil; may he—whom you have saved from death—endure tortures compared to which a thousand deaths were nothing! Be it so! you shall have your wish!"

Impetuous as fire, Falkner did not pause: something, some emotion devouring as fire, was lighted up in his heart—there must be no delay!— never had he seen the effects of his crime in so vivid a light; avoiding the name of Neville, he had never heard that of his victim coupled with shame— she was unfortunate, but he persuaded himself that she was not thought guilty; dear injured saint! had then her sacred name been bandied about by the vulgar—she pronounced unworthy by the judges of her acts—ignominy heaped upon the grave he had dug for her? Was her beloved son the victim of his belief in her goodness? Had his youthful life been blighted by his cowardly concealments? Oh, rather a thousand deaths than such a weight of sin upon his soul! He would declare all; offer his life in expiation—what more could be demanded?

And again—this might be thought a more sordid motive; and yet it was not—Gerard was vowed to the discovery of the true criminal; he would discover him—earth would render up her secrets, Heaven lead the son to the very point—by slow degrees his crime would be unveiled—Elizabeth called upon to doubt and to believe. His vehement disposition was not calculated to bear the slow process of such discoveries; he would meet them, avow all—let the worst fall on him: it was happiness to know and feel the worst.

Lost for ever, he would deliver himself up to reprobation and the punishment of his guilt. Too long he had delayed—now all his motives for concealment melted away like snow overspread by volcanic fire. Fierce, hurrying destiny seized him by the hair of his head—crying aloud, "Murderer, offer up thy blood—shade of Alithea, take thy victim!"

He wrote instantly to Elizabeth to meet him at their home at Wimbledon, and proceeded thither himself. Unfortunately, the tumult of his thoughts acted on his health; after he had proceeded a few miles, he was taken ill— for three days he was confined to his bed, in a high fever. He thought he was about to die—his secret untold. Copious bleeding, however, subdued the violence of the attack—and weak and faint, he, despite his physician's advice, proceeded homeward; weak and faint, an altered man—life had no charms, no calls, but one duty. Hitherto he had lived in contempt of the chain of effects which ever links pain to evil and of the Providence which will not let the innocent be for ever traduced. It had fallen on him; now his punishment had begun, not as he, in the happier vehemence of passion, had determined, not by sudden, self-inflicted, or glorious death—but the slow grinding of the iron wheels of destiny, as they passed over him, crushing him in the dust.

Yet his heart, despite its sufferings, warmed with something like pleasure when, after a tedious journey of three days, he drew near his home, where he hoped to find Elizabeth. He had misgivings; he had asked her to return, but she might have written to request a delay—no! she was there; she had been there two days, anxiously expecting him. It is so sweet a thing to hear the voice of one we love welcoming us on our return home! It seems to assure us of a double existence; not only in our own identity—which we bear perpetually about with us—but in the heart we leave behind, which has thought of us—lived for us, and now beats with warm pleasure on beholding the expected one. On the whole earth Falkner loved none but Elizabeth. He hated himself; the past—the present—the future, as they appertained to him, were all detestable; remorse, grief, and loathsome anticipation made up the sum of feelings with which he regarded them: but here, bright and beautiful; without taint; all affection and innocence—a monument of his own good feelings, a lasting rock to which to moor his every hope, stood before him the child of his adoption; his heart felt bursting when he thought of all she was to him.

Yet a doubt entered to mar his satisfaction—was she changed? If love had insinuated itself into her heart, he was rejected; at least the plenteous, abundant fountain, that gave from its own source, would be changed to the still waters that neither received increase nor bestowed any overflowing. Worse than this—she loved Gerard Neville, the son of his victim, he whose life was devastated by him, who would regard him with abhorrence. He would teach Elizabeth to partake this feeling. The blood stood chilled in Falkner's heart when he thought of thus losing the only being he loved on earth.

He mastered these feelings when he saw her. The first moment, indeed, when she flew to his arms, and expressed with eager fondness her delight in seeing him again, was all happiness. She perceived the traces of suffering on his brow, and chided herself for having remained away so long; she promised never to absent herself thus again. Every remembered look and tone of her dear face and voice, now brought palpably before him, was a medicine to Falkner. He repressed his uneasiness, he banished his fears; for a few hours he made happiness his own again.

The evening was passed in calm and cheering conversation. No word was said of the friends whom Elizabeth had left. She had forgotten them, during the first few hours she spent with her father; and when she did allude to her visit, Falkner said, "We will talk of these things to-morrow; to-night let us only think of ourselves." Elizabeth felt a little mortified; the past weeks, the fortunes of her friends, and the sentiments they excited, had become a part of herself; and she was pained that so much of disjunction existed between her and Falkner, as to make that which was so vivid and present to her vacant of interest to him; but she checked her disappointment: soon he would know her new friend, sympathize in his devotion towards his injured mother, enter as warmly as she did into the result of his endeavours for her exculpation. Meanwhile she yielded to his wish, and they talked of scenes and countries they had visited together, and all the feelings and opinions engendered by the past; as they were wont to do in days gone by, before a stranger influence had disturbed a world in which they lived for each other only—father and daughter—without an interest beyond.

Nothing could be more pure and entire than their affection, and there was between them that mingling of hearts which words cannot describe; but which, whenever it is experienced, in whatever relation in life, is unalloyed happiness. There was a total absence of disguise, of covert censure, of mutual diffidence; perfect confidence gave rise to the fearless utterance of every idea, and there was a repose, and yet an enjoyment in the sense of sympathy and truth, which filled and satisfied. Falkner was surprised at the balmy sense of joy that, despite everything, stole over him; and he kissed and blessed his child, as she retired for the night, with more grateful affection, a fuller sense of her merits, and a more fervent desire of preserving her always near him, than he had ever before been conscious of experiencing.

# CHAPTER XXV

Elizabeth rose on the following morning, her bosom glowing with a sensation of acknowledged happiness. So much of young love brooded in her heart, as quickened its pulsations, as gave lightness and joy to her thoughts. She had no doubts, nor fears, nor even hopes: she was not aware that love was the real cause of the grateful sense of happiness, with which she avowed, to Heaven and herself, that all was peace. She was glad to be reunited to Falkner, for whom she felt an attachment at once so respectful, and yet, on account of his illness and melancholy, so watchful and tender, as never allowed her to be wholly free from solicitude when absent from him. Also she expected on that morning to see Gerard Neville. When Falkner's letter came to hasten her departure from Oakly, she felt grieved at the recall, at the moment when she was expecting him to join her, so to fill up the measure of her enjoyments; with all this, she was eager to obey, and anxious to be with him again. Lady Cecil deputed Miss Jervis to accompany her. On the very morning of their departure, Neville asked for a seat in the carriage; they travelled to town together; and when they separated, Neville told her of his intention of immediately securing a passage to America, and since then had written a note to mention that he should ride over to Wimbledon on that morning.

The deep interest that Elizabeth took in his enterprise made her solicitous to know whether he had procured any further information; but her paramount desire was to introduce him to Falkner, to inspire him with her sentiments of friendship, and to see two persons whom she considered superior to the rest of the world bound to each other by a mutual attachment; she wanted to impart to her father a pity for Alithea's wrongs, and an admiration for her devoted son. She walked in the shrubbery before breakfast, enjoying nature with the enthusiasm of love; she gathered the last roses of the departing season, and mingling them with a few carnations, hung, with a new sense of rapture, over these fairest children of nature; for it is the property of love to enhance all our enjoyments, "to paint the lily, and add a perfume to the rose." When she returned to the house, she was told that Falkner still slept, and begged not to be disturbed. She breakfasted, therefore, by herself, sitting by the open casement, and looking on the waving trees, her flowers shedding a sweet atmosphere around; sometimes turning to her open book, where she read of

"The heavenly Una with her milk white lamb,"

and sometimes leaning her cheek upon her hand, in one of those reveries where we rather feel than think, and every articulation of the frame thrills with a living bliss.

The quick canter of a horse, the stopping at the gate, the ringing of the bell, and the entrance of Neville, made her heart beat and her eyes light up with gladness. He entered with a lighter step, a more cheerful and animated mien, than usual. He was aware that he loved. He was assured that Elizabeth was the being selected from the whole world who could make him happy; while he regarded her with all the admiration, the worship, due to her virtues. He had never loved before. The gloom that absorbed him, the shyness inspired by his extreme sensitiveness, had hitherto made him avoid the society of women; their pleasures, their gayety, their light airy converse, were a blank to him; it was Elizabeth's sufferings that first led him to remark her: the clearness of her understanding, her simplicity, tenderness, and dignity of soul won him; and, lastly, the unbounded, undisguised sympathy she felt for his endeavours, which all else regarded as futile and insane, riveted him to her indissolubly.

Events were about to separate them, but her thoughts would accompany him across the Atlantic—stand suspended while his success was dubious, and hail his triumph with a joy equal to his own. The very thought gave fresh ardour to his desire to fulfil his task; he had no doubt of success, and, though the idea of his mother's fate was still a cloud in the prospect, it only mellowed, without defacing the glowing tints shed over it by love.

They met with undisguised pleasure; he sat near her, and gazed with such delight as, to one less inexperienced than Elizabeth, would have at once betrayed the secret of his heart. He told her that he had found a vessel about to sail for New-York, and that he had engaged a passage on board. He was restless and uneasy, he feared a thousand chances; he felt as if he were neglecting his most sacred duty by any delay; there was something in him urging him on, telling him that the crisis was at hand; and yet, that any neglect on his part might cause the moment to slip by for ever. When arrived at New-York, he should proceed with all speed to Washington, and then, if Osborne had not arrived, he should set forward to meet him. So much might intervene to balk his hopes! Osborne might die, and his secret die with him. Every moment's delay was crime. The vessel was to drop down the river that very night, and to-morrow he was to join her at Sheerness. He had come to say farewell.

This sudden departure led to a thousand topics of interest; to his hopes—his certainty that all would soon be revealed, and he rewarded for his long suffering. Such ideas led him to speak of the virtues of his mother, which were the foundation of his hopes. He spoke of her as he remembered her; he described her watchful tenderness, her playful but well-regulated treatment of himself. Still in his dreams, he said, he sometimes felt pressed in her arms, and kissed with all the passionate affection of her maternal heart; in such sweet visions her cry of agony would mingle; it seemed the last shriek of wo and death. "Can you wonder," continued Neville, "can my father, can Sophia wonder, that, recollecting all these things, I will not bear without a struggle that my mother's name should be clouded, her fate encompassed by mystery and blame, her very warm, kind feelings and enchanting sensibility turned into accusations against her? I do indeed hope and believe that I shall learn the truth whither I am going, and that the unfortunate victim of lawless violence, of whom Osborne spoke, is my lost mother; but, if I am disappointed in this expectation, I shall not for that give up my pursuit; it will only whet my purpose to seek the truth elsewhere."

"And that truth may be less sad than you anticipate," said Elizabeth; "yet I cannot help fearing that the miserable tragedy which you have heard is connected with your mother's fate."

"That it is a tragedy may well dash my eagerness," replied Neville; "for, right or wrong, I cannot help feeling, that to see her again—to console her for her sufferings—to show that she is remembered, loved, idolized by her son, would be a dearer reward to me than triumph over the barbarous condemnation of the world, if that triumph is to be purchased by having lost her for ever. This is not an heroic feeling, I confess—"

"If it be heroism," said Elizabeth, "to find our chief good in serving others; if compassion, sympathy, and generosity be greater virtues, as I believe, than cold self-absorbed severity, then is your feeling founded on the purest portion of our nature."

While they were thus talking, seated near each other, Elizabeth's face beaming with celestial benignity, and Neville, in the warmth of his gratitude for her approval, had taken her hand and pressed it to his lips, the door opened, and Falkner slowly entered. He had not heard of the arrival of the stranger; but seeing a guest with Elizabeth, he divined in a moment who it was. The thought ran through his frame like an ice-bolt—his knees trembled under him—cold dew gathered on his brow—for a moment he leaned against the doorway, unable to support himself; while Elizabeth, perceiving his entrance, blushing, she knew not why, and now frightened by the ghastly pallor of his face, started up, exclaiming, "My father! Are you ill?"

Falkner struggled a moment longer, and then recovered his self-possession. The disordered expression of his countenance was replaced by a cold and stern look, which, aided by the marble paleness that settled over it, looked more like the chiselling of a statue than mortal endurance. A lofty resolve to bear unflinchingly was the spirit that moulded his features into an appearance of calm. From this moment he acquired the strength of body, as well as of mind, to meet the destiny before him. The energy of his soul did not again fail. Every instant—every word, seemed to add to his courage—to nerve him to the utmost height of endurance; to make him ready to leap, without one tremour, into the abyss which he had so long and so fearfully avoided.

The likeness of Neville to his mother had shaken him more than all. His voice, whose tones were the same with hers, was another shock. His very name jarred upon his sense, but he betrayed no token of suffering. "Mr. Neville," said Elizabeth, "is come to take leave of me. To-morrow he sails to America."

"To America! Wherefore?" asked Falkner.

"I wrote to you," she replied; "I explained the motives of this voyage. You know—"

"I know all," said Falkner; "and this voyage to America is superfluous."

Neville echoed the word with surprise, while Elizabeth exclaimed, "Do you think so? You must have good reasons for this opinion. Tell them to Mr. Neville. Your counsels, I am sure, will be of use to him. I have often wished that you had been with us. I am so glad that he sees you before he goes—if he does go. You say his voyage is superfluous; tell him wherefore; advise him. Your advice will, I am sure, be good. I would give the world that he did the exact thing that is best—that is most likely to succeed."

Neville looked gratefully at her as she spoke thus eagerly; while Falkner, still standing, his eyes fixed on and scanning the person of the son of his victim, marble pale, but displaying feeling by no other outward sign, scarcely heard what she said, till her last words drew his attention. He smiled, as in scorn, and said, "Oh, yes, I can advise; and he shall succeed—and he will not go."

"I shall be happy," said Neville, with surprise. "I am willing to be advised—that is, if your advice coincides with my wishes."

"It shall do so," interrupted Falkner.

"Then," exclaimed Neville, impetuously, "the moments that I linger here will appear to you too many. You will desire that I should be on board already—already under sail—already arrived. You will wish the man whom I seek should be waiting on the sands when I reach the shore!"

"He is much nearer," said Falkner, calmly; "he is before you. I am he!"

Neville started; "You! What mean you? You are not Osborne."

"I am Rupert Falkner; your mother's destroyer."

Neville glanced at Elizabeth—his eye met hers—their thought was the same, that this declaration proceeded from insanity. The fire that flashed from Falkner's eyes as he spoke—the sudden crimson that died his cheeks—the hollow though subdued tone of his voice, gave warrant for such a suspicion.

Elizabeth gazed on him with painful solicitude.

"I will not stay one moment longer," continued Falkner, "to pain you by the sight of one so accursed as I. You will hear more from me this very evening. You will hear enough to arrest your voyage; and remember that I shall remain ready to answer any call—to make any reparation—any atonement you may require."

He was gone—the door closed; it was as if a dread spectre had vanished, and Neville and Elizabeth looked at each other to read in the face of either whether both were conscious of having been visited by the same vision.

"What does he mean? Can you tell me what to think?" cried Neville, almost gasping for breath.

"I will tell you in a few hours," said Elizabeth. "I must go to him now; I fear he is very ill. This is madness. When your mother died, Mr. Neville, my father and I were travelling together in Russia or Poland. I remember dates—I am sure that it was so. This is too dreadful. Farewell. You sail tomorrow—you shall hear from me to-night."

"Be sure that I do," said Neville; "for there is a method in his speech—a dignity and a composure in his manner, that enforces a sort of belief. What can he mean?"

"Do you imagine," cried Elizabeth, "that there is any truth in these unhappy ravings? That my father, who would not tread upon a worm—whose compassionate disposition and disinterestedness have been known to me since early childhood—the noblest and yet the gentlest of human beings—do you imagine that he is a murderer? Dear Mr. Neville, he never could have seen your mother!"

"Is it indeed so?" said Neville; "yet he said one word—did you not remark?—he called himself Rupert. But I will not distress you. You will write; or rather, as my time will be occupied in preparations for my voyage, and I scarcely know where the day will be spent, I will call here this evening at nine. If you cannot see me, send me a note to the gate, containing some information, either to expedite or delay my journey. Even if this strange scene be the work of insanity, how can I leave you in distress? and if it be true what he says—if he be the man I saw tear my mother from me—how altered—how turned to age and decrepitude! Yet, if he be that man, then I have a new and horrible course to take."

"Is it so?" cried Elizabeth, with indignation; "and can a man so cloud his fair fame, so destroy his very existence, by the wild words of delirium, that my dear father should be accused of being the most odious criminal?"

"Nay," replied Neville, "I make no accusation. Do not part from me in anger. You are right, I do not doubt; and I am unjust. I will call to-night."

"Do so without fail. Do not lose your passage. I little knew that personal feeling would add to my eagerness to learn the truth. Do not stay for my sake. Come to-night and learn how false and wild my father's words were; and then hasten to depart—to see Osborne—to learn all! Farewell till this evening."

She hurried away to Falkner's room, while stunned—doubting—forced, by Elizabeth, to entertain doubts, and yet convinced in his heart; for the name of Rupert brought, conviction home—Neville left the house. He had entered it fostering the sweetest dreams of happiness, and now he dared not look at the reverse.

Elizabeth, filled with the most poignant inquietude with regard to his health, hastened to the sitting-room which Falkner usually occupied. She found him seated at the table, with a small box—a box she well remembered—open before him. He was looking over the papers it contained. His manner was perfectly composed—the natural hue had returned to his cheeks—his look was sedate. He was, indeed, very different from the man who, thirteen years before, had landed in Cornwall. He was then in the prime of life; and if passion defaced his features, still youth, and health, and power animated his frame. Long years of grief and remorse, with sickness superadded, had made him old before his time. The hair had receded from the temples, and what remained was sprinkled with gray; his figure was bent and attenuated; his face careworn; yet, at this moment, he had regained a portion of his former self. There was an expression on his face of satisfaction, almost of triumph; and, when he saw Elizabeth, the old, sweet smile she knew and loved so well lighted up his countenance. He held out his hand; she took it. There was no fever in the palm—his pulse was equable; and when he spoke his voice did not falter. He said, "This blow has fallen heavily on you, my dear girl; yet all will be well soon, I trust. Meanwhile it cannot be quite unexpected."

Elizabeth looked her astonishment—he continued:—"You have long known that a heavy crime weighs on my conscience. It renders me unfit to live; yet, I have not been permitted to die. I sought death—but we are seldom allowed to direct our fate. I do not, however, complain; I am well content with the end which will speedily terminate all."

"My dearest father," cried Elizabeth, "I cannot guess what you mean. I thought—but no—you are not ill—you are not—"

"Not mad, dearest? was that your thought? It is a madness, at least, that has lasted long—since first you stayed my hand on your mother's grave. You are too good, too affectionate to regret having saved me, even when you hear who I am. You are too resigned to Providence not to acquiesce in the way chosen to bring all things to their destined end."

Elizabeth put her arm round his neck and kissed him. "Thank you," said Falkner, "and God bless you for this kindness. I shall indeed be glad if you, from your heart, pardon and excuse me. Meanwhile, my love, there is something to be done. These papers contain an account of the miserable past; you must read them, and then let Mr. Neville have them without delay."

"Nay," said Elizabeth, "spare me this one thing—do not ask me to read the history of any one error of yours. In my eyes you must ever be the first and best of human beings—if it has ever been otherwise, I will not hear of it. You shall never be accused of guilt before me, even by yourself."

"Call it, then, my justification," said Falkner. "But do not refuse my request—it is necessary. If it be pain, pardon me for inflicting it; but bear it for my sake—I wrote this narrative when I believed myself about to die in Greece, for the chief purpose of disclosing the truth to you. I have told my story truly and simply; you can have it from no one else, for no human being breathes who knows the truth except myself. Yield, then—you have ever been yielding to me—yield, I beseech you, to my solemn request; do not shrink from hearing of my crimes—I hope soon to atone them. And then perform one other duty: send these papers to your friend—you know where he is."

"He will call here this evening at nine."

"By that time you will have finished; I am going to town now, but shall return to-night. Mr. Neville will be come and gone before then, and you will know all. I do not doubt but that you will pity me—such is your generosity, that perhaps you may love me still—but you will be shocked and wretched, and I the cause. Alas! how many weapons do our errors wield, and how surely does retribution aim at our defenceless side! To know that I am the cause of unhappiness to you, my sweet girl, inflicts a pang I cannot endure with any fortitude. But there is a remedy, and all will be well in the end."

Elizabeth hung over him as he spoke, and he felt a tear warm on his cheek, fallen from her eye—he was subdued by this testimony of her sympathy—he strained her to his heart; but, in a moment after, he reassumed his self-command, and, kissing her, bade her farewell, and then left her to the task of sorrow he had assigned.

She knew not what to think, what image to conjure up. His words were free from all incoherence; before her, also, were the papers that would tell all—she turned from them with disgust; and then again she thought of Neville, his departure, his promised return, and what she could say to him. It was a hideous dream, but there was no awakening; she sat down, she took out the papers; the number of pages written in her father's hand seemed a reprieve; she should not hear all the dreadful truth in a few short, piercing words—there was preparation. For a moment she paused to gather her thoughts—to pray for fortitude—to hope that the worst was not there, but, in its stead, some venial error that looked like crime to his sensitive mind; and then—she began to read.

# CHAPTER XXVI

## FALKNER'S NARRATIVE

"To palliate crime, and, by investigating motive, to render guilt less odious—such is not the feeling that rules my pen; to confer honour upon innocence, to vindicate virtue, and announce truth—though that offer my own name as a mark for deserved infamy—such are my motives. And if I reveal the secrets of my heart, and dwell on the circumstances that led to the fatal catastrophe I record, so that, though a criminal, I do not appear quite a monster, let the egotism be excused for her dear sake—within whose young and gentle heart I would fain that my memory should be enshrined without horror, though with blame.

"The truth, the pure and sacred truth, will alone find expression in these pages. I write them in a land of beauty, but of desolation—in a country whose inhabitants are purchasing by blood and misery the dearest privileges of human nature—where I have come to die! It is night; the cooing aziolo, the hooting owl, the flashing fire-fly, the murmur of time-honoured streams, the moonlit foliage of the gray olive woods, dark crags, and rugged mountains, throwing awful shadows, and the light of the eternal stars—such are the objects around me. Can a man speak false in the silence of night, when God and his own heart alone keep watch! when conscience hears the moaning of the dead in the pauses of the breeze, and sees one pale, lifeless figure float away on the current of the stream! My heart whispers that before such witnesses the truth will be truly recorded; and my blood curdles, and my nerves, so firm amid the din of battle, shrink and shudder at the tale I am about to narrate.

"What is crime?

"A deed done injurious to others—forbidden by religion, condemned by morality, and which human laws are enacted to punish.

"A criminal feels all mankind to be his foes, the whole frame of society is erected for his especial ruin. Before he had a right to choose his habitation in the land of his forefathers—and, placing the sacred name of liberty between himself and power, none dared check his freeborn steps—his will was his law; the limits of his physical strength were the only barriers to his wildest wanderings—he could walk erect and fear the eye of no man. He who commits a crime forfeits these privileges. Men from out the lowest grade of society can say to him, 'You must come with us!'—they can drag him from those he loves, immure him in a loathsome cell, dole out scant portions of the unchartered air, make a show of him, lead him to death, and throw his body to the dogs; and society, which for the innocent would have raised one cry of horror against the perpetrators of such outrages, look on and clap their hands with applause.

"This is a vulgar aspect of the misery of which I speak—a crime may never be discovered. Mine lies buried in my own breast. Years have passed, and none point at me and whisper, 'There goes the murderer!' But do I not feel that God is my enemy, and my own heart whispers condemnation? I know that I am an impostor—that any day may discover the truth; but more heavy than any fear of detection is the secret hidden in my own heart; the icy touch of the death I caused creeps over me during the night. I am pursued by the knowledge that naught I do can prosper, for the cry of innocence is raised against me, and the earth groans with the secret burden I have committed to her bosom. That the death-blow was not actually dealt by my hand in no manner mitigates the stings of conscience. My act was the murderer, though my intention was guiltless of death.

"Is there a man who at some time has not desired to possess, by illegal means, a portion of another's property, or to obey the dictates of an animal instinct, and plant his foot on the neck of his enemy? Few are so cold of blood or temperate of mood as not, at some one time, to have felt hurried beyond the demarcations set up by conscience and law; few but have been tempted without the brink of the forbidden; but they stopped, while I leaped beyond—there is the difference between us. Falsely do they say who allege that there is no difference in guilt between the thought and act; to be tempted is human; to resist temptation—surely, if framed like me, such is to raise us from our humanity into the sphere of angels.

"Many are the checks afforded us. Some are possessed by fear; others are endowed by a sensibility so prophetic of the evil that must ensue, that perforce they cannot act the thing they desire; they tremble at the idea of being the cause of events over whose future course they can have no control; they fear injuring others—and their own remorse.

"But I disdained all these considerations—they occurred but faintly and ineffectually to my mind. Piety, conscience, and moral respect yielded before a feeling which decked its desires in the garb of necessity. Oh, how vain it is to analyze motive! Each man has the same motives; but it is the materials of each mind—the plastic or rocky nature, the mild or the burning temperament—that rejects the alien influence, or receives it into its own essence and causes the act. Such an impulse is as a summer healthy breeze just dimpling a still lake to one—while to another it is the whirlwind that rouses him to spread ruin around.

"The Almighty who framed my miserable being made me a man of passion. They say that of such are formed the great and good. I know not that—I am neither; but I will not arraign the Creator. I will hope that in feeling my guilt—in acknowledging the superexcellence of virtue, I fulfil, in part, his design. After me, let no man doubt but that to do what is right is to ensure his own happiness; or that self-restraint, and submission to the voice of conscience implanted in our souls, impart more dignity of feeling, more true majesty of being, than a puerile assertion of will and a senseless disregard of immutable principles.

"Is passion known in these days? Such as I felt, has any other experienced it? The expression has fled from our lips; but it is as deep-seated as ever in our hearts. Who, of created beings, has not loved? Who, of my sex, has not felt the struggle, and the yielding in the struggle, of the better to the worse parts of our nature? Who so dead to nature's influence as not, at least for some brief moments, to have felt that body and soul were a slight sacrifice to obtain possession of the affections of her he loved? Who, for some moments in his life, would not have seen his mistress dead at his feet rather than wedded to another? To feel this tyranny of passion is to be human; to conquer it is to be virtuous. He who conquers himself is, in my eyes, the only true hero. Alas, I am not such! I am among the vanquished, and view the wretch I am, and learn that there is nothing so contemptible, so pitiable, so eternally miserable, as he who is defeated in his conflict with passion.

"That I am such, this very scene—this very occupation testifies. Once the slave of headlong impulse, I am now the victim of remorse. I am come to seek death, because I cannot retrieve the past; I long for the moment when the bullet shall pierce my flesh, and the pains of dissolution gather round me. Then I may hope to be, that for which I thirst, free! There is one who loves me. She is pure and kind as a guardian angel—she is as my own child—she implores me to live. With her my days might pass in a peace and innocence that saints might envy; but so heavy are the fetters of memory, so bitter the slavery of my soul, that even she cannot take away the sting from life.

"Death is all I covet. When these pages are read, the hand that traces them will be powerless—the brain that dictates will have lost its functions. This is my last labour—my legacy to my fellow-beings. Do not let them disdain the outpourings of a heart which for years has buried its recollections and remorse in silence. The waters were pent up by a dam—now they rush impetuously forth—they roar as if pursued by a thousand torrents—their turmoil deafens heaven; and what though their sound be only conveyed by the little implement that traces these lines—not less headlong than the swelling waves is the spirit that pours itself out in these words.

"I am calmer now—I have been wandering beside the stream—and, despite the lurking foe and deceptive moonbeams, I have ascended the steep mountain's side—and looked out on the misty sea, and sought to gain from reposing nature some relief to my sense of pain. The hour of midnight is at hand—all is still—I am calm, and with deliberation begin to narrate that train of circumstances, or rather of feelings, that hurried me first to error, then to crime, and, lastly, brought me here to die.

"I lost my mother before I can well remember. I have a confused recollection of her crying—and of her caressing me—and I can call to mind seeing her ill in bed, and her blessing me; but these ideas are rather like revelations of an ante-natal life, than belonging to reality. She died when I was four years old. My childhood's years were stormy and drear. My father, a social, and, I believe, even a polite man in society, was rough and ill-tempered at home. He had gambled away his own slender younger brother's fortune and his wife's portion, and was too idle to attend to a profession, and yet not indolent enough for a life devoid of purpose and pursuit. Our family was a good one; it consisted of two brothers, my father, and my uncle. This latter, favoured of birth and fortune, remained long unmarried; and was in weak health. My father expected him to die. His death, and his own consequent inheritance of the family estate, was his constant theme; but the delayed hope irritated him to madness. I knew his humour even as a child, and escaped it as I could. His voice, calling my name, made my blood run cold; his epithets of abuse, so frequently applied, filled me with boiling but ineffectual rage.

"I am not going to dwell on those painful days when, a weak, tiny boy, I felt as if I could contend with the paternal giant; and did contend, till his hand felled me to the ground, or cast me from his threshold with scorn and seeming hate. I dare say he did not hate me; but certainly no touch of natural love warmed his heart.

"One day he received a letter from his brother—I was but ten years old, but rendered old and careworn by suffering; I remember that I looked on him as he took it and exclaimed, 'From Uncle John! What have we here?' with a nervous tremour as to the passions the perusal of it might excite. He chuckled as he broke the seal—he fancied that he called him to his dying bed—'And that well over, you shall go to school, my fine fellow,' he cried;

'we shall have no more of your tricks at home.' He broke the seal, he read the letter. It announced his brother's marriage, and asked him to the wedding. I let fall the curtain over the scene that ensued: you would have thought that a villanous fraud had been committed, in which I was implicated. He drove me with blows from his door; I foamed with rage, and then I sat down and wept, and crept away to the fields, and wondered why I was born, and longed to kill my uncle, who was the cause to me of so much misery.

"Everything changed for the worse now. Hitherto my father had lived on hope—now he despaired. He took to drinking, which exalted his passions and debased his reason. This at times gave me a superiority over him—when tipsy, I could escape his blows—which yet, when sober, fell on me with double severity. But even the respite I gained through his inebriety afforded me no consolation—I felt at once humbled and indignant at the shame so brought on us. I, child as I was, expostulated with him—I was knocked down, and kicked from the room. Oh, what a world this appeared to me! a war of the weak with the strong—and how I despised everything except victory.

"Time wore on. My uncle's wife bore him in succession two girls. This was a respite. My father's spirits rose—but, fallen as he was, he could only celebrate his reawakened hopes by deeper potations and coarse jokes. The next offspring was a boy—he cost my father his life. Habits of drink had inflamed his blood—and his violence of temper made him nearly a maniac. On hearing of the birth of the heir, he drank to drown thought; wine was too slow a medicine; he quaffed deeply of brandy, and fell into a sleep, or rather torpor, from which he never after awoke. It was better so—he had spent everything—he was deeply in debt—he had lost all power of raising himself from the state of debasement into which he had fallen—the next day would have seen him in prison.

"I was taken in by my uncle. At first the peace and order of the household seemed to me paradise—the comfort and regularity of the meals was a sort of happy and perpetual miracle. My eye was no longer blasted by the sight of frightful excesses, nor my ear wounded by obstreperous shouts. I was no longer reviled—I no longer feared being felled to the ground—I was not any more obliged to obtain food by stratagem or by expostulations, which always ended by my being the victim of personal violence. The mere calm was balmy, and I fancied myself free, because I was no longer in a state of perpetual terror.

"But soon I felt the cold—and rigid atmosphere that, as far as regarded me, ruled this calm. No eye of love ever turned on me, no voice ever spoke a cheering word. I was there on sufferance, and was quickly deemed a troublesome inmate; while the order and regularity required of me, and the law passed that I was never to quit the house alone, became at last more tormenting than the precarious, but wild and precious liberty of my former life. My habits were bad enough; my father's vices had fostered my evil qualities—I had never learned to lie or cheat, for such was foreign to my nature; but I was rough, self-willed, lazy, and insolent. I have a feeling, such was my sense of bliss on first entering the circle of order and peace, that a very little kindness would have subdued my temper and awakened a desire to please. It was not tried. From the very first I was treated with a coldness to which a child is peculiarly sensitive; the servants, by enforcing the rules of the house, became first my tormentors, and then my enemies. I grew imperious and violent—complaint, reprehension, and punishment despoiled my paradise of its matin glow—and then I returned at once to my own bad self; I was disobedient and reckless; soon it was decreed that I was utterly intolerable, and I was sent to school.

"This, a boy's common fate, I had endured without a murmur, had it not been inflicted as a punishment, and I made over to my new tyrants, even in my own hearing, as a little blackguard, quite irreclaimable, and only to be kept in order by brute force. It is impossible to describe the effect of this declaration of my uncle—followed up by the master's recommendation to the usher to break my spirit if he could not bend it—had on my heart, which was bursting with a sense of injury, panting for freedom, and resolved not to be daunted by the menaces of the tyrants before me. I declared war with my whole soul against the world; I became all I had been painted; I was sullen, vindictive, desperate. I resolved to run away; I cared not what would befall me; I was nearly fourteen—I was strong, and could work—I could join a gang of gipsies, I could act their life singly, and, subsisting by nightly depredation, spend my days in liberty.

"It was at an hour when I was meditating flight that the master sent for me. I believed that some punishment was in preparation. I hesitated whether I should not instantly fly—a moment's thought told me that was impossible, and that I must obey. I went with a dogged air, and a determination to resist. I found my tyrant with a letter in his hand. 'I do not know what to do with you,' he said; 'I have a letter here from a relation, asking you to spend the day. You deserve no indulgence, but for this once you may go. Remember, any future permission depends upon your turning over an entirely new leaf. Go, sir; and be grateful to my lenity, if you can. Remember, you are to be home at nine.' I asked no questions—I did not know where I was to go; yet I left him without a word. I was sauntering back to the prison-yard which they called a playground, when I was told that there was a pony-chaise at the door ready to take me. My heart leaped at the word; I fancied that, by means of this conveyance, I could proceed on the first stage of my flight. The pony-carriage was of the humblest description; an old man drove. I got in, and away we trotted, the little cob that drew it going much faster than his looks gave warrant. The driver was deaf—I was sullen—not a word did we exchange. My plan was, that he should take me to the farthest point he intended, and then that I should leap out and take to my heels. As we proceeded, however, my rebel fit somewhat subsided. We left the town in which the school was situated, and the dreary, dusty roads I was accustomed to perambulate under the superintendence of the ushers. We entered shady lanes and umbrageous groves; we perceived extensive prospects, and saw the winding of romantic streams; a curtain seemed drawn from before the scenes of nature; and my spirits rose as I gazed on new objects, and saw earth spread wide and free around. At first this only animated me to a keener resolve to fly; but, as we went on, a vague sentiment possessed my soul. The skylarks winged up to heaven, and the swallows skimmed the green earth; I felt happy because nature was gay, and all things free and at peace. We turned from a lane redolent with honeysuckle into a little wood, whose short thick turf was interspersed with moss and starred with flowers. Just as we emerged I saw a little railing, a rustic green gate, and a cottage clustered over with woodbine and jessamine, standing secluded among, yet peeping out from the overshadowing trees. A little peasant boy threw open the gate, and we drove up to the cottage door.

"At a low window which opened on the lawn, in a large arm-chair, sat a lady, evidently marked by ill health, yet with something so gentle and unearthly in her appearance as at once to attract and please. Her complexion had faded into whiteness—her hair was nearly silver, yet not a grizzly grayish white, but silken still in its change; her dress was also white—and there was something of a withered look about her—redeemed by a soft, but bright gray eye, and more by the sweetest smile in the world, which she wore, as, rising from her chair, she embraced me, exclaiming, 'I know you from your likeness to your mother—dear, dear Rupert.'

"That name of itself touched a chord which for many years had been mine. My mother had called me by that name; so indeed had my father, when any momentary softness of feeling allowed him to give me any other appellation except 'You sir!' 'You dog, you!' My uncle, after whom I was also called John, chose to drop what he called a silly, romantic name; and in his house, and in his letters, I was always John. Rupert breathed of a dear home and my mother's kiss; and I looked inquiringly on her who gave it me, when my attention was attracted, riveted by the vision of a lovely girl, who had glided in from another room, and stood near us, radiant in youth and beauty. She was, indeed, supremely lovely—exuberant in all the charms of girlhood—and her beauty was enhanced by the very contrast to the pale lady by whom she stood—an houri she seemed, standing by a disimbodied spirit—black, soft, large eyes, overpowering in their lustre, and yet more so from the soul that dwelt within—a cherub look—a fairy form; with a complexion and shape that spoke of health and joy. What could it mean? Who could she be? And who was she who knew my name? It was an enigma, but one full of promise to me, who had so long been exiled from the charities of life; and who, 'as the hart panteth for the water brooks,' panted for love."

# CHAPTER XXVII

"After a little explanation, I discovered who my new friends were. The lady and my mother were remotely related; but they had been educated together, and separated only when they married. My mother's death had prevented my knowing that such a relation existed; far less that she took the warmest interest in the son of her earliest friend. Mrs. Rivers had been the poorer of the two, and for a long time considered that her childhood's companion was moving in an elevated sphere of life, while she had married a lieutenant in the navy; and while he was away, attending the duties of his profession, she lived in retirement and economy, in the rustic, low-roofed, yet picturesque and secluded cottage, whose leaf-shrouded casements and flowery lawn even now are before me, and speak of peace. I never call to mind that abode of tranquillity without associating it with the poet's wish:—

'Mine be a cot beside the hill—
A beehive's hum shall sooth my ear;
A willowy brook, that turns a mill,
With many a fall shall linger near.'

To any one who fully understands and appreciates the peculiar beauties of England—who knows how much elegance, content, and knowledge can be sheltered under such a roof, these lines must ever, I think, as to me, have a music of their own, and, unpretending as they are, breathe the very soul of happiness. In this imbowered cot, near which a clear stream murmured—which was clustered over by a thousand odoriferous parasites—which stood in the seclusion of a beech wood—there dwelt something more endearing even than all this—and one glance at the only daughter of Mrs. Rivers served to disclose that an angel dwelt in the paradise.

"Alithea Rivers—there is music, and smiles, and tears—a whole life of happiness—and moments of intensest transport in the sound. Her beauty was radiant; her dark eastern eye, shaded by the veined and darkly-fringed lid, beamed with a soft but penetrating fire; her face of a perfect oval, and lips which were wreathed into a thousand smiles, or softly and silently parted, seemed the home of every tender and poetic expression which one longed to hear them breathe forth; her brow clear as day; her swan throat and symmetrical and fairy-like form disclosed a perfection of loveliness, that the youngest and least susceptible must have felt, even if they did not acknowledge.

"She had two qualities which I have never seen equalled separately, but which, united in her, formed a spell no one could resist—the most acute sensitiveness to joy or grief in her own person, and the most lively sympathy with these feelings in others. I have seen her so enter heart and soul into the sentiments of one in whom she was interested, that her whole being took the colour of their mood; and her very features and complexion appeared to alter in unison with theirs. Her temper was never ruffled; she could not be angry; she grieved too deeply for those who did wrong; but she could be glad; and never have I seen joy, the very sunshine of the soul, so cloudlessly expressed as in her countenance. She could subdue the stoutest heart by a look—a word; and were she ever wrong herself, a sincere acknowledgment, an ingenuous shame—grief to have offended, and eagerness to make reparation, turned her very error into a virtue. Her spirits were high, even to wildness; but, at their height, tempered by such thought for others, such inbred feminine softness, that her most exuberant gayety resembled heart-cheering music, and made each bosom respond. All, everything loved her; her mother idolized her; each bird of the grove knew her; and I felt sure that the very flowers she tended were conscious of, and rejoiced in, her presence.

"Since my birth—or at least since I had lost my mother in early infancy, my path had been cast upon thorns and brambles—blows and stripes, cold neglect, reprehension, and debasing slavery; to such was I doomed. I had longed for something to love—and in the desire to possess something whose affections were my own, I had secreted at school a little nest of field mice on which I tended; but human being there was none who marked me, except to revile, and my proud heart rose in indignation against them. Mrs. Rivers had heard a sad story of my obduracy, my indolence, my violence; she had expected to see a savage, but my likeness to my mother won her heart at once, and the affection I met transformed me at once into something worthy of her. I had been told I was a reprobate till I half believed. I felt that there was war between me and my tyrants, and I was desirous to make them suffer even as they made me. I read in books of the charities of life—and the very words seemed only a portion of that vast system of imposture with which the strong oppressed the weak. I did not believe in love or beauty; or if ever my heart opened to it, it was to view it in external nature, and to wonder how all of perceptive and sentient in this wondrous fabric of the universe was instinct with injury and wrong.

"Mrs. Rivers was a woman of feeling and sense. She drew me out—she dived into the secrets of my heart; for my mother's sake she loved me, and she saw that to implant sentiments of affection was to redeem a character not ungenerous, and far, far from cold—whose evil passions had been fostered as in a hotbed, and whose better propensities were nipped in the bud. She strove to awaken my susceptibility to kindness, by lavishing a thousand marks of favour. She called me her son—her friend; she taught me to look upon her regard as a possession of which nothing could deprive me, and to consider herself and her daughter as near and dear ties that could not be rent away. She imparted happiness, she awoke gratitude, and made me in my innermost heart swear to deserve her favour.

"I now entered on a new state of being, and one of which I had formed no previous idea. I believed that the wish to please one who was dear to me would render every task easy; that I did wrong merely from caprice and revenge, and that if I chose, I could with my finger stem and direct the tide of my passions. I was astonished to find that I could not even bend my mind to attention—and I was angry with myself, when I felt my breast boiling with tumultuous rage, when I promised myself to be meek, enduring, and gentle. My endeavours to conquer these evil habits were indeed arduous. I forced myself by fits and starts to study sedulously—I yielded obedience to our school laws; I taxed myself to bear with patience the injustice and impertinence of the ushers, and the undisguised tyranny of the master. But I could not for ever string myself to this pitch. Meanness, and falsehood, and injustice again and again awoke the tiger in me. I am not going to narrate my boyhood's wrongs; I was doomed. Sent to school with a bad character, which at first I had taken pains to deserve, and afterward doing right in my own way, and still holding myself aloof from all, scorning their praise, and untouched by their censure, I gained no approbation, and was deemed a dangerous savage, whose nails must be kept close pared, and whose limbs were still to be fettered, lest he should rend his keepers.

"From such a scene I turned, each Sunday morning, my willing steps to the cottage of Mrs. Rivers. There was something fascinating to me in the very peculiarities of her appearance. Ill health had brought premature age upon her person—but her mind was as active and young—her feelings as warm as ever. She could only stand for a few minutes, and could not unassisted walk across the room—she took hardly any nourishment, and looked, as I have said, more like a spirit than a woman. Thus deprived of every outward resource, her mind acquired, from habits of reflection and resignation, aided by judicious reading, a penetration and delicacy quite unequalled. There was a philosophical truth in all her remarks, adorned by a feminine tact and extreme warmth of heart, that rendered her as admirable as she was endearing. Sometimes she suffered great pain, but, for the most part, her malady, which was connected with the spine, had only the effect of extreme weakness, and at the same time of rendering her sensations acute and delicate. The odour of flowers, the balmy air of morning, the evening breeze almost intoxicated her with delight; any dissonant sound appeared to shatter her—peace was within, and she coveted peace around; and it was her dearest pleasure when we—I and her lovely daughter—were at her feet, she playing with the sunny ringlets of Alithea's hair, and I listening, with a thirst for knowledge—and ardour to be taught; while she with eloquence mild and cheering, full of love and wisdom, charmed our attentive ears, and caused us to hang on all she said as on the oracles of a divinity.

"At times we left her, and Alithea and I wandered through the woods and over the hills; our talk was inexhaustible, now canvassing some observation of her mother, now pouring out our own youthful bright ideas, and enjoying the breezes and the waterfalls, and every sight of nature, with a rapture unspeakable. When we came to rugged uplands, or some swollen brook, I carried my young companion over in my arms; I sheltered her with my body from the storms that, sometimes overtook us. I was her protector and her stay; and the very office filled me with pride and joy. When fatigued by our rambles, we returned home, bringing garlands of wild flowers for the invalid, whose wisdom we revered, whose maternal tenderness was our joy; and yet, whose weakness made her, in some degree, dependant on us, and gave the form of a voluntary tribute to the attentions we delighted to pay her.

"Oh, had I never returned to school, this life had been a foretaste of heaven! but there I returned, and there again I found rebuke, injustice, my evil passions, and the fiends who tormented me. How my heart revolted from the contrast! with what inconceivable struggles I tried to subdue my hatred, to be as charitable and forgiving as Mrs. Rivers implored me to be; but my tormentors had the art of rousing the savage again, and, despite good resolves, despite my very pride, which urged me merely to despise, I was again violent and rebellious; again punished, again vowing revenge, and longing to obtain it. I cannot imagine—even the wild passions of my after life do not disclose—more violent struggles than those I went through. I returned from my friends, my heart stored with affectionate sentiments and good intentions; my brow was smooth, my mind unruffled; my whole soul set upon at once commanding myself, and proving to my tyrants that they could not disturb the sort of heavenly calm with which I was penetrated.

"On such a day, and feeling thus, I came back one evening from the cottage. I was met by one of the ushers, who, in a furious voice, demanded the key of my room, threatening me with punishment if I ever dared lock it again. This was a sore point; my little family of mice had their warm nest in my room, and I knew that they would be torn from me if the animal before me penetrated into my sanctuary before I could get in to hide them; but the fellow had learned from the maids that I had some pets, and was resolute to discover them. I cannot dwell on the puerile yet hideous minutiæ of such a scene; the loud voice, the blow, the key torn from me, the roar of malice with which my pets were hailed, the call for the cat. My blood ran cold; some slave—among boys even there are slaves—threw into the room the tiger animal; the usher showed her prey; but before she could spring I caught her up, and whirled her out of the window The usher gave me a blow with a stick; I was a well-grown boy, and a match for him unarmed; he struck me on the head, and then drew out a knife, that he might himself commence the butcher's work on my favourites: stunned by the blow, but casting aside all the cherished calm I had hitherto maintained, my blood boiling, my whole frame convulsed with passion, I sprung on him. We both fell on the ground, his knife was in hand, open; in our struggle I seized the weapon, and the fellow got cut in the head—of course I inflicted the wound; but had, neither before nor at that time, the intention; our struggle was furious; we were both in a state of phrensy, and an open knife at such a moment can hardly fail to do injury; I saw the blood pouring from his temple, and his efforts slacken. I jumped up, called furiously for help, and when the servants and boys rushed into the room, I made my escape. I leaped from the window, high as it was, and alighted, almost by a miracle, unhurt on the turf below; I made my way with all speed across the fields. Methought the guilt of murder was on my soul, and yet I felt exultation that at last I, a boy, had brought upon the head of my foe some of the tortures he had so often inflicted upon me. By this desperate act I believed that I had severed the cords that bound me to the vilest servitude. I knew not but that houseless want would be my reward, but I felt light as air and free as a bird.

"Instinctively my steps took the direction of my beloved cottage; yet I dared not enter it. A few hours ago I had left it in a pure and generous frame of mind. I called to mind the conversation of the evening before, the gentle eloquence of Mrs. Rivers, inculcating those lessons of mild forbearance and lofty self-command which had filled me with generous resolve; and how was I to return?—my hands died in blood.

"I hid myself in the thicket near her house, sometimes I stole near it; then, as I heard voices, I retreated farther into the wild part of the wood. Night came on at last, and that night I slept under a tree, but at a short distance from the cottage.

"The cool morning air woke me; and I began seriously to consider my situation; destitute of friends and money, whither should I direct my steps? I was resolved never to return to my school. I was nearly sixteen; I was tall and athletic in my frame, though still a mere boy in my thoughts and pursuits; still, I told myself that, such as I, many a stripling was cast upon the world, and that I ought to summon courage, and to show my tyrants that I could exist independent of them. My determination was to enlist as a soldier; I believed that I should so distinguish myself by my valour as speedily to become a great man. I saw myself singled out by the generals, applauded, honoured, and rewarded. I fancied my return, and how proudly I should present myself before Alithea, having carved out my own fortune, and become all that her sweet mother entreated me to be—brave, generous, and true. But could I put my scheme in execution without seeing my young companion again? Oh, no! my heart, my whole soul led me to her side, to demand her sympathy, to ask her prayers, to bid her never forget me; at the same time that I dreaded seeing her mother, for I feared her lessons of wisdom. I felt sure, I knew not why, that she would wholly disapprove of my design.

"I tore a leaf from my pocketbook, and, with the pencil, implored Alithea to meet me in the wood, whence I resolved not to stir till I should see her. But how was I to convey my paper without the knowledge of her mother? or being seen by the servants? I hovered about all day; it was not till nightfall that I ventured near, and, knowing well the casement of her room, I wrapped my letter round a stone, and threw it in. Then I retreated speedily.

"It was night again; I had not eaten for twenty-four hours; I knew not when Alithea could come to me, but I resolved not to move from the spot I had designated till she came. I hunted for a few berries, and a turnip that had fallen from a cart was as the manna of the desert. For a short half hour it stilled the gnawings of my appetite, and then I lay down unable to sleep. Eying the stars through the leafy boughs above, thinking alternately of a prisoner deserted by his jailer, and starved to death, while at each moment he fancied the far step approaching, and the key turning in the lock; and then, again, of feasts, of a paradise of fruits, of the simple, cheerful repasts at the cottage, which, for many a long year, I was destined never again to partake of.

"It was midnight; the air was still, not a leaf moved; sometimes I believed I dosed; but I had a sense of being awake always present to my mind; the hours seemed changed to eternity. I began suddenly to think I was dying; I thought I never should see the morrow's sun. Alithea would come, but her friend would not answer to her call; he would never speak to her more. At this moment I heard a rustling; was there some animal about? it drew near, it was steps; a white figure appeared between the trunks of the trees; again I thought it was a dream, till the dearest of all voices spoke my name, the loveliest and kindest face in the world bent over me; my cold, clammy hand was taken in hers, so soft and warm. I started up, I threw my arms around her, I pressed her to my bosom. She had found my note on retiring for the night; fearful of disobeying my injunctions of secrecy, she had waited till all was at rest before she stole out to me; and now, with all the thoughtfulness that characterized her, when another's wants and sufferings were in question, she brought food with her, and a large cloak to wrap my shivering limbs. She sat beside me as I ate, smiling through her tears; no reproach fell from her lips, it was only joy to see me, and expressions of kind encouragement.

"I dwell too much on these days; my tale grows long, and I must abridge the dear recollections of those moments of innocence and happiness. Alithea easily persuaded me to see her mother, and Mrs. Rivers received me as a mother would a son who has been in danger of death, and is recovering. I saw only smiles, I heard only congratulations. I wondered where the misery and despair which gathered so thickly around me had flown—no vestige remained; the sun shone unclouded on my soul.

"I asked no questions, I remained passive; I felt that something was being done for me, but I did not inquire what. Each day I spent several hours in study, so to reward the kindness of my indulgent friend. Each day I listened to her gentle converse, and wandered with Alithea over hill and dale, and poured into her ear my resolutions to become great and good. Surely in this world there are no aspirations so noble, pure, and godlike as those breathed by an enthusiastic boy, who dreams of love and virtue, and who is still guarded by childlike innocence.

"Mrs. Rivers, meanwhile, was in correspondence with my uncle, and, by a fortunate coincidence, a cadetship long sought by him was presented at this moment, and I was removed to the East Indian military college. Before I went, my maternal friend spoke with all the fervour of affection of my errors, my duties, the expectation she had that I should show myself worthy of the hopes she entertained of me. I promised to her and to Alithea—I vowed to become all they wished; my bosom swelled with generous ambition and ardent gratitude; the drama of life, methought, was unrolling before me—the scene on which I was to act appeared resplendent in fairy and gorgeous colours; neither vanity nor pride swelled me up; but a desire to prove myself worthy of those adored beings who were all the world to me, who had saved me from myself, to restore me to the pure and happy shelter of their hearts. Can it be wondered that, from that day to the present hour, they have seemed to me portions of heaven incarnate upon earth?—that I have prized the thought of them as a rich inheritance? And how did I repay? Cold, wan figure of the dead! reproach me not thus with your closed eyes, and the dank strings of your wet clinging hair. Give me space to breathe, that I may record your vindication and my crime.

"I was placed at the military college. Had I gone there at once, it had been well; but first I spent a month at my uncle's, where I was treated like a reprobate and a criminal. I tried to consider this but as a trial of my promises and good resolution to be gentle—to turn one cheek when the other was smitten. It is not for me to accuse others or defend myself; but yet I think that I had imbibed so much of the celestial virtues of my instructress, that, had I been treated with any kindness, my heart must have warmed towards my relatives; as it was, I left my uncle's, having made a vow never to sleep beneath his roof again.

"I reached the military college, and here I might fairly begin a new career. I exerted myself to study—to obey—to conciliate. The applause that followed my endeavours gave me a little pleasure; but when I wrote to Alithea and her mother, and felt no weight on my conscience, no drawback to my hope, that I was rendering myself worthy of them, then indeed my felicity was without alloy; and when my fiery temper kindled, when injustice and meanness caused my blood to boil, I thought of the mild, appealing look of Mrs. Rivers, and the dearer smiles of her daughter, and I suppressed every outward sign of anger and scorn.

"For two whole years I did not see these dear, dear friends, while I lived upon the thought of them—alas! when have I ceased to do that?—I wrote constantly and received letters. Those dictated by Mrs. Rivers, traced by her sweet daughter's hand, were full of all that generous benevolence, and enlightened sensibility which rendered her the very being to instruct and rule me; while the playful phrases of Alithea—her mention of the spots we had visited together, and history of all the slight events of her innocent life, breathed so truly of the abode of peace from which they emanated, that they carried the charm of a soft repose even to my restless spirit. A year passed, and then tidings of misery came. Mrs. Rivers was dying. Alithea wrote in despair—she was alone—her father distant. She implored my assistance— my presence. I did not hesitate. Her appeal came during the period that preceded an examination; I believed that it would be useless to ask leave to absent myself, and I resolved at once to go without permission. I wrote a letter to the master, mentioning that the sickness of a friend forced me to this step; and then, almost moneyless and on foot, I set out to cross the country. I do not record trivialties—I will not mention the physical sufferings of that journey, they were so much less than the agony of suspense I suffered, the fear that I should not find my maternal friend alive. Life burnt low indeed—when I, at last, stepped within the threshold of her sick chamber; yet she smiled when she saw me, and tried to hold out her hand—one already clasped that of Alithea. For hours we thus watched her, exchanging looks, not speech. Alithea, naturally impetuous, and even vehement, now controlled all sign of grief, except the expression of wo, that took all colour from her face, and clouded her brow with anguish. She knelt beside her mother—her lips glued to her hand, as if to the last to feel her pulse of life, and assure herself that she still existed. The room was darkened; a broken ray tinged the head of the mourner, while her mother lay in shadow—a shadow that seemed to deepen as the hue of death crept over her face; now and then she opened her eyes—now and then murmured inarticulately, and then she seemed to sleep. We neither moved—sometimes Alithea raised her head and looked on her mother's countenance, and then, seeing the change already operated, it drooped over the wan hand she held. Suddenly there was a slight sound—a slight convulsion in the fingers. I saw a shade darken over the face—something seemed to pass over, and then away—and all was marble still—and the lips, wreathed into a smile, became fixed and breathless. Alithea started up, uttered a shriek, and threw herself on her mother's body—such name I give—the blameless soul was gone for ever.

"It was my task to console the miserable daughter; and such was the angelic softness of Alithea's disposition, that when the first burst of grief was over, she yielded to be consoled. There was no hardness in her regrets. She collected every relic, surrounded herself with every object that might keep alive the memory of her parent. She talked of her continually; and together we spoke of her virtues, her wisdom, her ardent affection, and felt a thrilling, trembling pleasure in recalling every act and word that most displayed her excellence. As we were thus employed, I could contemplate and remark the change the interval of my absence had operated in the beautiful girl—she had sprung into womanhood; her figure was surrounded by a thousand graces; a tender charm was diffused over each lineament and motion that intoxicated me with delight. Before I loved—now I revered her; her mother's angelic essence seemed united to hers, forming two in one. The sentiments these beings had divided were now concentrated in her; and added to this, a breathless adoration, a heart's devotion, which still even now dwells beside her grave, and hallows every memory that remains.

"The cold tomb held the gentle form of Mrs. Rivers: each day we visited it, and each day we collected fresh memorials, and exhausted ourselves in talk concerning the lost one. Immediately on my arrival I had written to my uncle, and the cause of my rash act pleading my excuse, it was visited less severely than I expected; I was told that it was well that I displayed affection and gratitude towards a too indulgent friend, though my depravity betrayed itself in the manner even in which I fulfilled a duty. I was bid at once return to the college—after a fortnight had passed I obeyed; and now I lived on Alithea's letters, which breathed only her eloquent regrets— already my own dream of life was formed to be for ever her protector, her friend, her servant, her all that she could deign to make me; to devote myself day after day, year after year, through all my life to her only. While with her, oppressed by grief as we both were, I did not understand my own sensations, and the burning of my heart, which opened as a volcano when I heard her only speak my name, or felt the touch of her soft hand. But, returned to college, a veil fell from my eyes. I knew that I loved her, I hailed the discovery with transport; I hugged to my bosom the idea that she was the first and last being to awaken the tumultuous sensations that took away my breath, dimmed my eyes, and dissolved me into tenderness.

"Soon after her mother's death she was placed as a parlour boarder at a school. I saw her once there, but I did not see her alone. I could not speak—I could only gaze on her unexampled loveliness; nor, strange to say, did I wish to disclose the passion that agitated me: she was so young, so confiding, so innocent, I wished to be but as a brother to her, for I had a sort of restless presentiment that distance and reserve would ensue on my disclosing my other feeling. In fact, I was a mere boy; I knew myself to be a friendless one and I desired time and consideration, and the fortunate moment to occur, before I exchanged our present guileless, but warm and tender attachment, for the hopes and throes of a passion which demands a future, and is therefore full of peril. True, when I left her I reproached myself for my cowardice; but I would not write, and deferred, till I saw her, all explanation of my feelings.

"Some months after, the time arrived when I was to embark for India. Captain Rivers had returned, and inhabited the beloved cottage, and Alithea dwelt with him. I went to see her previous to my departure. My soul was in tumults: I desired to take her with me, but that was impossible; and yet to leave her thus, and go into a far and long exile away from her, was too frightful. I could not believe that I could exist without the near hope and expectation of seeing her—without that constant mingling of hearts which made her life-blood but as a portion of my own. My resolution was easily made to claim her as mine, my betrothed, my future bride; and I had a vague notion that, if I were accepted, Captain Rivers would form some plan to prevent my going to India, or to bring me back speedily. I arrived at the cottage, and the first sight of her father was painful to me. He was rough and uncouth; and though proud of his daughter, yet treated her with little of that deference to which she had a right even from him—the more reason, I thought, to make her mine; and that very evening I expressed my desire to Captain Rivers: a horselaugh was the reply; he treated me partly as a mad boy, partly as an impertinent beggar. My passions were roused, my indignation burst all the fetters I sought to throw over it; I answered haughtily—insolently—our words were loud and rude; I laughed at his menaces and scoffed at his authority. I retorted scorn with scorn, till the fiery old sailor was provoked to knock me down. In all this I thought not of him in the sacred character of Alithea's father—I knew but one parent for her; she had, as it were, joined us by making us companions and friends—both children of her heart; she was gone, and the rude tyrant who usurped her place excited only detestation and loathing, from the insolence of his pretensions. Still, when he struck me, his age and his infirmities—for he was lame—prevented my returning the blow. I rose, and folding my arms, and looking at him with a smile of ineffable contempt, I said, 'Poor, miserable man! do you think to degrade me by a blow? but for pity, I could return it so that you would never lift up your head again from that floor—I spare you—farewell. You have taught me one lesson—I will die rather than leave Alithea in the hands of a ruffian, such as you.' With these words I turned on my heel, and walked out of the house.

"I repaired to a neighbouring public house, and wrote to Alithea, asking, demanding an interview; I claimed it in her mother's name. Her answer came, it was wetted with her tears—dear gentle being!—so alien was her nature from all strife, that the very idea of contention shook her delicate frame, and seemed almost to unhinge her reason. She respected her father, and she loved me with an affection nourished by long companionship and sacred associations. She promised to meet me if I would abstain from again seeing her father.

"In the same wood, and at the same midnight hour as when before she came to bring assistance and consolation to the outcast boy three years before, I saw her again, and for the last time, before I left England. Alithea had one fault, if such name may be given to a delicacy of structure that rendered every clash of human passion terrifying. In physical danger she could show herself a heroine; but awaken her terror of moral evil, and she was hurried away beyond all self-command by spasms of fear. Thus, as she came now clandestinely, under the cover of night, her father's denunciations still sounding in her ears—the friend of her youth banished—going away for ever; and that departure disturbed by strife, her reason almost forsook her—she was bewildered—clinging to me with tears—yet fearful at every minute of discovery. It was a parting of anguish. She did not feel the passion that ruled my bosom. Hers was a gentler, sisterly feeling; yet not the less intwined with the principles of her being, and necessary to her existence. She lavished caresses and words of endearment on me: she could not tear herself away; yet she rejected firmly every idea of disobedience to her father; and the burning expressions of my love found no echo in her bosom.

"Thus we parted; and a few days afterward I was on the wide sea, sailing for my distant bourn. At first I had felt disappointed and angry; but soon imagination shed radiance over what had seemed chilly and dim. I felt her dear head repose on my heart; I saw her bright eyes overbrimming with tears; and heard her sweet voice repeat again and again her vow never to forget her brother, her more than brother, her only friend; the only being left her to love. No wonder that, during the various changes of a long voyage— during reveries indulged endlessly through calm nights, and the mightier emotions awakened by storm and danger, that the memory of this affection grew into a conviction that I was loved, and a belief that she was mine for ever.

"I am not writing my life; and, but for the wish to appear less criminal in my dear child's eyes, I had not written a word of the foregone pages, but leaped at once to the mere facts that justify poor Alithea, and tell the tragic story of her death. Years have passed, and oblivion has swept away all memory of the events of which I speak. Who recollects the wise, white lady of the secluded cot, and her houri daughter? This heart alone; there they live enshrined. My dreams call up their forms. I visit them in my solitary reveries. I try to forget the ensuing years, and to become the heedless half-savage boy who listened with wonder, yet conviction, to lessons of virtue; and to call back the melting of the heart which the wise lady's words produced, and the bounding, wild joy I felt beside her child. If there is a hell, it need no other torment but memory to call back such scenes as these, and bid me remember the destruction that ensued.

"I remained ten years in India, an officer in a regiment of the company's cavalry. I saw a good deal of service; went through much suffering; and doing my duty on the field of battle, or at the hour of attack, I gained that approbation in the field which I lost when in quarters by a sort of systematized insubordination, which was a part of my untameable nature. In action even I went beyond my orders—however, that was forgiven; but when in quarters, I took part with the weak, and showed contempt for the powerful. I was looked upon as dangerous; and the more so, that the violence of my temper often made my manner in a high degree reprehensible. I attached myself to several natives; that was a misdemeanor. I strove to inculcate European tastes and spirit, enlightened views, and liberal policy, to one or two native princes, whom, from some ill luck, the English governors wished to keep in ignorance and darkness. I was for ever entangled in the intimacy, and driven to try to serve the oppressed; while the affection I excited was considered disaffection on my part to the rulers. Sometimes also I met with ingratitude and treachery: my actions were misrepresented, either by prejudice or malice; and my situation, of a subordinate officer, without fortune, gave to the influence I acquired, through learning the language and respecting the habits and feelings of the natives, an air of something so inexplicable, as might, in the dark ages, have been attributed to witchcraft, and in these enlightened times was considered a tendency to the most dangerous intrigues. Having saved an old rajah's life, and having taken great pains to extricate him from a difficulty in which the Europeans had purposely entangled him, it became rumoured that I aspired to succeed to a native principality, and I was peremptorily ordered off to another station. My views were in diametrical opposition to the then Indian government. My conversation was heedless—my youthful imagination exalted by native magnificence; I own I often dreamed of the practicability of driving the merchant sovereigns from Hindostan. There was, as is the essence of my character, much boyish folly joined to dangerous passion; all of which took the guise in my own heart of that high heroic adventure with which I longed to adorn my life. A subaltern in the company's service, I could never gain my Alithea, or do her the honour with which I longed to crown her. The acquisition of power, of influence, of station, would exalt me in her father's eyes—so much of what was selfish mingled in my conduct—but I was too young and impetuous to succeed. Those in power watched me narrowly. The elevation of a day was always followed by a quick transfer to an unknown and distant province.

"In all my wildest schemes the thought of Alithea reigned paramount. My only object was to prove myself worthy of her; and my only dream for the future was to make her mine for ever.

"A constancy of ten years, strung perpetually up to the height of passion, may appear improbable; yet it was so. It was my nature to hold an object with tenacious grasp—to show a proud contempt of obstacles—to resolve on ultimate triumph. Besides this, the idea of Alithea was so kneaded up and incorporate with my being, that my living heart must have been searched and anatomized to its core, before the portion belonging to her could have been divided from the rest. I disdained the thought of every other woman. It was my pride to look coldly on every charm, and to shut my heart against all but Alithea. During the first years of my residence in India, I often wrote to her, and pouring out my soul on paper, I conjured her to preserve herself for me. I told her how each solitary jungle or mountain ravine spoke to me of a secluded home with her; how every palace and gorgeous hall seemed yet a shrine too humble for her. The very soul of passion breathed along the lines I traced—they were such as an affianced lover would have written, pure in their tenderness; but heartfelt, penetrating, and eloquent; they were my dearest comfort. After long, wearisome marches—after the dangers of an assault or a skirmish—after a day spent among the sick or dying—in the midst of many disappointments and harassing cares—during the storms of pride and the languor of despair, it was my consolation to fly to her image and to recall the tender happiness of reunion—to endeavour to convey to her how she was my hope and aim—my fountain in the desert—the shadowy tree to shelter me from the burning sun—the soft breeze to refresh me—the angelic visitor to the unfortunate martyr. Not one of these letters ever reached her—her father destroyed them all: on his head be the crime and the remorse of his daughter's death! Fool and coward! would I shift to other shoulders the heavy weight? No! no! crime and remorse still link me to her. Let them eat into my frame fiery torture; they are better than forgetfulness!

"I had two hopes in India: one was, to raise myself to such a station as would render me worthy of Alithea in the eyes of Captain Rivers; the other, to return to England—to find change there—to find love in her heart—and to move her to quit all for me. By turns these two dreams reigned over me; I indulged in them with complacency—I returned to them with ardour—I nourished them with perseverance. I never saw a young Indian mother with her infant, but my soul dissolved in tender fancies of domestic union and bliss with Alithea. There was something in her soft dark eye, and in the turn of her countenance, purely eastern; and many a lovely, half-veiled face I could have taken for hers; many a slight, symmetrical figure, round, elegant, and delicate, seemed her own, as, with elastic, undulating motion, they passed on their way to temple or feast. I cultivated all these fancies; they nourished my fidelity, and made the thought of her the absolute law of my life.

"Ten years passed, and then news came that altered my whole situation. My uncle and his only son died; the family estate devolved on me. I was rich and free. Rich in my own eyes, and in the eyes of all to whom competence is wealth. I felt sure that, with this inheritance, Captain Rivers would not disdain me for his child. I gave up my commission immediately, and returned to England.

"England and Alithea! How balmy, how ineffably sweet was the idea of once more beholding the rural spot where she resided; of treading the woodland paths with her—of visiting her dear mother's grave—of renewing our old associations, and knitting our destinies inextricably in one. It was a voyage of bliss. I longed for its conclusion; but feeling that a pathway was stretched across the ocean, leading even into her very presence, I blessed each wave or tract of azure sea we passed over. The limitless Atlantic was my road to her, and became glorified as the vision of the Hebrew shepherd boy; and yet loved with the same homefelt sweetness as that with which I used to regard the lime-tree walk that led to her garden-gate. I forgot the years that had elapsed since we met; it was with difficulty that I forced my imagination to remember that I should not find her pale mother beside her to sanctify our union."

# CHAPTER XXVIII

"On landing in England, I at once set off to the far northern county where she resided. I arrived at the well-known village; all looked the same; I recognised the cottages and their flower-gardens, and even some of the elder inhabitants looking, methought, no older than when I left them. My heart hailed my return home with rapture, and I quickened my steps towards the cottage. It was shut up and abandoned. This was the first check my sanguine spirit had met. Hitherto I had not pronounced her name or asked a question—I longed to return, as from a walk, and to find all things as I had left it. Living in a dream, I had not considered the chances and the storms, or even the mere changes, of the seasons of life.

"My pen lags in its task—I dilate on things best hurried over, yet they serve as a screen between me and fate. A few inquiries revealed the truth. Captain Rivers was dead—his daughter married. I had lived in a fool's paradise. None of the obstacles existed that I expected to meet and conquer, but in their stead a fourfold brazen door had risen, locked, barred, and guarded, and I could not even shake a hinge, or put back a bolt.

"I hurried from the fatal spot; it became a hell to me. And oh, to think that I had lived in vain—vainly dreamed of the angel of my idolatry, vainly hoped—and most vainly loved; called her mine when another held her, sold myself to perpetual slavery to her shadow, while her living image enriched the shrine of another's home! The tempest that shook my soul did not permit me to give form, or, indeed, to dwell consecutively on such desolating thoughts. As a man who arrives from a pleasant journey, and turns the corner where he expects to view the dwelling in which repose his wife, his children—all dear to him—and when he gains the desired spot, beholds it smouldering in ashes, and is told that all are consumed, and that their bones lie beneath the ruins; thus was I—my imagination had created home, and bride, and fair being sprung from her side, who called me father, and one word defaced my whole future life and widowed me for ever.

"Now began that chain of incidents that led to a deed I had not thought of. Incidents or accidents; acts, done I know not why; nothing in themselves; but meeting, and kindled by the fiery spirit that raged in my bosom, they gave such direction to its ruinous powers as produced the tragedy for ever to be deplored.

"Bewildered and overwhelmed by the loss which to me had all the novelty and keenness of a disaster of yesterday, though I found that many years had gone by since, in reality, it was completed, I fled from the spot I had so fondly sought, and hurried up to London on no fixed errand, with no determined idea, yet vaguely desiring to do something. Scarcely arrived, I met a man whom I had known in India. He asked me to dine with him, and I complied; because to refuse would have required explanation, and the affirmative was more easily given. I did not mean to keep my engagement; yet when the hour came, so intolerable had I become to myself—so poignant and loathsome were my thoughts—that I went, so to lose for a few moments the present sense of ill. It was a bachelor's dinner, and there were, in addition to myself, three or four other guests—among them a Mr. Neville. From the moment this man opened his lips to speak, I took a violent dislike to him. He was, and always must have been, the man whom among ten thousand I should have marked out to abhor. He was cold, proud, and sarcastic, withal a decayed dandy, turned cynic—who, half despising himself, tried wholly to disdain his fellow-creatures. A man whose bosom never glowed with a generous emotion, and who took pride in the sagacity which enabled him to detect worms and corruption in the loveliness of virtue. A poor, mean-spirited fellow, despite his haughty outside; and then when he spoke of women, how base a thing he seemed! his disbelief in their excellence, his contemptuous pity, his insulting love, made my blood boil. To me there was something sacred in a woman's very shadow. Was she evil, I regarded her with the pious regret with which I might view a shrine desecrated by sacrilegious hands—the odour of sanctity still floated around the rifled altar; I never could regard them as mere fellow-creatures—they were beings of a better species, sometimes gone astray in the world's wilderness, but always elevated above the best among us. For Alithea's sake I respected every woman. How much good I knew of them! Generous, devoted, delicate— their very faults were but misdirected virtues; and this animal dared revile beings of whose very nature he could form no conception. A burden was lifted from my soul when he left us.

"'It is strange,' said our host, 'that Neville should indulge in this kind of talk; he is married to the most beautiful, and the best woman in the world. Much younger than himself, she yet performs her duties as a wife with steadiness and cheerfulness; lovely beyond her sex, she is without its weakness; to please some jealous freak of his, she has withdrawn herself from the world, and buried herself alive at his seat in the North. How she can endure an eternal tête-à-tête with that empty, conceited, and arrogant husband of hers is beyond any guessing.'

"I made some observation expressive of my abhorrence of Mr. Neville's character, and my friend continued—'Disagreeable and shallow as he is, one would have thought that the society of so superior, so perfect a woman, would reconcile him to her sex, but I verily believe he is jealous of her surpassing excellence; and that it is not so much a natural, and I might almost call it generous, fear of losing her affections, as a dislike of seeing her admired, and knowing that she is preferred to him, especially now that he absolutely looks an old fellow. Poor Alithea Rivers—hers is a hard fate!'

"I had a glass of wine in my hand; my convulsive grasp shivered the brittle thing, but I gave no other outward sign; before, I was miserable, I had lost all that made life dear; but to know that she was lost to herself, bound for life to a human brute, curdled my heart's blood, and spread an unnatural chilliness through my frame.

"What a sacrifice was there; a sacrifice of how much more than life, of the heart's sweetest feelings, when a spirit, sent to gladden the world, and cast one drop of celestial nectar into the bitterness of existence, was made garbage for that detested animal; from that moment, from the moment I felt assured that I had seen Alithea's husband, something departed from the world, such as I had once known it, never to return again. A sense of acquiescence in the decrees of Providence, of confidence in the benevolence and beauty of the universe, of pride, despite all my misfortunes, in being man, of pleasure in the loveliness of nature, all departed! I had lost her— that was nothing; it was my disaster, but did not injure the order and grace of the creation; she was, I fondly trusted, married to a better man than I; but, bound to that grovelling and loathsome type of the world's worst qualities, the devil usurped at once the throne of God, and life became a hell.

"'You are miserable, Alithea! you must be miserable! For you there is no sympathy, no mingling of hearts, no generous confidence in another's esteem and kindness, no indulgence in golden imaginations of the beauty of life. You are tied to a foul, corrupting corpse. You are cut off from the dear associations of the social hearth, from the dignified sense of having exchanged virgin purity for a sweeter and more valuable possession in another's heart; coldly and listlessly you look on the day which brings no hope to you, if, indeed, you do not rave and blaspheme in your despair. Oh! with me, the brother of your soul, your servant, lover, untiring friend, how differently had your lot been cast!'"

"I rushed from my friend's house; I entered no roof that night; my passions were awake, my fierce volcanic passions! Had I encountered Neville, I had assuredly murdered him; my soul was chaos, yet a tempestuous ray gave a dark light amid the storm; a glimmering, yet permanent irradiation mantled over the ruins among which I stood. I said to myself, 'I am mad, driven to desperation;' but, beneath this outward garb of my thought, I knew and recognised an interior form. I knew what I desired, what I intended, and what, though I tried to cheat myself into the belief that I wavered, I henceforth steadily pursued. There is, perhaps, no more dangerous mood of mind than when we doggedly pursue means, recklessly uncertain of their end.

"Thus was I led to the fatal hour; a life of love, and a sudden bereavement, with such a thing the instrument of my ruin! A contempt for the order of the universe, a stern, demoniacal braving of fate, because I would rule, and put that right which God had let go wrong. Oh, let me not again blaspheme. God made the stars, and the green earth, within whose bosom Alithea lies. She also is his, and I will believe, despite the hellish interference that tainted and deflowered her earthly life, that now she is with the source of all good, reaping the reward of her virtues, the compensation for her suffering. Else, why are we created! To crawl forth, to suffer and die? I cannot believe it. Spirit of the blessed, omnipotence did not form perfection to shatter and dissipate the elements like broken glass! But I rave and wander; Alithea still lives and suffers at the time of which I write, and I erecting myself into a providence, resolved to put that right which was wrong, and cure the world's misrule. From that moment I never paused to look back; I set my soul upon the cast, and I am here. And Alithea! her mysterious grave you shall now approach.

"Bent upon a dangerous purpose, fate led before me an instrument, without which I should have found it difficult to execute my plan. I got a letter from a man in great distress, asking for some small help; he was on the point of quitting England for America, and working his passage; slight assistance would be of inestimable benefit in furthering his plans. The petitioner followed his petition quickly, and was ushered in before me. I scrutinized his shrewd yet down-looking countenance; I scanned his supple yet uncertain carriage; I felt that he was a coward, yet knew he would tamper with roguery, in all safety, for a due reward. I had known the fellow in India; James Osborne was his name; he dabbled in various disreputable money transactions, both with natives and Englishmen, and at last, having excited the suspicion of government, got thrown into prison. He had then written to me, who was considered a sort of refuge for the destitute, and I went to see him. There was no great harm in the man; on the contrary, he was soft-hearted and humane; the infection of dishonesty, caught in bad company, and fostered in poverty, was his ruin; and he joined to this a strong desire to be respectable, if he could only contrive to subsist without double-dealing. I thought, that by extricating him from his embarrassments, and removing him from temptation, I might save him from ignominy; so I paid his passage to England; where he told me that he had friends and resources. But his old habits pursued him, and even now, though poverty was the alleged motive for his emigration, I saw that there was secret fear of legal pursuit for dishonest practices; he had been inveigled, he said, to lend his name to a transaction which turned out a knavish one. With all this, Osborne was not a villain, and scarcely a rogue; there was truth in what he said; he had always an aspiration for a better place in society, but he saw no way of attaining it except by money, and no way of gaining money except by cheating.

"I listened to his story. 'You are an incorrigible fellow,' said I. 'How can I give ear to your promises? Still I am willing to assist you. I am myself going to America; you shall accompany me.' By degrees I afterward explained the service I needed; yet I only half disclosed the truth. Osborne never knew the name or position of the lady who was to be my companion across the Atlantic. A man's notions of the conduct of others are always coloured by his own ruling passion. Osborne thought I was intent on carrying off an heiress.

"With this ally I proceeded to Cumberland—my mind more intent on the result of my schemes than their intermediate detail. I learned before I went that Mr. Neville was still in town. This was a golden opportunity, and I hastened to use it. I reached the spot that Alithea inhabited—I entered the outer gate of the demesne—I rode up to the avenue that led to the house—I was ushered into the room where I knew that I should find her. I summoned every power to calm the throbbing of my heart. I expected to find her changed; but when I saw her, I discovered no alteration. It was strange that so much of girlish appearance should remain. Her figure was light and airy; her rich clustering ringlets abundant as before; her face—it was Alithea! All herself! That soft, loving eye—that clear brow—those music-breathing lips—time had not harmed her—it was herself.

"She did not at once recognise me; the beardless stripling was become a weather-beaten, thought-worn man; but when I told her who I was—the name so long forgotten—never heard since last she spoke it, 'Rupert!' burst from her lips—it united our severed lives; and her look of rapture, her accent all breathless with joy, told me that her heart was still the same—ardent, affectionate, and true.

"We sat together, hand linked in hand, looking at each other with undisguised delight. At first, with satanic cunning, I assumed the brother's part. I questioned her concerning her fate—her feelings; and seeing that she was averse to confess the truth of her disappointed, joyless married state,

I led her back to passed days. I spoke of her dear mother. I said that often had the image of that pale, wise spirit checked, guided, and whispered sage lessons to me in my banishment. I recalled a thousand scenes of our childhood, when we wandered together—hand in hand—heart linked to heart—confiding every pain—avowing every wild or rebellious thought, or discussing the mighty secrets of nature and of fate, which to our young hearts were full of awe and mystery, and yet of beauty and joy. As I spoke, I examined her more narrowly. At first she had appeared to me the same; now I marked a difference. Her mouth, the home of smiles, had ever its sweet, benignant expression; but her eyes, there was a heaviness in the lids, a liquid melancholy in their gaze, which said that they were acquainted with tears; her cheeks, once round, peachlike, and downy, were not fallen, yet they had lost their rich fulness. She was more beautiful; there was more reflection, more sentiment in her face; but there was far, far less happiness. Before, smiles sprung up wherever she turned to gaze; now, an interest akin to pity and tears made the spectator's heart ache as he watched the turns of a countenance which was the faithful mirror of the truest heart that ever beat. Worse than this, there ever and anon shot across her face a look that seemed like fear. Oh, how unlike the trusting, dreadless Alithea!

"My talk of other days at first soothed, then excited, and threw her off her guard. By degrees I approached the object of all my talk, and drew her to speak of her father, and the motives that induced her marriage. My knowledge and vivid recollections of all that belonged to her made her unawares speak, as she had not done since we parted, the undisguised truth; and before she knew what she had said, I had led her to confess that she had never loved her husband; that she found no sympathy, and little kindness in him; that her life had been one of endurance of faults alien to her own temperament. Had I been more cautious, I had allowed this to pass off at first, and won her entire confidence before I laid bare my own thoughts; for all she said had never before been breathed into any living ear but mine. It was her principle to submit, and to hide her sense of her husband's defective disposition; and had I not, with a serpent's subtlety, glided on imperceptibly; had I not brought forward her mother's name, and the memory of childhood's cloudless years, she had been mute with me. But now I could contain myself no longer. I told her that I had seen the miserable being to whom she was linked. I uttered curses on the fate that had joined them together. She laid her hand on my arm, and looking in my face with confiding innocence, 'Hush, Rupert,' she said, 'you make me mean more than I would willingly have you think. He is not unkind; I have no right to complain; it is not in every man that we can find a brother's or a friend's heart. Neville does not understand these things; but he is my husband; as such I honour him.'

"I saw the internal feeling that led her to speak thus; I saw the delicate forbearance that filled her noble mind. She thought of her virgin faith plighted—long years spent at his side—her children—her fidelity, which, if it had ceased to cling to him, had never wandered, even in thought, to another; duties exemplarily fulfilled—earnest strivings to forget his worthlessness. All this honour for her own pure nature, she cheated herself into believing was honour paid to him. I resolved to tear the veil which her gentleness and sense of right had drawn before the truth, and I exclaimed, impetuously, 'Wrong yourself not so much, dear girl! do not fancy that your high soul can really bow down to baseness. You pay reverence to your own sense of duty; but you hate—you must hate that man.'

"She started, and her face and neck became died in blushes, proceeding half from anger at being urged beyond her wish, half from native modesty at hearing her husband thus spoken of. As for myself, I grew mad as I looked on her, and felt the sweet, transporting influences that gathered round; here indeed was the creature whom I had loved through so many years, who was mine in my dreams, whose faith and true affection I fancied I held for ever; and she was torn from me, given away, not to one who, like me, knew and felt her matchless excellence, but to a base-minded thing, from whom she must shrink as from an animal of another species. All that her soul contained of elevated thoughts and celestial aspirations, all of generous, high, and heroic that warmed her heart, what were they before a blind, creeping worm, who held a matchless jewel in his hand, and deemed it dross? He even could not understand, or share the more sober affections—mutual trust and mutual forbearance; the utterance of love, the caresses of tenderness, what were these to a wretch who saw baseness and deceit in the most lofty and pure feelings of a woman's heart?

"I expressed these thoughts, or rather, they burst from me. She interrupted me. 'I do not deny,' she said, 'for I know not how you have cheated me of my secret, but that repinings have at times entered my mind; and I have shed foolish tears, to think that the dreams of my girlhood were as a bright morning, quickly followed by a dim, cloudy day. But I have reproved myself for this discontent, and you do very wrong to revive it; the heart will rebel, but religion, and philosophy, and the very tears I shed, sooth its ruffled mood, and make me remember that we do not live to be happy, but to perform our duties; to fulfil mine is the aim of my life; teach me how to do that more completely, more entirely to resign myself, and you will be my benefactor. It is true that my husband does not understand the childish overflowings of my heart, which is too ready to seek its joys among the clouds; he does not dwell with rapture on the thoughts and sentiments which give me so much life and happiness—he is a stronger and sterner nature; a slower one also, I acknowledge, one less ready to sympathize and feel. But if I have in my intercourse with him regretted that lively, cheering interchange of sentiment which I enjoyed with you, you are now here to bestow it, and my life, hitherto defective, your return may render complete.'

"I laughed bitterly. 'Poor innocent bird,' I cried; 'think you at once to be free, and in a cage? at once to feel the fowler's grasp, and fly away to heaven? Alithea, you miserably deceive yourself; hitherto you have but half guessed the secrets of a base grovelling spirit—have you never seen your husband jealous?'

"She shuddered—and I saw a spasm of exquisite pain cloud her features as she averted her head from me, and the look of trembling fear I had before remarked crept over her. I was shocked to see so much of the slave had entered her soul. I told her this; I told her she was being degraded by the very duties which she was devoting herself, body and soul, to perform; I told her that she must be free; she looked wonderingly, but I continued. 'Is not the very name of liberty dear and exhilarating? does it not draw you irresistibly onward? is not the very thought of casting your heavy chains from off you full of new and inexpressible joy? Poor prisoner, do you not yearn to breathe without a fear? would you not with transport escape from your jailer to a home of love and freedom?'

"Hitherto she had fancied that I but regretted her sorrows as she did, and repined as she did over a fate whose real misery she alone could entirely feel; she repented having spoken so openly—yet she loved me for my unfeigned sympathy; but now she saw that something more was meant; she looked earnestly at me, as if to read my heart; she saw its wishes in my eyes, and shrunk from them as from a snake, as she exclaimed, 'Never, dear Rupert, speak thus to me again, or we must again part—I have a son.'

"The radiance of angelic love lighted up her face as she uttered these words; and then, my error and weakness being her strength, she resumed the self-possession she had lost during our previous conversation; with bewitching grace she held out her hand to me, and in a voice modulated by the soul of persuasion, said, 'Let us be friends, Rupert, such as we once were, brother and sister; I will not believe that you are returned only to pain and injure me—I am happy in my children—stay but a little, and you will see how foolish I have been to complain at all. You also will love my boy.'

"Would you not think that these words had sufficed to cure my madness and banish every guilty project? Had you seen her, her inimitable grace of attitude, the blushing, tender expression of her face, and her modest, earnest manner, a manner which spoke the maternal nature, such as Catholics imagine it, without a tincture of the wife, a girlish, yet enthusiastic rapture at the very thought of her child, you would have known that every scheme I meditated was riveted faster, every desire to make her my own for ever more fixed and eager. I went on to urge her, till I saw every feature give token of distress; and at last she suddenly left me, as if unable any longer to bear my pertinacity. She left me without a word, but I saw her face bathed in tears. I was indeed insane. These tears, which sprung from anguish of soul to think that her childhood's companion should thus show himself an injurer instead of a friend, I interpreted into signs of relenting—into a struggle with her heart."

# CHAPTER XXIX

"I called again the following morning, but she was denied to me; twice this happened. She feared me, I believed; and still more franticly I was driven to continue my persecutions. I wrote to her; she did not answer my letters. I entered the grounds of her house clandestinely; I lay in wait for her; I resolved to see her again. At length one afternoon I found her alone, walking and musing in the more solitary part of the park; I stood suddenly before her, and her first emotion was pleasure, so true was she to her affections, so constant to her hope that at last I should be persuaded not to pain her by a renewal of my former conversation. But I believed that I had a hold on her that I would not forego. When she offered to renew our childhood's compact of friendship, I asked her how that could be if she refused me her confidence; I asked how she could promise me happiness, whose every hope was blighted. I told her that it was my firm conviction that her mother had intended us for one another, that she had brought her up for me, given her to me, and that thus she was indeed mine. Her eyes flashed fire at this. 'My mother,' she said, 'brought me up for a higher purpose than even conducing to your happiness. She brought me up to fulfil my duties, to be a mother in my turn. I do not deny,' she continued, 'that I share in some sort my mother's fate, and am more maternal than wife-like; and as I fondly wish to resemble her in all her virtues, I will not repine at the circumstances that lead me rather to devote my existence to my children, than to be that most blessed creature, a happy wife—I do not ask for that happiness; I am contented with my lot; my very girlish, romantic repinings do not really make me unhappy.'

"'Nor your fears, nor his base jealousy, his selfishness, his narrow soul, and brutish violence? I know more than you think, Alithea—I read your heart—you must be miserable; submissive, yet tyrannized over; wedded to your duty, yet watched, suspected, accused. There are traces of tears on your cheeks, my poor girl; your neck is bowed by the yoke, your eyes have no longer the radiance of conscious rectitude, and yet you are innocent.'

"'God knows I am,' she replied, as a shower of tears fell from her eyes—but she was ashamed, and brushed them away—'I am, and will be, Rupert, though you would mislead me. Where, indeed, can I find a consciousness of rectitude, except in my heart? My husband mistrusts me, I acknowledge it—by torture you force the truth—he does not understand, and you would pervert me; in God and my own heart I put my trust, and I will never do that which my conscience tells me is wrong—and despite both I shall be happy. A mother is, in my eyes, a more sacred name than wife. My life is wrapped in my boy; in him I find blameless joy, though all the rest pierce my heart with poisoned arrows.'

"'You shall, sweet Alithea,' I cried, 'preserve him, and every other blessing. You were not born to inherit this maimed, poverty-stricken life, the widowed mother of an orphan child—such are you now; I will be a father to him for your sake, and many other joys will be yours, and the fondest, truest heart that ever warmed man's bosom shall be all your own. Alithea, you must not offer yourself up a living sacrifice to that base idol, but belong to one whose love, and honour, and eternal devotion merit you, though he possess no other claim. Let me save you from him, I ask no more.'

"I felt a tear, for many long years forgotten, steal down my cheek—my heart worshipped her excellence, and pity and grief mingled with my deep regrets; she saw how sincerely I was moved, and tried to comfort me. She wept also, for, despite her steadier thoughts, she knew the cruelty of her destiny, and I do believe her heart yearned to taste, once more before she died, the full joy of complete sympathy. But, if indeed her tears were partly shed for herself, yet she never wavered; she deplored my unhappiness, but she reproved my perversion of principle; she tried to awaken patience, piety, or philosophic fortitude—any of the noble virtues that might enable me to combat the passion by which I was enslaved.

"Time was forgotten as we thus talked with the same openness of heart as in former days, yet those hearts how saddened and wounded since then! I would not let her go: while the moon rose high, shedding its silvery light over the forest trees, and casting dark shadows on our path, still we indulged in what she deemed our last conference. As I must answer my crimes before God, I swear I could discern no wavering thought, no one idea that strayed to the forbidden ground, towards which I strove to lead her. She told me that she had intended not to see me again till her husband returned; she said that she must implore me not again to seek her in this way, or I should make her a prisoner in her house. I listened—I answered, I knew not what—I was more resolved than ever not to lose her—despite all, I still was mad enough to hope. She left me at last, hoping to have conquered, yet resolved not to see me again, she said, till her husband returned. This determination on her part was in absolute contradiction to what I resolved should be. I had decreed to see her again; nay, more, I would see her, not within the precincts of her home, where all spoke against me; but where she should be free, where, seeing nothing to remind her of the heavy yoke to which she bent her neck, I fondly dreamed I might induce her wholly to throw it aside. If it so pleased her, I would detain her but a few short hours, and restore her to her home in all liberty; but, could I induce her to assert her freedom, and follow me voluntarily—then—to think that possible, the earth reeled under me, and my passion gained strength from its very folly.

"I prepared all things for my plan; I went to Liverpool, and bought two fleet horses and a light foreign calèche suited to my purpose. Returning northward towards Dromore, I sought a solitary spot, for the scene of our last interview, or of the first hour of my lasting bliss. What more solitary than the wild and drear seashore of the south of Cumberland? Landward it is screened by a sublime back-ground of mountains; but in itself presenting to the view a wide extent of uninhabited sands, intersected by rivers which, when the tide is up, presents a dreary expanse of shallow water, and at ebb are left, except in the channels of the rivers, a barren extent of mud and marsh; the surrounding waste being variegated only by a line of sand-hills thrown up to the height of thirty or forty feet, shutting in the view from shore, while seaward no boat appeared ever to spread its sail on that lonely sea. On these sands, near the mouth of one of the rivers, there was a small hut deserted, but not in ruins; it was probably occasionally inhabited by guides who are used in this part of the country to show the track of the fords when the tide is full, and any deviation from the right path is attended by peril, the beds of the rivers being full of ruts and deep holes; that hut I selected as the spot where all should be determined. If she consented to accompany me, we would proceed rapidly forward to Liverpool, and embark for America; if she resolved to return, this spot was but five miles from her home, and I could easily lead her back without suspicion being excited. I was anxious to put my scheme in execution, as her husband was shortly expected.

"It seemed a feasible one. In my own heart I did not expect to induce her to forsake her home; but I might; and the very doubt maddened me. And if I did not, yet for a few hours to have her near me, not in any spot that called her detested husband master, but in the wide, free scenes of nature, the ocean, parent of all liberty, spread at our feet; the way easy to escape, no eye, no ear, to watch and spy out the uncontrolled and genuine emotions of her heart, or no hand to check our progress if she consented to follow. In this plan Osborne, whom I had left at the miserable town of Ravenglass—and who, indeed, had been the man to find and point out to me the solitary hut, was necessary. My explanation and directions to him were few and peremptory: he was to appear with the calèche, he acting as postillion, at a certain spot; the moment he saw me arrive, as soon as I had placed the lady who was to be my companion in the carriage, he was to put spurs to his horses, and not by any cry of hers, nor command of mine, nor interference of strangers, to be induced to stop till he reached the hut: there she should be free; till then I would have her a prisoner even beyond my own control, lest her entreaties should cheat me out of my resolves. Osborne looked frightened at some portion of these orders, but I glossed over any inconsistency; my bribe was high, and he submitted.

"At every step I took in this mad and guilty scheme, I became more resolved to carry it on. Here is my crime—here the tale of sin, I have to relate. The rest is disaster and endless remorse. What moved me to this height of insanity—what blinded me to the senseless as well as the unpardonable nature of my design, I cannot tell; except that, for years, I had lived in a dream, and waking in the real world, I refused to accommodate myself to its necessities, but resolved to bend its laws to my desires. I loved Alithea—I had loved her through years of absence; she was the wife of my reveries, my hopes, my heart. I could no more part with the thought of her as such, than with a consciousness of my own identity. To see her married and a mother, might be supposed capable of dissipating these fancies; far from it. Her presence, her beauty, the witchery of her eye, her heart-subduing voice, her sensibility, the perfection of her nature, which her inimitable loveliness only half expressed, but which reached my soul, through a sort of inner sense that acknowledged it with worship; all this added to my phrensy, and steeped me to the very lips in intoxication.

"What right had I to call this matchless creature mine? None! That I acknowledged—but that he, the man without a soul, the incarnate Belial, should claim her, was not to be endured. Mad as I was, I aver, and He who reads all hearts be now my testimony, that it was more my wish to set her free from him than to bind her to myself, that urged me on. I had in the solitary shades of her park, during the arguments and struggles of our last interview, sworn, that if she would suffer me to take her, and her boy too if she chose, away from him, I would place her in some romantic spot, build a home worthy of her, surrounded with all the glory of nature, and only see her as a servant and a slave. I pledged my soul to this, and I would have kept my oath. Those who have not loved may look on this as the very acme of my hallucination; it might be—I cannot tell—but so it was.

"All was ready; and I wrote to her to meet me for the last time. In this also I was, in one sense, sincere; for I had determined, if I should fail in my persuasions, never to see her more. She came, but several hours later than I intended, which, to a certain degree, deranged my plans. The weather had a sultriness about it all day, portending storm, occasioning a state of atmosphere that operates to render the human frame uneasy and restless. I paced the lane that bounded the demesnes of Dromore for hours; I threw myself on a grassy bank. The rack in the upper sky sped along with fearful impetuosity; it traversed the heavens from west to east, driven by a furious wind which had not yet descended to us; for below on earth, no breath of air moved the herbage, or could be perceived amid the topmost boughs of the trees. Everything in nature, acted upon by these contrary influences, had a strange and wild appearance. The sun descended red towards the ocean before Alithea opened the private gate of the grounds, and stood in all her loveliness before me.

"She brought her son with her. At first this annoyed me; but at a second thought it seemed to render my whole design more conclusive. She had spoken of this child with such rapture that it would have been a barbarity beyond my acting to separate her from him. By making him her companion, she completed my purpose; I would take them away together. I met her, I thought, with self-possession, but she read the conflict of passion in my face, and, half fearful, asked what disturbed me. I attributed my agitation to our approaching parting; and drawing her hand through my arm, walked forward along the lane. At the moment of executing my project, its wickedness and cruelty became so apparent, that a thousand times I was about to confess all, solicit her forgiveness, and leave her for ever: but that hardness, which in the ancient religions is deemed the immediate work of God, crept over my heart, turning its human misgiving to stony resolution. I endeavoured to close every aperture of my soul against the relenting moods that assailed me; yet they came with greater power each time, and at length wholly mastering me, I consented to be subdued. I determined to relinquish my schemes, to bid her an eternal adieu; and, moved by self-pity at the desolate lot I was about to encounter, I spoke of separation and absence, and the death of hope with such heartfelt pathos as moved her to tears.

"Surely there is no greater enemy to virtue and good intentions than that want of self-command, the exterior of which, though I had acquired, no portion existed in the inner substance of my mind. Calm, proud, and stern as I seemed to others, capable of governing the vehemence of my temper, within I was the same slave of passion I had ever been. I never could force myself to do the thing I hated; I never could persuade myself to relinquish the thing I desired. There is the secret of my crimes; there the vice of my disposition, which produced for her I loved a miserable death, and for myself endless, unutterable wo. For a moment I had become virtuous and heroic. We reached the end of the lane—my emissary appeared with the carriage. I had worked myself up by this time to determine to restore her to her home; to part with her for ever. She believed this. The despair written on my brow—my sombre, mute, yet heart-broken mien—my thoughts which had totally relinquished their favourite project, and consented to be widowed of her for ever, expressed in brief, passionate sentences, proved to her, who had never suspected that I meant otherwise, that I took my last look and spoke my last words. We reached the end of the lane; Osborne drove up. 'Be not surprised,' I said. 'Yes, it is there, Alithea; the carriage that is to convey me far, far away. Gracious God, do I live to see this hour!'

"The carriage stopped; we walked up to it. A devil at that moment whispered in my ear, a devil, who feeds on human crimes and groans, prompted my arm. Coward and dolt! to use such words—my own hellish mind was the sole instigator. In a moment it was done. I lifted her light figure into the carriage; I jumped in after her; I bade her boy follow. It was too late. One cry from him, one long, piercing shriek from her, and we were gone. With the swiftness of the winds we descended the eminence towards the shore, and left child and all return far behind.

"At that moment the storm burst over us; but the thunder was unheard amid the rattling of the wheels. Even her cries were lost in the uproar; but, as the thickening clouds changed twilight into night, the vivid lightning showed me Alithea at my feet, in convulsions of fear and anguish. There was no help. I raised her in my arms; and she struggled in them without meaning, without knowledge. Spasm succeeded to spasm; I saw them, by the flashes of the frequent lightning, distort her features with agony, but I could not even hear her groans; the furious haste at which we went, the thunder from above, the plash of the rain, suspended only by the howlings of the rising wind, drowned every other sound. I called to Osborne to stop; he gave no heed to my cries. Methought the horses had taken fright, and held the bit in their teeth, with such unimaginable speed we swept along. The roar of ocean, torn up by the wild west wind, now mingled with the universal uproar—hell had broken loose upon earth—yet what was every other and more noisy tempest compared to that which shook my soul, as I pressed Alithea to my heart in agony, vainly hoping to see the colour revisit her cheeks, and her dear eyes open! Was she already a corpse! I tried to feel her breath upon my cheek; but the speed of our course, and the uproar of the elements, prevented my being able to ascertain whether she was alive or dead. And thus I bore her—thus I made her my bride, thus I, her worshipper, emptied the vials of pain on her beloved head!"

# CHAPTER XXX

"At last I became aware that the wheels of the carriage passed through water. Hope revived with the thought. The hut where Osborne was to stop was to the south of the river we were now crossing: the tide was ebbing, and, despite the wind and storm, we passed the ford in safety; a moment more, and the carriage stopped amid the sands. I took the unfortunate lady in my arms, and carried her into the hut; then, fetching the cushions of the carriage, I bade Osborne take the horses on to a covered shed about half a mile off, which he had prepared for them, and return immediately.

"I re-entered the hut—still Alithea lay motionless on the ground where I had placed her. The lightning showed me her pale face; and another flash permitted me to discover a portion of luggage brought here by Osborne—necessary if we fled. Among other things which, soldier-like, I always carried with me, I saw my canteen; it contained the implements for striking a light, and tapers. By such means I could at last discover that my victim still lived; and sometimes also she groaned and sighed heavily. What, had happened to her I could not tell, nor by what means consciousness might be restored. I chafed her head and hands in spirituous waters; I made her swallow some—in vain. For a moment she somewhat revived, but relapsed again; and the icy cold of her hands and feet seemed to portend instant dissolution. Osborne returned, as I had ordered; he was totally unaware of the state to which my devilish machinations had brought my victim. He found me hanging over her—calling her by every endearing name—chafing her hands in mine—watching in torture for such signs of returning sense as would assure me that I was not about to see her expire before my eyes. He was scared by what he saw; but I silenced him, and made him light a fire, and heat sand, which I placed at her feet; and then, by degrees, with help of large doses of sal-volatile and other drugs, circulation was restored. She opened her eyes and gazed wildly round, and tears gushed from under the lids in large slow drops! My soul blessed God! Every mad desire and guilty scheme had faded before the expectation of her death. All I asked of Heaven was her life, and leave to restore her to her child and her home. Heaven granted, as I thought, my prayer. The livid streaks which had settled round her mouth and eyes disappeared; her features lost the rigidity of convulsions, a slight colour tinged her cheeks; her hands, late chill and stiff, now had warmth and voluntary motions of their own. Once or twice she looked round and tried to speak. 'Gerard!' that word, the name of her boy, was murmured; I caught the sound as I bent eagerly over her. 'He is safe—he is well,' I whispered. 'All is well; be comforted, Alithea.' The poor victim smiled; yes, her own sweet smile dawned upon her face. 'She too is safe,' I thought. Once again I felt my heart beat freely and at ease.

"She continued, however, in a state of torpor. There were two rooms in the hut. I prepared a sort of couch for her in the inner one. I placed her on it; I covered her with her cloak. By degrees the sort of insensibility in which she sunk changed to sleep. We left her then, and sat watching in the outer room. I kept my eyes fixed on her, and saw that each hour added to the tranquillity of her repose; I could not hear her breathe; for though the thunder and rain had ceased, the wind howled and the near ocean roared; its billows, driven by the western gale, encroached upon the sands almost to the threshold of the hut.

"A revulsion had taken place within me; I felt that there was something dearer to me than the fulfilment of my schemes, which was her life. She appeared almost miraculously restored, and my softened heart thanked God and blessed her. I believed I could be happy even in eternal absence, now that the guilt of her death was taken from my soul. Well do I remember the kind of rapture that flowed in upon my heart, as at dawn of day I crept noiselessly to her side, and marked the regular heaving of her bosom; and saw her eyelids, heavy and dark with suffering, it is true, yet gently closed over the dear orbs which again and for many a long year would enjoy the light of day. I felt a new man, I felt happy. In a few short hours I should receive her pardon—convey her home—declare my own guilt; and while absolving her, offer myself as the mark of whatever vengeance her husband might choose to take. Me!—oh, what was I? I had no being; it was dissolved into a mere yearning for her life—her contentment. I was about to render myself up as a criminal to a man whose most generous act would be to meet me in the field; but that was nothing; I thought not of it, either with gladness or regret. She lives—she shall be restored to all she loves—she once again will be at peace.

"These were my dreams as I hung over her, and gradually the break of day became more decided; by the increasing light I could perceive that I had not deceived myself, she slept a healthy, profound, healing sleep: I returned to the outer room; Osborne had wrapped himself in his great-coat, and lay stretched on the floor. I roused him, and told him to go for the horses and carriage immediately, so that the first thing that might welcome Alithea's awakening should be the offer of an immediate return home. He gladly obeyed, and left the hut; but scarcely was he gone than a sort of consciousness came over me, that I would not remain with her alone; so I followed him at some little distance towards the shed where the carriage and horses were.

"The wind had scattered every cloud, and still howled through the clear gray morning sky; the sea was in violent commotion, and huge surges broke heavily and rapidly on the beach. The tide was flowing fast, and the bed of the river we had crossed so safely the night before was covered by the waves; in a little time the ford would be impassable, and this was another reason to hasten the arrival of the horses. To the east each crag and precipice, each vast mountain-top, showed in dark relief against the golden eastern sky; seaward the horizon was misty from the gale, and the ocean stretched out inimitably; curlews and gulls screamed as they skimmed the crested waves, and breaker after breaker dashed furiously at my feet. It was a desolate, but a magnificent spectacle, and my throbbing heart was in unison with its vast grandeurs. I blessed sea, and wind, and heaven, and the dawn; the guilt of my soul had passed from me, and without the grievous penalty I had dreaded; all again was well. I walked swiftly on, I reached the shed. Osborne was busy with the horses; he had done what he could for them the night before, and they seemed tolerably fresh. I spoke cheerfully to the man, as I helped to harness them. Osborne was still pale with fright; but when I told him that I was going to carry the lady back to her friends, and that there was nothing to fear, he took heart; I bade him come slowly along, that the noise of the wheels might not waken her, if she still slept, and I walked beside, my hand on the neck of one horse while he bestrode the other, and we gazed around and pointed to each other signs of the recent tempest, which had been so much more violent than I in my preoccupation had known; and then as the idea of the ford being rendered impassable crossed me again, I bid him get on at a quicker rate, there was no fear of disturbing the sleeping lady, for the wheels were noiseless on the heavy sands.

"I have mentioned that huge sand-hills were thrown up here and there on the beach; two of the highest of these shut out all view of the hut, and even of the river, till we were close upon them. As we passed these mounds, my first glance was to see the state of the tide. The bed of the river was entirely filled with dashing crested waves, which poured in from the sea with inconceivable rapidity, and obliterated every trace of the ford. I looked anxiously round, but it was plain we must wait for the ebbing tide, or make a long detour to seek the upper part of the stream. As I gazed, something caught my eyes as peculiar. The foam of the breaking waves was white, and this object also was white; yet was it real, or but the mockery of a human form? For a moment my heart ceased to beat, and then with wings to my feet I ran to the hut: I rushed into the inner room—the couch was deserted, the whole dwelling empty! I hurried back to the river's brink and strained my eyeballs to catch a sight of the same fearful object; it was there! I could not mistake, a wave lifted up and then again overwhelmed and swallowed it in its abyss, the form, no longer living, the dead body of Alithea. I threw myself into the water, I battled with the waves, the tide bore me on. Again and again I was blinded and overwhelmed by the surges, but still I held on, and made my way into the middle of the roaring flood. As I rose gasping from one large billow that had, for more than a minute, ingulfed me in its strangling depths, I felt a substance strike against me; instinctively I clutched at it, and grasping her long streaming hair, now with renewed strength and frantic energy I made for shore. I was as a plaything to the foaming billows; but by yielding to them, by suffering myself to be carried up the tide to where the river grew shallower and the waves less powerful, I was miserable enough at last to escape. Fool! did I not know that she was dead!—why did I not, clasping her in my arms, resign my life to the waters? No! she had returned to me from the gates of death the night before, and I madly deemed the miracle would be twice performed.

"I reached the bank. Osborne, trembling and ghastly, helped me to lift her on shore; we endeavoured by various means to recall the spark of life— it was too late. She had been long in the water, and was quite dead!

"How can I write these words, how linger on these hideous details? Alas! they are for ever before me; no day, no hour passes but the whole scene is acted over again with startling vividness—and my soul shrinks and shudders from the present image of death. Even now that the dawn of Greece is breaking among the hills—that the balmy summer air fans my cheek—that the distant mountain-tops are gilded by the morning beams, and the rich, tranquil beauty of a southern clime is around—yet even now the roar of that distant ocean is in my ear, the desolate coast stretches out far away, and Alithea lies pale, drenched, and lifeless at my feet.

"I saw it all; and how often and for ever do I go over in my thoughts what had passed during the interval of my absence! She had awoke refreshed— she collected her scattered senses—she remembered the hideous vision of her carrying off. She knew not of my relenting—she feared my violence— she resolved to escape; she was familiar with that shore; its rivers and the laws which governed their tides were known to her. She believed that she could pass the water in safety, for often, when the bed of the estuary was apparently full, she knew that she had forded the stream on horseback, and the waters scarce covered the animal's fetlock. Intent on escaping the man of violence, of reaching her beloved home, she had entered the stream without calculating the difference of a calm neap tide, and the mass of irresistible waves borne up by the strong western wind; they perhaps seemed less terrible than I; to fly from me, she encountered, delivered herself up to them! and there she lay, destroyed, dead, lost for ever!

"No more of this! What then I did may, I now conceive, appear more shocking to my countrymen than all that went before. But I knew little of English customs. I had gone out an inexperienced stripling to India, and my modes of action were formed there. I now know that when one dies in England, they keep the lifeless corpse, weeping and watching beside it, for many days, and then, with lingering ceremonies and the attendance of relations and friends, lay it solemnly in the dismal tomb. But I had seen whole armies mown down by the sword and disease; I was accustomed to the soldier's hastily-dug grave in a climate where corruption follows fast upon death. To hide the dead with speed from every eye was the Indian custom.

"And then, should I take the corpse of Alithea, wet with the ocean tide, ghastly from the throes of recent death, and bear her to her home, and say, here she is—she enjoyed life and happiness yester-evening; I bore her away, behold my work! Should I present myself to her husband, answer his questions, detail the various stages of my crime, and tamely await his vengeance or his pardon! Never!

"Or should I destroy myself at her side, and leave our bodies to tell a frightful tale of mystery and horror? The miserable terrors of my associate would of itself have prevented this catastrophe. I had to reassure and protect him.

"My resolution was quickly made not to outlive my victim—and, making atonement by my death, what other penalty could I be called upon to pay? But my death should not be a tale to appal or amuse the vulgar, or to swell with triumph the heart of Alithea's tyrant husband. Secrecy and oblivion should cover all. My plan was laid, and I acted accordingly.

"Osborne entered into the design with alacrity. He was moved by other feelings, he was possessed by an agony of fear; he did not doubt but that we should be accused of murdering the hapless lady, and the image of the gallows flitted before his eyes.

"Understanding each other without many words, Osborne said that in the shed where we had placed the horses he had remarked a spade; it was so early that no one was about to observe him, and he went to fetch it. He returned in about half an hour; I sat keeping watch the while by the dead, and feasted my eyes with the sight of my pale victim as she lay at my feet. Of what tough materials is man formed, that my heart-strings did not break, and that I outlived that hour!

"Osborne returned, and we went to work. Some ten yards above high-water mark there was a single leafless, moss-grown, skeleton tree, with something like soil about its roots, and sheltered from the spray and breeze by the vicinity of a sand-hill; close to it we dug a deep grave. I placed the cushions in it on which her fair form, all warm and soft, had reposed, during the preceding night. Then I composed her stark limbs, banding the long wet tresses of her abundant hair across her eyes, for ever closed, crossing her hands upon her pure, death-cold bosom; I touched her reverently—I did not even profane her hand by a kiss; I wrapped her in her cloak, and laid her in the open grave. I tore down some of the decaying boughs of the withered tree, and, arching them above her body, threw my own cloak above, so with vain care to protect her lifeless form from immediate contact with the soil. Then we filled up the grave, and, scattering dry sand above, removed every sign of recent opening. This was performed in silence, or with whispered words—the roaring waves were her knell, the rising sun her funeral torch; I was satisfied with the solemnity of the scene around, and I was composed, for I was resolved on death. Osborne trembled in every limb, and his face rivalled in hue her wan, bloodless countenance.

"We carefully removed every article from the hut, and put all in the same state as when we found it. I did not, indeed, fear discovery; who would imagine that my course would be to the desolate seabeach? and if they did, and found all, I should be far, I should be dead. But Osborne was eager to obliterate every mark of the hut having been visited. When he was satisfied that he had accomplished this, without looking behind, I got into the carriage, we drove with what speed we could to Lancaster, and thence to Liverpool. Osborne was in a transport of fear till he got on board an American vessel: fortunately, the wind having veered towards the north, there was one about to weigh anchor. I placed a considerable sum of money in my accomplice's hands, and recommended discretion. He would have questioned me as to my own designs, but he respected my stern silence, and we parted never to meet again. A small coasting vessel, bound for Plymouth, was at that moment making her way out of harbour; I hailed a man on board, and threw myself on to the deck.

"Elizabeth can tell the rest. She knows how I landed in a secluded village of Cornwall, with the intent there to make due sacrifice to the outraged manes of Alithea. Still I grieve for the unaccomplished purpose; still I repine that I did not there die. She stopped my hand. An angel, in likeness of a human child, arrested my arm; and winning my wonder by her extraordinary loveliness, and my interest by her orphan and desolate position, I seemed called upon to live for her sake. The struggle was violent, for I longed to make atonement by my death; and I longed to forget my crimes and their consequences in the oblivious grave. At first I thought that the respite I granted myself would be short; but it lasted for years; and I dragged out a living death, having survived love and hope: remorse my follower; ghastly images of crime and death my comrades. I travelled from place to place, pursued by Alithea's upbraiding ghost and my own torturing thoughts. By frequent change of place, I sought to assuage my pangs; I believe that I increased them. They might perhaps have been mitigated by the monotony of a stationary life. But a traveller's existence is all sensation, and every emotion is rendered active and penetrating by the perpetual variation of the appearances of natural objects. Thought and feeling awaken with the sun, and dewy eve and the radiant stars cause the eyes to turn towards the backward path; while darkness, felt palpably, as one proceeds onward in an unknown land, awakens the snakes of conscience. The storm and expected wreck are images of retribution; while yet the destruction I pined for receded from before my thirsting lips.

"Yet still I dragged on life, most unworthily and unworthy, till on a day I saw the son of my victim at Baden. I witnessed misery, widely spread, through my means; and felt that her disimbodied spirit must curse me for the evil I had brought on her beloved child. I remembered all she had fondly said of him: and the cloudless beauty of his face, his joyous laugh, and free step when last I saw him at her side. He was blighted and destroyed by me; gloomy, savage, and wild, eternal sorrow was written on his brow, fear and hatred gleamed in his eyes. Such by my means had the son of Alithea become; such had his base-minded father rendered him; but mine the guilt—mine be the punishment! What a wretch was I, to live in peace and security, ministered to by an angel—while this dearest part of herself was doomed to anguish, and to the unmitigated influence of the demon for ever at his side, through my accursed means.

"From that hour I became thrice hateful to myself; I had tried to live for my Elizabeth; but that idea passed away with every other solace, in which hitherto I had iniquitously indulged. I resolved to die; but as a taint has been cast by the most villanous heart in the world upon her hallowed name, my first task was to redeem that out of her unworthy husband's hands; and yet I could not, I would not, while living, disclose the truth and give a triumph to my enemy. But soon, oh, very soon, will the soil of Greece drink up my life-blood! and while this writing proclaims her innocence, I shall be sheltered by the grave from the taunts and revilings of men.

"And you, dear child of my affection, who have been to me as a blessing immediate from Heaven, who have warmed my heart with your love and smoothed the fierceness of my temper by your unalterable sweetness; who having blessed me with your virtues, clinging to the ruin with a fidelity I believed impossible, how shall I say farewell to you? Forgive your friend that he deserts you; long ago he deserted himself and the better part of life; it is but the shell of him that remains; and that corroded by remorse, and the desire to die. You deserve better than to have your young days clouded by the shadow of my crime thrown over them. Forget me, and be happy; you must be so, while I—The sun is up; the martial trumpet sounds. It is a joy to think that I shall have a soldier's grave."

# CHAPTER XXXI

Such was the tale presented to the young, enthusiastic, innocent Elizabeth, unveiling the secret of the life of him whom she revered above all the world. Her soul was in her eyes as she read, or rather devoured, page after page, till she arrived at the catastrophe; when a burst of passionate tears relieved her swelling bosom, and carried away upon their stream a thousand, trembling, unspeakable fears that had gathered in wild multitude around her heart. "He is innocent! He, my benefactor, my father, when he accused himself of murder, spoke, as I thought, of a consequence, not an act; and if the chief principle of religion be true, that repentance washes away sin, he is pardoned, and the crime forgotten. Noble, generous heart! What drops of anguish have you not shed in atonement! What glorious obsequies you pay your victim. For she also is acquitted. Gerard's mother is more than innocent. She was true to him, and to the purest sentiments of nature, to the end; nay, more, her life was sacrificed to them." And Elizabeth went over in her mind, as Falkner had often done, the emotions that actuated her to attempt the dangerous passage across the ford. She fancied her awakening on the fatal morning, her wild look around. No familiar object met her view—nor did any friendly voice reassure her; the strange scene and solitary hut were testimonies that she did not dream, and that she had really been torn from home and all she loved by a violence she could not resist. At first she must have listened tremblingly, and fancied her lover-enemy at hand. But all is still. She rises; she ventures to examine the strange dwelling to which she has been carried—no human being presents himself. She quits the threshold of the hut—a familiar scene is before her eyes, the ocean and the dreary but well-known shore—the river which she has so often crossed—and among the foldings of the not distant hills, imbosomed in trees, she sees Dromore, her tranquil home. She knows that it is but a few miles distant; and while she fancies her enemy near at hand, yet the hope animates her that she may cross the stream unseen, and escape. Elizabeth imaged all her hopes and fears; she seemed to see the hapless lady place her uncertain feet, her purpose being stanch and unfaltering, within the shallow wave, which she believed she could traverse in safety; the roar of the advancing tide was in her ears, the spray dashed round her, and her footing grew uncertain, as she sought to find her way across the rugged bed of the river. But she thought only of her child, from whom she had been torn, and her fears of being, through the deed of violence which had carried her off, excluded from her home for ever. To arrive at that home was all her desire. As she advanced she still fixed her eyes on the clustering woods of Dromore, sleeping stilly in the gray, quiet dawn: and she risked her life unhesitatingly to gain the sacred shelter. All depended on her reaching it, quickly and alone; and she was doomed never to see it more. She advances resolutely, but cautiously. The waves rise higher—she is in the midst of the stream—her footing becomes more unsteady—does she look back?—there is no return—her heart proudly repels the very thought of desiring it. She gathers her garments about her—she looks right onward—she steps more carefully—the surges buffet her—they rise higher and higher—the spray is dashed over her head, and blinds her sight—a false step—she falls—the waters open to ingulf her—she is borne away. One thought of her Gerard— one prayer to Heaven, and the human eye can pursue the parting soul no farther. She is lost to earth—none upon it can any longer claim a portion in her.

But she is innocent. The last word murmured in her last sleep—the last word human ears heard her utter, was her son's name. To the last she was all mother; her heart filled with that deep yearning, which a young mother feels to be the very essence of her life, for the presence of her child. There is something so beautiful in a young mother's feelings. Usually a creature to be fostered and protected—taught to look to another for aid and safety; yet a woman is the undaunted guardian of her little child. She will expose herself to a thousand dangers to shield his fragile being from harm. If sickness or injury approach him, her heart is transfixed by terror: readily, joyfully, she would give her own blood to sustain him. The world is a hideous desert when she is threatened to be deprived of him; and when he is near, and she takes him to the shelter of her bosom, and wraps him in her soft, warm embrace, she cares for nothing beyond that circle; and his smiles and infantine caresses are the life of her life. Such a mother was Alithea; and in Gerard she possessed a son capable of calling forth in its intensity, and of fully rewarding, her maternal tenderness. What wonder, when she saw him cast pitilessly down on the road-side—alive or dead she knew not—the wheel of the carriage that bore her away might have crushed and destroyed his tender limbs—what wonder that she should be threatened by instant death, through the excess of her agony? What wonder that, reviving from death, her first and only thought was to escape—to get back to him—to clasp him to her heart—never to be severed more?

How glad, and yet how miserable, Gerard would be to read this tale. His proudest and fondest assertions certified as true, and yet to feel that he had lost her for ever, whose excellence was proved to be thus paramount. Elizabeth's reflections now rested on him—and now turned to Falkner—and now she opened the manuscript again, and read anew—and then again her heart made its commentary, and she wept and rejoiced; and longed to comfort her father, and congratulate Neville, all in a breath.

She never thought of herself. This was Elizabeth's peculiarity. She could be so engrossed by sympathy for others, that she could forget herself wholly. At length she remembered her father's directions, that his manuscript should be given to Neville when he called. She had no thought of disobeying; nor could she help being glad that Gerard's filial affection should receive its reward, even while she was pained to think that Falkner should be changed at once into an enemy in her new friend's eyes. Still her generous nature led her instantly to ally herself to the weaker side. Neville was triumphant—Falkner humiliated and fallen; and thus he drew her closer to him, and riveted the chain of gratitude and fidelity by which she was bound. She had shed many tears for Alithea's untimely fate; for the virtues and happiness hurried to a mysterious end—buried in an untold grave. But she had her reward. Long had she been there, where there is no trouble, no strife—her pure soul received into the company of kindred angels. Her heroism would now be known; her actions justified; she would be raised above her sex in praise; her memory crowned with unfading glory. It was Falkner who needed the exertion of present service, to forgive and console. He must be raised from his self-abasement; his despair must be cured. He must feel that the hour of remorse was past; that of repentance and forgiveness come. He must be rewarded for all his goodness to her, by being made to love life for her sake. Neville, whose heart was free from every base alloy, would enter into these feelings. Content to rescue the fame of his mother from the injury done it; happy in being assured that his faithful, filial love had not been mistaken in its reliance, the first emotion of his generous soul would be to forgive. Yet Elizabeth fancied that, borne away by his ardour in his mother's cause, he might altogether pass over and forget the extenuating circumstances that rendered Falkner worthy of pardon; and she thought it right to accompany the narrative with an explanatory letter. Thus she wrote:—

> "My father has given me these papers for the purpose of transmitting them to you. I need not tell you that I read them this day for the first time: that till now I was in total ignorance of the facts they disclose.
>
> "It is most true that I, a little child, stopped his arm as he was about to destroy himself. Moved by pity for my orphan state, he consented to live. Is this a crime? Yet I could not

reconcile him to life, and he went to Greece, seeking death. He went there in the pride of life and health. You saw him at Marseilles; you saw him to-day—the living effigy of remorse and wo.

"It is hard, at the moment you discover that he was the cause of your mother's death, to ask your sympathy for his sufferings and high-minded contrition. I leave you to follow the dictates of your own heart with regard to him. For myself, attached to him as I am by every sentiment of affection and gratitude, I am, from this moment, more than ever devoted to his service, and eager to prove to him my fidelity.

"These words come from myself. My father knows not what I write. He simply told me to inform you that he should remain here; and if you desired aught of him, he was ready at your call. He thinks, perhaps, you may require further explanation—further guidance to your mother's grave. Oh, secret and obscure as it is, is it not guarded by angels? Have you not been already led to it?"

She left off abruptly—she heard a ring at the outer gate—the hour had come—it must be Neville! She placed the papers in the writing-case, and directing and sealing the letter, gave both to the servant, to be delivered to him. Scarcely was this done, when suddenly it flashed across her how the relative situations of Neville and herself were changed. That morning she had been his chosen friend—into her ear he poured the history of his hopes and fears—he claimed her sympathy—and she felt that from her he derived a happiness never felt before. Now he must regard her as the daughter of his mother's destroyer, and should she ever see him more? Instinctively she rushed to the highest room of the house to catch one other glimpse. By the time she reached the window, the act was fulfilled that changed both their lives—the packet given. Dimly, in the twilight, she saw a horseman emerge from under the wall of the garden, and slowly cross the heath; slowly at first, as if he did not comprehend what had happened, or what he was doing. There is something that excites unspeakable tenderness when the form of the loved one is seen, even from far; and Elizabeth, though unaware of the nature and depth of her sensations, yet felt her heart soften and yearn towards her friend. A blessing fell from her lips; while the consciousness of all of doubtful and sad that he must at that moment experience, at being sent from her door with a written communication only, joined to the knowledge that each succeeding hour would add to the barriers that separated them, so overcame her, that when at last he put spurs to his horse, and was borne out of sight into the thickening twilight, she burst into a passion of tears, and wept for some time, not knowing what she did, nor where she was; but feeling that from that hour the colour of her existence was changed—its golden hue departed—and that patience and resignation must henceforth take place of gladness and hope.

She roused herself after a few minutes from this sort of trance, and her thoughts reverted to Falkner. There are few crimes so enormous but that, when we undertake to analyze their motives, they do not find some excuse and pardon in the eyes of all except their perpetrators. Sympathy is more of a deceiver than conscience. The stander-by may dilate on the force of passion and the power of temptation, but the guilty are not cheated by such subterfuges; he knows that the still voice within was articulate to him. He remembers that at the moment of action he felt his arm checked, his ear warned; he could have stopped, and been innocent. Perhaps of all the scourges wielded by the dread Eumenides, there is none so torturing as the consciousness of the wilfulness of the act deplored. It is a mysterious principle, to be driven out by no reasonings, no commonplace philosophy. It had eaten into Falkner's soul; taken sleep from his eyes, strength from his limbs, every healthy and self-complacent sentiment from his soul.

Elizabeth, however, innocent and good as she was, fancied a thousand excuses for an act, whose frightful catastrophe was not foreseen. Falkner called himself a murderer; but, though the untimely death of the unfortunate Alithea was brought about by his means, so far from being guilty of the deed, he would have given a thousand lives to save her. Since her death, she well knew that sleep had not refreshed, nor food nourished him. He was blighted, turned from all the uses and enjoyments of life; he desired the repose of the grave; he had sought death; he had made himself akin to the grim destroyer.

That he had acted wrongly, nay, criminally, Elizabeth acknowledged. But by how many throes of anguish, by what repentance and sacrifice of all that life holds dear, had he not expiated the past! Elizabeth longed to see him again, to tell him how fondly she still loved him, how he was exalted, not debased, in her eyes; to comfort him with her sympathy, cherish him with her love. It was true that she did not quite approve of the present state of his mind; there was too much of pride, too much despair. But when he found that, instead of scorn, his confession met with compassion and redoubled affection, his heart would soften, he would no longer desire to die, so to escape from blame and retribution; but be content to endure, and teach himself that resignation which is the noblest and most unattainable temper of mind to which humanity may aspire.

# CHAPTER XXXII

While these thoughts, founded on a natural piety, pure and gentle as herself, occupied Elizabeth, Falkner indulged in far other speculations. He triumphed. It is strange, that although perpetually deceived and led astray by our imagination, we always fancy that we can foresee, and in some sort command, the consequences of our actions. Falkner, while he deplored his beloved victim with the most heartfelt grief, yet at no time experienced a qualm of fear, because he believed that he held the means of escape in his own hands, and could always shelter himself from the obloquy that he now incurred, in an unapproachable tomb. Through strange accidents, that resource had failed him; he was alive, and his secret was in the hands of his enemies. But as he confronted the injured son of a more injured mother, another thought, dearer to his lawless yet heroic imagination, presented itself. There was one reparation he could make, and doubtless it would be demanded of him. The law of honour would be resorted to, to avenge the death of Alithea. He did not for a moment doubt but that Neville would challenge him. His care must be to fall by the young man's hand. There was a sort of poetical justice in this idea, a noble and fitting ending to his disastrous story, that solaced his pride, and filled him, as it has been said, with triumph.

Having arrived at this conclusion, he felt sure also that the consummation would follow immediately on Neville's perusal of the narration put into his hands, This very day might be his last, and it was necessary to make every preliminary arrangement. Leaving Elizabeth occupied with his fatal papers, he drove to town to seek Mr. Raby's solicitor, to place in his hands the proofs of his adopted child's birth, so to secure her future acknowledgment by her father's family. She was not his child; no drop of his blood flowed in her veins; his name did not belong to her. As Miss Raby, Neville would gladly seek her, while as Miss Falkner, an insuperable barrier existed between them; and though he fell by Gerard's hand, yet he meant to leave a letter to convince her that this was but a sort of cunning suicide, and that it need place no obstacle between two persons whom he believed were formed for each other. What more delightful than that his own Elizabeth should love the son of Alithea? If he survived, indeed, this mutual attachment would be beset by difficulties; his death was like the levelling of a mountain—all was plain, easy, happy, when he no longer deformed the scene.

He had some difficulty in meeting with Mr. Raby's man of business. He found him, however, perfectly acquainted with all the circumstances, and eager to examine the documents placed in his hands. He had already written to Treby, and received confirmation of all Falkner's statements. This activity had been imparted by Mrs. Raby, then at Tunbridge Wells, who was anxious to render justice to the orphan, the moment she had been informed of her existence; Falkner heard with great satisfaction of the excellent qualities of this lady, and the interest she showed in poor Edwin Raby's orphan child. The day was consumed, and part of the evening, in these arrangements, and a final interview with his own solicitor. His will was already made: he divided his property between Elizabeth and his cousin, the only surviving daughter of his uncle.

Something of shame was in his heart when he returned and met again his adopted child, a shame ennobled by the sense that he was soon to offer up his life as atonement; while she, who had long been reflecting on all that occurred, yet felt it brought home more keenly when she again saw him, and read in his countenance the tale of remorse and grief, more legibly than in the written page. Passionately and gratefully attached, her heart warmed towards him, his very look of suffering was an urgent call upon her fidelity; and though she felt all the change that his disclosures operated, though she saw the flowery path she had been treading at once wasted and barren, all sense of personal disappointment was merged in her desire to prove her affection at that moment; silently, but with heroic fervour, she offered herself up at the shrine of his broken fortunes: love, friendship, good name, life itself, if need were, should be set at naught; weighed in a balance against her duty to him, they were but as a feather in the scale.

They sat together as of old, their looks were affectionate, their talk cheerful; it seemed to embrace the future as well as the present, and yet to exclude every painful reflection. The heart of each bore its own secret without betrayal. Falkner expected in a few hours to be called upon to expiate with his life the evils he had caused, while Elizabeth's thoughts wandered to Neville. Now he was reading the fatal narrative; now agonized pity for his mother, now abhorrence of Falkner, alternated in his heart; her image was cast out, or only called up to be associated with the hated name of the destroyer. Her sensibility was keenly excited. How ardently had she prayed, how fervently had she believed that he would succeed in establishing his mother's innocence; in what high honour she had held his filial piety—these things were still the same; yet how changed were both towards each other! It was impossible that they should ever meet again as formerly, ever take counsel together, that she should ever be made happy by the reflection that she was his friend and comforter.

Falkner called her attention by a detail of his journey to Belleforest, and the probability that she would soon have a visit from her aunt. Here was a new revulsion; Elizabeth was forced to remember that her name was Raby. Falkner described the majestic beauties of the ancestral seat of her family, tried to impress her with the imposing grandeur of its antiquity, to interest her in its religion and prejudices, to gild the reality of pride and desertion with the false colours of principle and faith. He spoke of Mrs. Raby, as he had heard her mentioned, as a woman of warm feeling, strong intellect, and extreme generosity. Elizabeth listened, but her eyes were fondly fixed on Falkner's face, and at last she exclaimed with spontaneous earnestness, "For all this I am your child, and we shall never be divided!"

It was now near midnight; at each moment Falkner expected a message from the son of his victim. He engaged Elizabeth to retire to her room, that her suspicions might not be excited by the arrival of a visitor at that unaccustomed hour. He was glad to see her wholly unsuspicious of what he deemed the inevitable consequence of his confession; for though her thoughts evidently wandered, and traces of regret clouded her brow, it was regret, not fear, that inspired sadness; she tried to cheer, to comfort for the past, and gain fortitude to meet the future; but that future presented no more appalling image than the never seeing Gerard Neville more.

She went, and he remained waiting and watching the livelong night, but no one came. The following day passed, and the same mysterious silence was observed. What could it mean? It was impossible to accuse Alithea's child of lukewarmness in her cause, or want of courage. A sort of dark, mysterious fear crept over Falkner's heart; something would be done; some vengeance taken. In what frightful shape would the ghost of the past haunt him? He seemed to scent horror and disgrace in the very winds, yet he was spell-bound; he must await Neville's call, he must remain as he had promised, to offer the atonement demanded. He had felt glad and triumphant when he believed that reparation to be his life in the field; but the delay was ominous; he knew not why, but at each ring at the gate, each step along the passages of the house, his heart grew chill, his soul quailed. He despised himself for cowardice, yet it was not that; but he knew that evil was at hand; he pitied Elizabeth, and he shrunk from himself as one doomed to dishonour and unspeakable misery.

# CHAPTER XXXIII

On arriving in London from Hastings, Neville had repaired, as usual, to his father's house; which, as was to be supposed at that season of the year, he found empty. On the second day, Sir Boyvill presented himself unexpectedly. He looked cold and stern as ever. The father and son met as they were wont: the latter anticipating rebuke and angry, unjust commands; the other assuming the lofty tone of legitimate authority, indignant at being disputed. "I hear from Sophia," said Sir Boyvill, "that you are on the point of sailing for America, and this without deigning to acquaint me with your purpose. Is this fair? Common acquaintances act with more ceremony towards each other."

"I feared your disapproval, sir," replied Neville.

"And thought it less faulty to act without than against a father's consent: such is the vulgar notion; but a very erroneous one. It doubles the injury, both to disobey me, and to keep me in the dark with regard to my danger."

"But if the danger be only imaginary?" observed his son.

Sir Boyvill replied, "I am not come to argue with you, nor to dissuade, nor to issue commands. I come with the more humble intention of being instructed. Sophy, though she evidently regrets your purposed journey, yet avers that it is not so wild and aimless as your expeditions have hitherto been; that the letters from Lancaster did lead to some unlooked-for disclosure. You little know me if you are not aware that I have the question, which you debate in so rash and boyish a manner, as deeply and more sorely at heart than you. Let me then hear the tale you have heard."

Surprised, and even touched to find his father unbend so far as to listen to him, Neville related the American's story, and the information that it seemed probable that Osborne could afford. Sir Boyvill listened attentively, and then observed, "It will be matter of triumph to you, Gerard, to learn that your strange perseverance has a little overcome me. You are no longer a mere lad; and though inexperienced and headstrong, you have shown talents and decision; and I am willing to believe, though perhaps I am wrong, that you are guided by conviction, and not by a blind wish to disobey. Your conduct has been consistent throughout, and so far is entitled to respect. But you are, as I have said (and forgive a father for saying so), inexperienced—a mere child in the world's ways. You go straightforward to your object, reckless of the remark that you excite, and the gall and wormwood that such remark imparts. Why will you not in some degree be swayed by me? Our views, if you would deign to inquire into mine, are not so dissimilar."

Neville knew not what to answer, for every reply and explanation were likely to offend. "Hitherto," continued Sir Boyvill, "in disgust at your wilfulness, I have only issued disregarded commands. But I am willing to treat my son as my friend, if he will let me; but it must be on one condition. I exact one promise."

"I am ready, sir," replied Neville, "to enter into any engagement that does not defeat my purpose."

"It is simply," said Sir Boyvill, "that you shall do nothing without consulting me. I, on the other hand, will promise not to interfere by issuing orders which you will not obey. But if there is any sense in your pursuit, my counsels may assist. I ask no more than to offer advice, and to have opportunity afforded me to express my opinion. Will you not allow that so much is due to me? Will you not engage to communicate your projects, and to acquaint me unreservedly with every circumstance that falls to your knowledge? This is the limit of my exactions."

"Most willingly I make this promise," exclaimed Neville. "It will indeed be my pride to have your participation in my sacred task."

"How far I can afford that," replied Sir Boyvill, "depends on the conduct you will pursue. With regard to this Osborne, I consent at once that his story should be sifted; nay, that you should go to America for that purpose, while you are ready to engage that you will not act on any information you may gather, without my knowledge."

"You may depend," said Gerard, "that I will keep to the letter of my promise; and I pledge my honour, gladly and unreservedly, to tell you everything, to learn your wishes, and to endeavour throughout to act with your approbation."

This concession made on both sides, the father and son conversed on more unreserved and kinder terms than they had ever before done. They passed the evening together, and though the arrogance, the wounded pride, the irritated feelings, and unredeemed selfishness of Sir Boyvill betrayed themselves at every moment, Gerard saw with surprise the weakness masked by so imposing an exterior. His angry commands and insulting blame had been used as batteries to defend the accessible part. He still loved and regretted Alithea; he pined to be assured of her truth; but he despised himself for these emotions—calling them feebleness and credulity. He felt assured that his worst suspicions would be proved true. She might now be dead; he thought it probable, that ere this her faults and sorrows were hushed in the grave: but had she remained voluntarily one half hour in the power of the man who had carried her from her home, no subsequent repentance, no remorse, no suffering could exculpate her. What he feared, was the revival of a story so full of dishonour—the dragging a mangled half-formed tale again before the public, which would jeer his credulity, and make merry over the new gloss of a time-worn subject. When such a notion occupied his brain, his heart swelled with uncontrollable emotions of pride and indignation.

Neville cared little for the world. He thought of his mother's wrongs and sufferings. He conjured up the long years which might have been spent in wretchedness; he longed, whatever she had done, to feel her maternal embrace, to show his gratitude for her early care of him. This was one view, one class of emotions present to his mind, when any occurrence tended to shake his belief in her unblemished honour and integrity, which was the religion of his heart. At the same time he, as much as his father, abhorred that the indifferent and light-hearted, the levelling and base, should have any food administered to their loathsome appetite for slander. So far as his father's views were limited to the guarding Alithea's name from further discussion, Neville honoured them. He showed Sir Boyvill that he was not so imprudent as he seemed, and brought him at last to allow that some discovery might ensue from his voyage. This open-hearted and peaceful interchange of sentiment between them was very cheering to both; and when Gerard visited Elizabeth the following day, his spirit was lighter and happier than it had ever been, and love was there to mingle its roseate visions with the sterner calls of duty. He entered Falkner's house with much of triumph, and more of hope gladdening his heart; he left it horror-struck, aghast, and almost despairing.

He would not return to his father. Elizabeth's supposition that Falkner spoke under a delusion, produced by sudden insanity; and his reluctance that while doubt hung over the event, that her dear name should be needlessly mixed up with the tragedy of his mother's death, restrained him. He resolved at once to take no final step till the evening, till he had again seen Elizabeth, and learned what foundation there was for the tremendous avowal that still rung in his ears. The evening—he had mentioned the evening—but would it ever come? till then he walked in a frightful dream. He first went to the docks, withdrew his luggage, and yet left word that by possibility he might still join the vessel at Sheerness. He did this, for he was glad to give himself something to do; and yet, soon after, how gladly would he have exchanged those hours of suspense for the certainty that too quickly came like a sudden ray of light, to show that he had long been walking at the edge of a giddy precipice. He received the packet and letter from the servant; dizzy and confounded he rode away; by the light of the first lamp he read Elizabeth's letter; it disordered the current of his blood, it confused and maddened the functions of reason; putting spurs to his horse, he galloped furiously on till he reached his father's house.

Sir Boyvill was seated solitarily in his drawing-room, sipping his coffee, and indulging in various thought. His wedded life with Alithea—her charms, her admirable qualities, and sweet, endearing disposition—occupied him as they had never done before since her flight. For the first time, the veil, woven by anger and vanity, fell from his eyes, and he saw distinctly the rashness and injustice of his past actions. He became convinced that deceit could never have had a part in her; did not her child resemble her, and was he not truth itself? He had nourished an aversion to his son, as her offspring; now he looked on his virtues as an inheritance derived from his sweet mother, and his heart instinctively, unaccountably, warmed towards both.

Gerard opened the door of the room and looked in; Sir Boyvill could hardly have recognised him, his face whiter than marble, his eyes wild and wandering, his whole countenance convulsed, his person shrunk up and writhing. He threw the packet on the table, crying out, "Victory, my father, victory!" in a voice so shrill and dissonant, so near a shriek, as to inspire his auditor with fear rather than triumph: "Read! read!" he continued, "I have not yet—I keep my word, you shall know all, even before me—and yet, I *do* know all, I have seen my mother's destroyer! She is dead!"

Sir Boyvill now, in some degree, comprehended his son's agitation. He saw that he was too much excited to act with any calmness; he could not guess how he had discovered the villain on whom both would desire to heap endless, unsatiable revenge; but he did not wonder, that if he had really encountered this man, and learned his deeds, that he should be transported into a sort of phrensy. He took up the packet—he cut the string that tied it—he turned over the papers, and his brow darkened. "Here is a long narrative," he said; "there is much of excuse, and much of explanation here. The story ought to be short that exculpates her; I do not like these varnishings of the simple truth."

"You will find none," said Neville; "at least, I heard none. His words were direct—his avowal contained no subterfuge."

"Of whom do you speak?" asked Sir Boyvill.

"Read," said Neville, "and you will know more than I; but half an hour ago those papers were put into my hands. I have not read them. I give them to you before I am aware of their contents, that I might fully acquit myself of my promise. They come from Rupert Falkner, my mother's destroyer."

"Leave me then to my task," said Sir Boyvill, in an altered and subdued tone. "You speak of strange things; facts to undo a frightful past, and to generate a future dedicated to a new revenge. Leave me; let me remain alone while I read—while I ponder on what credit I may give—what course I must pursue. Leave me, Gerard. I have long injured you, but at last you will be repaid. Come back in a few hours; the moment I am master of the contents of the manuscript I will see you."

Gerard left him. He had scarcely been aware of what he was doing when he carried the packet, unopened, unexamined, to his father. He had feared that he might be tempted—to what?—to conceal his mother's vindication? Never! Yet the responsibility sat heavy on him; and, driven by an irresistible impulse, he had resolved to deprive himself of all power of acting basely by giving at once publicity to all that passed. When he had done this, he felt as if he had applied a match to some fatal rocket which would carry destruction to the very temple and shrine of his dearest hopes—to Elizabeth's happiness and life. But the deed was done; he could but shut his eyes and let the mortal ball proceed towards its destined prey.

Gerard was young. He aspired to happiness with all the ardour of youth. While we are young we feel as if happiness were the birthright of humanity; after a long and cruel apprenticeship, we disengage ourselves from this illusion—or from (a yet more difficult sacrifice) the realities that produce felicity—for on earth there are such, though they are too often linked with adjuncts that make the purchase of them cost in the end peace of mind and a pure conscience. Thus was it with Gerard. With Elizabeth, winning her love and making her his own, he felt assured of a life of happiness; but to sacrifice his mother's name—the holy task to which he had dedicated himself from childhood—for the sake of obtaining her—it must not be!

With this thought came destruction to the fresh-sprung hopes that adorned his existence. Gerard's poetic and tender nature led him to form sweet dreams of joys derived from a union which would be cemented by affection, sympathy, and enthusiastic admiration of the virtues of his companion. In Elizabeth he had beheld the imbodying of all his wishes; in her eyes he had read their accomplishment. Her love for her father had first awakened his love. Her wise, simple, upright train of thinking—the sensibility ennobled by self-command, yet ever ready to spring forth and comfort the unhappy—her generosity—her total abnegation of self—her understanding so just and true, yet tempered with feminine aptitude to adapt itself to the situation and sentiments of others—all these qualities, discovered one by one, and made dear by the friendship she displayed towards him, had opened the hitherto closed gates of the world's only paradise; and now he found that, as the poet says, evil had entered even there—"and the trail of the serpent" marked with slimy poison the fairest and purest of Eden's flowers. [1]

Neville had looked forward to a life of blameless but ecstatic happiness, as her friend, her protector, her husband. Youth, without being presumptuous, is often sanguine. Prodigal of self, it expects, as of right, a full return. Ready to assist Elizabeth in her task of watching over her father's health—who, in his eyes, was wasting gradually away—he felt that he should be near to soften her regrets, and fill his place, and sooth her sinking spirits when struck by a loss which to her would seem so dire.

And now—Falkner! He believed him to be in a state of health that did not leave him many years to live. He recollected him at Marseilles, stretched on his couch, feeble as an infant, the hues of death on his brow. He thought of him as he had seen him that morning—his figure bent by disease—his face ashy pale and worn. He was the man whom, thirteen years before, he remembered in upright, proud, and youthful strength; wo and disease had brought on the ravages of age—he was struck by premature decay—a few years, by the course of nature, he would be laid in his grave. But Gerard could not leave him this respite—he must at once meet him in such encounter as must end in the death of one of the combatants—whichever that might be, there was no hope for Elizabeth—in either case she lost her all—in either case Falkner would die, and an insuperable barrier be raised between her and her only other friend. Neville's ardent and gentle spirit quivered with agony as he thought of these things. "Oh ye destructive powers of nature!" he cried; "come all! Storm, flood, and fire, mingled in one dire whirlwind; or bring the deadlier tortures tyrants have inflicted and martyrs undergone, and say, can any agony equal that which convulses the human heart when writhing under contending passions—torn by contrary purposes! This very morning Elizabeth was all the universe of hope and joy. I would not for worlds have injured one hair of her dear head—and now I meditate a deed that is to consign her to eternal grief."

Athwart this tumult of thought came the recollection that he was still in ignorance of the truth. He called to mind the narrative which his father was then reading; would it reveal aught that must alter the line of conduct which he now considered inevitable? A devouring curiosity was awakened. Leaving his father, he had rushed into the open air, in obedience to the instinct that always leads the unquiet mind to seek the solace of bodily activity. He had hurried into Hyde Park, which then, in the dimness of night, appeared a wide expanse—a limitless waste. He hurried to and fro on the turf—he saw nothing, he was aware of nothing, except the internal war that shook him. Now, as he felt the eager desire to get quit of doubt, he fancied that several hours must have elapsed, and that his father must be waiting for him. The clocks of London struck—he counted—it was but eleven—he had been there scarcely more than an hour.

[1] "Alas, for man! said the pitying spirit,
Dearly you pay for your primal fall!
Some flowers of Eden you still inherit,
But the trail of the serpent is over them all."

*Paradise and the Peri.*

# CHAPTER XXXIV

Neville returned home—he paused at the drawing-room door—a slight noise indicated that his father was within—his hand was on the lock, but he retreated; he would not intrude uncalled for—he wandered through the dark, empty rooms, till a bell rang. Sir Boyvill inquired for him—he hurried into his presence—he devoured the expression of his countenance with his eyes, trying to read the thought within. Sir Boyvill's face was usually stamped with an unvarying expression of cold self-possession, mingled with sarcasm. These feelings were now at their height—his aged countenance, withered and deep lined, was admirably calculated to depict the concentrated, disdain that sat upon his lips and elevated his brows. He pointed to the papers before him, and said in a composed, yet hollow voice, "Take these away—read, for it is necessary you should—the amplified confession of the murderer."

Gerard's blood ran cold. "Yet why call it a confession," continued Sir Boyvill, his assumed contempt rising into angry scorn; "from the beginning to the end it is a lie. He would varnish over his unparalleled guilt—he would shelter himself from its punishment, but in vain. Read, Gerard—read and be satisfied. I have wronged your mother—she was innocent—murdered. Be assured that her vindication shall be heard as loudly as her accusation, and that her destroyer shall die to expiate her death."

"Be that my task," said Gerard, trembling and pale from the conflict of passion; "I take the office of vengeance on myself—I will meet Mr. Falkner."

"Ha! you think of a duel!" cried his father. "Remember your promise, young man—I hold you strictly to it—you do nothing without first communicating with me. You must read these papers before you decide; I have decided—be not afraid, I shall not forestall your purpose, I will not challenge the murderer: but, in return for this pledge, give me your word that you have no communication with the villain till you see me again. I will not balk you of your revenge, be sure of that; but you must see me first."

"I promise," said Gerard.

"And one word more," continued Sir Boyvill; "is there any possibility of this man's escape? Is he wrapped in the security which his lie affords, or has he even now fled beyond our vengeance?"

"Be his crimes what they may," replied Neville, "I believe him to entertain a delicate sense of worldly honour. He has promised to remain in his home till he hears from me. He doubtless expects to be challenged, and I verily believe desires to die. I feel convinced that the idea of flight has not crossed his mind."

"Enough; good-night. We are now one, Gerard; united by our love and honour for your wronged mother's memory, and by our revenge; dissimilar only in this, that my desire to repair her injuries is more vehement even than yours." Sir Boyvill pressed his son's hand, and left him. A few minutes afterward, it would seem, he quitted the house.

"Now to my task," thought Neville; "and O, thou God, who watchest over the innocent, and yet gavest the innocent into the hands of the destroyer, rule thou the throbbings of my heart; that neither mad hate nor hunger for revenge take away my human nature, and turn me into a fiend!"

He took up the manuscript; at first the words seemed written in fire, but he grew calmer as he found how far back the narration went; and curiosity succeeding to devouring impatience, he became attentive.

He read and pitied. All that awoke Sir Boyvill's ire; Falkner's presumption in daring to love, and his long-cherished constancy, excited his compassion. When he came to the account of the meeting of the forsaken lover and happy husband, he found, in the epithets so liberally bestowed in the contemptuous description of his father, a cause for his augmented desire for vengeance. When he read that his mother herself repined, herself spoke disparagingly of her husband, he wondered at the mildness of Sir Boyvill's expressions with regard to her, and began to suspect that some strange and appalling design must be working in his head to produce this unnatural composure. The rest was madness, madness and misery, thus to take a wife and mother from her home, to gratify the insane desire to exert for one half hour a power he had lost for ever; the vain hope of turning her from her duties, which at least, as far as her children were concerned, were the dearest part of herself; her terror, her incapacity of mastering her alarm, the night of insensibility which she passed in the hut—with a start, Gerard felt sure that he had seen and marked that very spot; all wrought him up to the height of breathless interest; till, when he read the sad end of all, cold dew gathered on his brow, the tears that filled his eyes changed to convulsive sobbings, and, despite his manhood, he wept with the agony of a child.

He ended the tale, and he thought—"Yes, there is but one termination to this tragedy; I must avenge my sweet mother, and, by the death of Falkner, proclaim her innocence." But wherefore, it came across his mind, had his father called him murderer? in intention and very deed he was none; why term the narrative a lie? He followed it word by word, and felt that truth was stamped in every line.

The house was still; it was two in the morning. Had his father retired to rest? He had been so absorbed by his occupation, that he had heard no sound, knew nothing that might have been passing around. He remembered at last Sir Boyvill's good-night, and believing, as all was hushed, that all slept, he retired to his own room. He could not think of Elizabeth, or of the projected duel; he could think only of the narrative he had read. When in bed, unable to sleep, he rose, lighted his candle, and read much of it again: he pondered over every word in the concluding pages; it was all true, he would have staked his existence on the accuracy of every word: was it not stamped on Falkner's brow, as he had seen him but a few hours ago? sad, and worn with grief and suffering, but without the stain of concealed guilt, lofty in its very wo. It was break of day, just as Gerard was thinking of rising to find and consult with his father, that sleep crept unawares over him. Sleep will visit the young unbidden; he had suffered so much fatigue of mind and body, that nature sought relief; sleep, at first disturbed, but soon profound and refreshing, steeped his distracted thoughts in peace, his wearied limbs in delightful repose.

The morning was far advanced when he awoke, refreshed, ready to meet the necessities of the hour, grieved, but composed, sad, but strengthened and resolved. He inquired for his father, and heard, to his infinite astonishment, that he had left town: he had set out in his travelling carriage at four that morning; a note from him was put into Neville's hands. It contained few words: "Remember your engagement—that you take no steps with regard to Mr. Falkner till you have seen me. I am setting out for Dromore; on my return, which will be speedy, I will communicate my wishes, to which I do not doubt you will accede."

Neville was startled; he guessed at once Sir Boyvill's aim in the sudden journey; but was he not a fit partner in such an act? ought he not to share in the duty of rendering honour to his mother's grave? He felt that he ought to be at his father's side, and, ordering his own chariot, set out with the hope of overtaking him.

But Sir Boyvill travelled with equal speed, and was many miles and many hours in advance. Gerard hoped to come up with him when he stopped at night. But the old gentleman was so eager in his pursuit, that he prosecuted his journey without rest. Gerard continued in the same way; travelling alone, he revolved again and again all that must be, all that might have been. Whatever happened, he was divided from Elizabeth for ever. Did she love him? he had scarcely questioned the return his affection would one day meet, till now that he had lost her for ever; and like a true lover, earnestly desirous to preserve some property in her he loved, he cherished the hope that she would share his deep regrets, and so prove that in heart they were one. How pleasant were the days they had passed at Oakly; all his sorrows there, and his passionate desire to unveil the mystery of his mother's fate, how had it given an interest to each hour, and imparted an untold and most sweet grace to the loved Elizabeth, that she should sympathize with so much fervour and kindness.

How strange the chance that led the daughter of the destroyer to share the feelings of the unhappy victim's son; yet stranger still that destroyer had a child. Rambling among many tangled thoughts, Gerard started when first this idea suggested itself. Where was Falkner's boasted fidelity, on which he laid claim to compassion and pardon; where his assertion, that all his soul was centred in Alithea? and this child, an angel from her birth, was even then born to him; he opened the writing-case which contained the papers, and which he carried with him; he referred to them for explanation. Yes, Elizabeth then lived, and was not far from him; her hand had staid his arm, raised against his life. It was not enough that the phrensy of passion urged him to tear Alithea from her home and children, but even the existence of his own daughter was no restraint, he was willing to doom her from very childhood to a partnership in guilt and misery. Hitherto, despite all, and in despite of his resolve to meet him in mortal encounter, Neville had pitied Falkner; but now his heart grew hard against him; he began to revolve thoughts similar to those expressed by Sir Boyvill, and to call Elizabeth's father an impostor, his tale a lie. He reread the manuscript with a new feeling of skepticism; this time he was against the writer, he detected exaggeration, where, before, he had only found the energy of passion; he saw an attempt to gloss over guilt, where, before, he had read merely the struggles of conscience, the innate innocence of profound feeling, combating with the guilt, which circumstances may impart to our loftiest emotions; his very sufferings became but the just visitation of angry Heaven; he was a wretch, whom to kill were mercy—and Elizabeth, beautiful, generous, and pure, was his child!

# CHAPTER XXXV

That night was spent in travelling, and without any sleep. Neville saw the day break in melancholy guise, struggling with the clouds, with which a southeast wind veiled the sky. Nature looked bleak and desolate, even though she was still dressed in her summer garments. It was only the latter end of August, but so changeable is our climate, that the bright festive days which he had lately enjoyed in Sussex were already followed by chill and dreary precursors of the year's decline. Gerard reached Dromore at about noon. He learned that his father had arrived during the night—he had slept a few hours, but was already gone out; it appeared that he had ridden over to a neighbour, Mr. Ashley; for he had inquired if he were in the county, and had, with his groom, both on horseback, taken the road that led toward his house.

Neville hastily took some refreshment, while he ordered a horse to be saddled. His heart led him to seek and view a spot which he had once before visited, and which seemed accurately described in Falkner's narrative. He left behind him the woods of Dromore, and the foldings of the green hills in which it was situated—he descended towards the barren, dreary shore—the roar of ocean soon met his ear, and he reached the waste sands that border that melancholy coast—he saw the line of sand-hills, which formed a sort of bulwark against the tide—he reached at length a rapid, yet shallow stream, which was but about twenty yards wide, flowing over a rough bottom of pebbles; the eye easily reached its utmost depth, it could not be more than two feet. Could that be the murderous, furious estuary in which his mother had been borne away? he looked across—there stood the hut—there the moss-grown, leafless oak, and gathered round it was a crowd of men. His father, and two or three other gentlemen on horseback, were stationed near— while some labourers were throwing up the sand beneath the withered trunk. When we have long thought of and grieved over an incident—if any outward object bring the image of our thoughts bodily before us, it is strange what an accession of emotion stirs the depths of the heart. For many hours Neville's mind had dwelt upon the scene in all its parts—the wild waste sea, dark and purple beneath the lowering clouds—the dreary extent of beach— the far, stupendous mountains, thrown up in sublime, irregular grandeur, with cloud-capped peaks, and vast gulfs between—a sort of Cyclopean screen to the noble landscape, which they encompassed with their wide majestic extent—his reflections had selected the smaller objects—the river, the hut, the monumental tree; and it seemed as if actual vision could not bring it home more truly; but when he actually beheld these objects, and the very motive of his coming was revealed, as it were, by the occupation of the men at work, his young heart, unhardened by many sufferings, sickened, the tears rushed into his eyes, and the words—"Oh my mother!" burst, from his lips. It was a spasm of uncontrollable pain—an instant afterward he had mastered it, and guiding his horse through the ford, with tranquil mien, though pale and sad, he took his station abreast with his father. Sir Boyvill turned as he rode up; he manifested no surprise, but he looked thankful, and even triumphant, Gerard thought; and the young man himself, as he contemplated the glazed eyes and attenuated form of his parent, which spoke of the weight of years, despite his still upright carriage, and the stern expression of his face, felt that his right place was at his side, to render the support of his youthful strength and active faculties. The men went on with their work in silence, nor did any speak; the sand was thrown up in heaps, the horses pawed the ground impatiently, and the hollow murmurs of the neighbouring breakers filled every pause with sound, but no voice spoke; or if one of the labourers had a direction to give, it was done in whispers. At length some harder substance opposed their progress, and they worked more cautiously. Mingled with sand they threw out pieces of dark substance like cloth or silk, and at length got out of the wide long trench they had been opening. With one consent, though in silence, every one gathered nearer, and looked in—they saw a human skeleton. The action of the elements, which the sands had not been able to impede, had destroyed every vestige of a human frame, except those discoloured bones, and long tresses of dark hair, which were wound around the scull. A universal yet suppressed groan burst from all. Gerard felt inclined to leap into the grave, but the thought of the many eyes all gazing acted as a check; and a second instinctive feeling of pious reverence induced him to unfasten his large black horseman's cloak, and to cast it over the opening. Sir Boyvill then broke the silence: "You have done well, my son: let no man lift that covering, or in any way disturb the remains beneath. Do you know, my friends, who lies there? Do you remember the night when Mrs. Neville was carried off? The country was raised, but we sought for her in vain. On that night she was murdered, and was buried here."

    A hollow murmur ran through the crowd, already augmented by several stragglers, who had heard that something strange was going on. All pressed forward, though but to see the cloak, now become an object of curiosity and interest. Several remembered the lady, whose mouldered remains were thus revealed, in the pride of youth and beauty, warm of heart, kind, beloved; and this was all left of her! these unseemly bones were all earth had to show of the ever sweet Alithea!

"Mr. Ashley kindly assists me," continued Sir Boyvill; "we are both magistrates. The coroner is already sent for, a jury will be summoned; when that duty is performed, the remains of my unfortunate, much-wronged wife will be fitly interred. These ceremonies are necessary for the punishment of the murderer. We know him, he cannot escape; and you, every one of you, will rejoice in that vengeance which will be mine at last."

Execrations against the villain burst from every lip; yet even then each eye turned from old Sir Boyvill, whose vindictive nature had been showed before towards the hapless victim herself, to the young man, the son, whose grief and pious zeal had been the theme of many a gossip's story, and who now, pale and mute as he was, showed, in his intent and wo-struck gaze, more true touch of natural sorrow than Sir Boyvill's wordy harangue could denote.

"We must appoint constables to guard this place," said Sir Boyvill.

Mr. Ashley assented; the proper arrangements were made; the curious were to be kept off, and two servants from Dromore were added to the constables; then the gentlemen rode off. Neville, bewildered, desirous to stay to look once again on what had been his mother, yet averse to the vulgar gaze, followed them at a slower pace, till Mr. Ashley, taking leave of Sir Boyvill, rode away, and he perceived that his father was waiting for him, and that he must join him.

"Thank you, my son," said Sir Boyvill, "for your zeal and timely arrival. I expected it of you. We are one now; one to honour your mother; one in our revenge. You will not this time refuse your evidence."

"Do you then believe that Mr. Falkner is actually a murderer?" cried Neville.

"Let the laws of his country decide on that question," replied Sir Boyvill, with a sneering laugh. "I bring forward the facts only—you do the same; let the laws of his country and a jury of his equals acquit or condemn him."

"Your design, then, is to bring him to a trial?" asked Gerard. "I should have thought that the publicity—"

"I design," cried Sir Boyvill, with uncontrolled passion, "to bring him to a fate more miserable than his victim's; and I thank all-seeing Heaven, which places such ample revenge in my hands. He will die by the hands of the hangman, and I shall be satisfied."

There was something horrible in the old man's look and voice; he gloated on the foul disgrace about to be heaped on his enemy. The chivalrous notions of Gerard, a duel between the destroyer and his victim's son, was a paltry, trifling vengeance, compared with the ignominy he contemplated. "Was not the accusation against your mother loud," continued Sir Boyvill, "public, universal? Did not the assembled parliament pronounce upon her guilt, and decree her shame? And shall her exculpation be hushed up and private? I court publicity. A less august tribunal, but one whose decisions are no less widely circulated, shall proclaim her innocence. This idea alone would decide my course, if I could so far unman my soul as to forget that vengeance is due. Let it decide yours, if so much milk still mingle with your blood that it sicken at the thought of justice against a felon."

Transported by rage, Sir Boyvill sought for words bitter and venomous enough to convey his meaning; and Neville discerned at once how much he was incensed by the language used with regard to him in Falkner's manuscript. Wounded vanity sought to ape injured feelings; in such petty, selfish passions, Gerard could take no share, and he observed: "Mr. Falkner is a gentleman. I confess that his narration has won belief from me. His crime, dressed in his own words, is frightful enough; and heavily, if it be left to me, shall I visit it; but the plan you adopt is too discordant with the habits of persons of our rank of life, for me to view it without aversion. There is another which I prefer adopting."

"You mean," replied Sir Boyvill, "that you would challenge him—risk your life on the chance of taking his. Pardon me; I can by no means acquiesce in the propriety of such an act. I look on the wrongs he has done us as depriving him of the right to be treated with courtesy; nor do I wish him to add the death of my only son to the list of the injuries I have sustained."

The old man paused: his lip quivered—his voice dropped. Neville fancied that tenderness of feeling caused these indications; he was deceived; his father continued: "I am endeavouring so far to command myself as to speak with moderation. It is difficult to find words to express implacable hatred, so let that go by; and let us talk, since you can, and believe doubtless that I ought, calmly and reasonably. You would challenge this villain, this gentleman, as you name him. You would put your life on a par with his. He murdered your mother, and, to repay me, you would die by the same hand.

"If you speak the truth—if he possess a spark of those feelings which, as a soldier, you have a right to believe may animate him, do you think that he would return your fire? He raves about remorse in that tissue of infamous falsehoods which you put into my hands; if he be human, he must have some touch of that; and he could not, if he would, raise his weapon against the child of poor Alithea. He will therefore refuse to meet you, or, meeting you, refuse to fire; and either it will end in a farce for the amusement of the world, or you will shoot a defenceless man. I do not see the mercy of this proceeding."

"Of that, sir," said Neville, "we must take our chance."

"I will take no chance," cried his father. "My unfortunate wife was borne off forcibly from her home; you can bear witness to that. Two men carried her away, and no tidings ever again reached us of her fate. And now one of these men, the arch criminal, chooses to gloss over these circumstances, events, as pleases him; tells his own story, giving it such graces of style as may dupe the inexperienced, and we are to rest satisfied, and say, It is so. The absurdity of such conduct would mark us as madmen. Enough of this; I have reasoned with you as if the decision lay with me; when, in fact, I have no voice on the subject. It is out of my hands; I have made it over to the law, and we can but stand by and view its course. I believe, and before Heaven and your country you must assert the same, that the remains we have uncovered are all that is left us of your lost mother; the clandestine burial at once declares the guilt of murder; such must be the opinion of impartial judges, if I mistake not. I can interfere no further. The truth will be sifted by three juries; this is no hole-and-corner vengeance; let our enemy escape, in God's name, if they acquit him; but, if he be guilty, then let him die, as I believe he will, a felon's death."

Sir Boyvill looked on his son with glassy eyes, but a sneering lip, that spoke of the cruel triumph he desired. "There is Ravenglass," he added, "there the coroner is summoned—there the court meets. We go to give our deposition. We shall not lie, nor pervert facts; we tell who it was revealed to us your mother's unknown grave; it rests with them to decide whether he, who by his own avowal placed her therein, has not the crime of murder on his soul."

# CHAPTER XXXVI

Sir Boyvill quickened his pace; Neville followed. He was still the same being who in his youth had been driven to the verge of insanity by the despotism of his father. His free and feeling heart revolted from arbitrary commands and selfishness. It was not only that his thoughts flew back, wounded and sore, to Elizabeth, and figured her agony, but he detested the fierce and vulgar revenge of his father. It is true that he had seen Falkner, and in the noble though tarnished grandeur of his countenance he had read the truth of the sad tale he related; and he could not treat him with the contempt Sir Boyvill evinced; to whom he was an image of the mind— unseen, unfelt. And then Falkner had loved his mother; nay, more, she as a sister had loved him; and faulty and cruel as had been his return for her kindness, he, through her, was endued with sacredness in his eyes.

To oppose these softening feelings came a sort of rage that Elizabeth was his child; that through him a barrier was raised to separate him from the chosen friend of his heart, the one sweet, angel who had first whispered peace to his soul. The struggle was violent—he did not see how he could refuse his evidence at the inquest already summoned; in every way his motives might be misunderstood, and his mother's fame might suffer. This idea became the victor—he would do all that he was called upon to do—to exculpate her; the rest he must leave to the mysterious guidance of Providence.

He arrived at the poverty-stricken town of Ravenglass—the legal authorities were assembled—and while preliminaries were being arranged, he was addressed by Sir Boyvill's solicitor, who asked him to relate what he knew, that his legal knowledge might assist in framing his evidence briefly and conclusively. Neville recounted his story simply, confining himself, as much as possible, to the bare outline of the facts. The man of law was evidently struck by the new turn he gave to the tale; for Sir Boyvill had unhesitatingly accused Falkner of murder. "This Falkner," he said, "had concealed himself for the space of thirteen years, till his accomplice Osborne was discovered—and till he heard of Gerard's perseverance in sifting the truth—then, fearful the tale might be disclosed in America, he came forward with his own narrative, which glossed over the chief crime, and yet, by revealing the burial-place of his victim, at once demonstrated the truth of the present accusation. It is impossible that the facts could have occurred as he represents them, plausible as his account is. Could a woman as timid as Alithea have rushed on certain death, as he describes? Why should she have crossed the stream in its fury? A bare half mile would have carried her to a cottage where she had been safe from Falkner's pursuit. What lady in a well-known country, where every face she met must prove a friend, but would not have betaken herself to the nearest village, instead of to an estuary renowned for danger. The very wetting her feet in a brook had terrified her—never could she have encountered the roar of waves sufficient to overwhelm and destroy her."

Such were the observations of Sir Boyvill; and though Gerard, by his simple assertion that he believed Falkner's tale, somewhat staggered the solicitor, yet he could not banish his notion that a trial was the inevitable and best mode of bringing the truth to light. The jury were now met, and Sir Boyvill gave such a turn to his evidence as at once impressed them unfavourably towards the accused. In melancholy procession they visited poor Alithea's grave. A crowd of country people were collected about it— they did not dare touch the cloak, but gazed on it with curiosity and grief. Many remembered Mrs. Neville, and their rude exclamations showed how deeply they felt her injuries. "When I was ill," said an old woman, "she gave me medicine with her own hand." "When my son James was lost at sea," said another, "she came to comfort me, and brought young Master Gerard—and cried, bless her! When she saw me take on—rich and grand as she was, she cried for poor James—and that she should be there now!" "My dear mistress," cried another, "never did she speak a harsh word to me—but for her, I could not have married—if she had lived, I had never known sorrow!"

Execrations against the murderer followed these laments. The arrival of the jury caused a universal murmur—the crowd was driven back—the cloak lifted from the grave—the men looked in; the scull, bound by her long hair—hair whose colour and luxuriance many remembered—attracted peculiar observation; the women, as they saw it, wept aloud—fragments of her dress were examined, which yet retained a sort of identity, as silk or muslin—though stained and colourless. As farther proof, among the bones were found a few ornaments—among them, on the skeleton hand, was her wedding-ring, with two others—both of which were sworn to by Sir Boyvill as belonging to his wife. No doubt could exist concerning the identity of the remains; it was sacrilege to gaze on them a moment longer than was necessary—while each beholder, as they contemplated so much beauty and excellence reduced to a small heap of bones, abhorrent to the eye, imbibed a heartfelt lesson on the nothingness of life. Stout-hearted men wept—and each bosom glowed with hatred against her destroyer.

After a few moments the cloak was again extended—the crowd pressed nearer—the jury retired, and returned to Ravenglass. Neville's evidence was only necessary to prove the name and residence of the assassin—there was no hesitation about the verdict. That of wilful murder against Falkner was unhesitatingly pronounced—a warrant issued for his apprehension, and proper officers despatched to execute it.

The moment that the verdict was delivered, Sir Boyvill and his son rode back to Dromore. Mr. Ashley and the solicitor accompanied them—and all the ordinary mechanism of life, which intrudes so often for our good, so to justle together discordant characters and wear off poignant impressions, now forced Neville, who was desirous to give himself up to meditation, to abide for several hours in the society of these gentlemen. There was a dinner to be eaten—Mr. Ashley partook of it, and Gerard felt that his absence would be indecorous. After dinner he was put to a trial—more severe to a sensitive, imaginative mind than any sharp strokes of commonplace adversity. He was minutely questioned as to the extent of his acquaintance with Falkner— how he came to form it—how often he had seen him—and what had drawn confession from him they named the criminal. These inquiries had been easily answered, but that the name of Elizabeth must be introduced—and, as he expected, at the mention of a daughter, a world of inquiry followed— and coarse remarks fell from his father's lips—which harrowed up his soul; while he felt that he had no exculpation to offer, nor any explanation that might take from her the name and association of the child of a murderer.

As soon as he could he burst away. He rushed into the open air, and hurried to the spot where he could best combat with and purify the rebellious emotions of his heart—none but the men placed as watch were near his mother's grave. Seeing the young squire, they retreated—and he who had come on foot at such quick pace that he scarcely felt the ground he trod, threw himself on the sands, grateful to find himself alone with nature. The moon was hurrying on among the clouds—now bright in the clear ether, now darkened by heavy masses—and the mirroring ocean was sometimes alive with sparkling silver, now veiled and dim, so that you could hear, but not see, the breaking of the surge.

An eloquent author has said, in contempt of such a being: "Try to conceive a man without the ideas of God and eternity; of the good, the true, the beautiful, and the infinite." Neville was certainly not such. There was poetry in his very essence; and enthusiasm for the ideal of the excellent gave his character a peculiar charm, to any one equally exalted and refined. His mother's decaying form lay beneath the sands on which he was stretched, death was there in its most hideous form; beauty, and even form had deserted that frame-work which once was the dear being, whose caresses, so warm and fond, it yet often thrilled him to remember. He had demanded from Heaven the revelation of his mother's fate, *here* he found it, here in the narrow grave lay the evidence of her virtues and her death; did he thank Heaven? even while he did, he felt with bitterness that the granting of his prayer was inextricably linked with the ruin of a being, as good and fair as she whose honour he had so earnestly desired to vindicate.

He thought of all the sordid, vulgar, but heart-thrilling misery which by his means was brought on Elizabeth; and he sought his heart for excuses for the success for which he had pined. They came ready; no desire of vulgar vengeance had been his; his motives had been exalted, his conduct straightforward. The divine stamp on woman is her maternal character—it was to prove that his idolized mother had not deserted the first and most sacred duty in the world that had urged him—and he could not foresee that the innocent would suffer through his inquiries. The crime must fall on its first promoter—on Falkner's head must be heaped the consequences of his act; all else were guiltless. These reflections, however, only served to cheat his wound of its pain for a time—again other thoughts recurred, the realities, the squalid realities of the scene, in which she, miserable, was about to take a part. The thief-takers and the gyves—the prison, and the public ignominious trial—Falkner was to be subjected to all these indignities, and he well knew that his daughter would not leave his side. "And I, her son, the offspring of these sainted bones—placed here by him—how can I draw near his child! God have mercy on her, for man will have none!"

Still he could not be satisfied. "Surely," he thought, "something can be done, and something I will do. Already men are gone, who are to tear him from his home, and to deliver him up to all those vile contrivances devised for the coercion of the lowest of mankind—she will accompany him, while I must remain here. To-morrow these remains will be conveyed to our house—on the following day they are to be interred in the family vault, and I must be present—I am tied, forced to inaction—the privilege of free action taken from me."

Hope was awakened, however, as he pursued these thoughts, and recollected the generous, kindly disposition of Lady Cecil, and her attachment to her young friend. He determined to write to her. He felt assured that she would do all in her power to alleviate Elizabeth's sufferings—what she could do, he did not well understand—but it was a relief to him to take some step for the benefit of the devoted daughter. Bitterly as he thought of these things, did he regret that he had ever seen Elizabeth? So complicated was the web of event, that he knew not how to wish any event to have occurred differently; except that he had not trusted to the hollow pretences of his father. He saw at once how the generous and petty-minded can never coalesce—he ought to have acted for himself, by himself; and miserable as in any case the end must have been, he felt that his own open, honourable revenge would have been less cruel in its effects than the malicious pursuit of his vindictive father.

# CHAPTER XXXVII

There is an impatient spirit in the young, that will not suffer them to take into consideration the pauses that occur between events. That which they do not see move, they believe to be stationary. Falkner was surprised by the silence of several days on the part of Neville; but he did not the less expect and prepare for the time, when he should be called upon to render an account for the wrong he had done. Elizabeth, on the contrary, deemed that the scene was closed, the curtain fallen. What more could arise? Neville had obtained assurance of the innocence and miserable end of his mother. In some manner this would be declared to the world; but the echo of such a voice would not penetrate the solitude in which she and her guardian were hereafter to live. Silence and exclusion were the signal and seal of discovered guilt—other punishment she did not expect. The name of Falkner had become abhorrent to all who bore any relationship to the injured Alithea. She had bid an eternal adieu to the domestic circle at Oakly—to the kind and frank-hearted Lady Cecil—and, with her, to Gerard. His mind, fraught with a thousand virtues—his heart, whose sensibility had awoke her tenderness, were shut irrevocably against her.

Did she love Gerard? This question never entered her own mind. She felt, but did not reason on, her emotions. Elizabeth was formed to be alive to the better part of love. Her enthusiasm gave ideality, her affectionate disposition warmth, to all her feelings. She loved Falkner, and that with so much truth and delicacy, yet fervour of passion, that scarcely could her virgin heart conceive a power more absolute, a tie more endearing, than the gratitude she had vowed to him; yet she intimately felt the difference that existed between her deep-rooted attachment for him she named and looked on as her father, and the spring of playful, happy, absorbing emotions that animated her intercourse with Neville. To the one she dedicated her life and services; she watched him as a mother may a child; a smile or cheerful tone of voice was warmth and gladness to her anxious bosom, and she wept over his misfortunes with the truest grief.

But there was more of the genuine attachment of mind for mind in her sentiment for Neville. Falkner was gloomy and self-absorbed. Elizabeth might grieve for, but she found it impossible to comfort him. With Gerard it was far otherwise. Elizabeth had opened in his soul an unknown spring of sympathy, to relieve the melancholy which had hitherto overwhelmed him. With her he gave way freely to the impulses of a heart which longed to mingle its hitherto checked stream of feeling with other and sweeter waters. In every way he excited her admiration as well as kindness. The poetry of his nature suggested expressions and ideas at once varied and fascinating. He led her to new and delightful studies, by unfolding to her the pages of the poets of her native country, with which she was little conversant. Except Shakspeare and Milton, she knew nothing of English poetry. The volumes of Chaucer and Spenser, of ancient date; of Pope, Gray, and Burns; and, in addition, the writings of a younger, but divine race of poets, were all opened to her by him. In music, also, he became her teacher. She was a fine musician of the German school. He introduced her to the simpler graces of song; and brought her the melodies of Moore, so "married to immortal verse," that they can only be thought of conjointly. Oh, the happy days of Oakly! How had each succeeding hour been gilded by the pleasures of a nascent passion, of the existence of which she had never before dreamed—and these were fled for ever! It was impossible to feel assured of so sad a truth, and not to weep over the miserable blight. Elizabeth commanded herself to appear cheerful, but sadness crept over her solitary hours. She felt that the world had grown, from being a copy of paradise, into a land of labour and disappointment; where self-approbation was to be gained through self-sacrifice; and duty and happiness became separate, instead of united objects at which to aim.

From such thoughts she took refuge in the society of Falkner. She loved him so truly, that she forgot her personal regrets—she forgot even Neville when with him. Her affection for her benefactor was not a stagnant pool, mantled over by memories existing in the depths of her soul, but giving no outward sign; it was a fresh spring of overflowing love—it was redundant with all the better portion of our nature—gratitude, admiration, and pity for ever fed it, as from a perennial fountain.

It was on a day, the fifth after the disclosure of Falkner, that she had been taking her accustomed ride, and, as she rode, given herself up to those reveries—now enthusiastic, now drooping and mournful—that sprung from her singular and painful position. She returned home, eager to forget in Falkner's society many a rebel thought, and to drive away the image of her younger friend, by gazing on the wasted, sinking form of her benefactor, in whose singularly noble countenance she ever found new cause to devote her fortunes and her heart. To say that he was "not less than archangel ruined," is not to express the peculiar interest of Falkner's appearance. Thus had he seemed, perhaps, thirteen years before at Treby;

but gentle and kindly sentiments, the softening intercourse of Elizabeth, the improvement of his intellect, and the command he had exercised over the demonstration of passion, had moulded his face into an expression of benevolence and sweetness, joined to melancholy thoughtfulness; an abstracted, but not sullen seriousness, that rendered it interesting to every beholder. Since his confession to Neville, since the die was cast, and he had delivered himself up to his fate to atone for his victim, something more was added; exalted resolution and serene lofty composure had replaced his usual sadness; and the passions of his soul, which had before deformed his handsome lineaments, now animated them with a beauty of mind which struck Elizabeth at once with tenderness and admiration.

Now, longing to behold, to contemplate this dear face, and to listen to a voice that always charmed her out of herself, and made her forget her sorrows—she was disappointed to find his usual sitting-room empty—it appeared even as if the furniture had been thrown into disorder; there were marks of several dirty feet upon the carpet; on the half-written letter that lay on the desk the pen had hastily been thrown, blotting it. Elizabeth wondered a little, but the emotion was passing away, when the head servant came into the room, and informed her that his master had gone out, and would not return that night.

"Not to-night!" exclaimed Elizabeth; "what has happened? who have been here?"

"Two men, miss."

"Men! gentlemen?"

"No, miss, not gentlemen."

"And my father went away with them?"

"Yes, miss," replied the man, "he did indeed. He would not take the carriage; he went in a hired post-chaise. He ordered me to tell you, miss, that he would write directly, and let you know when you might expect him."

"Strange, very strange is this!" thought Elizabeth. She did not know why she should be disturbed, but disquiet invaded her mind; she felt abandoned and forlorn, and, as the shades of evening gathered round, even desolate. She walked from room to room, she looked from the window, the air was chill, and from the east, yet she repaired to the garden; she felt restless and miserable; what could the event be that took Falkner away? She pondered vainly. The most probable conjecture was, that he obeyed some summons from her own relations. At length one idea rushed into her mind, and she returned to the house, and rang for the servant. Falkner's wandering life had prevented his having any servant of long-tried fidelity about him—but this man was good-hearted and respectable—he felt for his young mistress, and consulted with her maid as to the course they should take under the present painful circumstances; and had concluded that they should preserve silence as to what had occurred, leaving her to learn it from their master's expected letter. Yet the secret was in some danger, when, fixing her eyes on him, Elizabeth said, "Tell me truly, have you no guess what this business is that has taken your master away?"

The man looked confused; but, like many persons not practised in the art of cross-questioning, Elizabeth balked herself, by adding another inquiry before the first was answered; saying with a faltering voice, "Are you sure, Thompson, that it was not a challenge—a duel?"

The domestic's face cleared up: "Quite certain, miss, it was no duel—it could not be—the men were not gentlemen."

"Then," thought Elizabeth, as she dismissed the man, "I will no longer torment myself. It is evidently some affair of mere business that has called him away. I shall learn all to-morrow."

Yet the morrow and the next day came, and Falkner neither wrote nor returned. Like all persons who determine to conjecture no more, Elizabeth's whole time was spent in endeavouring to divine the cause of his prolonged absence and strange silence. Had any communication from Neville occasioned his departure? was he sent for to point out his victim's grave? That idea carried some probability with it; and Elizabeth's thoughts flew fast to picture the solitary shore, and the sad receptacle of beauty and love. Would Falkner and Neville meet at such an hour? without a clew to guide her, she wandered for ever in a maze of thought, and each hour added to her disquietude. She had not gone beyond the garden for several days, she was fearful of being absent when anything might arise; but nothing occurred, and the mystery became more tantalizing and profound.

On the third day she could endure the suspense no longer; she ordered horses to be put to the carriage, and told the servant of her intention to drive into town, and to call on Falkner's solicitor, to learn if he had any tidings; that he was ill she felt assured—where and how? away from her, perhaps deserted by all the world: the idea of his sick-bed became intolerably painful; she blamed herself for her inaction; she resolved not to rest till she saw her father again.

Thompson knew not what to say; he hesitated, begged her not to go; the truth hovered on his lips, yet he feared to give it utterance. Elizabeth saw his confusion; it gave birth to a thousand fears, and she exclaimed, "What frightful event are you concealing? Tell me at once. Great God! why this silence? Is my father dead?"

"No, indeed, miss," said the man, "but my master is not in London, he is a long way off. I heard he was taken to Carlisle."

"Taken to Carlisle! Why taken? What do you mean?"

"There was a charge against him, miss," Thompson continued, hesitating at every word, "the men who came—they apprehended him for murder."

"Murder!" echoed his auditress; "then they fought! Gerard is killed!"

The agony of her look made Thompson more explicit. "It was no duel," he said, "it was done many years ago; it was a lady who was murdered, a Mrs. or Lady Neville."

Elizabeth smiled—a painful, yet a genuine smile; so glad was she to have her worst fears removed, so futile did the accusation appear; the smile passed away, as she thought of the ignominy, the disgraceful realities of such a process—of Falkner torn from his home, imprisoned, a mark for infamy. Weak minds are stunned by a blow like this, while the stronger rise to the level of the exigency, and grow calm from the very call made upon their courage. Elizabeth might weep to remember past or anticipated misfortunes, but she was always calm when called upon to decide and act; her form seemed to dilate, her eyes flashed with a living fire, her whole countenance beamed with lofty and proud confidence in herself. "Why did you not tell me this before?"' she exclaimed. "What madness possessed you to keep me in ignorance? How much time has been lost! Order the horses! I must begone at once, and join my father."

"He is in jail, miss," said Thompson. "I beg your pardon, but you had better see some friend before you go."

"I must decide upon that," replied Elizabeth. "Let there be no delay on your part, you have caused too much. But the bell rings; did I not hear wheels? perhaps he is returned." She rushed to the outer door; she believed that it was her father returned; the garden-gate opened—two ladies entered; one was Lady Cecil. In a moment Elizabeth felt herself embraced by her warm-hearted friend; she burst into tears. "This is kind, more than kind!" she exclaimed; "and you bring good news, do you not? My father is liberated, and all is again well!"

# CHAPTER XXXVIII

The family of Raby must be considered collectively, as each member united in one feeling, and acted on one principle. They were Catholics, and never forgot it. They were not bent on proselytism; on the contrary, they rather shunned admitting strangers into their circle: but they never ceased to remember that they belonged to the ancient faith of the land, and looked upon their fidelity to the tenets of their ancestors as a privilege, and a distinction far more honourable than a patent of nobility. Surrounded by Protestants, and consequently, as they believed, by enemies, it was the aim of their existence to keep their honour unsullied; and that each member of the family should act for the good and glory of the whole, unmindful of private interests and individual affections. The result of such a system may be divined. The pleasures of mediocrity—toiling merit—the happy home—the cheerful family union, where smiles glitter brighter than gold; all these were unknown or despised. Young hearts were pitilessly crushed; young hopes blighted without remorse. The daughters were doomed, for the most part, to the cloister; the sons to foreign service. This, indeed, was not to be attributed entirely to the family failing—a few years ago, English Catholics were barred out from every road to emolument and distinction in their native country.

Edwin Raby had thus been sacrificed. His enlightened mind disdained the trammels thrown over it; but his apostacy doomed him to become an outcast. He had previously been the favourite and hope of his parents; from the moment that he renounced his religion he became the opprobrium. His name was never mentioned; and his death hailed as a piece of good fortune, that freed his family from a living disgrace. The only person among them who regretted him was the wife of his eldest brother; she had appreciated his talents and virtues, and had entertained a sincere friendship for him; but even she renounced him.

Her heart, naturally warm and noble, was narrowed by prejudice; but while she acted in conformity with the family principle, she suffered severely from the shock thus given to her better feelings. When Edwin died, her eyes were a little opened; she began to suspect that human life and human suffering deserved more regard than articles of belief. The "late remorse of love" was awakened, and she never wholly forgot the impression. She had not been consulted concerning, she knew nothing of, his widow and orphan child. Young at that time, the weight of authority pressed also on her, and she had been bred to submission. There was a latent energy, however, in her character that developed itself as she grew older. Her husband died, and her consequence increased in old Oswi Raby's eyes. By degrees her authority became paramount; it was greatly regulated by the prejudices and systems cherished by the family, as far as regarded the world in general; but it was softened in her own circle by the influence of the affections. Her daughters were educated at home—not one was destined for the cloister. Her only son was brought up at Eton; the privileges granted of late years to the Catholics made her entertain the belief, that it was no longer necessary to preserve the old defences and fortifications which intolerance had forced its victims to institute; still pride—pride of religion, pride of family, pride in an unblemished name, were too deeply rooted, too carefully nurtured, not to form an integral part of her character.

When a letter from her father-in-law revealed to her the existence of Elizabeth, her heart warmed towards the orphan and deserted daughter of Edwin. She felt all the repentance which duties neglected bring on a well-regulated mind—her pride revolted at the idea that a daughter of the house of Raby was dependant on the beneficence of a stranger—she resolved that no time should be lost in claiming and receiving her, even while she trembled to think of how, brought up as an alien, she might prove rather a burden than an acquisition. She had written to make inquiries as to her niece's abode. She heard that she was on a visit at Lady Cecil's at Hastings—Mrs. Raby was at Tunbridge—she instantly ordered horses, and proceeded to Oakly.

On the morning of her visit, Lady Cecil had received a letter from Gerard: it was incoherent, and had been written by snatches in the carriage on his way to Dromore. Its first words proclaimed his mother's innocence, and the acknowledgment of her wrongs by Sir Boyvill himself. As he went on, his pen lingered—he trembled to write the words, "Our friend, our Elizabeth, is the daughter of the destroyer." It was unnatural, it was impossible—the very thought added acrimony to his detestation of Falkner—it prevented the compassion his generous nature would otherwise have afforded, and yet roused every wish to spare him, as much as he might be spared, for his heroic daughter's sake. He felt deceived, trepanned, doomed. In after life we are willing to compromise with fate—to take the good with the bad—and are satisfied if we can at all lighten the burden of life. In youth we aim at completeness and perfection. Ardent and single-minded, Neville disdained prejudices; and his impulse was, to separate the idea of father and daughter, and to cherish Elizabeth as a being totally distinct from her parentage. But she would not yield to this delusion—she would cling to her father—and if he died by his hand, he would for ever become an object of detestation. Well has Alfieri said, "There is no struggle so vehement as when an upright but passionate heart is divided between inclination and duty." Neville's soul was set upon honour and well-doing; never before had he found the execution of the dictates of his conscience so full of bitterness and impatience. Something of these feelings betrayed themselves in his letter. "We have lost Elizabeth," he wrote; "for ever lost her! Is there no help for this? No help for her? None! She clings to the destroyer's side, and shares his miserable fate—lost to happiness—to the innocence and sunshine of life. She will live a victim and die a martyr to her duties; and she is lost to us for ever!"

Lady Cecil read again and again—she wondered—she grieved—she uttered impatient reproaches against Gerard for having sought the truth; and yet her heart was with him, and she rejoiced in the acknowledged innocence of Alithea. She thought of Elizabeth with the deepest grief—had they never met—had she and Gerard never seen each other, neither had loved, and half this wo had been spared. How strange and devious are the ways of fate—how difficult to resign one's self to its mysterious and destructive course! Naturally serene, though vivacious—kind-hearted, but not informed with trembling insensibility—yet so struck was Lady Cecil by the prospects of misery for those she best loved, that she wept bitterly, and wrung her hands in impatient, impotent despair. At this moment Mrs. Raby was announced.

Mrs. Raby had something of the tragedy queen in her appearance. She was tall and dignified in person. Her black full eyes were melancholy— her brow shadowing them over had a world of thought and feeling in its sculpture-like lines. The lower part of her face harmonized, though something of pride lurked about her beautiful mouth—her voice was melodious, but deep-toned. Her manners had not the ease of the well-bred Lady Cecil—something of the outcast was imprinted upon them, which imparted consciousness, reserve, and alternate timidity and haughtiness. There was nothing embarrassed, however, in her mien, and she asked at once for Elizabeth with obvious impatience. She heard that she was gone with regret. The praises Lady Cecil almost involuntarily showered on her late guest at once dissipated this feeling; and caused her, with all the frankness natural to her, to unfold at once the object of her visit—the parentage of the orphan—the discovery of her niece. Lady Cecil clasped her hands in a transport, which was not all joy. There was so much of wonder, almost of disbelief, at the strange tale—had a fairy's wand operated the change, it had not been more magical in her eyes. Heaven's ways were vindicated—all of evil vanished from the scene—her friend snatched from ignominy and crime, to be shrined for ever in their hearts and love.

She poured out these feelings impetuously. Mrs. Raby was well acquainted with Alithea's story, and was familiar with Gerard Neville's conduct; all that she now heard was strange indeed. She did not imbibe any of Lady Cecil's gladness, but much of her eagerness. It became of paramount importance in her mind to break at once the link between Elizabeth and her guardian, before the story gained publicity, and the name of Raby became mingled in a tale of horror and crime, which, to the peculiar tone of Mrs. Raby's mind, was singularly odious and disgraceful. No time must be lost—Elizabeth must be claimed—must at once leave the guilty and tainted one, while yet her name received no infection; or she would be disowned for ever by her father's family. When Lady Cecil learned Mrs. Raby's intention of proceeding to London to see her niece, she resolved to go also, to act as mediator, and to soften the style of the demands made, even while she persuaded Elizabeth to submit to them. She expressed her intention, and the ladies agreed to travel together. Both were desirous of further communication. Lady Cecil wished to interest Mrs. Raby still more deeply in her matchless kinswoman's splendid qualities of heart and mind; while Mrs. Raby felt that her conduct must be founded on the character and worth of her niece; even while she was more convinced, at every minute, that no half measures would be permitted by Oswi Raby, and others of their family and connexion, and that Elizabeth's welfare depended on her breaking away entirely from her present position, and throwing herself unreservedly upon the kindness and affection of her father's relations.

Strange tidings awaited their arrival in London, and added to the eagerness of both. The proceedings of Sir Boyvill, the accusation of Falkner, and his actual arrest, with all its consequent disgrace, made each fear that it was too late to interpose. Mrs. Raby showed most energy. The circumstances were already in the newspapers, but there was no mention of Elizabeth. Falkner had been taken from his home, but no daughter accompanied him, no daughter appeared to have any part in the shocking scene. Had Falkner had the generosity to save her from disgrace? If so, it became her duty to cooperate in his measures. Where Elizabeth had taken refuge, was uncertain; but, on inquiry, it seemed that she was still at Wimbledon. Thither the ladies proceeded together. Anxiety possessed both to a painful degree. There was a mysteriousness in the progress of events which they could not unveil—all depended on a clear and a happy explanation. The first words and first embrace of Elizabeth reassured her friend; all indeed would be well, she restored to her place in society, and punishment would fall on the guilty alone.

# CHAPTER XXXIX

The first words that Elizabeth spoke, as she embraced Lady Cecil, "You are come, then all is well," seemed to confirm her belief that the offered protection of Mrs. Raby would sound to the poor orphan as a hospitable shore to the wrecked mariner. She pressed her fondly to her heart, repeating her own words, "All is well—dear, dear Elizabeth, you are restored to us, after I believed you lost for ever."

"What, then, has happened?" asked Elizabeth, "and where is my dear father?"

"Your father! Miss Raby," repeated a deep, serious, but melodious voice; "whom do you call your father?"

Elizabeth, in her agitation, had not caught her aunt's name, and turned with surprise to the questioner, whom Lady Cecil introduced as one who had known and loved her real father; as her aunt, come to offer a happy and honourable home—and the affection of a relative to one so long lost, so gladly found.

"We have come to carry you off with us," said Lady Cecil; "your position here is altogether disagreeable; but everything is changed now, and you will come with us."

"But my father," cried Elizabeth; "for what other name can I give to my benefactor? Dear Lady Cecil, where is he?"

"Do you not then know?" asked Lady Cecil, hesitatingly.

"This very morning I heard something frightful, heart-breaking; but since you are here, it must be all a fiction, or at least the dreadful mistake is put right. Tell me, where is Mr. Falkner?"

"I know less than you, I believe," replied her friend; "my information is only gathered from the hasty letters of my brother, which explain nothing."

"But Mr. Neville has told you," said Elizabeth, "that my dear father is accused of murder; accused by him who possesses the best proof of his innocence. I had thought Mr. Neville generous, unsuspicious—"

"Nor is it he," interrupted Lady Cecil, "who brings this accusation. I tell you I know little; but Sir Boyvill is the origin of Mr. Falkner's arrest. The account he read seemed to him unsatisfactory, and the remains of poor Mrs. Neville. Indeed, dear Elizabeth, you must not question me, for I know nothing; much less than you. Gerard puts much faith in the innocence of Mr. Falkner."

"Bless him for that!" cried Elizabeth, tears gushing into her eyes. "Oh yes, I knew that he would be just and generous. My poor, poor father! by what fatal mistake is your cause judged by one incapable of understanding or appreciating you?"

"Yet," said Lady Cecil, "he cannot be wholly innocent; the flight, the catastrophe, the concealment of his victim's death; is there not guilt in these events?"

"Much, much; I will not excuse or extenuate. If ever you read his narrative, which, at his desire, I gave Mr. Neville, you will learn from that every exculpation he can allege. It is not for me to speak, nor to hear even of his past errors; never was remorse more bitter, contrition more sincere. But for me, he had not survived the unhappy lady a week; but for me, he had died in Greece, to expiate his fault. Will not this satisfy his angry accusers?

"I must act from higher motives. Gratitude, duty, every human obligation bind me to him. He took me, a deserted orphan, from a state of miserable dependance on a grudging, vulgar woman; he brought me up as his child; he was more to me than father ever was. He has nursed me as my own mother would in sickness; in perilous voyages he has carried me in his arms, and sheltered me from the storm, while he exposed himself for my sake; year after year, while none else have cared for, have thought, of me, I have been the object of his solicitude. He has consented to endure life, that I might not be left desolate, when I knew not that one of my father's family would acknowledge me. Shall I desert him now? Never!"

"But you cannot help him," said Lady Cecil; "he must be tried by the laws of his country. I hope he has not in truth offended against them; but you cannot serve him."

"Where is he, dear Lady Cecil? tell me where he is."

"I fear there can be no doubt he is in prison at Carlisle."

"And do you think that I cannot serve him there? in prison as a criminal! Miserable as his fate makes me, miserable as I too well know that he is, it is some compensation to my selfish heart to know that I can serve him, that I can be all in all of happiness and comfort to him. Even now he pines for me; he knows that I never leave his side when in sorrow; he wonders I am not already there. Yes, in prison, in shame, he will be happy when he sees me again. I shall go to him, and then, too, I shall have comfort."

She spoke with a generous animation, while yet her eyes glistened, and her voice trembled with emotion. Lady Cecil was moved, while she deplored; she caressed her; she praised, while Mrs. Raby said, "It is impossible not to honour your intentions, which spring from so pure and noble a source. I think, indeed, that you overrate your obligations to Mr. Falkner. Had he restored you to us after your mother's death, you would have found, I trust, a happy home with me. He adopted you, because it best pleased him so to do. He disregarded the evil he brought upon us by so doing; and only restored you to us when the consequence of his crimes prevented him from being any longer a protection."

"Pardon me," said Elizabeth, "if I interrupt you. Mr. Falkner is a suffering, he believed himself to be a dying, man; he lived in anguish till he could declare his error, to clear the name of his unhappy victim; he wished first to secure my future lot, before he dared fate for himself; chance altered his designs; such were his motives, generous towards me as they ever were."

"And you, dear Elizabeth," said Lady Cecil, "must act in obedience to them and to his wishes. He anticipated disgrace from his disclosures—a disgrace which you must not share. You speak like a romantic girl of serving him in prison. You cannot guess what a modern jail is, its vulgar and shocking inhabitants: the hideous language and squalid sights are such that their very existence should be a secret to the innocent: be assured that Mr. Falkner, if he be, as I believe him, a man of honour and delicacy, will shudder at the very thought of your approaching such contamination; he will be best pleased to know you safe and happy with your family."

"What a picture do you draw!" cried Elizabeth, trying to suppress her tears; "my poor, poor father, whose life hangs by a thread! how can he survive the accumulation of evil? But he will forget all these horrors when I am with him. I know, thank God, I do indeed know, that I have power to cheer and support him, even at the worst."

"This is madness!" observed Lady Cecil, in a tone of distress.

Mrs. Raby interposed with her suggestions. She spoke of her own desire, the desire of all the family, to welcome Elizabeth; she told her that with them, belonging to them, she had new duties; her obedience was due to her relatives; she must not act so as to injure them. She alluded to their oppressed religion; to the malicious joy their enemies would have in divulging such a tale as that would be, if their niece's conduct made the whole course of events public. And, as well as she could, she intimated that if she mixed up her name in a tale so full of horror and guilt, her father's family could never after receive her.

Elizabeth heard all this with considerable coldness. "It grieves me," she said, "to repay intended kindness with something like repulse. I have no wish to speak of the past; nor to remind you that if I was not brought up in obedience to you all, it was because my father was disowned, my mother abandoned; and I, a little child, an orphan, was left to live and die in dependance. I, who then bore your name, had become a subject of niggard and degrading charity. Then, young as I was, I felt gratitude, obedience, duty, all due to the generous benefactor who raised me from this depth of want, and made me the child of his heart. It is a lesson I have been learning many years; I cannot unlearn it now. I am his; bought by his kindness; earned by his unceasing care for me, I belong to him—his child—if you will, his servant—I do not quarrel with names—a child's duty I pay him, and will ever. Do not be angry with me, dear aunt, if I may give you that name—dearest Lady Cecil, do not look so imploringly on me—I am very unhappy. Mr. Falkner a prisoner, accused of the most hideous crime—treated with ignominy—he whose nerves are agonized by a touch—whose frame is even now decaying through sickness and sorrow—and I, and every hope, away. I am very unhappy. Do not urge me to what is impossible, and thrice, thrice wicked. I must go to him; day and night I shall have no peace till I am at his side; do not, for my sake do not, dispute this sacred duty."

It was not thus that the two ladies could be led to desist; they soothed her, but again returned to the charge. Lady Cecil brought a thousand arguments of worldly wisdom, of feminine delicacy. Mrs. Raby insinuated the duty owed to her family, to shield it from the disgrace she was bringing on it. They both insisted on the impossibility, on the foolish romance of her notions. Had she been really his daughter, her joining him in prison was impracticable—out of all propriety. But Elizabeth had been brought up to regard feelings, rather than conventional observances; duties, not proprieties. All her life Falkner had been her law, rule, every tie to her; she knew and felt nothing beyond. When she had followed him to Greece—when she had visited the Morea, to bear him, dying, away—when at Zante she had watched by his sick couch, the world, and all the Rabys it contained, were nothing to her; and now, when he was visited by a far heavier calamity, when, in solitude and misery, he had, besides her, no one comfort under heaven, was she to adopt a new system of conduct, become a timid, home—bred young lady, tied by the most frivolous rules, impeded by fictitious notions of propriety and false delicacy? Whether they were right and she were wrong—whether, indeed, such submission to society—such useless, degrading dereliction of nobler duties, was adapted for feminine conduct, and whether she, despising such bonds, sought a bold and dangerous freedom, she could not tell; she only knew and felt, that for her, educated, as she had been, beyond the narrow paling of boarding-school ideas, or the refinements of a lady's boudoir, that, where her benefactor was, there she ought, to be; and that to prove her gratitude, to preserve her faithful attachment to him amid dire adversity, was her sacred duty—a virtue before which every minor moral faded and disappeared.

The discussion was long; and, even when they found her proof against every attack, they would not give up. They entreated her to go home with them for that day. A wild light beamed from her eyes. "I am going home," she cried; "an hour hence, and I shall be gone to where my true home is. How strange it is that you should imagine that I could linger here!

"Be not afraid for me, dear Lady Cecil," she continued; "all will go well with me; and you will, after a little reflection, acknowledge that I could not act other than I do. And will you, Mrs. Raby, forgive my seeming ingratitude? I acknowledge the justice of your demands. I thank you for your proposed kindness. The name of Raby shall receive no injury; it shall never escape my lips. My father will preserve the same silence. Be not angry with me; but—except that I remember my dear parents with affection—I would say, I take more joy and pride in being his daughter, his friend at this need, than in the distinction and prosperity your kindness offers. I give up every claim on my family; the name of Raby shall not be tainted: but Elizabeth Falkner, with all her wilfulness and faults, shall, at least, prove her gratitude to him who bestowed that appellation on her."

And thus they parted. Lady Cecil veiling her distress in sullenness; while Mrs. Raby was struck and moved by her niece's generosity, which was in accordance with her own noble mind. But she felt that other judges would sit upon the cause, and decide from other motives. She parted from her as a pagan relative might from a young Christian martyr—admiring, while she deplored her sacrifice, and feeling herself wholly incapable of saving.

## CHAPTER XL

Elizabeth delayed not a moment proceeding on her journey; an exalted enthusiasm made her heart beat high, and almost joyously. This buoyancy of spirit, springing from a generous course of action, is the compensation provided for our sacrifices of inclination—and at least, on first setting out, blinds us to the sad results we may be preparing for ourselves. Elated by a sense of acting according to the dictates of her conscience, despite the horror of the circumstances that closed in the prospect, her spirits were light, and her eyes glistened with a feeling at once triumphant and tender, while reflecting on the comfort she was bringing to her unfortunate benefactor. A spasm of horror seized her now and then, as the recollection pressed that he was in prison—accused as a murderer—but her young heart refused to be cowed, even by the ignominy and anguish of such a reflection.

A philosopher not long ago remarked, when adverting to the principle of destruction latent in all works of art, and the overthrow of the most durable edifices; "but when they are destroyed, so as to produce only dust, Nature asserts an empire over them; and the vegetative world rises in constant youth, and in a period of annual successions, by the labours of man, providing food, vitality and beauty adorn the wrecks of monuments, which were once raised for purposes of glory." Thus when crime and wo attack and wreck an erring human being, the affections and virtues of one faithfully attached decorate the ruin with alien beauty; and make that pleasant to the eye and heart which otherwise we might turn from as a loathsome spectacle.

It was a cold September day when she began her journey, and the solitary hours spent on the road exhausted her spirits. In the evening she arrived at Stony Stratford, and here, at the invitation of her servant, consented to spend the night. The solitary inn-room, without a fire, and her lonely supper, chilled her; so susceptible are we to the minor casualties of life, even when we meet the greater with heroic resolution. She longed to skip the present hour, to be arrived—she longed to see Falkner, and to hear his voice—she felt forlorn and deserted. At this moment the door was opened, "a gentleman" was announced, and Gerard Neville entered. Love and nature at this moment asserted their full sway—her heart bounded in her bosom, her cheek flushed, her soul was deluged at once with a sense of living delight—she had never thought to see him more—she had tried to forget that she regretted this; but he was there, and she felt that such a pleasure were cheaply purchased by the sacrifice of her existence. He also felt the influence of the spell. He came agitated by many fears, perplexed by the very motive that led him to her—but she was there in all her charms, the dear object of his nightly dreams and waking reveries—hesitation and reserve vanished in her présence, and they both felt the alliance of their hearts.

"Now that I am here, and see you," said Neville, "it seems to me the most natural thing in the world that I should have followed you as I have done. While away, I had a thousand misgivings—and wherefore? did you not sympathize in my sufferings, and desire to aid me in my endeavours; and I feel convinced that fate, while by the turn of events it appeared to disunite, has, in fact, linked us closer than ever. I am come with a message from Sophia—and to urge also, on my own part, a change in your resolves; you must not pursue your present journey."

"You have, indeed, been taking a lesson from Lady Cecil, when you say this," replied Elizabeth; "she has taught you to be worldly for me—a lesson you would not learn on your own account—she did not seduce me in this way; I gave you my support when you were going to America."

Elizabeth began to speak almost sportively, but the mention of America brought to her recollection the cause of his going and the circumstances that prevented him; and the tears gushed from her eyes as she continued, in a voice broken by emotion, "Oh, Mr. Neville, I smile while my heart is breaking—my dear, dear father! What misery is this that you have brought on him—and now, while he treated you with unreserve, have you falsely— you must know—accused him of crime, and pursued your vengeance in a vindictive and ignominious manner? It is not well done!"

"I pardon your injustice," said Neville, "though it is very great. One of my reasons for coming was to explain the exact state of things, though I believed that your knowledge of me would have caused you to reject the idea of my being a party to my father's feelings of revenge."

Neville then related all that had passed; the discovery of his mother's remains in the very spot Falkner had indicated, and Sir Boyvill's resolve to bring the whole train of events before the public. "Perhaps," he continued, "my father believes in the justice of his accusation—he never saw Mr. Falkner, and cannot be impressed as I am by the tokens of a noble mind, which, despite his errors, are indelibly imprinted on his brow. At all events, he is filled with a sense of his own injuries—stung by the disdain heaped on him in that narration, and angry that he had been led to wrong a wife, the memory of whose virtues and beauty now revives bitterly to reproach him. I cannot wonder at his conduct, even while I deplore it: I do deplore it on your account; for Mr. Falkner, God knows I would have visited his crime in another mode; yet all he suffers he has brought on himself—he must feel it due—and must bear it as best he may: forgive me if I seem harsh—I compassionate him through you—I cannot for his own sake."

"How falsely do you reason," cried Elizabeth; "and you also are swayed and perverted by passion. He is innocent of the hideous crime laid to his charge—you know and feel that he is innocent; and were he guilty—I have heard you lament that crime is so hardly visited by the laws of society. I have heard you say, that even where guilt is joined to the hardness of habitual vice, that it ought to be treated with the indulgence of a correcting father, not by the cruel vengeance of the law. And now, when one whose very substance and flesh are corroded by remorse—one whose conscience acts as a perpetual scourge—one who has expiated his fault by many years spent in acts of benevolence and heroism; this man, because his error has injured you, you, forgetting your own philosophy, would make over to a fate which, considering who and what he is, is the most calamitous human imagination can conceive."

Neville could not hear this appeal without the deepest pain. "Let us forget," he at last said, "these things for a few minutes. They did not arise through me, nor can I prevent them; indeed, they are now beyond all human control. Falkner could as easily restore my mother, whose remains we found mouldering in the grave which he dug for them; he could as easily bring her back to the life and happiness of which he deprived her, as I, my father, or any one, free him from the course of law to which he is made over. We must all abide by the issue—there is no remedy. But you—I would speak of you—"

"I cannot speak, cannot think of myself," replied Elizabeth, "except in one way—to think all delays tedious that keep me from my father's side, and prevent me from sharing his wretchedness."

"And yet you must not go to him," said Neville; "yours is the scheme of inexperience—but it must not be. How can you share Mr. Falkner's sorrows? you will scarcely be admitted to see him. And how unfit for you is such a scene! You cannot guess what these things are; believe me, they are most unfit for one of your sex and age. I grieve to say in what execration the supposed murderer of my mother is held. You would be subjected to insult, you are alone and unprotected—even your high spirit would be broken by the evils that will gather round you."

"I think not," replied Elizabeth; "I cannot believe that my spirit can be broken by injustice, or that it can quail while I perform a duty. It would indeed—spirit and heart would both break—were my conscience burdened with the sin of deserting my father. In prison—amid the hootings of the mob—if for such I am reserved—I shall be safe and well guarded by the approbation of my own mind."

"Would that an angel from heaven would descend to guard you!" cried Neville, passionately; "but in this inexplicable world, guilt and innocence are so mingled, that the one reaps the blessings deserved by the other; and the latter sinks beneath the punishment incurred by the former. Else why, removed by birth, space, and time from all natural connexion with the cause of all this misery, are you cast on this evil hour? Were you his daughter, my heart would not rebel—blood calls to blood, and a child's duty is paramount. But you are no child of his; you spring from another race—honour, affection, prosperity await you in your proper sphere. What have you to do with that unhappy man?

"Yet another word," he continued, seeing Elizabeth about to reply with eagerness; "and yet how vain are words to persuade. Could I but take you to a tower, and show you, spread below, the course of events, and the fatal results of your present resolves, you would suffer me to lead you from the dangerous path you are treading. If once you reach Cumberland, and appear publicly as Falkner's daughter, the name of Raby is lost to you for ever; and if the worst should come, where will you turn for support? Where fly for refuge? Unable to convince, I would substitute entreaty, and implore you to spare yourself these evils. You know not, indeed you do not know, what you are about to do."

Thus impetuously urged, Elizabeth was for a few minutes half bewildered; "I am afraid," she said, "I suppose, indeed, that I am something of a savage—unable to bend to the laws of civilization. I did not know this—I thought I was much like other girls—attached to their home and parents—fulfilling their daily duties, as the necessities of those parents demand. I nursed my father when sick: now that he is in worse adversity, I still feel my proper place to be at his side, as his comforter and companion, glad if I can be of any solace to him. He is my father—my more than father—my preserver in helpless childhood from the worst fate. May I suffer every evil when I forget that! Even if a false belief of his guilt renders the world inimical to him, it will not be so unjust to one as unoffending as I; and if it is, it cannot touch me. Methinks we speak two languages—I speak of duties the most sacred; to fail in which would entail self-condemnation on me to the end of my days. You speak of the conveniences, the paint, the outside of life, which is as nothing in comparison. I cannot yield—I grieve to seem eccentric and headstrong—it is my hard fate, not my will, so to appear."

"Do not give such a name," replied Neville, deeply moved, "to an heroic generosity, only too exalted for this bad world. It is I that must yield, and pray to God to shield and recompense you as you deserve—he only can—he and your own noble heart. And will you pardon me, Miss Raby?"

"Do not give me that name," interrupted Elizabeth. "I act in contradiction to my relations' wishes—I will not assume their name. The other, too, must be painful to you. Call me Elizabeth—"

Neville took her hand. "I am," he said, "a selfish, odious being; you are full of self-sacrifice, of thought for others, of every blessed virtue. I think of myself—and hate myself while I yield to the impulse. Dear, dear Elizabeth, since thus I may call you, are you not all I have ever imagined of excellent? I love you beyond all thought or word; and have for many, many months, since first I saw you at Marseilles. Without reflection, I knew and felt you to be the being my soul thirsted for. I find you, and you are lost!"

Love's own colour died deeply the cheeks of Elizabeth—she felt recompensed for every suffering in the simple knowledge of the sentiment she inspired. A moment before, clouds and storms had surrounded her horizon; now the sun broke in upon it. It was a transcendent though a transient gleam. The thought of Falkner again obscured the radiance, which, even in its momentary flash, was as if an angel, bearing with it the airs of paradise, had revealed itself, and then again become obscured.

Neville was less composed. He had never fully entered into his father's bitter thoughts against Falkner—and Elizabeth's fidelity to the unhappy man made him half suspect the unexampled cruelty and injustice of the whole proceeding. Still compassion for the prisoner was a passive feeling; while horror at the fate preparing for Elizabeth stirred his sensitive nature to its depths, and filled him with anguish. He walked impatiently about the room—and stopped before her, fixing on her his soft lustrous eyes, whose expression was so full of tenderness and passion. Elizabeth felt their influence; but this was not the hour to yield to the delusions of love, and she said—"Now you will leave me, Mr. Neville—I have far to travel tomorrow—good-night."

"Have patience with me yet a moment longer," said Neville; "I cannot leave you thus—without offering from my whole heart, and conjuring you to accept my services. Parting thus, it is very uncertain when we meet again, and fearful sufferings are prepared for you. I believe that you esteem, that you have confidence in me. You know that my disposition is constant and persevering. You know that the aim of my early life being fulfilled, and my mother's name freed from the unworthy aspersions cast upon it, I at once transfer every thought, every hope, to your well-being. At a distance, knowing the scene of misery in which you are placed, I shall be agitated by perpetual fears, and pass unnumbered hours of bitter disquietude. Will you promise me, that, despite all that divides us, if you need any aid or service, you will write to me, commanding me, in the full assurance that all you order shall be executed in its very spirit and letter?"

"I will indeed," replied Elizabeth, "for I know that whatever happens you will always be my friend."

"Your true, your best, your devoted friend," cried Neville; "it will always be my dearest ambition to prove all this. I will not adopt the name of brother—yet use me as a brother—no brother ever cherished the honour, safety, and happiness of a sister as I do yours."

"You knew," said Elizabeth, "that I shall not be alone—that I go to one to whom I owe obedience, and who can direct me. If in his frightful situation he needs counsel and assistance, it is not you, alas, that can render them; still in the world of sorrow in which I shall soon be an inhabitant, it will be a solace and support to think of your kindness, and rely upon it as unreservedly as I do."

"A world of sorrow, indeed!" repeated Neville; "a world of ignominy and wo, such as ought never to have visited you, even in a dream. Its duration will be prolonged also beyond all fortitude or patience. Of course Mr. Falkner's legal advisers will insist on the necessity of Osborne's testimony—he must be sent for, and brought over. This demands time; it will be spring before the trial takes place."

"And all this time my father will be imprisoned as a felon in a jail," cried Elizabeth, tears, bitter tears springing into her eyes. "Most horrible! Oh how necessary that I should be with him, to lighten the weary, unending hours. I thought all would soon be over—and his liberation at hand; this delay of justice is indeed beyond my fears.

"Thank God, that you are thus sanguine of the final result," replied Neville. "I will not say a word to shake your confidence, and I fervently hope it is well placed. And now indeed good-night, I will not detain you longer. All good angels guard you—you cannot guess how bitterly I feel the necessity that disjoins us in this hour of mutual suffering."

"Forgive me," said Elizabeth, "but my thoughts are with my father. You have conjured up a whole train of fearful anticipations; but I will quell them, and be patient again—for his, and all our sakes."

They separated, and at the moment of parting, a gush of tenderness smoothed the harsher feelings inspired by their grief—despite herself, Elizabeth felt comforted by her friend's faithful and earnest attachment; and a few minutes passed in self-communion restored her to those hopes for the best, which are the natural growth of youth and inexperience. Neville left the inn immediately on quitting her; and she, unable to sleep, occupied by various reveries, passed a few uneasy, and yet not wholly miserable, hours. A hallowed calm at last succeeded to her anxious fears; springing from a reliance on Heaven, and the natural delight of being loved by one so dear; it smoothed her wrinkled cares and blunted her poignant regrets.

At earliest dawn she sprung from her bed, eager to pursue her journey—nor did she again take rest till she arrived at Carlisle.

# CHAPTER XLI

In the best room that could be allotted to him consistently with safe imprisonment, and with such comforts around as money might obtain, Falkner passed the lingering days. What so forlorn as the comforts of a prison! the wigwam of the Indian is more pleasing to the imagination — that is in close contiguity with Nature, and partakes her charm — no barrier exists between it and freedom — and Nature and freedom are the stanch friends of unsophisticated man. But a jail's best room sickens the heart in its very show of accommodation. The strongly-barred windows, looking out on the narrow court, surrounded by high frowning walls; the appalling sounds that reach the ear, in such close neighbourhood to crime and wo; the squalid appearance given to each inhabitant by the confined air — the surly, authoritative manners of the attendants — not dependant on the prisoner, but on the state — the knowledge that all may come in, while he cannot get out — and the conviction that the very unshackled state of his limbs depends upon his tame submission and apparent apathy; there is no one circumstance that does not wound the free spirit of man, and make him envy the meanest animal that breathes the free air, and is at liberty.

Falkner, by that strange law of our nature which makes us conceive the future, without being aware of our foreknowledge, had acquainted his imagination with these things — and while writing his history amid the far-stretched mountains of Greece, had shrunk and trembled before such an aspect of slavery; and yet now that it had fallen on him, he felt in the first instance more satisfied, more truly free, than for many a long day before.

There is no tyranny so hard as fear; no prison so abhorrent as apprehension; Falkner was not a coward, yet he feared. He feared discovery — he feared ignominy, and had eagerly sought death to free him from the terror of such evils, with which, perhaps — so strangely are we formed — Osborne had infected him. It had come — it was here — it was his life, his daily bread; and he rose above the infliction calmly, and almost proudly. It is with pride that we say that we endure the worst — there is a very freedom in the thought, that the animosity of all mankind is roused against us — and every engine set at work for our injury — no more can be done — the gulf is passed — the claw of the wild beast is on our heart — but the spirit soars more freely still. To this was added the singular relief which confession brings to the human heart. Guilt hidden in the recesses of the conscience assumes gigantic and distorted dimensions. When the secret is shared by another, it falls back at once into its natural proportion.

Much had this man of wo endured—the feeling against him throughout the part of the country where he now was was vehement. The discovery of poor Alithea's remains—the inquest, and its verdict—the unhappy lady's funeral—had spread far and wide his accusation. It had been found necessary to take him into Carlisle by night; and even then, some few remained in waiting, and roused their fellows, and the hootings of execration were raised against him. "I end as I began," thought Falkner; "amid revilings and injustice—I can surely suffer now that which was so often my lot in the first dawn of boyhood."

His examination before the magistrates was a more painful proceeding. There was no glaring injustice, no vindictive hatred here, and yet he was accused of the foulest crime in nature, and saw in many faces the belief that he was a murderer. The murderer of Alithea! He could have laughed in scorn, to think that such an idea had entered a man's mind. She, an angel whom he worshipped—whom to save he would have met ten thousand deaths—how mad a world—how insane a system must it be, where such a thought was not scouted as soon as conceived!

Falkner had no vulgar mind. In early youth he experienced those aspirations after excellence which betoken the finely moulded among our fellow-creatures. There was a type of virtue engraved in his heart, after which he desired to model himself. Since the hour when the consequences of his guilt revealed its true form to him, he had striven, like an eagle in an iron-bound cage, to free himself from the trammels of conscience. He felt within how much better he might be than anything he was. But all this was unacknowledged and uncared for in the present scene—it was not the heroism of his soul that was inquired into, but the facts of his whereabouts; not the sacred nature of his worship for Alithea, but whether he had had opportunity to perpetrate crime. When we are conscious of innocence, what so heart-sickening as to combat circumstances that accuse us of guilt which we abhor. His prison-room was a welcome refuge after such an ordeal.

His spirit could not be cowed by misfortune, and he felt unnaturally glad to be where he was; he felt glad to be the victim of injustice, the mark of unspeakable adversity; but his body's strength failed to keep pace with the lofty disdain of his soul—and Elizabeth, where was she? He rejoiced that she was absent when torn from his home; he had directed the servants to say nothing to Miss Falkner—he would write; and he had meant to fulfil this promise, but each time he thought to do so he shrunk repugnant. He would not for worlds call her to his side, to share the horrors of his lot; and feeling sure that she would be visited by some member of her father's family, he thought it best to let things take their course—unprotected and alone, she would gladly accept refuge there where it was offered—and the tie snapped between them—happiness and love would alike smile on her.

He had it deeply at heart that she should not be mingled in the frightful details of his present situation, and yet drearily he missed her, for he loved her with a feeling which, though not paternal, was as warm as ever filled a father's breast. His passions were ardent, and all that could be spared from remorse were centred in his adopted child. He had looked on her, as the prophet might on the angel who ministered to his wants in the desert: in the abandonment of all mankind, in the desolation to which his crime had led him, she had brought love and cheer. She had been his sweet household companion, his familiar friend, his patient nurse—his soul had grown to her image, and when the place was vacant that she had filled, he was excited by eager longings for her presence, that even made his man's heart soft as a woman's with very desire.

By degrees, as he thought of her and the past, the heroism of his soul was undermined and weakened. To every eye he continued composed, and even cheerful, as before. None could read in his impassive countenance the misery that dwelt, within. He spent his time in reading and writing, and in necessary communications with the lawyers who were to conduct his defence; and all this was done with a calm eye and unmoved voice. No token of complaint or impatience ever escaped; he seemed equal to the fortune that attacked him. He grew, indeed, paler and thinner—till his handsome features stood out in their own expressive beauty; he might have served for a model of Prometheus—the vulture at his heart producing pangs and spasms of physical suffering; but his will unconquered—his mind refusing to acknowledge the bondage to which his body was the prey. It was an unnatural combat; for the tenderness which was blended with his fiercer passions, and made the charm of his character, sided with his enemies, and made him less able to bear, than one more roughly and hardly framed.

He loved nature—he had spent his life among her scenes. Nothing of her visited him now, save a star or two that rose above the prison wall into the slip of sky his window commanded; they were the faintest stars in heaven, and often were shrouded by clouds and mist. Thus doubly imprisoned, his body barred by physical impediments—his soul shut up in itself—he became, in the energetic language of genius, the cannibal of his own heart. Without a vent for any, thoughts revolved in his brain with the velocity and action of a thousand mill-wheels, and would not be stopped. Now a spasm of painful emotion covered his brow with a cold dew—now self-contempt made every portion of himself detestable in his own eyes—now he felt the curse of God upon him, weighing him down with heavy, relentless burden; and then again he was assailed by images of freedom, and keen longings for the free air. "If even, like Mazeppa, I might seek the wilds, and career along, though death was the bourn in view, I were happy!" These wild thoughts crossed him, exaggerated into gasping desire to achieve such a fate, when the sights and sounds of a prison gathered thick around, and made the very thought of his fellow-creatures one of disgust and abhorrence.

Thus sunk in gloom, far deeper internally than in outward show—warring with remorse and the sense of unmerited injury—vanquished by fate, yet refusing to yield, nature had reached the acme of suffering. He grew to be careless of the result of his trial, and to neglect the means of safety. He pondered on self-destruction—though that were giving the victory to his enemies. He looked round him; his cell appeared a tomb. He felt as if he had passed out of life into death; strange thoughts and images flitted through his mind, and the mortal struggle drew to a close—when, on a day, his prison-door opened, and Elizabeth stepped within the threshold.

To see the beloved being we long for inexpressibly, and believe to be so far—to hear the dear voice, whose sweet accent we imagined to be mute to us for ever—to feel the creature's very soul in real communion with us, and the person we dote on visible to our eyes, such are moments of bliss, which the very imperfections of our finite nature render immeasurably dear. Falkner saw his child, and felt no longer imprisoned. She was freedom and security. Looking on her sweet face, he could not believe in the existence of evil. Wrongs and wo, and a torturing conscience, melted and fled away before her; while fresh-springing happiness filled every portion of his being.

# CHAPTER XLII

Elizabeth arrived at the moment of the first painful crisis of Falkner's fate. The assizes came on—busy faces crowded into his cell, and various consultations took place as to the method of his defence; and here began a series of cares, mortifications, and worse anxieties, which brought home to the hearts of the sufferers the horrors of their position.

The details of crime and its punishment are so alien to the individuals placed in the upper classes of society, that they read them as tales of another and a distant land. And it is like being cast away on a strange and barbarous country to find such become a part of our own lives. The list of criminals—the quality of their offences—the position Falkner held among them, were all discussed by the men of law; and Falkner listened, impassive in seeming apathy—his eagle eye bent on vacancy—his noble brow showing no trace of the rush of agonizing thought that flowed through his brain; it was not till he saw his child's earnest, searching eyes bent on him that he smiled, so to soften the keenness of her lively sympathy. She listened too, her cheek alternately flushed and pale, and her eyes brimming over with tears, as she drew nearer to her unfortunate friend's side, as if her innocence and love might stand between him and the worst.

The decision of the grand jury was the first point to be considered. There existed no doubt but that would go against the accused. The lawyers averred this, but still Elizabeth hoped; men could not be so blind, or some unforeseen enlightenment might dawn on their understandings. The witnesses against him were Sir Boyvill and his son; the latter, she well knew, abhorred the course pursued; and if some touch could reach Sir Boyvill's heart, and show him the unworthiness and falsehood of his proceedings, through the mode in which their evidence might be given, all would alter—the scales would drop from men's eyes, the fetters from Falkner's limbs, and this strange and horrible entanglement be dissipated like morning mist. She brooded for ever on these thoughts; sometimes she pondered on writing to Neville—sometimes on seeing his father; but his assertion was recollected that nothing now could alter the course of events, and that drove her back upon despair.

For ever thinking on these things and hearing them discussed, it was yet a severe blow to both when, in the technical language of the craft, it was announced that a true bill was found against Rupert Falkner.

Such is the nature of the mind, that hitherto Falkner had never looked on the coming time in its true proportions or colours. The decision of the preliminary jury, which *might* be in his favour, had stood as a screen between him and the future. Knowing himself to be innocent, abhorring the very image of the crime of which he was accused, how could twelve impartial, educated men agree that any construction put upon his actions should cast the accusation on him? The lawyers had told him that so it would be—he had read the fearful expectation in Elizabeth's eyes—but it could not! Justice was not a mere word—innocence bore a stamp not to be mistaken; the vulgar and senseless malice of Sir Boyvill would be scouted and reprobated; such was his intimate conviction, though he had never expressed it; but this was all changed now. The tale of horror was admitted, registered as a probability, and had become a rule for future acts. The ignominy of a public trial would assuredly be his. And going, as is usual, from one extreme to the other, the belief entered his soul that he should be found guilty and die the death. A dark veil fell over life and nature. Ofttimes he felt glad even to escape thus from a hideous system of wrong and suffering; but the innate pride of the heart rebelled, and his soul struggled as in the toils.

Elizabeth heard the decision with even more dismay; her head swam, and she grew sick at heart. Would his trial come on in a few days? would all soon, so soon, be decided? was the very moment near at hand to make or mar existence, and turn this earth from a scene of hope into a very hell of torture and despair? for such to her it must be if the worst befell Falkner. The worst! oh, what a worst! how hideous, squalid, unredeemed! There was madness in the thought, and she hurried to his cell to see him and hear him speak, so to dissipate the horror of her thoughts; her presence of mind, her equanimity, all deserted her; she looked bewildered—her heart beat as if it would burst her bosom—her face grew ashy pale—her limbs unstrung of every strength—and her efforts to conceal her weakness from Falkner's eyes but served the more to confuse.

She found him seated near his window, looking on so much of the autumnal sky as could be perceived through the bars of the high narrow opening. The clouds traversed the slender portion of heaven thus visible; they fled fast to other lands, and the spirit of liberty rode upon their outstretched wings; away they flew far from him, and he had no power to reach their bourn, nor to leave the dingy walls that held him in. Oh, Nature! while we possess thee, thy changes ever lovely, thy vernal airs or majestic storms, thy vast creation spread at our feet, above, around us, how can we call ourselves unhappy? There is brotherhood in the growing, opening flowers, love in the soft winds, repose in the verdant expanse, and a quick spirit of happy life throughout, with which our souls hold glad communion. But the poor prisoner was barred out from these; how cumbrous the body felt, how alien to the inner spirit of man the fleshy bars—that allowed it to become the slave of his fellows.

The stunning effects of the first blow had passed away, and there was in Falkner's face that lofty expression that resembled coldness, though it was the triumph over sensibility; something of disdain curled his lip, and his whole air denoted the acquisition of a power superior to fate. Trembling, Elizabeth entered; never before had she lost self-command; even now she paused at the threshold to resume it, but in vain; she saw him, she flew to his arms, she dissolved in tears, and became all woman in her tender fears. He was touched—he would have soothed her; a choking sensation arose in his throat: "I never felt a prisoner till now," he cried: "can you still cling to one struck with infamy?"

"Dearer, more beloved than ever!" she murmured: "surely there is no tie so close and strong as misery?"

"Dear, generous girl." said Falkner, "how I hate myself for making such large demand on your sympathy. Let me suffer alone. This is not the place for you, Elizabeth. Your free step should be on the mountain's side; these silken tresses the playthings of the unconfined winds. While I thought that I should speedily be liberated, I was willing to enjoy the comfort of your society; but now I, the murderer, am not a fit mate for you. I am accursed, and pull disaster down on all near me. I was born to destroy the young and beautiful."

With such talk they tried to baffle this fierce visitation of adversity. Falkner told her that on that day it would be decided whether the trial should take place at once, or time be given to send for Osborne from America. The turn Neville had given to his evidence had been so favourable to the accused as to shake the prejudice against him, and it was believed that the judges would at once admit the necessity of waiting for so material a witness; and yet their first and dearest hope had been destroyed, so they feared to give way to a new one.

As they conversed, the solicitor entered with good tidings. The trial was put off till the ensuing assizes in March, to give time for the arrival of Osborne. The hard dealing of destiny and man relented a little, and despair receded from their hearts, leaving space to breathe, to pray, to hope. No time was to be lost in sending for Osborne. Would he come? It could not be doubted. A free pardon was to be extended to him; and he would save a fellow-creature, and his former benefactor, without any risk of injury to himself.

The day closed, therefore, more cheeringly than it had begun. Falkner conquered himself, even to a show of cheerfulness; and recalled the colour to his tremulous companion's cheeks, and half a smile to her lips, by his encouragement. He turned her thoughts from the immediate subject, narrating the events of his first acquaintance with Osborne, and describing the man; a poltron, but kindly hearted—fearful of his own skin to a contemptible extent, but looking up with awe to his superiors, and easily led by one richer and of higher station to any line of conduct; an inborn slave, but with many of a slave's good qualities. Falkner did not doubt that he would put himself eagerly forward on the present occasion; and whatever his evidence were good for, it would readily be produced.

There was no reason, then, for despair. While the shock they had undergone took the sting from the present—fearing an immediate and horrible catastrophe—the wretchedness of their actual state was forgotten— it acquired comfort and security by the contrast—each tried to cheer the other, and they separated for the night with apparent composure. Yet that night Elizabeth's pillow, despite her earnest endeavours to place reliance on Providence, was watered by the bitterest tears that ever such young eyes shed; and Falkner told each hour of the livelong night, as his memory retraced past scenes, and his spirit writhed and bled to feel that, in the wantonness and rebellion of youth, he had been the author of so widespreading, so dark a web of misery.

From this time their days were spent in that sort of monotony which has a peculiar charm to the children of adversity. The recurrence of one day after the other, none being marked by disaster, or indeed any event, imparted a satisfaction, gloomy indeed, and sad, but grateful to the heart wearied by many blows, and by the excitement of mortal hopes and fears. The mind adapted itself to the new state of things, and enjoyments sprung up in the very home of desolation—circumstances that, in happier days, were but the regular routine of life, grew into blessings from Heaven; and the thought, "Come what will, this hour is safe," made precious the mere passage of time—months were placed between them and the dreaded crisis—and so are we made, that when once this is an established, acknowledged fact, we can play on the eve of danger almost like the unconscious animal destined to bleed.

Their time was regularly divided, and occupations succeeded one to another. Elizabeth rented apartments not far from the prison. She gave the early morning hours to exercise, and the rest of the day was spent in

Falkner's prison. He read to her as she worked at the tapestry frame, or she took the book while he drew or sketched; nor was music wanting, such as suited the subdued tone of their minds, and elevated it to reverence and resignation; and sweet still hours were spent near their fire; for their hearth gleamed cheerfully, despite surrounding horrors—gayety was absent, but neither was the voice of discontent heard; all repinings were hidden in the recesses of their hearts; their talk was calm, abstracted from matters of daily life, but gifted with the interest that talent can bestow on all it touches. Falkner exerted himself chiefly to vary their topics, and to enliven them by the keenness of his observations, the beauty of his descriptions, and the vividness of his narrations. He spoke of India, they read various travels, and compared the manners of different countries—they forgot the bars that checkered the sunlight on the floor of the cell—they forgot the cheerless gloom of each surrounding object. Did they also forget the bars and bolts between them and freedom? the thoughtful tenderness which had become the habitual expression of Elizabeth's face—the subdued manner and calm tones of Falkner were a demonstration that they did not. Something they were conscious of at each minute, that checked the free pulsations of their hearts; a word in a book, brought by some association home to her feelings, would cause Elizabeth's eyes to fill with unbidden tears—and proud scorn would now and then dilate the breast of Falkner, as he read some story of oppression, and felt, "I also am persecuted, and must endure."

In this position they each grew unutterably dear to the other—every moment, every thought, was full to both of the image of either. There is something inexpressibly winning in beauty and grace—it is a sweet blessing when our household companion charms our senses by the loveliness of her person, and makes the eye gladly turn to her, to be gratified by such a form and look as we would travel miles to see depicted on canvass. It soothed many a spasm of pain, and turned many an hour of suffering into placid content, when Falkner watched the movements of his youthful friend. You might look in her face for days, and still read something new, something sublime in the holy calm of her brow, in her serious, yet intelligent eyes; while all a woman's softness dwelt in the moulding of her cheeks and her dimpled mouth. Each word she said, and all she did, so became her, that it appeared the thing best to be said and done—and was accompanied by a fascination, both for eye and heart, which emanated from her purity and truth. Falkner grew to worship the very thought of her. She had not the wild spirits and trembling sensibility of her he had destroyed, but in her kind she was no way inferior.

Yet though each, as it were, enjoyed the respite given by fortune to their worst fears, yet this very sense of transitory security was in its essence morbid and unnatural. A fever preyed nightly on Falkner, and there were ghastly streaks upon his brow that bespoke internal suffering and decay. Elizabeth grew paler and thinner—her step lost its elasticity, her voice became low-toned—her eyes were acquainted with frequent tears, and the lids grew heavy and dark. Both lived for ever in the presence of misery—they feared to move or speak, lest they should awaken the monster, then for a space torpid; but they spent their days under its shadow—the air they drew was chilled by its icy influence—no wholesome light-hearted mood of mind was ever theirs—they might pray and resign themselves, they might congratulate themselves on the safety of the passing moment; but each sand that flowed from the hourglass was weighed—each thought that passed through the brain was examined—every word uttered was pondered over. They were exhausted by the very vividness of their unsleeping endeavours to blunt their sensations.

The hours were very sad that they spent apart. The door closed on Elizabeth, and love, and hope, and all the pride of life vanished with her. Falkner was again a prisoner, an accused felon—a man over whom impended the most hideous fate—whom the dogs of law barked round, and looked on as their prey. His high heart often quailed. He laid his head on his pillow, desiring never again to raise it—despair kept his lids open the livelong nights, while naught but palpable darkness brooded over his eyeballs; he rose languid—dispirited—revolving thoughts of death; till at last she came who by degrees dispelled the gloom, and shed over his benighted soul the rays of her pure spirit.

She also was miserable in solitude; the silent evening hours spent apart from him were melancholy and drear. Nothing interrupted their stillness. She felt deserted by every human being, and was indeed reduced to the extremity of loneliness. In the town and neighbourhood many pitied, many admired her, and some offered their services; but none visited or tried to cheer the solitary hours of the devoted daughter. As the child of a man accused of murder, there was a barrier between her and the world. The English are generous to their friends, but they are never kind to strangers; the tie of brotherhood, which Christ taught as uniting all mankind, is unacknowledged by them. They so fear that their sullen fireside should be unduly invaded, and so expect to be ill-treated, that each man makes a Martello tower of his home, and keeps watch against the gentler charities of life, as from an invading enemy. Hour after hour, therefore, Elizabeth spent—thought her only companion.

From Falkner and his miserable fortunes, sometimes her reflections strayed to Gerard Neville—the generous friend on whom she wholly relied, yet who could in no way aid or comfort her. They were divided. He thought of her, she knew: his constant and ardent disposition would cause her to be for ever the cherished object of his reveries; and now and then, as she took her morning ride, or looked from her casement at night upon the high stars, and pale, still moon, Nature spoke to her audibly of him, and her soul overflowed with tenderness. Still he was far—no word from him reached her—no token of living remembrance. Lady Cecil also—she neither wrote nor sent. The sense of abandonment is hard to bear, and many bitter tears did the young sufferer shed—and many a yearning had she to enter, with her ill-starred father, the silent abode of the tomb—scarcely more still or dark than the portion of life which was allotted to them, even while existence was warm in their hearts, and the natural impulse of their souls was to seek sympathy and receive consolation.

# CHAPTER XLIII

The varied train of hopes and fears which belonged to the situation of the prisoner and his faithful young companion, stood for some time suspended. In some sort, they might be said neither to hope nor fear; for, reasoning calmly, they neither expected that the worst would befall; and the actual and impending evil was certain. Like shipwrecked sailors, who have betaken themselves to a boat, and are tossed upon a tempestuous sea, they saw a ship nearing; they believed that their signal was seen, and that it was bearing down towards them. What if, with sudden tack, the disdainful vessel should turn its prow aside, and leave them to the mercy of the waves. They did not anticipate such a completion to their disasters.

Yet, as time passed, new anxieties occurred. Falkner's solicitor, Mr. Colville, had despatched an agent to America to bring Osborne over. The pardon promised ensured his coming; and yet it was impossible not to feel inquietude with regard to his arrival. Falkner experienced least of this. He felt sure of Osborne, his creature; the being whose life he had heretofore saved, whose fortunes he had created. He knew his weakness, and how easily he was dealt with. The mere people of business were not so secure. Osborne enjoyed a comfortable existence, far from danger—why should he come over to place himself in a disgraceful situation, to be branded as a pardoned felon? In a thousand ways he might evade the summons. Perhaps there was nothing to prove that the Osborne whom Hoskins named was the Osborne who had been employed by Falkner, and was deemed an accessory in Mrs. Neville's death.

Hillary, who had been sent, to Washington in September, had written immediately on his arrival. His passage had been tedious, as autumnal voyages to America usually are; he did not arrive till the last day of October; he announced that Osborne was in the town, and that on the morrow he should see him. This letter had arrived towards the end of November, and there was no reason wherefore Hillary and Osborne should not quickly follow it. But November passed away, and December had begun, and still the voyagers did not arrive; the southwest wind continued to reign with slight variation; except that as winter advanced it became more violent: packets perpetually arrived in Liverpool from America, after passages of seventeen and twenty days; but Hillary did not return, nor did he write.

The woods were despoiled of their leaves; but still the air was warm and pleasant; and it cheered Elizabeth, as favourable to her hopes: the sun shown at intervals, and the misty mornings were replaced by cheerful days. Elizabeth rode out each morning, and this one day, the sixteenth of December, she found a new pleasure in her solitary exercise. The weather was calm and cheerful; a brisk canter gave speed to the current of her blood; and her thoughts, though busy, had a charm in them that she was half angry with herself for feeling, but which glowed all warm and bright, despite every effort. On the preceding evening she had observed on her return home at nine o'clock from the prison, the figure of a man, which passed her hastily, and then stood aloof, as if guarding and watching her at a distance. Once, as he stood under an archway, a flickering lamp threw his shadow across her path. It was a bright moonlight night, and as he stood in the midst of an open space, near which her house was situated, she recognised, muffled as he was, the form of Gerard Neville. No wonder, then, that her heart was lightened of its burden; he had not forgotten her—he could no longer command himself to absence; if he might not converse with her, at least he might look upon her as she passed.

On the same morning she entered her father's prison-room—she found two visiters already there, Colville and his agent, Hillary. The faces of both were long and serious. Elizabeth turned anxiously to Falkner, who looked stern and disdainful. He smiled when he saw her, and said, "You must not be shocked, my love, at the news which these gentlemen bring. I cannot tell how far it influences my fate; but it is impossible to believe that it is irrevocably sealed by it. But who can express the scorn that a man must feel, to know that so abject a poltron wears the human form. Osborne refuses to come."

Such an announcement naturally filled her with dismay. At the request of Falkner, Hillary began again to relate the circumstances of his visit to America. He recounted, that finding that Osborne was in Washington, he lost no time in securing an interview. He delivered his letters to him, and said that he came from Mr. Falkner, on an affair of life and death. At the name, Osborne turned pale; he seemed afraid of opening the letters, and muttered something about there being a mistake. At length he broke the seals. Fear, in its most abject guise, blanched his cheek as he read, and his hand trembled so that he could scarcely hold the paper. Hillary, perceiving at last that he had finished reading, and was hesitating what to say, began himself to enter on the subject; when, faltering and stammering, Osborne threw the letter down, saying, "I said there was a mistake—I know nothing—all this affair is new to me—I never had concern with Mr. Falkner—I do not know who Mr. Falkner is."

But for the pale quivering lips of the man, and his tremulous voice, Hillary might have thought that he spoke truth; but he saw that cowardice was the occasion of the lie he told, and he endeavoured to set before him the perfect safety with which he might comply with the request he conveyed. But the more he said, Osborne, gathering assurance, the more obstinately denied all knowledge of the transactions in question, or their principal actor. He changed, warmed by his own words, from timid to impudent, in his denials, till Hillary's conviction began to be shaken a little; and at the same time he grew angry, and cross-questioned him, with a lawyer's art, about his arrival in America; questions which Osborne answered with evident trepidation. At last, he asked him if he remembered such and such a house, and such a journey, and the name of his companion on the occasion; and if he recollected a person of the name of Hoskins. Osborne started at the word as if he had been shot. Pale he was before, but now his cheeks grew of a chalky white, his limbs refused to support him, and his voice died away; till, rousing himself, he pretended to fly into a violent passion at the insolence of the intrusion and impertinence of the questions. As he spoke, he unwarily betrayed that he knew more of the transaction than he would willingly have allowed; at last, after running on angrily and incoherently for some time, he suddenly broke away, and (they were at a tavern) left the room, and also the house.

Hillary hoped that, on deliberation, he would come to his senses. He sent the letters after him to his house, and called the next day; but he was gone; he had left Washington the evening before, by the steamer to Charlestown. Hillary knew not what to do. He applied to the government authorities; they could afford him no help. He also repaired to Charlestown. Some time he spent in searching for Osborne—vainly; it appeared plain that he travelled under another name. At length, by chance, he found a person who knew him personally, who said that he had departed a week before for New-Orleans. It seemed useless to make this further journey, yet Hillary made it, and with like ill success. Whether Osborne was concealed in that town; whether he had gone to Mexico, or lurked in the neighbouring country, could not be discovered. Time wore away in fruitless researches, and it became necessary to come to a decision. Hopeless of success, Hillary thought it best to return to England—with the account of his failure—so that no time might be lost in providing a remedy, if any could be found, to so fatal an injury to their cause.

While this tale was being told, Falkner had leisure to recover from that boiling of the blood which the first apprehension of unworthy conduct in one of our fellow-creatures is apt to excite, and now spoke with his usual composure. "I cannot believe," he said, "that this man's evidence is of the import which is supposed. No one, in fact, believes that I am a murderer; every one knows that I am innocent. All that we have to do is to prove this in a sort of technical and legal manner; and yet hardly that—for we are not to address the deaf ear of law, but the common sense of twelve men, who will not be slow, I feel assured, in recognising the truth. All that can be done to make my story plain, and to prove it by circumstances, of course must be done; and I do not fear but that, when it is ingenuously and simply told, it will suffice for my acquittal."

"It is right to hope for the best," said Mr. Colville; "but Osborne's refusal to come is, in itself, a bad fact; the prosecutor will insist much upon it—I would give a hundred pounds to have him here."

"I would not give a hundred pence," said Falkner, dryly.

The other stared—the observation had an evil effect on his mind; he fancied that his client was even glad that a witness so material refused to appear, and this to him had the aspect of guilt. He continued, "I am so far of a different opinion, that I should advise sending a second time. Had you a friend sufficiently zealous to undertake a voyage across the Atlantic for the purpose of persuading Osborne—"

"I would not ask him to cross a ditch for the purpose," interrupted Falkner, with some asperity. "Let such men as would believe a dastard like Osborne in preference to a gentleman and a soldier, take my life, if they will. It is not worth this pains in my own eyes—and thirsted for by my fellow-men, it is a burden I would willingly lay down."

The soft touch of Elizabeth's hand placed on his recalled him—he looked on her tearful eyes, and became aware of his fault—he smiled to comfort her. "I ought to apologize to these gentlemen for my hastiness," he said, "and to you, my dear girl, for my apparent trifling—but there is a degradation in these details that might chafe a more placid temper. I cannot, I will not descend to beg my life; I am innocent; this all men must know, or at least will know, when their passions are no longer in excitement against me—I can say no more—I cannot win an angel from heaven to avouch my guiltlessness of her blood—I cannot draw this miserable fellow from his cherished refuge. All must fall on my own shoulders—I must support the burden of my fate; I shall appear before my judges; if they, seeing me, and hearing me speak, yet pronounce me guilty, let them look to it—I shall be satisfied to die, so to quit at once a blind, bloodthirsty world!"

The dignity of Falkner as he spoke these words, the high, disdainful, yet magnanimous expression of his features, the clear though impassioned tone of his voice, thrilled the hearts of all. "Thank God, I do love this man even as he deserves to be loved," was the tender sentiment that lighted up

Elizabeth's eyes; while his male auditors could not help, both by countenance and voice, giving token that they were deeply moved. On taking their leave soon after, Mr. Colville grasped Falkner's hand cordially, and bade him rest assured that his zeal, his utmost endeavours should not be wanting to serve him. "And," he added, in obedience rather to his newly awakened interest than his judgment, "I cannot doubt but that our endeavours will be crowned with complete success."

A man of real courage always finds new strength unfold within him to meet a larger demand made upon it. Falkner was now, perhaps, for the first time, thoroughly roused to meet the evils of his lot. He threw off every natural, every morbid sensibility, and strung himself at once to a higher and firmer tone of mind. He renounced the brittle hopes before held out to him—of this or that circumstance being in his favour—he intrusted unreservedly his whole cause to the mighty irresistible power who rules human affairs, and felt calm and free. If by disgrace and death he were to atone for the destruction of his victim, so let it be—the hour of suffering would come, and it would pass away—and leaving him a corpse, the vengeance of his fellow-creatures would end there. He felt that the decree for life or death having received already the irrefragable fiat—he was prepared for both; and he resolved from that hour to drive all weak emotions, all struggle, all hope or fear from his soul. "Let God's will be done!" something of Christian resignation—something (derived from his Eastern life) of belief in fatality—and something of philosophic fortitude, composed the feeling that engraved this sentiment in his heart in ineffaceable characters.

He now spoke of Osborne to Elizabeth without acrimony. "My indignation against that man was all thrown away," he said; "we do not rebuke the elements when they destroy us, and why should we spend our anger against men?—a word from Osborne, they say, would save me—the falling of the wind, or the allaying of the waves, would have saved Alithea—both are beyond our control. I imagined in those days that I could guide events—till suddenly the reins were torn from my hands. A few months ago I exulted, in expectation that the penalty demanded for my crime would be the falling by the hands of her son—and here I am an imprisoned felon!—and now we fancy that this thing or that might preserve me; while in truth all is decreed, all registered, and we must patiently await the appointed time. Come what may, I am prepared—from this hour I have taught my spirit to bend, and to be content to die. When all is over, men will do me justice, and that poor fellow will bitterly lament his cowardice. It will be agony to him to remember that one word would have preserved my life then, when no power on earth can recall me to existence. He is not a bad man—and could he now have represented to him his after remorse, he would cease to exhibit such lamentable cowardice—a cowardice, after all, that has its origin in the remnants of good feeling. The fear of shame; horror at having participated in so fearful a tragedy; and a desire to throw off the consequences of his actions, which is the perpetual and stinging accompaniment of guilt, form his motives; but could he be told how immeasurably his sense of guilt will be increased if his silence occasions my death, all these would become minor considerations, and vanish on the instant."

"And would it be impossible," said Elizabeth, "to awaken this feeling in him?"

"By no means," replied Falkner; "though it is out of our power. We sent a mercenary, not indeed altogether lukewarm, but still not penetrated by that ardour, nor capable of that eloquence, which is necessary to move a weak man, like the one he had to deal with. Osborne is, in some sort, a villain; but he is too feeble-minded to follow out his vocation. He always desired to be honest. Now he has the reputation of being such; from being one of those miserable creatures, the refuse of civilization, preying upon the vices, while they are the outcasts of society, he has become respectable and trustworthy in the eyes of others. He very naturally clings to advantages dearly earned—lately gained. He fancies to preserve them by deserting me. Could the veil be lifted—could the conviction be imparted of the wretch he will become in his own eyes, and of the universal execration that will be heaped on him after my death, his mind would entirely change, and he would be as eager, I had almost said, to come forward, as now he is set upon concealment and silence."

# CHAPTER XLIV

Elizabeth listened in silence. All that had passed made a deep impression—from the moment that the solicitor had expressed a wish that Falkner had a zealous friend to cross the Atlantic—till now, that he himself dilated on the good that would result from representations being clearly and fervently made to Osborne, she was revolving an idea that absorbed her whole faculties.

This idea was no other than going to America herself. She had no doubt that, seeing Osborne, she could persuade him, and the difficulties of the journey appeared slight to her who had travelled so much. She asked Falkner many questions, and his answers confirmed her more and more in her plan. No objection presented itself to her mind; already she felt sure of success. There was scarcely time, it was true, for the voyage; but she hoped that the trial might be again deferred, if reasonable hopes were held out of Osborne's ultimate arrival. It was painful to leave Falkner without a friend, but the object of her journey was paramount even to this consideration; but it must, it should be undertaken. Still she said nothing of her scheme, and Falkner could not guess at what was passing in her mind.

Wrapped in the revery suggested by such a plan, she returned home in the evening, without thinking of the apparition of Neville, which had so filled her mind in the morning. It was not till at her own door that the thought glanced through her mind, and she remembered that she had seen nothing of him—she looked across the open space where he had stood the evening before. It was entirely vacant. She felt disappointed and saddened; and she began to reflect on her total friendlessness—no one to aid her in preparations for her voyage—none to advise—her sole resource was in hirelings. But her independent, firm spirit quickly threw off this weakness, and she began a note to Mr. Colville, asking him to call on her, as she wished to arrange everything definitively before she spoke to Falkner. As she wrote, she heard a rapid, decided step in her quiet street, followed by a hurried yet gentle knock at her door. She started up. "It is he!" the words were on her lips, when Gerard entered; she held out her hand, gladness thrilling through her whole frame, her heart throbbing wildly—her eyes lighted up with joy. "This is indeed kind," she cried. "Oh, Mr. Neville, how happy your visit makes me!"

He did not look happy; he had grown paler and thinner, and the melancholy which had sat on his countenance before, banished for a time by her, had returned, with the addition of a look of wildness, that reminded her of the youth of Baden; Elizabeth was shocked to remark these traces of suffering; and her next impulse was to ask, "What has happened? I fear some new misfortune has occurred."

"It is the property of misfortune to be ever new," he replied, "to be always producing fresh and more miserable results. I have no right to press my feelings on you; your burden is sufficient; but I could not refrain any longer from seeing in what way adversity had exerted its pernicious influence over you."

His manner was gloomy and agitated; she, resigned, devoted to her duties; commanding herself, day by day, to fulfil her task of patience, and of acquiring cheerfulness for Falkner's sake; she imagined that some fresh disaster must be the occasion of these marks of emotion. She did not know that fruitless struggles to alleviate the evils of her situation, vain broodings over its horrors, and bitter regret at losing her, had robbed him of sleep, of appetite, of all repose. "I despise myself for my weakness," he said, "when I see your fortitude. You are more than woman, more than human being ever was, and you must feel the utmost contempt for one whom fortune bends and breaks as it does me. You are well, however, and half my dreams of misery have been false and vain. God guards and preserves you: I ought to have placed more faith in him."

"But tell me, dear Mr. Neville, tell me, what has happened?"

"Nothing!" he replied; "and does not that imply the worst? I cannot make up my mind to endure the visitation of ill fallen upon us; it drives me from place to place like an unlaid ghost. I am very selfish to speak in this manner. Yet it is your sufferings that fill my mind to bursting; were all the evil poured on my own head, while you were spared, welcome, most welcome would be the bitterest infliction! but you, Elizabeth, you are my cruel father's victim, and the future will be more hideous than the hideous present!"

Elizabeth was shocked and surprised; what could he mean? "The future," she replied, "will bring my dear father's liberation; how then can that be so bad?"

He looked earnestly and inquiringly on her. "Yes," she continued, "my sorrows, heavy as they are, have not that additional pang; I have no doubt of the ultimate justice that will be rendered my father. We have much to endure in the interim, much that undermines the fortitude and visits the heart with sickening throes; there is no help but patience; let us have patience, and this adversity will pass away; the prison and the trial will be over, and freedom and security again be ours."

"I see how it is," replied Neville; "we each live in a world of our own, and it is wicked in me to give you a glimpse of the scene as it is presented to me."

"Yet speak; explain!" said Elizabeth; "you have frightened me so much that any explanation must be better than the thoughts which your words, your manner, suggest."

"Nay," said Neville, "do not let my follies infect you. Your views, your hopes, are doubtless founded on reason. It is, if you will forgive the allusion that may seem too light for so sad a subject, but the old story of the silver and brazen shield. I see the dark, the fearful side of things; I live among your enemies—that is, the enemies of Mr. Falkner. I hear of nothing but his guilt, and the expiation prepared for it. I am maddened by all I hear.

"I have implored my father not to pursue his vengeance. Convinced as I am of the truth of Mr. Falkner's narration, the idea that one so gifted should be made over to the fate that awaits him is abhorrent; and when I think that you are involved in such a scene of wrong and horror, my blood freezes in my veins. I have implored my father, I have quarrelled with him, I have made Sophia advocate the cause of justice against malice; all in vain. Could you see the old man—my father I mean; pardon my irreverence—how he revels in the demoniacal hope of revenge, and with what hideous delight he gloats upon the detail of ignominy to be inflicted on one so much his superior in every noble quality, you would feel the loathing I do. He heaps sarcasm and contempt on my feeble spirit, as he names my pardon of my mother's destroyer, my esteem for him, and my sympathy for you; but that does not touch me. It is the knowledge that he will succeed, and you be lost and miserable for ever, that drives me to desperation.

"I fancied that these thoughts must pursue you even more painfully than they do me. I saw you writhing beneath the tortures of despair, wasting away under the influence of intense misery. You haunted my dreams, accompanied by every image of horror—sometimes you were bleeding, ghastly, dying—sometimes you took my poor mother's form, as Falkner describes it, snatched cold and pale from the waves—other visions flitted by, still more frightful. Despairing of moving my father, abhorring the society of every human being, I have been living for the last month at Dromore. A few days ago my father arrived there. I wondered till I heard the cause. The time for expecting Osborne had arrived. As vultures have instinct for carrion, so he swooped down at the far off scent of evil fortune; he had an emissary at Liverpool, on the watch to hear of this man's arrival. Disgusted at this foul appetite for evil, I left him. I came here—only to see you, to gaze on you afar, was to purify the world of the 'blasts from hell' which the bad passions I have so long contemplated spread round me. My father learned whither I had gone; I had a letter from him this morning—you may guess at its contents."

"He triumphs in Osborne's refusal to appear," said Elizabeth, who was much moved by the picture of hatred and malice Neville had presented to her; and trembled from head to foot as she listened, from the violent emotions his account excited, and the vehemence of his manner as he spoke.

"He does indeed triumph," replied Neville; "and you—you and Mr. Falkner, do you not despair?"

"If you could see my dear father," said Elizabeth, her courage returning at the thought, "you would see how innocence and a noble mind can sustain; at the worst, he does not despair. He bears the present with fortitude, he looks to the future with resignation. His soul is firm, his spirit inflexible."

"And you share these feelings?"

"Partly I do, and partly I have other thoughts to support me. Osborne's cowardice is a grievous blow, but it must be remedied. The man we sent to bring him was too easily discouraged. Other means must be tried. I shall go to America, I shall see Osborne, and you cannot doubt of my success."

"You?" cried Neville; "you to go to America? you to follow the traces of a man who hides himself? Impossible! This is worse madness than all. Does Falkner consent to so senseless an expedition?"

"You use strong expressions," interrupted Elizabeth.

"I do," he replied; "and I have a right to do so—I beg your pardon. But my meaning is justifiable—you must not undertake this voyage. It is as useless as improper. Suppose yourself arrived on the shores of wide America. You seek a man who conceals himself, you know not where: can you perambulate large cities, cross wide extents of country, go from town to town in search of him? It is by personal exertion alone that he can be found; and your age and sex wholly prevent that."

"Yet I shall go," said Elizabeth, thoughtfully; "so much is left undone, because we fancy it impossible to do; which, upon endeavour, is found plain and easy. If insurmountable obstacles oppose themselves, I must submit, but I see none yet; I have not the common fears of a person whose life has been spent in one spot; I have been a traveller, and know that, but for the fatigue, it is as easy to go a thousand miles as a hundred. If there are dangers and difficulties, they will appear light to me, encountered for my dear father's sake."

She looked beautiful as an angel as she spoke; her independent spirit had nothing rough in its texture. It did not arise from a love of opposition, but from a belief that, in fulfilling a duty, she could not be opposed or injured. Her fearlessness was that of a generous heart, that could not believe in evil intentions. She explained more fully to her friend the reasons that induced her determination. She repeated Falkner's account of Osborne's character, the injury that it was believed would arise from his refusal to appear, and the probable facility of persuading him, were he addressed by one zealous in the cause.

Neville listened attentively. She paused—he was lost in thought, and made no reply—she continued to speak, but he continued mute, till at last she said, "You are conquered, I know—you yield, and agree that my journey is a duty, a necessity."

"We are both apt, it would seem," he replied, "to see our duties in a strong light, and to make sudden, or they may be called rash, resolutions. Perhaps we both go too far, and are in consequence reprehended by those about us: in each other, then, let us find approval—you must not go to America, for your going would be useless—with all your zeal you could not succeed. But I will go. Of course this act will be treated as madness, or worse, by Sir Boyvill and the rest—but my own mind assures me that I do right. For many years I devoted myself to discovering my mother's fate. I have discovered it. Falkner's narrative tells all. But clear and satisfactory as that is to me, others choose to cast frightful doubts over its truth, and conjure up images the most revolting. Have they any foundation? I do not believe it—but many do—and all assert that the approaching trial alone can establish the truth. This trial is but a mockery, unless it is fair and complete—it cannot be that without Osborne. Surely, then, it neither misbecomes me as her son, nor as the son of Sir Boyvill, to undertake any action that will tend to clear up the mystery.

"I am resolved—I shall go—be assured that I shall not return without Osborne. You will allow me to take your place, to act for you—you do not distrust my zeal?"

Elizabeth had regarded her own resolves as the simple dictates of reason and duty. But her heart was deeply touched by Neville's offer; tears rushed into her eyes as she replied, in a voice faltering with emotion, "I fear this cannot be; it will meet with too much opposition; but never, never can I repay your generosity in but imagining so great a service."

"It is a service to both," he said; "and as to the opposition I shall meet, that is my affair. You know that nothing will stop me when once resolved. And I am resolved. The inner voice that cannot be mistaken assures me that I do right—I ask no other approval. A sense of justice, perhaps of compassion, for the original author of all our wretchedness, ought probably to move me; but I will not pretend to be better than I am; were Falkner alone concerned, I fear I should be lukewarm. But not one cloud, nor the shadow of a cloud, shall rest on my mother's fate. All shall be clear, all universally acknowledged; nor shall your life be blotted and your heart-broken by the wretched fate of him to whom you cling with matchless fidelity. He is innocent, I know; but if the world thinks and acts by him as a murderer, how could you look up again? Through you I succeeded in my task; to you I owe unspeakable gratitude, which it is my duty to repay. Yet, away with such expressions. You know that my desire to serve you is boundless; that I love you beyond expression; that every injury you receive is trebled upon me—that vain were every effort of self-command; I must do that thing that would benefit you, though the whole world rose to forbid. You are of more worth in your innocence and nobleness, than a nation of men such as my father. Do you think I can hesitate in my determinations thus founded, thus impelled?"

More vehement, more impassioned than Elizabeth, Neville bore down her objections, while he awakened all her tenderness and gratitude: "Now I prove myself your friend," he said, proudly; "now Heaven affords me opportunity to serve you, and I thank it."

He looked so happy, so wildly delighted, while a more still but not less earnest sense of joy filled her heart. They were young, and they loved—this of itself was bliss; but the cruel circumstances around them added to their happiness by drawing them closer together, and giving fervour and confidence to their attachment; and now that he saw a mode of serving her, and she felt entire reliance on his efforts, the last veil and barrier fell from between them, and their hearts became united by that perfect love which can result alone from entire confidence and acknowledged unshackled sympathy.

Always actuated by generous impulses, but often rash in his determinations, and impetuous in their fulfilment; full of the warmest sensibility, hating that the meanest thing that breathed should endure pain, and feeling the most poignant sympathy for all suffering, Neville had been maddened by his own thoughts, while he brooded over the position in which Elizabeth was placed. Not one of those various circumstances that alleviate disaster to those who endure it, presented themselves to his imagination—he saw adversity in its most hideous form, without relief or disguise—names and images appending to Falkner's frightful lot, which he and Elizabeth carefully banished from their thoughts, haunted him. The fate of the basest felon hung over the prisoner—Neville believed that it must inevitably fall on him; he often wondered that he did not contrive to escape; that Elizabeth, devoted and heroic, did not contrive some means of throwing open his dungeon's doors. He had endeavoured to open his father's eyes, to soften his heart, in vain. He had exerted himself to discover whether any trace of long past circumstances existed that might tend to acquit Falkner. He had gone to Treby, visited the graves of the hapless parents of Elizabeth, seen Mrs. Baker, and gathered there the account of his landing; but nothing helped to elucidate the mystery of his mother's death; Falkner's own account was the only trace left behind; that bore the stamp of truth in every line, and appeared to him so honourable a tribute to poor Alithea's memory, that he looked with disgust on his father's endeavours to cast upon it suspicions and interpretations the most hideous and appalling.

In the first instance, he had been bewildered by Sir Boyvill's sophistry, and half conquered by his plausible arguments. But a short time, and the very circumstance of Elizabeth's fidelity to his cause sufficed to show him the baseness of his motives, and the real injury he did his mother's fame.

Resolved to clear the minds of other men from the prejudice against the prisoner thus spread abroad, and at least to secure a fair trial, Neville made no secret of his belief that Falkner was innocent. He represented him everywhere as a gentleman—a man of humanity and honour—whose crime ought to receive its punishment from his own conscience, and at the hand of the husband or son of the victim in the field; and whom, to pursue as his father did, was at once futile and disgraceful. Sir Boyvill, irritated by Falkner's narrative; his vanity wounded to the quick by the avowed indifference of his wife, was enraged beyond all bounds by the opposition of his son. Unable to understand his generous nature, and relying on his previous zeal for his mother's cause, he had not doubted but that his revenge would find a' ready ally in him. His present arguments, his esteem for their enemy, his desire that he should be treated with a forbearance which, between gentlemen, was but an adherence to the code of honour—appeared to Sir Boyvill insanity, and worse—a weakness the most despicable, a want of resentment the most low-minded. But he cared not—the game was in his hands—revelling in the idea of his enemy's ignominious sufferings, he more than half persuaded himself that his accusation was true, and that the punishment of a convicted felon would at last satisfy his thirst for revenge.

A feeble old man, tottering on the verge of the grave, he gloried to think that his grasp was still deadly, his power acknowledged in throes of agony, by him by whom he had been injured.

Returning to Dromore from Carlisle, Gerard sought his father. Osborne's refusal to appear crowned Sir Boyvill's utmost hopes; and his sarcastic congratulations, when he saw his son, expressed all the malice of his heart. Gerard replied with composure, that he did indeed fear that this circumstance would prove fatal to the course of justice; but that it must not tamely be submitted to, and that he himself was going to America to induce Osborne to come, that nothing might be wanting to elucidate the mystery of his mother's fate, and to render the coming trial full, fair, and satisfactory. Such an announcement rendered, for a moment, Sir Boyvill speechless with rage. A violent scene ensued. Gerard, resolved, and satisfied of the propriety of his resolution, was calm and firm. Sir Boyvill, habituated to the use of vituperative expressions, boiled over with angry denunciations and epithets of abuse. He called his son the disgrace of his family—the opprobrium of mankind—the detractor of his mother's fame. Gerard smiled; yet, at heart, he deeply felt the misery of thus for ever finding an opponent in his father, and it required all the enthusiasm and passion of his nature to banish the humiliating and saddening influence of Sir Boyvill's indignation.

They parted worse friends than ever. Sir Boyvill set out for town; Gerard repaired to Liverpool. The wind was contrary—there was little hope of change. He thought that it would conduce to his success in America, if he spent the necessary interval in seeing Hoskins again; and also in consulting with his friend, the American minister; so, in all haste, having first secured his passage on board a vessel that was to sail in four or five days, he also set out for London.

## CHAPTER XLV

The philosophy of Falkner was not proof against the intelligence that Gerard Neville was about to undertake the voyage to America for the sake of inducing Osborne to come over. Elizabeth acquainted him with her design, and her friend's determination to replace her, with sparkling eyes, and cheeks flushed by the agitation of pleasure—the pure pleasure of having such proof of the worth of him she loved. Falkner was even more deeply touched; even though he felt humiliated by the very generosity that filled him with admiration. His blood was stirred, and his feelings tortured him by a sense of his own demerits, and the excellence of one he had injured. "Better die without a word, than purchase my life thus!" were the words hovering on his lips—yet it was no base cost that he paid—and he could only rejoice at the virtues of the son of her whom he had so passionately loved. There are moments when the past is remembered with intolerable agony; and when to alter events, which occurred at the distance of many years, becomes a passion and a thirst. His regret at Alithea's marriage seemed all renewed—his agony that thence—forth she was not to be the half of his existence, as he had hoped; that her child was not his child; that her daily life, her present pleasures, and future hopes were divorced from his—all these feelings were revived, together with a burning jealousy, as if, instead of being a buried corpse, she had still adorned her home with her loveliness and virtues.

Such thoughts lost their poignancy by degrees, and he could charm Elizabeth by dwelling on Gerard's praises; and he remarked with pleasure that she resumed her vivacity, and recovered the colour and elasticity of motion, which she had lost. She did not feel less for Falkner; but her contemplations had lost their sombre hue—they were full of Neville—his voyage—his exertions—his success—his return; and the spirit of love that animated each of these acts were gone over and over again in her waking dreams; unbidden smiles gleamed in her countenance; her ideas were gayly coloured, and her conversation gained a variety and cheerfulness that lightened the burden of their prison hours.

Meanwhile Neville arrived in London. He visited the American minister, and learned from him that Osborne had given up the place he held, and had left Washington—no one knew whither he was gone—these events being still too recent to leave any trace behind. It was evident that to seek and find him would be a work of trouble and time, and Neville felt that not a moment must be lost—December was drawing to a close. The voyages to and from America might, if not favourable, consume the whole interval that still remained before the spring assizes. Hoskins, he learned, was gone to Liverpool.

He visited Lady Cecil before he left town. Though somewhat tainted by worldliness, yet this very feeling made her highly disapprove Sir Boyvill's conduct. A plausible, and, she believed, true account was given of Mrs. Neville's death—exonerating her—redounding indeed to her honour. It was injurious to all to cast doubts upon this tale—it was vulgar and base to pursue revenge with such malicious and cruel pertinacity. Falkner was a gentleman, and deserved to be treated as such; and now he and Elizabeth were mixed up in loathsome scenes and details, that made Lady Cecil shudder even to think of.

That Gerard should go to America as the advocate, as it were, of Falkner, startled her; but he represented his voyage in a simpler light, as not being undertaken for his benefit, but for the sake of justice and truth. Sir Boyvill came in upon them while they were discussing this measure. He was absolutely phrensied by his son's conduct and views; his exasperation but tended to disgust, and did not operate to shake their opinions.

Neville hastened back to Liverpool; a southwest wind reigned, whose violence prevented any vessel from sailing for America; it was evident that the passage would be long, and perhaps hazardous. Neville thought only of the delay; but this made him anxious. A portion of his time was spent in seeking for Hoskins; but he was not to be found. At last it was notified to him that the wind had a little changed, and that the packet was about to sail. He hurried on board—soon they were tossing on a tempestuous sea—they lost sight of land—sky and ocean, each dusky, and the one rising at each moment into more tumultuous commotion, surrounded them. Neville, supporting himself by a rope, looked out over the horizon—a few months before he had anticipated the same voyage over a summer sea—now he went under far other auspices—the veil was raised—the mystery explained; but the wintry storms that had gathered round him were but types of the tempestuous passions which the discoveries he had made raised in the hearts of all.

For three days and nights the vessel beat about in the Irish Channel, unable to make any way—three days were thus lost to their voyage—and when were they to arrive? Impatient—almost terrified by the delay which attended his endeavours, Neville, began to despair of success. On the fourth night the gale rose to a hurricane—there was no choice but to run before it—by noon the following day the captain thought himself very lucky to make the harbour of Liverpool; and though the gale had much abated, and the wind had veered into a more favourable quarter, it was necessary to run in to refit. With bitter feelings of disappointment, Neville disembarked; several days must elapse before the packet would be able to put to sea, so he abandoned the idea of going by her—and finding a New-York merchantman preparing to sail at an early hour the following morning, he resolved to take his passage on board. He hastened to the American coffee-house to see the captain, and make the necessary arrangements for his voyage.

The captain had just left the tavern; but a waiter came up to Neville, and told him that the Mr. Hoskins, concerning whom he had before inquired, was in the house—in a private room. "Show me to him," said Neville, and followed the man as he went to announce him.

Hoskins was not alone—he had a friend with him, and they were seated over their wine on each side of the fire. Neville could not help being struck with the confusion evinced by both as he entered. The person with Hoskins was a fair, light-haired, rather good-looking man, though past the prime of life—he had at once an expression of good-nature and cunning in his face, and, added to this, a timid, baffled look—which grew into something very like dismay when the waiter announced "Mr. Neville."

"Good-morning, sir," said Hoskins; "I hear that you have been inquiring for me. I thought all our business was settled."

"On your side, probably," replied Neville; "on mine I have reasons for wishing to see you. I have been seeking you in vain in London and here."

"Yes, I know," said the other, "I went round by Ravenglass to take leave of the old woman before I crossed—and here I am, my passage taken, with not an hour to lose. I sail by the Owyhee, Captain Bateman."

"Then we shall have time enough for all my inquiries," observed Neville. "I came here for the very purpose of arranging my passage with Captain Bateman."

"You, sir! are you going to America? I thought that was all at an end.'

"It is more necessary than ever. I must see Osborne—I must bring him over—his testimony is necessary to clear up the mystery that hangs over my mother's fate."

"You are nearer hanging Mr. Falkner without him than with him," said Hoskins.

"I would bring him over for the very purpose of saving a man whom I believe to be innocent of the crime he is charged with; for that purpose I go to America. I wish the truth to be established—I have no desire for revenge."

"And do you really go to America for that purpose?" repeated Hoskins.

"Certainly—I consider it my duty," replied Neville. "Nay, it may be said that I went for this design, for I sailed by the John Adams—which has been driven back by contrary winds. I disembarked only half an hour ago."

"That beats all!" cried Hoskins. "Why, do you know—I have more than half a mind to tell you—you had really sailed for America for the purpose of bringing Osborne over, and you now intend taking a passage on board the Owyhee?"

"Certainly; why not? What is there so strange in all this? I sought you for the sake of making inquiries that might guide me in my search for Osborne, who wishes to conceal himself."

"You could not have addressed a better man—by the Lord! He's a craven, and deserves no better; so I'll just let out, Mr. Neville, that Osborne sneaked out of this room at the instant he saw you come into it."

Neville had seen Hoskins's companion disappear—he thought it but an act of civility—the strangeness of this coincidence, the course of events at once so contrary and so propitious, staggered him for a moment. "They tell of the rattlesnake," said Hoskins, "that, fixing its eye on its prey, a bird becomes fascinated, and wheels round nearer and nearer till he falls into the jaws of the enemy—poor Osborne! He wishes himself on the shores of the Pacific, to be far enough off—and here he is, and turn and twist as he will, it will end by the law grasping him by the shoulder, and dragging him to the very noose he so fears to slip into; not that he helped to murder the lady—you do not believe that, Mr. Neville?—you do not think that the lady was murdered?"

"I would stake my existence that she was not," said Neville; "were it otherwise, I should have no desire to see Osborne, or to interfere. Strange, most strange it is, that he should be here; and he is come, you think, with no design of offering his testimony to clear Mr. Falkner?"

"He is come under a feigned name," replied Hoskins; "under pretence that he was sent by Osborne—he has brought a quantity of attested declarations, and hopes to serve Mr. Falkner without endangering his own neck."

It was even so. Osborne was a weak man, good-hearted, as it is called, but a craven. No sooner did he hear that Hillary had sailed for Europe, and that he might consider himself safe, than he grew uneasy on another score. He had still possession, even while he had denied all knowledge of the writer, of Falkner's letter, representing to him the necessity of coming over. It was simply but forcibly written; every word went to the heart of Osborne, now that he believed that his conduct would make over his generous benefactor to an ignominious end. This idea haunted him like an unlaid ghost; yet, if they hanged Falkner, what should prevent them from hanging him too? suspicion must fall equally on both.

When Hillary had urged the case, many other objections had presented themselves to Osborne's mind. He thought of the new honest course he had pursued so long, the honourable station he had gained, the independence and respectability of his present life; and he shrunk from giving up these advantages, and becoming again, in all men's eyes, the Osborne whose rascality he had left behind in England; it seemed hard that he should feel the weight of the chain that bound his former existence to his present one, when he fondly hoped that time had broken it. But these minor considerations vanished as soon as the idea of Falkner's danger fastened itself on his mind. It is always easy to fall back upon a state of being which once was ours. The uncertain, disreputable life Osborne had once led, he had gladly bidden adieu to; but the traces were still there, and he could fall into the way of it without any great shock. Besides this, he knew that Hillary had made his coming, and the cause of it, known to the legal authorities in Washington; and though he might persist in his denials, still he felt that he should be universally disbelieved.

A dislike at being questioned and looked askance upon by his American friends made him already turn his eyes westward. A longing to see the old country arose unbidden in his heart. Above all, he could neither rest, nor sleep, nor eat, nor perform any of the offices of life, for the haunting image of his benefactor, left by him to die a felon's death. Not that he felt tempted to alter his determination, and to come forward to save him: on the contrary, his blood grew chill, and his flesh shrunk at the thought; but still he might conceal himself in England; no one would suspect him of being there; he would be on the spot to watch the course of events; and if it was supposed that he could render any assistance, without compromising himself, he should at least be able to judge fairly how far he might concede: his vacillating mind could go no further in its conclusions. Hoskins had rightly compared him to the bird and the rattlesnake. He was fascinated; he could not avoid drawing nearer and nearer to the danger which he believed to be yawning to swallow him; ten days after Hillary left America, he was crossing the Atlantic. Hoskins was the first person he saw on landing, the second was Neville. His heart grew cold; he felt himself in the toils; how bitterly he repented his voyage. Coward as he was, he died a thousand deaths from fear of that one which, in fact, there was no danger of his incurring.

That Osborne should of his own accord have come to England appeared to smooth everything. Neville did not doubt that he should be able to persuade him to come forward at the right time. He instructed Hoskins to reassure him, and to induce him to see him; and, if he objected, to contrive that they should meet. He promised to take no measures for securing his person, but to leave him in all liberty to act as he chose; he depended that the same uneasy conscience that brought him from America to Liverpool would induce him at last, after various throes and struggles, to act as it was supposed he would have done at the beginning.

But day after day passed, and Osborne was not to be found; Hoskins had never seen him again, and it was impossible to say whither he was gone or where he was hid. The Owyhee, whose voyage had again been delayed by contrary winds, now sailed. Hoskins went with her. It was possible that Osborne might be on board, returning to the land of refuge. Neville saw the captain, and he denied having such a passenger; but he might be bound to secrecy, or Osborne might have disguised himself. Neville went on board; he carefully examined each person; he questioned both crew and passengers; he even bribed the sailors to inform him if any one were secreted. The Owyhee was not, however, the only vessel sailing; nearly thirty packets and merchantmen, who had been detained by foul winds, were but waiting for a tide to carry them out. Neville deliberated whether he should not apply to a magistrate for a search-warrant. He was averse to this—nay, repugnant. It was of the first importance to the utility of Osborne as a witness, that he should surrender himself voluntarily. The seizing him by force, as an accomplice in the murder, would only place him beside Falkner in the dock, and render his evidence of no avail; and his, Neville's, causing his arrest, could only be regarded as a piece of rancorous hostility against the accused; yet to suffer him to depart from the English shores was madness; and worse still, to be left in doubt of whether he had gone or remained. If the first were ascertained, Neville could take his passage also, and there might still be time to bring him back.

When we act for another, we are far more liable to hesitation than when our deeds regard ourselves only. We dread to appear lukewarm; we dread to mar all by officiousness. Ill success always appears a fault, and yet we dare not make a bold venture—such as we should not hesitate upon were it our own cause. Neville felt certain that Falkner would not himself deliberate, but risk all to possess himself of the person of Osborne; still he dared not take so perilous, perhaps so fatal, a step.

The tide rose, and the various docks filled. One by one the American-bound vessels dropped out and put to sea. It was a moment of agony to Neville to see their sails unfurl, swell to the wind, and make a speedy and distant offing. He now began to accuse himself bitterly of neglect—he believed that there was but one mode of redeeming his fault—to hurry on board one of the packets, and to arrive in America as soon as Osborne, whom, he felt convinced, was already on his way thither. Swift in his convictions, rash in execution, uncertainty was peculiarly hostile to his nature; and these moments of vacillation and doubt, and then of self-reproach at having lost all in consequence, were the most painful of his life. To determine to do something was some consolation, and now he resolved on his voyage. He hurried back to his hotel for a few necessaries and money. On his entrance, a letter was put into his hands—the contents changed the whole current of his ideas. His countenance cleared up—the tumult of his thoughts subsided into a happy calm. Changing all his plans, instead of undertaking a voyage to America, he the same evening set out for London.

# CHAPTER XLVI

The prisoner and his faithful companion knew nothing of these momentous changes. Day by day Elizabeth withdrew from the fire to the only window in her father's room; moving her embroidery table close to it, her eyes turned, however, to the sky, instead of to the flowers she was working; and leaning her cheek upon her hand, she perpetually watched the clouds. Gerard was already, she fancied, on the waste of waters; yet the clouds did not change their direction—they all sped one way, and that contrary to his destination. Thus she passed her mornings; and when she returned to her own abode, where her heart could more entirely spend its thoughts on her lover and his voyage, her lonely room was no longer lonely, nor the gloomy season any longer gloomy. More than happy—a breathless rapture quickened the beatings of her heart, as she told over again and again Neville's virtues, and, dearer than all, his claims on her gratitude.

Falkner saw with pleasure the natural effects of love and hope add to the cheerfulness of his beloved child, diffuse a soft charm over her person, her motions, and her voice, and impart a playful tenderness to her before rather serious manners. Youth, love, and happiness are so very beautiful in their conjunction. "God grant," he thought, "I do not mar this fair creature's life—may she be happier than Alithea; if man can be worthy of her, Gerard Neville surely is." As he turned his eyes silently from the book that apparently occupied him, and contemplated her pensive countenance, whose expression showed that she was wrapped in, yet enjoying her thoughts, retrospect made him sad. He went over his own life, its clouded morning, the glad beams that broke out to dissipate those clouds, and the final setting amid tempests and wreck. Was all life like this, must all be disappointed hope, baffled desires, lofty imaginations engendering fatal acts, and bringing the proud thus low? would she at his age view life as he did—a weary wilderness—a tangled, endless labyrinth, leading by one rough path or another to a bitter end? He hoped not, her innocence must receive other reward from Heaven.

It was on a day as they were thus occupied—Falkner refrained from interrupting Elizabeth's revery, which he felt was sweeter to her than any converse—and appeared absorbed in reading; suddenly she exclaimed,

"The wind has changed, dear father; indeed it has changed, it is favourable now. Do you not feel how much colder it is? the wind has got to the north, there is a little east in it; his voyage will not be a long one if this change only lasts!"

Falkner answered her by a smile; but it was humiliating to think of the object of that voyage, and her cheerful voice announcing that it was to be prosperous struck, he knew not why, a saddening chord. At this moment he heard the bolts of the chamber-door pushed back, and the key turn in the lock—the turnkey entered, followed by another man, who hesitated as he came forward, and then, as he glanced at the inhabitants of the room, drew back, saying, "There is some mistake; Mr. Falkner is not here."

But for his habitual self-command, Falkner had started up, and made an exclamation—so surprised was he to behold the person who entered—for he recognised his visitant on the instant—he himself was far more changed by the course of years; time, sickness, and remorse had used other than Praxitilean art, and had defaced the lines of grace and power which had marked him many years ago, before his hands had dug Alithea's grave. He was indeed surprised to see who entered; but he showed no sign of wonder, only saying with a calm smile, "No, there is no mistake, I am the man you seek."

The other now apparently recognised him, and advanced timidly, and in confusion—the turnkey left them, and Falkner then said, "Osborne, you deserve my thanks for this, but I did believe that it would come to this."

"No," said Osborne, "I do not deserve thanks—I—" and he looked confused, and glanced towards Elizabeth. Falkner followed his eye, and understanding his look, said, "You do not fear being betrayed by a lady, Osborne; you are safe here as in America. I see how it is, you are here under a false name; no one is aware that you are the man who a few weeks ago refused to appear to save a fellow-creature from death."

"I see no way to do that now," replied Osborne, hesitatingly; "I do not come for that, I come—I could not stay away—I thought something might be done."

"Elizabeth, my love," said Falkner, "you at least will thank Mr. Osborne for his spontaneous services—you are watching the clouds which were to bear along the vessel towards him, and beyond our hopes he is already here."

Elizabeth listened breathlessly—she feared to utter a word, lest it should prove a dream—now, gathering Falkner's meaning, she came forward, and with all a woman's grace addressed the trembling man, who already looked at the door as if he longed to be on the other side, fearful that he was caught in his own toils; for, as Hoskins said, the fascinated prey had wheeled yet nearer to his fate involuntarily—he had been unable to resist his desire to see Falkner, and learn how it was with him; but he still resolved not to risk anything; he had represented himself to the magistrates as coming from Osborne, showing false papers, and a declaration drawn up by him at Washington, and attested before official men there, setting forth Falkner's innocence; he had brought this over to see if it would serve his benefactor, and had thus got access to him: such was his reliance on the honour of his patron, that he had not hesitated in placing himself in his power, well aware that he should not be detained by him against his will; for still his heart quailed, and his soul shrunk from rendering him the service that would save his life.

His manner revealed his thoughts to the observant Falkner; but Elizabeth, less well read in men's hearts, younger and more sanguine, saw in his arrival the completion of her hopes; and she thanked him with so much warmth, and with such heartfelt praises of his kindness and generosity, that Osborne began to think that his greatest difficulty would be in resisting her fascination and disappointing her wishes. He stammered out at last some lame excuses. All he could do consistently with safety, they might command; he had shown this by coming over—more could not be asked, could not be expected—he himself, God knew, was innocent, so was Mr. Falkner, of the crime he was charged with. But he had no hand whatever in the transaction; he was not in his confidence; he had not known even who the lady was; his testimony, after all, must be worth nothing, for he had nothing to tell, and for this he was to expose himself to disgrace and death.

Acquiring courage at the sound of his own voice, Osborne grew fluent. Elizabeth drew back—she looked anxiously at Falkner, and saw a cloud of displeasure and scorn gather over his countenance—she put her hand on his, as if to check the outbreak of his indignation; yet she herself, as Osborne went on, turned her eyes flashing with disdain upon him. The miserable fellow cowed before the glances of both; he shifted from one foot to the other; he dared not look up; but he knew that their eyes were on him, and he felt the beams transfix him, and wither up his soul. There are weak men who yield to persuasion; there are weaker who are vanquished by reproaches and contempt; of such was Osborne. His fluency faded into broken accents; his voice died away—as a last effort, he moved towards the door.

"Enough, sir," said Falkner, in a calm, contemptuous voice; "and now begone—hasten away—do not stop till you have gained the shore, the ship, the waves of the Atlantic; be assured I shall not send for you a second time; I have no desire to owe my life to you."

"If I could save your life, Mr. Falkner," he began; "but—"

"We will not argue that point," interrupted Falkner; "it is enough that it is generally asserted that your testimony is necessary for my preservation. Were my crime as great as it is said to be, it would find its punishment in that humiliation. Go, sir; you are safe! I would not advise you to loiter here, return to America; walls have ears in abodes like these; you may be forced to save a fellow-creature against your will; hasten then away; go, eat, drink, and be merry—whatever betides me, not even my ghost shall haunt you. Meanwhile, I would beg you no longer to insult me by your presence—begone at once."

"You are angry, sir," said Osborne, timidly.

"I hope not," replied Falkner, who had indeed felt his indignation rise, and checked himself; "I should be very sorry to feel anger against a coward; I pity you—you will repent this when too late."

"Oh, do not say so," cried Elizabeth; "do not say he will repent when too late—but now, in time, I am sure that he repents; do you not, Mr. Osborne? You are told that your fears are vain; you know Mr. Falkner is far too noble to draw you into danger to save himself—you know even that he does not fear death, but ignominy, eternal, horrible disgrace; and the end, the frightful end prepared, even he must recoil from that—and you—no, you cannot in cold blood, and with calm forethought, make him over to it—you cannot, I see that you cannot—"

"Forbear, Elizabeth!" interrupted Falkner, in a tone of displeasure; "I will not have my life, nor even my honour, begged by you; let the worst come, the condemnation, the hangman—I can bear all, except the degradation of supplicating such a man as that."

"I see how it is," said Osborne. "Yes—you do with me as you will—I feared this, and yet I thought myself firm; do with me as you will—call the jailer—I will surrender myself." He turned pale as death, and tottered to a chair.

Falkner turned his back on him—"Go, sir!" he repeated, "I reject your sacrifice."

"No, father, no," cried Elizabeth, eagerly; "say not so—you accept it—and I also, with thanks and gratitude: yet it is no sacrifice, Mr. Osborne—I assure you that is not, at least, the sacrifice you fear—all is far easier than you think—there is no prison for you—your arrival need not yet be known—your consent being obtained, a pardon will be at once granted—you are to appear as a witness—not as a—" her voice faltered—she turned to Falkner, her eyes brimming over with tears. Osborne caught the infection;

he was touched—he was cheered also by Elizabeth's assurances, which he hoped that he might believe; hitherto he had been too frightened and bewildered to hear accurately even what he had been told—he fancied that he must be tried—the pardon might or might not come afterward—the youth, earnestness, and winning beauty of Elizabeth moved him; and now that his fears were a little allayed, he could see more clearly, he was even more touched by the appearance of his former benefactor. Dignity and yet endurance—suffering as well as fortitude—marked his traits; there was something so innately noble, and yet so broken by fortune, expressed in his commanding yet attenuated features and person—he was a wreck that spoke so plainly of the glorious being he had once been; there was so much majesty in his decay—such real innocence sat on his high and open brow, streaked though it was with disease—such lofty composure in his countenance, pale from confinement and suffering—that Osborne felt a mixture of respect and pity that soon rose above every other feeling.

Reassured with regard to himself, and looking on his patron with eyes that caught the infection of Elizabeth's tears, he came forward—"I beg your pardon, Mr. Falkner," he said, "for my doubts—for my cowardice, if you please so to name it; I request you to forget it, and to permit me to come forward in your behalf. I trust you will not disdain my offer; though late, it comes, I assure you, from my heart."

There was no mock dignity about Falkner; a sunny smile broke over his features as he held out his hand to Osborne. "And from my heart I thank you," he replied, "and deeply regret that you are to suffer any pain through me—mine was the crime, you the instrument; it is hard, very hard, that you should be brought to this through your complaisance to me; real danger for you there is none—or I would die this worst death rather than expose you to it."

Elizabeth now, in all gladness, wrote a hasty note; desiring Mr. Colville to come to them, that all might at once be arranged. "And Gerard, dear father," she said, "we must write to Mr. Neville, to recall him from his far and fruitless journey."

"Mr. Neville is in Liverpool," said Osborne; "I saw him the very day before I came away—he doubtless was on the look—out for me, and I dare swear Hoskins betrayed me. We must be on our guard—"

"Fear nothing from Mr. Neville," replied Elizabeth; "he is too good and generous not to advocate justice and truth. He is convinced of my father's innocence."

They were interrupted—the solicitor entered—Osborne's appearance was beyond his hopes—he could not believe in so much good fortune. He had begun to doubt, suspect, and fear—he speedily carried off his godsend, as he named him, to talk over, and bring into form his evidence, and all that appertained to his surrender—thus leaving Falkner with his adopted child.

Such a moment repaid for much; for Elizabeth's hopes were high, and she knelt before Falkner, embracing his knees, thanking Heaven in a rapture of gratitude. He also was thankful; yet mortification and wounded pride struggled in his heart with a sense of gratitude for unhoped-for preservation. His haughty spirit rebelled against the obligation he owed to so mean a man as Osborne. It required hours of meditation—of reawakened remorse for Alithea's fate—of renewed wishes that she should be vindicated before all the world—of remembered love for the devoted girl at his feet, to bring him back from the tumult of contending passions, to the fortitude and humility which he at every moment strove to cultivate.

Elizabeth's sweet voice dispelled such storms, and rewarded him for the serenity he at last regained. It was impossible not to feel sympathy in her happiness, and joy in possessing the affection of so gentle, yet so courageous and faithful a heart. Elizabeth's happiness was even more complete when she left, him, and sat in her solitary room—there, where Gerard had so lately visited her, and his image, and her gratitude towards him mingled more with her thoughts: her last act that night was to write to him, to tell him what had happened. It was her note that he received at Liverpool on the eve of his second departure, and which had changed his purpose. He had immediately set out for London to communicate the good tidings to Lady Cecil.

# CHAPTER XLVII

These had been hours of sunshine for the prisoner and his child, such as seldom visit the precincts of a jail; and soon, too soon, they changed, and the usual gloom returned to the abode of suffering. In misfortune various moods assail us. At first we are struck, stunned, and overwhelmed; then the elastic spirit rises; it tries to shape misery in its own way; it adapts itself to it; it finds unknown consolations arise out of circumstances which, in moments of prosperity, were unregarded. But this temper of mind is not formed for endurance. As a sick person finds comfort in a new posture at first, but after a time the posture becomes restrained and wearisome; thus, after mustering fortitude, patience, the calm spirit of philosophy, and the tender one of piety, and finding relief, suddenly the heart rebels, its old desires and old habits recur, and we are the more dissatisfied from being disappointed in those modes of support in which we trusted.

There was a perpetual struggle in Falkner's heart. Hatred of life, pride, a yearning for liberty, and a sore, quick spirit of impatience for all the bars and forms that stood between him and it, swelled like a tide in his soul. He hated himself for having brought himself thus low; he was angry that he had exposed Elizabeth to such a scene; he reviled his enemies in his heart; he accused destiny. Then, again, if he but shut his eyes—the stormy river, the desolate sands, and the one fair being dead at his feet, presented themselves, and remorse, like a wind, drove back the flood. He felt that he had deserved it all, that he had himself woven the chain of circumstances which he called his fate, while his innocence of the crime brought against him imparted a lofty spirit of fortitude, and even of repose.

Elizabeth, with an angel's love, watched the changes of his temper. Her sensibility was often wounded by his sufferings; but her benign disposition was so fertile of compassion and forbearance, that her own mood was never irritated by finding her attempts to console fruitless. She listened meekly when his overladen heart spent itself in invectives against the whole system of life; or, catching a favourable moment, she strove to raise his mind to nobler and purer thoughts—unobtrusive, but never weary—eagerly gathering all good tidings, banishing the ill; her smiles, her tears, her cheerfulness, or calm sadness, by turns relieved and comforted him.

Winter came upon them. It was wild and drear. Their abode, far in the north of the island, was cold beyond their experience, the dark prison-walls were whitened by snow, the bars of their windows were laden; Falkner looked out, the snow drifted against his face, one peep at the dusky sky was all that was allowed him; he thought of the wide steppes of Russia, the swift sledges, and how he longed for freedom! Elizabeth, as she walked home through the frost and sleet, gave a sigh for the soft seasons of Greece, and felt that a double winter gathered round her steps.

Day by day, time passed on. Each evening returning to her solitary fireside, she thought, "Another is gone, the time draws near;" she shuddered, despite her conviction that the trial would be the signal for the liberation of Falkner; she saw the barriers time had placed between him and fate fall off one by one with terror; January and February passed, March had come—the first of March, the very month when all was to be decided, arrived. Poor tempest-tossed voyagers! would the wished-for port be gained—should they ever exchange the uncertain element of danger for the firm land of security?

It was on the first of March that, returning home in the evening, she found a letter on her table from Neville. Poor Elizabeth! she loved with tenderness and passion—and yet how few of the fairy thoughts and visions of love had been hers—love with her was mingled with so dire a tragedy, such real oppressive griefs, that its charms seemed crimes against her benefactor; yet now, as she looked on the letter, and thought, *"from him,"* the rapture of love stole over her, her eyes were dimmed by the agitation of delight, and the knowledge that she was loved suspended every pain, filling her with soft triumph, and thrilling, though vague expectation.

She broke the seal—there was an inner envelope directed to Miss Raby—and she smiled at the mere thought of the pleasure Gerard must have felt in tracing that name—the seal, as he regarded it, of their future union; but when she unfolded the sheet, and glanced down the page, her attention was riveted by other emotions. Thus Neville wrote:—

"My own sweet Elizabeth, I write in haste, but doubt is so painful, and tidings fly so quickly, that I hope you will hear first by means of these lines the new blow fate has prepared for us. My father lies dangerously ill. This, I fear, will again delay the trial—occasion prolonged imprisonment—and keep you still a martyr to those duties you so courageously fulfil. We must have patience. We are impotent to turn aside irrevocable decrees, yet when we think how much hangs on the present moment of time, the heart—my weak heart at least—is wrung by anguish.

"I cannot tell whether Sir Boyvill is aware of his situation—he is too much oppressed by illness for conversation; the sole desire he testifies is to have me near him. Once or twice he has pressed my hand, and looked on me with affection. I never remember to have received before such testimonials of paternal love. Such is the force of the natural tie between us, that I am deeply moved, and would not leave him for the whole world. My poor father!—he has no friend, no relative but me; and now, after so much haughtiness and disdain, he, in his need, is like a little child, reduced to feel his only support in natural affections. His unwonted gentleness subdues my soul. Oh, who would rule by power, when so much more absolute a tyranny is established through love!

"Sophia is very kind—but she is not his child. The hour approaches when we should be at Carlisle. What will be the result of our absence—what the event of this illness? I am perplexed and agitated beyond measure; in a day or two all will be decided: if Sir Boyvill becomes convalescent, still it may be long before he can undertake so distant a journey.

"Do not fear that for a moment I shall neglect your interests; they are my own. For months I have lived only on the expectation of the hour when you should be liberated from the horrors of your present position; and the anticipation of another delay is torture. Even your courage must sink, your patience have an end. Yet a little longer, my Elizabeth, support yourself, let not your noble heart fail at this last hour, this last attack of adversity. Be all that you have ever been, firm, resigned, and generous; in your excellence I place all my trust. I will write again very speedily, and if you can imagine any service that I can do you, command me to the utmost. I write by my father's bedside; he does not sleep, but he is still. Farewell—I love you; in those words is summed a life of weal or wo for me and for you also, my Elizabeth! Do not call me selfish for feeling thus—even here."

"Yes, yes," thought Elizabeth; "busy fingers are weaving—the web of destiny is unrolling fast—we may not think, nor hope, nor scarcely breathe—we must await the hour—death is doing his work—what victim will he select?"

The intelligence in this letter, communicated on the morrow to all concerned in the coming trial, filled each with anxiety. In a very few days the assizes would commence; Falkner's name stood first on the list—delay was bitter, yet he must prepare for delay, and arm himself anew with resolution. Several anxious days passed—Elizabeth received no other letter—she felt that Sir Boyvill's danger was protracted, that Gerard was still in uncertainty—the post hour now became a moment of hope and dread—it was a sort of harassing inquietude hard to endure; at length a few lines from Lady Cecil arrived—they brought no comfort—all remained in the same state.

The assizes began—on the morrow the judges were expected in Carlisle—and already all that bustle commenced that bore the semblance of gayety in the rest of the town, but which was so mournful and fearful in the jail. There were several capital cases; as Elizabeth heard them discussed, her blood ran cold—she hated life, and all its adjuncts: to know of misery she could not alleviate was always saddening; but to feel the squalid, mortal misery of such a place and hour brought home to her own heart, was a wretchedness beyond all expression, poignant and hideous.

The day that the judges arrived, Elizabeth presented herself in Falkner's cell—a letter in her hand—her first words announced good tidings; yet she was agitated, tearful—something strange and awful had surely betided. It was a letter from Neville that she held, and gave to Falkner to read.

"I shall soon be in Carlisle, my dearest friend, but this letter will outspeed me, and bring you the first intelligence of my poor father's death. Thank God, I did my duty by him to the last—thank God, he died in peace—in peace with me and the whole world. The uneasiness of pain yielded at first to torpor, and thus we feared he would die; but before his death he recovered himself an hour or two, and though languid and feeble, his mind was clear. How little, dear Elizabeth, do we know of our fellow-creatures—each shrouded in the cloak of manner—that cloak of various dies—displays little of the naked man within. We thought my father vain, selfish, and cruel—he was all this, but he was something else that we knew not of—he was generous, humane, humble—these qualities he hid as if they had been vices—he struggled with them—pride prevented him from recognising them as the redeeming points of a faulty nature; he despised himself for feeling them, until he was on his deathbed.

"Then, in broken accents, he asked me, his only son, to pardon his mistakes and cruelties—he asked me to forgive him, in my dear mother's name—he acknowledged his injustices towards her. 'Would that I might live,' he said; 'for my awakened conscience urges me to repair a portion of the evils I have caused—but it is too late. Strange that I should never have given ear to the whisperings of justice—though they were often audible—till now, when there is no help! Yet is it so? cannot some reparation be made? There is one'—and as he spoke he half raised himself, and some of the wonted fire flashed from his glazed eye—but he sunk back again, saying, in a low but distinct voice, 'Falkner—Rupert Falkner—he is innocent, I know and feel his innocence—yet I have striven to bring him to the death. Let me record my belief that his tale is true, and that Alithea died the victim of her own heroism, not by his hand. Gerard, remember, report these words—save him—his sufferings have been great—promise me—that I may feel that God and Alithea will forgive me, as I forgive him; I act now as your mother would have had me act; I act to please her.'

"I speak it without shame, my eyes ran over with tears, and this softening of a proud heart before the remembered excellence of one so long dead, so long thought of with harshness and resentment, was the very triumph of the good spirit of the world; yet tears were all the thanks I could give for several minutes. He saw that I was moved—but his strength was fast leaving him, and pressing my hand and murmuring, 'My last duty is now performed—I will sleep,' he turned away his head; he never spoke more, except to articulate my name, and once or twice, as his lips moved, and I bent down to listen, I heard the name of my mother breathed at the latest hour.

"I cannot write more—the trial will take place, I am told, immediately—before the funeral. I shall be in Carlisle—all will go well, dear Elizabeth—and when we meet again, happier feelings will be ours. God bless you now and always, as you deserve."

# CHAPTER XLVIII

All things now assumed an anxious aspect; all was hurrying to a conclusion. *To-morrow the trial was to come on.* "Security" is not a word for mortal man to use, more especially when the issue of an event depends on the opinions and actions of his fellow-creatures. Falkner's acquittal was probable, but not certain; even if the impression went in general in his favour, a single juryman might hold out, and perverseness, added to obstinacy, would turn the scale against him. Sickening fears crept over Elizabeth's heart; she endeavoured to conceal them; she endeavoured to smile and repeat, "This is our last day of bondage."

Falkner cast no thought upon the worst—innocence shut out fear. He could not look forward to the ignominy of such a trial without acute suffering; yet there was an austere composure in his countenance, that spoke of fortitude and reliance on a power beyond the limit of human influence. His turn had come to encourage Elizabeth. There was a nobleness and simplicity of character, common to both, that made them very intelligible to each other. Falkner, however, had long been nourishing secret thoughts and plans, of which he had made no mention, till now, the crisis impending, he thought it best to lift a portion of the veil that covered the future.

"Yes," he said, in reply to Elizabeth, "to-morrow will be the last day of slavery; I regain my human privileges after to-morrow, and I shall not be slow to avail myself of them. My first act will be to quit this country. I have never trod its soil but to find misery; after to-morrow I leave it for ever."

Elizabeth started, and looked inquiringly: were her wishes, her destiny to have no influence over his plans? he knew of the hope, the affection, that rendered England dear to her. Falkner took her hand. "You will join me hereafter, dearest; but you will in the first instance yield to my request, and consent to a separation for a time."

"Never!" said Elizabeth; "you cannot deceive me; you act thus for my purposes, and not your own, and you misconceive everything. We will never part."

"Daughters when they marry," observed Falkner, "leave father, mother, all, and follow the fortunes of their husbands. You must submit to the common law of human society."

"Do not ask me to reason with you and refute your arguments," replied Elizabeth; "our position is different from that of any other parent and child. I will not say I owe you more than daughter ever owed father—perhaps the sacred tie of blood may stand in place of the obligations you have heaped on me; but I will not reason; I cannot leave you. Right or wrong in the eyes of others, my own heart would perpetually reproach me. I should image your solitary wanderings, your lonely hours of sickness and suffering, and my peace of mind would be destroyed."

"It is true," said Falkner, "that I am more friendless than most men; yet I am not so weak and womanish that I need perpetual support. Your society is dear to me, dearer, God, who reads my heart, knows, than liberty or life; I shall return to that society, and again enjoy it; but, for a time, do not fear but that I can form such transitory ties as will prevent solitary suffering. Men and women abound who will feel benevolently towards the lonely stranger; money purchases respect; blameless manners win kindness. I shall find friends in my need if I desire it, and I shall return at last to you."

"My dearest father," said Elizabeth, "you cannot deceive me. I penetrate your motives, but you wholly mistake. You would force me also to mistake your character, but I know you too well. You never form transitory friendships; you take no pleasure in the ordinary run of human intercourse. You inquire; you seek for instruction; you endeavour to confer benefits; but you have no happiness except such as you derive from your heart, and that is not easily impressed. Did you not for many long years continue faithful to one idea—adhere to one image—devote yourself to one, one only, despite all that separated you? Did not the impediment you found to the fulfilment of your visions blight your whole life, and bring you here? Pardon me if I allude to these things. I cannot be to you what she was, but you can no more banish me from your heart and imagination than you could her. I know that you cannot. We are not parent and child," she continued, playfully, "but we have a strong resemblance on one point—fidelity is our characteristic; we will not speak of this to others, they might think that we boasted. I am not quite sure that it is not a defect; at least in some cases, as with you it proved a misfortune. To me it can never be such: it repays itself. I cannot leave you, whatever befalls. If Gerard Neville is hereafter lost to me, I cannot help it; it would kill me to fall off from you. I must follow the natural, the irresistible bent of my character.

"To-morrow, the day after to-morrow, we will speak more of this. What is necessary for your happiness, be assured, I will fulfil without repining; but now, dearest father, let us not speak of the future now; my heart is too full of the present—the future appears to me a dream never to be arrived at. Oh, how more than blessed I shall be when the future, the long future, shall grow into interest and importance!"

They were interrupted. One person came in, and then another, and the appalling details of the morrow effectually banished all thoughts of plans, the necessity of which Falkner wished to impress on his young companion. He also was obliged to give himself up to present cares. He received all, he talked to all, with a serious but unembarrassed air: while Elizabeth sat shuddering by, wiping away her tears unseen, and turning her dimmed eyes from one to the other, pale and miserable. We have fortitude and resignation for ourselves; but when those beloved are in peril we can only weep and pray. Sheltered in a dusky corner, a little retreated behind Falkner, she watched, she listened to all, and her heart almost broke. "Leave him! after this leave him!" she thought, "a prey to such memories? Oh, may all good angels desert me when I become so vile a wretch!"

The hour came when they must part. She was not to see him on the morrow, until the trial was over; for her presence during the preliminary scenes was neither fitting nor practicable. Already great indulgences had been granted to the prisoner, arising from his peculiar position, the great length of time since the supposed crime had been committed, and the impression, now become general, that he was innocent. But this had limits—the morrow was to decide all, and send him forth free and guiltless, or doom him to all the horrors of condemnation and final suffering.

Their parting was solemn. Neither indulged in grief. Falkner felt composed—Elizabeth endeavoured to assume tranquillity; but her lips quivered, and she could not speak; it was like separating not to meet for years; a few short hours, and she would look again upon his face—but how much would happen in the interval! how mighty a change have occurred! What agony would both have gone through! the one picturing, the other enduring the scene of the morrow; the gaze of thousands—the accusation—the evidence—the defence—the verdict—each of these bearing with it to the well-born and refined a barbed dart, pregnant with thrilling poison; ignominy added to danger. How Elizabeth longed to express to the assembled world the honour in which she held him, whom all looked on as overwhelmed with disgrace; how she yearned to declare the glory she took in the ties that bound them, and the affection that she bore! She must be mute—but she felt all this to bursting; and her last words, "Best of men! excellent, upright, noble, generous, God will preserve you and restore you to me!" expressed in some degree the swelling emotions of her soul. They parted. Night and silence gathered round Falkner's pillow. With stoical firmness he banished retrospect—he banished care. He laid his hopes and fears at the feet of that Almighty power, who holds earth and all it contains in the hollow of his hand, and he would trouble himself no more concerning the inevitable though unknown decree. His thoughts were at first solemn and calm; and then, as the human mind can never, even in torture, fix itself unalterably on one point, milder and more pleasing reveries presented themselves. He thought of himself as a wild yet not worthless schoolboy—he remembered the cottage porch clustered over with odoriferous parasites, under whose shadow sat—the sick, pale lady, with her starry eyes and wise lessons, and her radiant daughter, whose soft hand he held as they both nestled close at her feet. He recalled his wanderings with that daughter over hill and dale, when their steps were light, and their hearts unburdened with a care, soared to that heaven which her blessed spirit had already reached. Oh, what is life, that these dreams of youth and innocence should have conducted her to an untimely grave—him to a felon's cell! The thought came with a sharp pang; again he banished it, and the land of Greece, his perils, and his wanderings with Elizabeth on the shores of Zante, now replaced his other memories. He then bore a burden on his heart, which veiled with dark crape the glories of a sunny climate, the heart-cheering tenderness of his adopted child—this was less bitter, this meeting of fate, this atonement. Sleep crept over him at last; and such is the force of innocence, that though a cloud of agony hung over his awakening, yet he slept peacefully on the eve of his trial.

Towards morning his sleep became less tranquil. He moved—he groaned—then, opening his eyes, he started up, struggling to attain full consciousness of where he was, and wherefore. He had been dreaming—and he asked himself what had been the subject of his dreams. Was it Greece—or the dreary waste shores of Cumberland? And why did that fair lingering shape beckon him? Was it Alithea or Elizabeth? Before these confused doubts could be solved, he recognised the walls of the cell, and saw the shadow of the bars of his windows on the curtain spread before it. It was morning—*the morning*—where would another sun find him?

He rose and drew aside the curtain—and there were the dark, high walls—weather-stained and huge; clear, but sunless daylight was spread over each object—it penetrated every nook, and yet was devoid of cheer. There is indeed something inexpressibly desolate in the sight of the early, gray, chill dawn dissipating the shadows of night, when the day which it harbingers is to bring misery. Night is a cloak—a shelter—a defence—all men sleep at night—the law sleeps, and its dread ministrants are harmless in their beds, hushed like cradled children. "Even now they sleep," thought

Falkner, "pillowed and curtained in luxury—but day is come, and they will soon resume their offices—and drag me before them—and wherefore?— because it is day—because it is Wednesday—because names have been given to portions of time, which otherwise might be passed over and forgotten."

To the surgeon's eye a human body sometimes presents itself merely as a mass of bones, muscles, and arteries—though that human body may contain a soul to emulate Shakspeare—and thus there are moments when the wretched dissect the forms of life—and contemplating only the outward semblance of events, wonder how so much power of misery, or the reverse, resides in what is after all but sleeping or waking—walking here or walking there—seeing one fellow-creature instead of another. Such were the morbid sensations that absorbed Falkner as day grew clearer and clearer—the narrow court more gloomy as compared with the sky, and the objects in his cell assumed their natural colour and appearances. "All asleep," he again thought, "except I, the sufferer; and does my own Elizabeth sleep? Heaven grant it, and guard her slumbers! May those dear eyes long remain closed in peace upon this miserable day!"

He dressed himself long before any one in the prison (and jailers are early risers) was awake; at last there were steps in the passage—bolts were drawn and voices heard. These familiar sounds recalled him to actual life, and approaching, inevitable events. His haughty soul awoke again—a dogged pride steeled his heart—he remembered the accusation—the execration in which he believed him—self to be held—and his innocence. "Retribution or atonement—I am ready to pay it as it is demanded of me for Alithea's sake—but the injustice of man is not lessened on this account; henceforth I am to be stamped with ignominy—and yet in what am I worse than my fellows? at least they shall not see that my spirit bends before them."

He assumed cheerfulness, and bore all the preliminaries of preparation with apparent carelessness; sometimes his eagle eye flashed fire— sometimes fixed on vacancy, a whole life of memories passed across his mental vision; but there was no haste, no trepidation, no faltering—he never thought of danger or of death—innocence sustained him. The ignominy of the present was all that he felt that he had to endure and master—that, and the desolation beyond, when branded through life as he believed he should be, even by acquittal, he was henceforth to be looked on as an outcast.

At length he was led forth to trial—pride in his heart—resolution in his eye; he passed out of the gloomy portal of the prison, and entered the sunlit street—houses were around; but through an opening he caught a glimpse of the country—uplands, and lawny fields, and tree-crested hills—the work of God himself. Sunshine rested on the scene—one used to liberty had regarded with contempt the restricted view presented by the opening; but to the prisoner, who for months had only seen his prison-walls, it seemed as if the creation lay unrolled in its majesty before him. What was man in comparison with the power that upheld the earth and bade the sun to shine? And man was to judge him? What mockery! Man and all his works were but a plaything in the hands of Omnipotence, and to that Falkner submitted his destiny. He rose above the degrading circumstances around him; he looked down upon his fate—a real, a lofty calm at last possessed his soul; he felt that naught said or done that day by his fellow-creatures could move him; his reliance was elsewhere—it rested on his own innocence, and his intimate sense that he was in no more danger now than if sheltered in the farthest, darkest retreat, unknown to man; he walked as if surrounded by an atmosphere which no storms from without could penetrate.

He entered the court with a serene brow, and so much dignity added to a look that expressed such entire peace of conscience, that every one who beheld him became prepossessed in his favour. His distinct, calm voice declaring himself "Not Guilty;" the confidence, untinged by vaunting, with which he uttered the customary appeal to God and his country, excited admiration at first, and then, when a second sentiment could be felt, the most heart-moving pity. Such a man, so unstained by vice, so raised above crime, had never stood there before; accustomed to the sight of vulgar rogues or hardened ruffians, wonder was mingled with a certain self-examination, which made each man feel that, if justice were done, he probably deserved more to be in that dock than the prisoner.

And then they remembered that he stood there to be consigned to life or death, as the jury should decide. A breathless interest was awakened, not only in the spectators, but even in those hardened by habit to scenes like this. Every customary act of the court was accompanied by a solemnity unfelt before. The feeling, indeed, that reigned was something more than solemn; thirsting curiosity and eager wonder gave way before thrilling awe, to think that man might be condemned to an ignominious end.

When once the trial had begun, and his preliminary part had been played, Falkner sat down. He became, to all appearance, abstracted. He was, indeed, thinking of things more painful than even the present scene; the screams and struggles of the agonized Alithea—her last sad sleep in the hut upon the shore—the strangling, turbid waves—her wet, lifeless form—her low, unnamed grave dug by him; had these been atoned for by long years of remorse and misery, or was the present ignomiy, and worse that might ensue, fitting punishment? Be it as it might, he was equal to the severest blows, and ready to lay down a life in compensation for that of which he, most unintentionally, and yet most cruelly, had deprived her. His thoughts were not recalled to the present scene till a voice struck his ear, so like hers—did the dead speak? Knit up as he was to the endurance of all, he trembled from head to foot; he had been so far away from that place, till the echo, as it were, of Alithea's voice recalled him; in a moment he recovered himself, and found that it was her child, Gerard Neville, who was giving his evidence.

He heard the son of his victim speak of him as innocent, and a thrill of thankfulness entered his soul; he smiled, and hope and sympathy with his fellow-creatures, and natural softening feelings, replaced the gloomy bitterness and harshness of his past reflections. He felt that he should be acquitted, and that it became him to impress all present favourably; it became him to conduct himself so as to show his confidence in the justice of those on whom his fate depended, and at once to assert the dignity of innocence. From that time he gave himself entirely up to the details of the trial; he became attentive, and not the less calm and resolute, because he believed that his own exertions would crown the hour with success. The spectators saw the change in him, and were roused to double interest. The court clock, meanwhile, kept measure of the time that passed; the hands travelled silently on—another turn, and all would be over—and what would then be?

# CHAPTER XLIX

Elizabeth meanwhile might envy the resolution that bore him through these appalling scenes. On the night after leaving him, she had not even attempted to rest. Wrapped in a shawl, she threw herself on a sofa, and told each hour during the livelong night; her reveries were wild, vague, and exquisitely painful. In the morning she tried to recall her faculties—she remembered her conviction that on that day Falkner would be liberated, and she dressed herself with care, that she might welcome him with the appearances of rejoicing. She expected with unconquerable trepidation the hour when the court would meet. Before that hour, there was a knock at her door, and a visiter was announced; it was Mrs. Raby.

It was indeed a solace to see a friendly face of her own sex—she had been so long deprived of this natural support. Lady Cecil had now and then written to her—her letters were always affectionate, but she seemed stunned by the magnitude of the blow that had fallen on her friend, and unable to proffer consolation. With kindness of heart, sweetness of temper, and much good sense, still Lady Cecil was commonplace and worldly. Mrs. Raby was of a higher order of being. She saw things too exclusively through one medium—and thus the scope of her exertions was narrowed; but that medium was a pure and elevated one. In visiting Elizabeth, on this occasion, she soared beyond it.

Long and heavily had her desertion of the generous girl weighed on her conscience. She could sympathize in her heroism, and warmly approve—it was in her nature to praise and to reward merit, and she had withheld all tribute from her abandoned niece. The interests of her religion, blended with those of family, actuated her, and while resisting a natural impulse of generosity she fancied that she was doing right. She had spoken concerning her with no one but Lady Cecil; and she, while she praised her young friend, forgot to speak of Falkner, and there lay the stumbling-block to every motion in her favour.

When Elizabeth repaired to Carlisle, Mrs. Raby returned to Belleforest. She scarcely knew how to introduce the subject to her father-in-law; and when she did, he, verging into dotage, only said, "Act as you please, my dear, I rely on you; act for the honour and welfare of yourself and your children." The old man day by day lost his powers of memory and reason; by the time of the trial he had become a mere cipher. Every responsibility fell on Mrs. Raby; and she, eager to do right and fearful to do wrong, struggled with her better nature—wavered, repented, and yet remained inactive.

Neville strongly reprobated the conduct of every one towards Elizabeth. He had never seen Mrs. Raby, but she in particular he regarded with the strongest disapprobation. It so happened, that, the very day after his father's death, he was at Lady Cecil's when Mrs. Raby called, and, by an exception in the general orders—made for Elizabeth's sake—she was let come up. Gerard was alone in the drawing-room when she was announced—he rose hastily, meaning to withdraw, when the lady's appearance changed his entire mind. We ridicule the minutiæ of the science of physiognomy—but who is not open to first impressions? Neville was prepossessed favourably by Mrs. Raby's countenance; her open, thoughtful brow, her large, dark, melancholy eyes, her dignity of manner, joined to evident marks of strong feeling, at once showed him that he saw a woman capable of generous sentiments and heroic sacrifice. He felt that there must have been some grievous error in Sophia's proceedings not to have awakened more active interest in her mind. While he was forming these conclusions, Mrs. Raby was struck by him in an equally favourable manner. No one could see Gerard Neville without feeling that something angelic—something nobly disinterested—unearthly in its purity, yet, beyond the usual nature of man, sympathetic, animated a countenance that was all sensibility, genius, and love. In a minute they were intimate friends. Lady Cecil, hearing that they were together, would not interrupt them; and their conversation was long. Neville related his first acquaintance with Elizabeth Raby—he sketched the history of Falkner—he described him—and the scene when he denounced himself as the destroyer of Alithea. He declared his conviction of his innocence—he narrated Sir Boyvill's dying words. Then they both dwelt on his long imprisonment, Elizabeth's faithful affection, and all that they must have undergone—enough to move the stoniest heart. Tears rushed into Gerard's eyes while he spoke—while he described her innocence, her integrity, her total forgetfulness of self. "And I have deserted her," exclaimed Mrs. Raby; "we have all deserted her—this must not continue. You go to Carlisle to-morrow for the trial; the moment it is over, and Mr. Falkner acquitted—when they have left that town, where all is so full of their name and story, I will see her, and try to make up for my past neglect."

"It will be too late," said Gerard; "you may then please yourself by admiring one so superior to every human being; but you will not benefit her—Falkner acquitted, she will have risen above all need of your support. Now is the hour to be of use. The very hour of the trial, when this unfortunate, heroic girl is thrown entirely on herself—wounded by her absolute friendlessness, yet disdaining to complain. I could almost wish that Sophia would disregard appearances, and hasten to her side; although her connexion with our family would render that too strange. But you, Mrs. Raby, what should stop you? she is your niece—how vain to attempt to conceal this from the world—it must be known—through me, I fondly trust, it will be known—who shall claim her as Miss Raby—when, as Elizabeth Falkner, I could never see her more. And, when it is known, will not your desertion be censured? Be wise, be generous—win that noblest and gentlest heart by your kindness now, and the very act will be your reward. Hasten to Carlisle; be with her in the saddest hour that ever one so young and innocent passed through."

Mrs. Raby was moved—she was persuaded; she felt a veil fall from before her eyes; she saw her duty, and she keenly felt the littleness of her past desertion; she did not hesitate; and now that she perceived how gladly her niece welcomed her in this hour of affliction, and how gratefully she appreciated her kindness, she found in the approval of her own heart the sweetest recompense for her disinterestedness.

Elizabeth's swollen eyes, and timid, hurried manner, betrayed how she had passed the night, and how she was possessed by the most agitating fears. Still she spoke of the acquittal of her father, as she took pride in calling him at this crisis, as certain; and Mrs. Raby, taking advantage of this, endeavoured to draw her mind from the torture of representing to herself the progress of the scene then acting at so short a distance from them, by speaking of the future. Elizabeth mentioned Falkner's determination to quit England, and her own to accompany him; the hinted dissuasion of Mrs. Raby she disregarded. "He has been a father to me—I am his child. What would you say to a daughter who deserted her father in adversity and sickness? And, dear Mrs. Raby, you must remember that my father is, in spite of all his courage, struck by disease; accustomed to my attentions, he would die if left to hirelings. Deserted by me, he would sink into apathy or despair."

Mrs. Raby listened—she admired the enthusiasm, and yet the softness, the sensibility, and firmness of her young kinswoman; but she was pained: many ideas assailed her, but she would not entertain them—they were too wild and dangerous; and yet her heart, formed for generosity, was tempted to trample upon the suggestions of prudence and the qualms of bigotry. To give diversion to her thoughts, she mentioned Gerard Neville. A blush of pleasure, a smile shown more in the eyes than on the lips, mantled over her niece's countenance. She spoke of him as of a being scarcely earthly in his excellence. His devotion to his mother first, and lately his generosity towards her—his resolution to go to America, to seek Osborne, for her sake and the sake of justice, were themes for eloquence; she spoke with warmth and truth. "Yet, if you follow Mr. Falkner's fortunes," said Mrs. Raby, "you will see him no more."

"I cannot believe that," replied Elizabeth; "yet, if it must be so, I am resigned. He will never forget me, and I shall feel that I am worthy of him, though separated; better that, than to remain at the sacrifice of all I hold honourable and good; he would despise me, and that were worse absence, an absence of the heart ten thousand times more galling, than mere distance of place—one would be eternal and irremediable, the other easily obviated when our duties should no longer clash. I go with my father because he is suffering; Neville may join us because he is innocent—he will not, I feel and know, either forget me or stay away for ever."

# CHAPTER L

While they were conversing, quick footsteps were heard in the street below. Mrs. Raby had succeeded in making the time pass more lightly than could be hoped; it was three o'clock—there was a knock at the door of the house. Elizabeth, breaking off abruptly, turned ashy pale, and clasped her hands in the agony of expectation. Osborne rushed into the room. "It is all over!" he exclaimed; "all is well!" Tears streamed from his eyes as he spoke and ran up to shake hands with Elizabeth, and congratulate her, with an ardour and joy that contrasted strangely with the frightened-looking being he had always before shown himself.

"Mr. Falkner is acquitted—he is free—he will soon be here! No one could doubt his innocence that saw him—no one did doubt it—the jury did not even retire." Thus Osborne ran on, relating the events of the trial. Falkner's mere appearance had prepossessed every one. The frankness of his open brow, his dignified, unembarrassed manner, his voice, whose clear tones were the very echo of truth, vouched for him. The barrister who conducted the prosecution narrated the facts rather as a mystery to be inquired into than as a crime to be detected. Gerard Neville's testimony was entirely favourable to the prisoner; he showed how Falkner, wholly unsuspected, safe from the shadow of accusation, had spontaneously related the unhappy part he took in his unfortunate mother's death, for the sake of restoring her reputation and relieving the minds of her relatives. The narrative written in Greece, and left as explanation in case of his death, was further proof of the truth of his account. Gerard declared himself satisfied of his innocence; and when he stated his father's dying words, his desire, at the last hour on the bed of death, to record his belief in Falkner's being guiltless of the charge brought against him—words spoken as it were yesterday, for he who uttered them still lay unburied—the surprise seemed to be that he should have suffered a long imprisonment and the degradation of a trial. Osborne's own evidence was clear and satisfactory. At last Falkner himself was asked what defence he had to make. As he rose every eye turned on him, every voice and breath were hushed—a solemn silence reigned. His words were few, spoken calmly and impressively; he rested his innocence on the very evidence brought against him. He had been the cause of the lady's death, and asked for no mercy; but for her sake, and the sake of that heroic feeling that led her to encounter death amid the waves, he asked for justice, and he did not for a moment doubt that it would be rendered him.

"Nor could you doubt it as you heard him," continued Osborne. "Never were truth and innocence written so clearly on human countenance as on his as he looked upon the jury with his eagle eyes, addressing them without pride, but with infinite majesty, as if he could rule their souls through the power of a clear conscience and a just cause; they did not hesitate—the jury did not hesitate a moment; I rushed here the moment I heard the words, and now—he is come."

Many steps were again heard in the street below, and one, which Elizabeth could not mistake, upon the stairs. Falkner entered—she flew to his arms, and he pressed her to his bosom, wrapping her in a fond, long embrace, while neither uttered a word.

A few moments of trembling almost to agony, a few agitated tears, and the natural gladness of the hour assumed its genuine aspect. Falkner, commanding himself, could shake hands with Osborne, and thank him, and Elizabeth presented him to Mrs. Raby. He at once comprehended the kindness of her visit, and acknowledged it with a heartfelt thankfulness that showed how much he had suffered while picturing Elizabeth's abandonment. Soon various other persons poured into the room, and it was necessary to pass through many congratulations, and to thank, and, what was really painful, to listen to the outpouring talk of those persons who had been present at the trial. Yet, at such a moment, the heart, warmed and open, acknowledges few distinctions. Among those whose evident joy in the result filled Elizabeth with gratitude, she and Falkner felt touched by none so much as the visit of a turnkey, who was ashamed to show himself, yet who, hearing they were immediately to quit Carlisle, begged permission to see them once again. The poor fellow, who looked on Elizabeth as an angel and Falkner as a demigod—for, not forgetting others in their adversity, they had discovered and assisted his necessities—the poor fellow seemed out of his mind with joy—ecstasy was painted on his face—there was no mistaking the clear language of a full and grateful heart.

At length the hurry and tumult subsided—all departed. Falkner and his beloved companion were left alone, and for a few short hours enjoyed a satisfaction so perfect that angels might have envied them. Falkner was humbled, it is true, and looked to the past with the same remorse; but in vain did he think that his pride ought to feel deeply wounded by the scene of that day; in vain did he tell himself that, after such a trial, the purity of his honour was tarnished—his heart told another tale. Its emphatic emotions banished every conventional or sophisticated regret. He was honestly though calmly glad, and acknowledged the homely feeling with the sincerity of a man who had never been nourished in false refinements or factitious woes.

In the evening, when it was dusk, said Falkner, "Let us, love, take a walk." The words made Elizabeth both laugh and cry for joy; he put on his hat, and, with her on his arm, they got quickly out of the town, and strolled down a neighbouring lane. The wind that waved the heads of the still leafless trees, the aspect of the starry sky, the wide-spread fields, were felt as blessings from Heaven by the liberated prisoner. "They all seem," he said, "created purely for my enjoyment. How sweet is nature—how divine a thing is liberty! Oh, my God! I dare not be so happy as I would—there is one thought to chill the genial glow; but for the image of lost, dead Alithea, I should enjoy a felicity too pure for frail humanity."

As they returned into the town, a carriage with four posters passed them; Elizabeth recognised at once Gerard Neville within—a pang shot through her heart to remember that they did not share their feelings, but were separated, perhaps for ever, at this very hour. On her return, worn out with fatigue and oppressed with this reflection, she bade good-night to Falkner; and he, happy in the idea that the same roof would cover them, kissed and embraced her. On entering her room she found a letter on her toilet—and smiles again dimpled her face—it was a letter from Neville. It contained a few words, a very few, of congratulation, reminding her that he must hurry back to town for the melancholy task of his father's funeral, and imploring that neither she nor Falkner would determine on any immediate step. "I cannot penetrate the cloud in which we are enveloped," he said; "but I know that I ought not, that I cannot lose you. A little time, a little reflection may show us how to accord our various duties with the great necessity of our not being separated. Be not rash, therefore, my own Elizabeth, nor let your friend be rash. Surely the worst is over, and we may be permitted at last to hate no more, and to be happy."

Elizabeth kissed the letter, and placed it beneath her pillow. That night she slept sweetly and well.

Early in the morning Mrs. Raby called on them. The same prepossession which Gerard had felt in her favour as soon as he saw her, had taken place in her on seeing Falkner. There is a sort of magnetism that draws like to like, and causes minds of fine and lofty tone to recognise each other when brought in contact. Mrs. Raby saw and acknowledged at once Falkner's superiority; whatever his faults had been, they were winnowed away by adversity, and he was become at once the noblest and gentlest of human beings. Mrs. Raby had that touch of generosity in her own character that never permitted her to see merit without openly acknowledging and endeavouring to reward it. The first thought of the plan she now entertained she had cast away as impracticable, but it returned; the desire to give and to benefit, a natural growth in her heart, made her look on it with complacency—by degrees she dismissed the objections that presented themselves, and resolved to act upon it. "We complain," she thought, "of the barrenness of life, and the tediousness and faults of our fellow-creatures; and when Providence brings before us two selected from the world as endowed with every admirable quality, we allow a thousand unworthy considerations, which assume the voice of prudence, to exile us from them. Where can I find a man like Falkner, full of honour, sensibility, and talent? where a girl like Elizabeth, who has proved herself to be the very type of virtuous fidelity? Such companions will teach my children better than volumes of moral treatises, the existence and loveliness of human goodness."

Mrs. Raby passed a sleepless night, revolving these thoughts. In the morning she called on her new friends; and then, with all the grace that was her peculiar charm, she invited them to accompany her to Belleforest, and to take up their residence there for the next few months.

Elizabeth's eyes sparkled with delight. Falkner at once accepted the invitation for her, and declined it for himself. "You hear him, my dear aunt," cried Elizabeth; "but you will not accept his refusal—you will not permit this perversity."

"You forget many things when you speak thus," said Falkner; "but Mrs. Raby remembers them all. I thank her for her kindness; but I am sure she will admit of the propriety of my declining her invitation."

"You imagine then," replied Mrs. Raby, "that I made it for form's sake—intending it should be refused. You mistake. I know what you mean, and all you would covertly suggest—let us cast aside the ceremonies of mere acquaintanceship—let us be friends, and speak with the openness natural to us—do you consent to this?"

"You are good, very good," said Falkner; "except this dear girl, who will deign to be my friend?"

"If I thought," replied Mrs. Raby, "that your heart was so narrowed by the disasters and injustice you have suffered, that you must hereafter shut yourself up with the remembrance of them, I should feel inclined to retract my offer, for friendship is a mutual feeling; and he who feels only for himself can be no one's friend. But this is not the case with you. You have a heart true to every touch of sympathy, as Elizabeth can testify—since you determined to live for her sake, when driven to die by the agony of your sufferings. Let us, then, at once dismiss notions which I must consider as unworthy of us. When we turn to the page of history, and read of men visited by adversity—what do we say to those of their fellow-creatures who fall off from them on account of their misfortunes? Do we not call them little-minded, and visit them with our contempt? Do not class me with such. I might pass you carelessly by if you had always been prosperous. It is your misfortunes that inspire me with friendship—that render me eager to cultivate an intimacy with one who has risen above the most frightful calamity that could befall a man, and shown himself at once repentant and courageous.

"You will understand what I mean without long explanation—we shall have time for that hereafter. I honour you. What my heart feels, my voice and actions will ever be ready to proclaim. For Elizabeth's sake, you must not permit the world to think that he who adopted and brought her up is unworthy of regard and esteem. Come with us to Belleforest—you must not refuse; I long to introduce my girls to their matchless cousin—I long to win her heart by my affection and kindness; and if you will permit me the enviable task, how proud and glad I shall be to repay a portion of what we owe you on her account, by endeavouring to compensate, by a few months of tranquillity and friendship, for the misery you have undergone."

Mrs. Raby spoke with sincerity and earnestness, and Elizabeth's eyes pleaded her cause yet more eloquently. "Where you go," she said to Falkner, "there also I shall be—I shall not repine however you decide—but we shall be very happy at Belleforest."

It was real modesty, and no false pride, that actuated Falkner. He felt happy, yet when he looked outward he fancied that hereafter he must be shut out from society—a branded man. He intimately felt the injustice of this. He accepted it as a punishment for the past, but he did not the less proudly rise above it. It was a real pleasure to find one entertaining the generous sentiments which Mrs. Raby expressed, and capable of acting on them. He felt worthy of her regard, and acknowledged that none but conventional reasons placed any barrier to his accepting her kind offers. Why then should he reject them? He did not; frankly, and with sincere thanks, he suffered himself to be overruled; and on the following day they were on their road to Belleforest.

# CHAPTER LI

It was one of those days which do sometimes occur in March—warm and balmy, and enlivening as spring always is. The birds were busy among the leafless boughs; and if the carriage stopped for a moment, the gushing song of the skylark attracted the eye to his blue ethereal bower; a joyous welcome was breathed by nature to every heart, and none answered it so fervently as Falkner. Sentiments of pleasure possessed all three travellers. Mrs. Raby experienced that exultation natural to all human beings when performing a generous action. Elizabeth felt that in going to Belleforest she drew nearer Neville—for there was no reason why he should not enter her grandfather's doors; but Falkner was happier than either. It was not the vulgar joy of having escaped danger; partly it was gladness to see Elizabeth restored to her family, where only, as things were, she could find happiness, and yet not divided from him. Partly it arose from the relief he felt, as the burden of heavy, long-endured care was lifted from his soul. But there was something more, which was incomprehensible even to himself. "His bosom's lord sat lightly on its throne"—he no longer turned a saddened, reproachful eye on nature, nor any more banished soft emotions, nourishing remorse as a duty. He was reconciled to himself and the world; the very circumstances of his prison and his trial being over, took with them the more galling portion of his retrospections—health again filled his veins. At the moment when he had first accused himself, Neville saw in him a man about to die. It was evident now that the seeds of disease were destroyed—his person grew erect—his eye clear and animated. Elizabeth had never, since they left Greece, seen him so free from suffering; during all her intercourse with him, she never remembered him so bland and cheerful in his mood. It was the reward of much suffering—the gift of Heaven to one who had endured patiently—opening his heart to the affections instead of cherishing pride and despair. It was the natural result of a noble disposition, which could raise itself above even its own errors—throwing off former evil as alien to its nature—embracing good as its indefeasible right.

They entered the majestic avenues and imbowered glades of Belleforest—where cedar, larch, and pine diversified the bare woods with a show of foliage—the turf was covered with early flowers—the buds were green and bursting on the boughs. Falkner remembered his visit the preceding summer. How little had he then foreseen impending events; and how far from his heart had then been the peace that at present so unaccountably possessed it. Then the wide demesne and stately mansion had appeared the abode of gloom and bigotry; now it was changed to a happy valley, where love and cheerfulness reigned.

Mrs. Raby was welcomed by her children—two elegant girls of fifteen and sixteen, and a spirited boy of twelve. They adored their mother, and saw in their new cousin an occasion for rejoicing. Their sparkling looks and gay voices dispelled the last remnant of melancholy from the venerable mansion. Old Oswi Raby himself—too much sunk in dotage to understand what was going on—yet smiled and looked glad on the merry faces about him. He could not exactly make out who Elizabeth was—he was sure that it was a relation, and he treated her with an obsequious respect, which, considering his former impertinent tone, was exceedingly amusing.

What was wanting to complete the universal happiness? Elizabeth's spirits rose to unwonted gayety in the society of her young relations—and her cousin Edwin in particular found her the most delightful companion in the world—for she was as fearless on horseback as himself, and was unwearied in amusing him by accounts of the foreign countries she had seen—and adventures, ridiculous or fearful, that she had encountered. In Mrs. Raby she found a beloved friend for serious hours; and Falkner's recovered health and spirits were a source of exhaustless congratulation.

Yet where was Gerard Neville? Where the looks of love and rapturous sense of sympathy, before which all the other joys of life fade into dimness? Love causes us to get more rid of our haunting identity, and to give ourselves more entirely away than any other emotion; it is the most complete, the most without veil or shadow to mar its beauty. Every other human passion occupies but a distinct portion of our being. This assimilates with all, and turns the whole into bliss or misery. Elizabeth did not fear that Gerard would forget her. He had remembered through the dark hours gone by— and now his shadow walked with her beneath the avenues of Belleforest, and the recollection of his love impregnated the balmy airs of spring with a sweetness unfelt before. Elizabeth had now leisure to love—and many an hour she spent in solitary yet blissful dreams—almost wondering that such happiness was to be found on earth. What a change—what a contrast between the deathgirt prison of Carlisle and the love-adorned glades of her ancestral park! Not long ago the sky appeared to bend over one universe of tears and wo—and now, in the midst, a piece of heaven had dropped down upon earth, and she had entered the enchanted ground.

Yet as weeks sped on, some thoughts troubled her repose. Gerard neither came nor wrote. At length she got a letter from Lady Cecil, congratulating her on Falkner's acquittal, and the kindness of her aunt; her letter was amiable, yet it was constrained; and Elizabeth, reading it again and again, and pondering on every expression, became aware that her friends felt less satisfaction than she did in the turn of fortune that placed her and Falkner together under her paternal roof. She had believed that, as Elizabeth Raby, Neville would at once claim her; but she was forced to recollect that Falkner was still at her side; and what intercourse could there be between him and his mother's destroyer?

Thus anxiety and sadness penetrated poor Elizabeth's new-found paradise. She strove to appear the same, but she stole away, when she could, to meditate alone on her strange lot. It doubled her regret to think that Neville also was unhappy. She figured the struggles he underwent. She almost thought that, if he were happy, she could bear all. She remembered him as she last saw him, agitated and wretched—she alone, she felt sure, could calm—she alone minister happiness—and were they never more to meet?

Falkner, who watched Elizabeth with all the jealousy of excessive affection, soon perceived the change. At first, her gayety had been spontaneous, her step free, her voice and laugh the very echo of joy: now, the forced smile, the frequent abstraction, the eagerness with which she watched for opportunities to steal into solitude, while her attentions to him became even more sedulous and tender; as if she wished to prove how ready she was to make every sacrifice for his sake—all these appearances he saw, and his heart ached to think how the effects of his errors still spread poison over his own life and that of one so dear.

He felt sure that Mrs. Raby shared his uneasiness. She and her niece were much less together than before. Elizabeth could not speak of the thoughts that occupied her; and she could not feign with her dear, wise friend, whose eyes read her soul, and whose counsels or consolations she alike feared. Falkner saw Mrs. Raby's regards fix anxiously on her young relative; he penetrated her thoughts, and again he was forced to abhor himself as the destroyer of the happiness of all who came within his sphere.

It was evident that some communication must take place between some one of the individuals thus misplaced and wretched. Elizabeth alone was resigned, and therefore silent. Falkner longed to act rather than to speak; to depart, to disappear for ever; he also, therefore, brooded mutely over the state of things. Mrs. Raby, seeing the wretchedness that was creeping over the hearts of those whose happiness she most desired, was the first to enter on the subject. One day, being alone with Falkner, she began: "The more I see and admire my dearest niece," she said, "the greater I feel our obligation to be to you, Mr. Falkner, for having made her what she is. Her natural disposition is full of excellence, but it is the care and the education you bestowed which give her character so high a tone. Had she come to us in her childhood, it is more than probable she would have been placed in a convent—and what nature, however perfect, but would be injured by the system that reigns in those places? To you we owe our fairest flower, and if gratitude could repay you, you would be repaid by mine; to prove it, and to serve you, must always be the most pleasing duty of my life."

"I should be much happier," said Falkner, "if I could regard my interference as you do; I fear I have injured irreparably my beloved girl, and that, through me, she is suffering pangs which she is too good to acknowledge, but which, in the end, may destroy her. Had I restored her to you, had she been brought up here, she and Gerard Neville would not now be separated."

"But they might never have met," replied Mrs. Raby. "It is indeed vain thus to regard the past; not only is it unalterable, but each link of the chain, producing the one that followed, seems, in our instance, to have been formed and riveted by a superior power for peculiar purposes. The whole order of events is inscrutable; one little change, and none of us would be as we are now. Except as a lesson or a warning, we ought not to contemplate the past, but the future certainly demands our attention. It is impossible to see Gerard Neville and not to feel an intense interest in him; he is worthy of our Elizabeth, and he is ardently attached to her, and has, besides, made a deep impression on her young heart, which I would not have erased or lessened; for I am sure that her happiness, as far as mortals can be happy, will be ensured by their marriage."

"I stand in the way of this union; of that I am well aware," said Falkner; "but be assured I will not continue to be an obstacle to the welfare of my angel girl. It is for this that I would consult you: how are contradictions to be reconciled, or rather, how can we contrive my absence so as to remove every impediment, and yet not to awaken Elizabeth's suspicions?"

"I dislike contrivances," replied Mrs. Raby, "and I hate all mystery— suffer me, therefore, to speak frankly to you—I have often conversed with Elizabeth; she is firm not to marry, so as to be wholly divided from you. She reasons calmly, but she never wavers: she will not, she says, commence new duties by, in the first place, betraying her old ones; she should be for ever miserable if she did, and therefore those who love her must not ask it. Sir Gerard entertains similar sentiments with regard to himself, though less resolute, and, I believe, less just than hers. I received a letter from him this morning. I was pondering whether to show it to you or to my niece; it seems to me best that you should read it, if it will not annoy you."

"Give it me," said Falkner; "and permit me also to answer it—it is not in my nature to dally with evils—I shall meet those that now present themselves, and bring the best remedy I can, at whatever cost."

Neville's letter was that of a man whose wishes were at war with his principles; and yet who was not convinced of the justice of the application of those principles. It began by deeply regretting the estrangement of Elizabeth from his family, by asking Mrs. Raby if she thought that she could not be induced to pay another visit to Lady Cecil. He said that lady was eager to see her, and only delayed asking her till she ascertained whether her friendship, which was warm and lively as ever, would prove as acceptable as formerly.

"I will at once be frank with you," the letter continued; "for your excellent understanding may direct us, and will suggest excuses for our doubts. You may easily divine the cause of our perplexities, though you can scarcely comprehend the extremely painful nature of mine. Permit me to treat you as a friend—be the judge of my cause—I have faith in the purity and uprightness of a woman's heart, when she is endowed with gifts such as you possess. I had once thought to refer myself to Miss Raby herself, but I dread the generous devotedness of her disposition. Will you, who love her, take therefore the task of decision on yourself?"

Neville went on to express, in few but forcible words, his attachment to Elizabeth, his conviction that it could never change, and his persuasion that she returned it. "It is not therefore my cause merely that I plead," he said, "but hers also. Do not call me presumptuous for thus expressing myself. A mutual attachment alone can justify extraordinary conduct; but where it is mutual, every minor consideration ought to give way before it; the happiness of both our lives depends upon our not trifling with feelings which I am sure can never change. They may be the source of perpetual felicity—if not, they will, they must be pregnant with misery to the end of our lives. But why this sort of explanation, when the meaning that I desire to convey is, that *if*—that *as*, may I not say—we love each other—no earthly power shall deprive me of her—sooner or later she must, she shall be mine; and meanwhile this continued separation is painful beyond my fortitude to bear.

"Can I take my mother's destroyer by the hand, and live with him on terms of intimacy and friendship? Such is the price I must pay for Elizabeth—can I—may I—so far forget the world's censure, and, I may say, the instigations of nature, as unreservedly to forgive?

"I will confess to you, dear Mrs. Raby, that when I saw Falkner in the most degrading situation in which a man can be placed, manacled, and as a felon, his dignity of mien, his majestic superiority to all the race of common mortals around, the grandeur of his calm yet piercing eye, and the sensibility of his voice—won my admiration; with such is peopled that heaven where the noble penitent is more welcome than the dull follower of a narrow code of morals, who never erred, because he never felt. I pardon him, then, from my heart, in my mother's name. These sentiments, the entire forgiveness of the injury done me, and the sense of his merits, still continue: but may I act on them? would not you despise me if I did? say but that you would, and my sentence is pronounced—I lose Elizabeth—I quit England for ever—it matters little where I go.

"Yet, before you decide, consider that this man possesses virtues of the highest order. He honoured as much as he loved my mother, and if his act was criminal, dearly has he paid the result. I persuade myself that there is more real sympathy between me and my mother's childhood's friend— who loved her so long and truly—whose very crime was a mad excess of love—than one who knew nothing of her—to whom her name conjures up no memories, no regret.

"I feel that I could lament with Falkner the miserable catastrophe, and yet not curse him for bringing it about. Nay—as with such a man there can be no half sentiments—I feel that if we are thrown together, his noble qualities will win ardent sentiments of friendship; were not his victim my mother, there does not exist a man whose good opinion I should so eagerly seek and highly prize as that of Rupert Falkner. It is that fatal name which forms the barrier between me and charity—shutting me out, at the same time, from hope and love.

"Thus incoherently I put down my thoughts as they rise—a tangled maze which I ask you to unravel. I will endeavour to abide by your decision, whatever it may be; yet I again ask you to pause. Is Elizabeth's happiness as deeply implicated as mine? if it be, can I abide by any sentence that shall condemn her to a wretchedness similar to that which has so long been an inmate of my struggling heart? no; sooner than inflict one pang on her, I will fly from the world. *We three* will seek some far obscure retreat and be happy, despite the world's censure, and even your condemnation."

Falkner's heart swelled within him as he read. He could not but admire Neville's candour—and he was touched by the feelings he expressed towards himself; but pride was stronger than regret, and prompted an instant and decisive reply. He rebelled against the idea that Gerard and Elizabeth should suffer through him, and thus he wrote:—

"You have appealed to Mrs. Raby; will you suffer me to answer that appeal, and to decide? I have a better right; for kind as she is, I have Elizabeth's welfare yet more warmly at heart.

"The affection that she feels for you will endure to the end of her life—for her faithful heart is incapable of change; on you therefore depends her happiness, and you are called upon to make some sacrifice to ensure it. Come here, take her at my hand—it is all I ask—from that hour you shall never see me more—the injured and the injurer will separate; my fortunes are of my own earning, and I can bear them. You must compensate to my dear child for my loss—you must be father as well as husband—and speak kindly of me to her, or her heart will break.

"We must be secret in our proceedings—mystery and deception are contrary to my nature—but I willingly adopt them for her sake. Mrs. Raby must not be trusted; but you and I love Elizabeth sufficiently even to sacrifice a portion of our integrity to secure her happiness. For her own sake we must blindfold her. She need never learn that we deceived her. She will naturally be separated from me for a short time—the period will be indefinitely prolonged—till new duties arise wholly to wean her from me—and I shall be forgotten.

"Come then at once—endure the sight of the guilty Falkner for a few short days—till you thus earn his dearest treasure—and do not fear that I shall intrude one moment longer than is absolutely necessary for our success; be assured that when once Elizabeth is irrevocably yours, wide seas shall roll between us. Nor will your condescension to my wish bring any stigma on yourself or your bride, for Miss Raby does not bear my tainted name. All I ask is, that you will not delay. It is difficult for me to cloak my feelings to one so dear—let my task of deception be abridged as much as possible.

"I shall give my Elizabeth to you with confidence and pleasure. You deserve her. Your generous disposition will enable you to endure her affection for me, and even her grief at my departure. Never speak unkindly of me to her. When you see me no more, you will find less difficulty in forgetting the injury I have done you; you must endeavour to remember only the benefit you receive in gaining Elizabeth."

# CHAPTER LII

The beautiful month of May had arrived, with her light budding foliage, which seems to hang over the hoar branches of the trees like a green aerial mist—the nightingales sung through the moonlight night, and every other feathered chorister took up the note at early dawn. The sweetest flowers in the year embroidered the fields; and the verdant corn-fields were spread like a lake, now glittering in the sun, now covered over by the shadows of the clouds. It appeared impossible not to hope—not to enjoy; yet a seriousness had again gathered over Falkner's countenance that denoted the return of care. He avoided the society even of Elizabeth—his rides were solitary—his evenings passed in the seclusion of his own room. Elizabeth, for the first time in her life, grew a little discontented. "I sacrificed all to him," she thought, "yet I cannot make him happy. Love alone possesses the sceptre and arbitrary power to rule; every other affection admits a parliament of thoughts—and debate and divisions ensue, which may make us wiser, but which sadly derogates from the throned state of what we fancy a master sentiment. I cannot make Falkner happy; yet Neville is miserable through my endeavours—and to such struggle there is no end—my promised faith is inviolable, nor do I even wish to break it."

One balmy, lovely day, Elizabeth rode out with her cousins; Mrs. Raby was driving her father-in-law through the grounds in the pony phaeton—Falkner had been out, and was returned. Several days had passed, and no answer arrived from Neville. He was uneasy and sad, and yet rejoiced at the respite afforded to the final parting with his child. Suddenly, from the glass doors of the saloon he perceived a gentleman riding up the avenue; he recognised him, and exclaimed, "All is over!" At that moment he felt himself transported to a distant land—surrounded by strangers—cut off from all he held dear. Such must be the consequence of the arrival of Gerard Neville; and it was he who, dismounting, in a few minutes after entered the room.

He came up to Falkner, and held out his hand, saying, "We must be friends, Mr. Falkner—from this moment I trust that we are friends. We join together for the happiness of the dearest and most perfect being in the world."

Falkner could not take his hand—his manner grew cold; but he readily replied, "I hope we do; and we must concert together to ensure our success."

"Yet there is one other," continued Neville, "whom we must take into our consultations."

"Mrs. Raby?"

"No! Elizabeth herself. She alone can decide for us all, and teach us the right path to take. Do not mistake me; I know the road she will point out, and am ready to follow it. Do you think I could deceive her? Could I ask her to give me her dear self, and thus generously raise me to the very height of human happiness, with deception on my lips? I were indeed unworthy of her, if I were capable of such an act.

"Yet, but for the sake of honest truth, I would not even consult her—my own mind is made up if you consent; I am come to you, Mr. Falkner, as a suppliant, to ask you to give me your adopted child, but not to separate you from her: I should detest myself if I were the cause of so much sorrow to either. If my conduct need explanation in the world, you are my excuse, I need go no further. We must both join in rendering Miss Raby happy, and both, I trust, remain friends to the end of our lives."

"You are generous," replied Falkner; "perhaps you are just. I am not unworthy of the friendship you offer, were you any other than you are."

"It is because I am such as I am that I venture to make advances which would be impertinent from any other."

At this moment, a light step was heard on the lawn without, and Elizabeth stood before them. She paused in utter wonder on seeing Falkner and Neville together; soon surprise was replaced by undisguised delight— her expressive countenance became radiant with happiness. Falkner addressed her: "I present a friend to you, dear Elizabeth; I leave you with him—he will best explain his purposes and wishes. Meanwhile I must remark, that I consider him bound by nothing that has been said; you must take counsel together—you must act for your mutual happiness—that is all the condition I make—I yield to no other. Be happy; and, if it be necessary, forget me, as I am very willing to forget myself."

Falkner left them; and they instinctively, so to prevent interruption, took their way into a woody glade of the park; and as they walked beneath the shadows of some beautiful lime-trees, on the crisp green turf, disclosed to each other every inner thought and feeling. Neville declared his resolve not to separate her from her benefactor. "If the world censure me," he said, "I am content; I am accustomed to its judgments, and never found them sway or annoy me. I do right for my own heart. It is a godlike task to reward the penitent. In religion and morality, I know that I am justified; whether I am in the code of worldly honour, I leave others to decide; and yet I believe that I am. I had once thought to have met Falkner in a duel, but my father's vengeance prevented that. He is now acquitted before all the world of being more than the accidental cause of my dear mother's death. Knights of old, after they fought in right good earnest, became friends, each finding, in the bravery of the other, a cause for esteem. Such is the situation of Rupert Falkner and myself; and we will both join, dear Elizabeth, in making him forget the past, and rendering his future years calm and happy."

Elizabeth could only look her gratitude. She felt, as was most true, that this was not a cause for words or reason. Falkner in himself offered, or did not offer, full excuse for the generosity of Neville. No one could see him, and not allow that the affectionate, duteous son in no way derogated from his reverence for his mother's memory, by entirely forgiving him who honoured her as an earthly angel, and had deplored, through years of unutterable anguish, the mortal injury done her. Satisfied in his own mind that he acted rightly, Neville did not seek for any other approval; and yet he gladly accepted it from Elizabeth, whose heart, touched to its very core by his nobleness, felt an almost painful weight of gratitude and love; she tried to express it: fortunately, between lovers mere language is not necessary ineffectually to utter that which transcends all expression. Neville felt himself most sweetly thanked; a more happy pair never trod this lovely earth than the two that, closely linked hand in hand, and with hearts open and true as the sunlight about them, enjoyed the sweetest hour of love, the first of acknowledged perpetual union, beneath the majestic, deep-shadowing thickets of Belleforest.

All that had seemed so difficult now took its course easily. They did not any of them seek to account for or to justify the course they took. They each knew that they could not do other than they did. Elizabeth could not break faith with Falkner—Neville could not renounce her; it might be strange—but it must be so; they three must remain together through life, despite all of tragic and miserable that seemed to separate them.

Even Lady Cecil admitted that there was no choice. Elizabeth must be won—she was too dear a treasure to be voluntarily renounced. In a few weeks, the wedding-day of Sir Gerard Neville and Miss Raby being fixed, she joined them at Belleforest, and saw, with genuine pleasure, the happiness of the two persons whom she esteemed and loved most in the world, secured. Mrs. Raby's warm heart reaped its own reward in witnessing this felicitous conclusion of her interference.

Whether the reader of this eventful tale will coincide with every other person, fully in the confidence of all, in the opinion that such was the necessary termination of a position full of difficulty, is hard to say—but so it was; and it is most certain that no woman who ever saw Rupert Falkner but thought Neville just and judicious; and if any man disputed this point, when he saw Elizabeth he was an immediate convert.

As much happiness as any one can enjoy, whose inner mind bears the unhealing wound of a culpable act, fell to the portion of Falkner. He had repented; and was forgiven, we may believe, in heaven, as well as on earth. He could not forgive himself—and this one shadow remained upon his lot—it could not be got rid of; yet perhaps in the gratitude he felt to those about him, in the softened tenderness inspired by the sense that he was dealt with more leniently than he believed that he deserved, he found full compensation for the memories that made him feel himself a perpetual mourner beside Alithea's grave.

Neville and Elizabeth had no drawback to their felicity. They cared not for the world, and when they did enter it, the merits of both commanded respect and liking; they were happy in each other, happy in a growing family, happy in Falkner; whom, as Neville had said, it was impossible to regard with lukewarm sentiments; and they derived a large store of happiness from his enlightened mind, from the elevated tone of moral feeling, which was the result of his sufferings, and from the deep affection with which he regarded them both. They were happy also in the wealth which gave scope to the benevolence of their dispositions, and in the talents that guided them rightly through the devious maze of life. They often visited Dromore, but their chief time was spent at their seat in Bucks, near which Falkner had purchased a villa. He lived in retirement: he grew a sage amid his books and his own reflections. But his heart was true to itself to the end, and his pleasures were derived from the society of his beloved Elizabeth, of Neville, who was scarcely less dear, and their beautiful children. Surrounded by these, he felt no want of the nearest ties; they were to him as his own. Time passed lightly on, bringing no apparent change; thus they still live—and Neville has never for a moment repented the irresistible impulse that led him to become the friend of him whose act had rendered his childhood miserable, but who completed the happiness of his maturer years.